OH, MAN, THIS WAS SO WRONG.
AND SO RIGHT.

"Ross," she whispered, her voice so damn sultry.

His mind told him to stop. But his heart had a completely different idea. His heart had been waiting decades to kiss Sabina Grey. And there she was, right in reach, and her mouth looked so ready to be kissed that he couldn't help himself.

He leaned down and pressed his mouth to her lips, and even though this wasn't exactly the hands-on, bodies-pressed-together, hot and heavy kiss he'd once fantasized about, the heat of the moment still swept through him.

He wanted to pull her close. He wanted to explore her mouth a little deeper. He wanted to do a lot more than dance with her.

But Sabina pushed back. "We can't do this."

"Last Chance is a place we've come to know as well as we know our own hometowns. It's become real, filled with people who could be our aunts, uncles, cousins, friends, or the crazy cat lady down the street. It's familiar, comfortable, welcoming."

—RubySlipperedSisterhood.com

"Hope Ramsay heats up romance to such a degree every reader will be looking for a nice, cool glass of sweet tea to cool off."

—*The Reading Reviewer*
(MaryGramlich.blogspot.com)

Last Chance Christmas

"Amazing...These lovely folks filled with Southern charm [and] gossip were such fun to get to know...This story spoke to me on so many levels about faith, strength, courage, and choices...If you're looking for a good Christmas story with a few angels, then *Last Chance Christmas* is a must-read. For fans of Susan Wiggs."

—TheSeasonforRomance.com

"Visiting Last Chance is always a joy, but Hope Ramsay has outdone herself this time. She took a difficult hero, a wounded heroine, familiar characters, added a little Christmas magic, and—voila!—gave us a story sure to touch the Scroogiest of hearts...It draws us back to a painful time when tensions—and prejudices—ran deep, compels us to remember and forgive, and reminds us that healing, redemption, and love are the true gifts of Christmas."

—RubySlipperedSisterhood.com

Last Chance Beauty Queen

"4½ stars! Enchantingly funny and heartwarmingly charming."   —*RT Book Reviews*

"Grab this today and get ready for a rollicking read."
—RomRevToday.com

"A little Bridget Jones meets *Sweet Home Alabama*."
—GrafWV.com

Home at Last Chance

"An enjoyable ride that will capture interest and hold it to the very end."   —RomRevToday.blogspot.com

"Full of small town charm and Southern hospitality... You will want to grab a copy."
—TopRomanceNovels.com

Welcome to Last Chance

"Ramsay's delicious contemporary debut introduces the town of Last Chance, SC, and its warmhearted inhabitants...[she] strikes an excellent balance between tension and humor as she spins a fine yarn."
—*Publishers Weekly* (starred review)

"[A] charming series, featuring quirky characters you won't soon forget."

—Barbara Freethy, *New York Times* bestselling author of *At Hidden Falls*

LAST CHANCE HERO

Also by Hope Ramsay

LAST CHANCE HERO

Hope Ramsay

FOREVER

NEW YORK   BOSTON

Forever
Hachette Book Group
1290 Avenue of the Americas
New York, NY 10104
forever-romance.com

Printed in the United States of America

First Edition: June 2015
10 9 8 7 6 5 4 3 2 1

OPM

Forever is an imprint of Grand Central Publishing.
The Forever name and logo are trademarks of Hachette Book Group, Inc.

The Hachette Speakers Bureau provides a wide range of authors for speaking events. To find out more, go to www.hachettespeakersbureau.com or call (866) 376-6591.

The publisher is not responsible for websites (or their content) that are not owned by the publisher.

ATTENTION CORPORATIONS AND ORGANIZATIONS:
Most HACHETTE BOOK GROUP books are available at quantity discounts with bulk purchase for educational, business, or sales promotional use. For information, please call or write:

Special Markets Department, Hachette Book Group
1290 Avenue of the Americas, New York, NY 10104
Telephone: 1-800-222-6747 Fax: 1-800-477-5925

To the people who volunteer, whether it's fighting fires, organizing PTA luncheons, or working to improve the world through nonprofit organizations. Where would we be without you?

Acknowledgments

Writing may be a solitary experience, but no author works alone. I'd like to begin with a big thank-you to the folks at www.firehouse.com for the wealth of information they provided online about hose lays, turnout suits, assessing fires, and more. I never realized how much I didn't know about firefighting until I started reading the various lessons for firefighters posted on that website.

I'd also like to give a huge shout-out to the members of the Last Chance Book Club, for helping me name my villain and my firehouse dog, and especially for coming up with the hilarious idea of having an ATF agent caught reading *Cosmo* in public. You ladies rock.

I'd also like to thank my critique partners Carol Hayes and Keely Thrall, who helped me negotiate the pitfalls of writing a book about one man and his relationship with two sisters.

As always, I must thank my thoughtful agent, Elaine English, my amazing editor, Alex Logan, and the whole team at Forever Romance who have given me such terrific support, not to mention the amazing artwork on the cover of this book. And finally many thanks to my husband, Bryan, who is the king of home renovation and a veritable font of knowledge on anything related to building construction. I love you more than words could ever express.

CHAPTER 1

Wednesdays were slow at the Last Chance Around Antique Mall. So Sabina Grey was alone. She sat behind the checkout counter surfing the Internet while the morning sun slanted through the front windows of what once had been a Woolworth five-and-ten-cent store.

Sabina was using this rare moment of inaction to daydream about the grand European tour she planned to take one day. She was flipping through images of the Parthenon and thinking of handsome, dark-eyed Greek men.

"Hey there." The voice wobbled like an ancient phonograph recording.

Sabina looked up with a start to find Miriam Randall blinking at her through her thick trifocals. Miz Miriam had to be eighty-five and, bless her heart, she was starting to lose her mind. Today she was wearing a house dress that might have been a nightgown or a robe. Her white hair looked a little lopsided, as if she'd had trouble putting it up in the crown braids she always wore.

"Hey, Miz Miriam, what brings you to Last Chance

Around this morning?" Sabina stood up behind the point-of-sale counter to get a better look at the old woman. Oh, good Lord, Miriam was wearing a pair of bedroom slippers. Had she walked all the way into town dressed like that?

This wasn't good. Sabina picked up her cell phone and started punching in the numbers for Miriam's niece Savannah. But before she could finish, Miriam leaned both elbows on the counter. "Honey, I need to talk with you."

Sabina's insides went all weightless like they did on the first dip of the big roller coaster at Six Flags Over Georgia. "You want to talk to me? What about?"

"What do you think it's about? I have some advice for you."

Advice? Oh, boy. This was unexpected. Before she started losing her mind, Miriam Randall had been Allenberg County's premier matchmaker. Not that Miriam actually matched people up. She was really more of a soothsayer or something. She would hand out vague advice, like the kind in fortune cookies. And danged if her advice always turned out to be true.

So if you were single and pining away for love, it was a red letter day when Miz Miriam darkened your door. "I, uh, well, I'm surprised." Sabina's breath chose that moment to go on vacation. Too bad the rest of her couldn't tag along.

"You didn't think you were going to end up a spinster, did you?"

"Well…" In fact she was kind of starting to worry about that.

Which was truly sad, since her high school had voted

her the girl most likely to require a shotgun wedding. An honor that was not really true then, but definitely out of the question now.

Events had changed the silly, boy-crazy girl she'd once been. And while she'd been maturing, all the eligible bachelors in her age group had gotten married or moved away. So the soulmate pickings in Allenberg County were slim at best, that was for sure. Besides, her activities with the Altar Guild, the book club, the Chamber of Commerce, and the new Discover Last Chance Association didn't give her much time for romance.

Miz Miriam spoke again in a voice as ancient as faded parchment. "I declare, you young people are so impatient. Well, you listen up now. I came over here to tell you that your soulmate will arrive just as soon as you set your mind to helping your sister tie the knot."

Well, that was sort of a letdown. For one glorious moment, Sabina had thought this visit was about her. But of course it made total sense that Miz Miriam would consult her about Lucy.

And yet, unwanted envy pricked Sabina like a lance. "Miz Miriam, I do appreciate this advice. You've made my day." The stiff, brittle words felt sour in Sabina's mouth.

"I have?" The old lady's white brows arched. "I would have thought you'd be annoyed with me, since I'm asking you to think about someone else."

Sabina's composure crumbled. How could anyone accuse her of not caring about Lucy? "I love my sister, Miz Miriam. I would do anything for her."

"If you love her, girl, then get out of her way. Let her discover the truth."

"The truth?"

The old woman gave her a stare so penetrating, it probably could have pierced the vault at Fort Knox. It was hard to believe that Miriam's mind (or eyesight) was going when her look was so keen. "Yes, the truth. You don't ask a fish about the water, do you?"

"Huh?"

"You know, a fish doesn't see the water. It's right there in front of his eyeballs. It's the God's honest truth that people never notice what's right in front of their faces. Your sister is like that. And I think you're part of the problem."

"I am? How?"

Just then Momma came striding through the front door, dressed in her usual shabby chic ensemble composed of a hand-sewn flowered skirt, a sleeveless jean jacket, and a vintage lace blouse. Momma also wore a pair of blinged-out cowboy boots she'd picked up in San Antonio last year on one of Daddy's business trips. Momma was trying hard not to grow old.

"Oh, hey, Miz Miriam. What brings you to Last Chance Around?" Momma's high-pitched voice sounded as young as she wished she still was.

"I came to give your daughter advice."

Momma lit up like the Vegas Strip at midnight. "You did? How wonderful."

"Well, maybe not." Miriam turned and gave Sabina another pointed look. "You need to give your sister space, you hear?"

"Space?" Momma blinked in befuddlement.

"That's what I said, isn't it? I always say what I mean."

That was a debatable point, but Sabina was not about to get into an argument with Miriam Randall. Not when she was delivering marital advice.

But Momma had been waiting a long, long time for Miriam to darken one of her daughters' doors. So as usual, Momma blundered ahead like a blind horse. "What did you tell her, Miriam?"

"I told her that she needed to make sure of her sister's happiness before she can ever find her own."

"Well, that's good news, isn't it?"

Before Miriam could say another word, Dash Randall came striding into the store. "Aunt Mim, what are you doing here in your house dress?" he asked.

Miz Miriam pulled herself up straight. "I had urgent business here."

Dash cast his gaze from Sabina to Momma and back again. "'Morning, ladies. I think I should caution you that Aunt Mim hasn't been herself the last few days."

He gave them both a charming, lopsided grin and then gently took his aunt's arm. "Come on, now. You need to get dressed for the senior center, and then there's the Purly Girls meeting later."

"I was helping them, Dash."

"I know, Aunt Mim." He nodded then looked up at Momma and Sabina. He gave them a little wink and a shrug.

And with that, Dash guided Miz Miriam out of the antiques mall.

"Well, isn't that something?" Momma said, looking after them with a glance that had gone all wistful. "Honey, we need to put our heads together and figure out a way to get Ross off his lazy backside. What in the name of all creation is he waiting for? Maybe I should tell him he's standing in the way of your happiness."

"Oh good Lord, Momma, I don't think that's a good plan. You heard Dash. Miriam hasn't been herself lately.

I think we should keep what just happened here to ourselves. I don't think it means one thing."

"You don't? Well I have more faith in Miriam Randall than you do, I guess. I want my girls to be happy. And right now I'm sick to death of the way Ross has been dragging his heels. He needs to propose to Lucy. Sooner rather than later. And Miriam has just given us the leverage we need."

Momma turned and headed toward the door. "Don't you worry now, honey. I'm going to talk to Elsie, and we'll figure out a way to light a fire under Ross."

Oh, no. This was bad. Very bad. Sabina didn't want Ross to think that he stood between her and happiness. It was embarrassing. Once a million years ago—before the fire that had scarred Lucy—Sabina had been the Davis High Homecoming Queen. She could have had her pick.

But she didn't want Ross thinking she was desperate. And she didn't want to be used as leverage against him, either.

"Momma, don't you dare tell the Altar Guild about this," Sabina said. "You tell Elsie Campbell what happened here this morning and the whole town will know about it before nightfall. You can't do that to Ross and Lucy." Not to mention herself. She was going to look pathetic, which was actually kind of true.

"I can't? You just watch me."

Chief Ross Gardiner sat in his small office at the Last Chance firehouse preparing the annual budget for the volunteer fire department. He was the only paid member of the force and the only member who had professional fire-fighting experience. Which explained why he got to do all the paperwork and deal with the county bureaucracy.

Budget time always made him grumpy. And this year, the county had imposed deep cutbacks. Ross supposed these might be popular with taxpayers, but the funding reductions were making it darn hard to provide fire and emergency medical services.

He was just thinking about ditching the paperwork and heading over to the doughnut shop for a cup of coffee when Matt Jasper, the lone officer of the Allenberg County Sheriff's Department K-9 unit, came through the open door. Matt's partner, Rex, a big German shepherd, trotted at his side.

"I come bearing the elixir of life," Matt said, holding up two paper coffee cups. "And this is *good* coffee, I bought it at the Garden of Eatin'."

"How did you know my caffeine tank was running on empty?" Ross said as he took one of the cups.

Matt sank into the ugly, 1960s-style plastic chair beside Ross's desk. He glanced down at the paperwork. "Because you and everyone else with any kind of authority has been stuck behind their desks doing budgets that are probably going to cost a lot of hardworking people their jobs."

Matt roughed up Rex's ears as he continued speaking. "In fact, Rex and I might be the first ones downsized." Matt continued to pet his dog and avoid eye contact.

"Jeez." Ross shook his head and leaned back. "I didn't think the Sheriff's Department would be hit with budget cuts."

"Sheriff Rhodes told me this morning that he's not sure he can save the K-9 department, such as it is." Matt chewed on his lower lip for an instant. He was working hard to keep it together.

"I'm really sorry."

Matt continued to rub Rex's ears. "Working with dogs is the one thing I know. The army trained me well. If I can't be a K-9 cop here, then I'll have to go somewhere else. There are departments in other places that would love to have a dog like Rex and an experienced handler. I just don't know how Annie is going to take the idea of leaving this town." He hunched his shoulders and pressed his lips into a hard line, as if saying any more would take him to a place too emotional to share.

Ross didn't know what to say, so he said nothing. Silence seemed right. Since Ross had returned to Last Chance two years ago, Matt, a newcomer, had become his best buddy. Buddies didn't need words to share the emotion of the moment.

"Well, it is what it is," Matt said on a gust of air after about half a minute. Rex settled at his feet with his big head on Matt's foot. "I didn't come over here to cry in my coffee. The truth is, I heard some gossip over at the hardware store that I figured you needed to hear." He finally looked up and made eye contact.

"Since when do you listen to gossip?" Ross asked.

"When it involves you."

"Me? I haven't done one thing gossip-worthy. Ever."

"Apparently that's the problem."

"What? Tell me." Ross braced himself.

"I gather Miriam Randall visited the antiques store this morning and told Sabina that if she ever wanted to find her soulmate, she needed to help Lucy get married. So naturally, the females of this town now believe that you are the person standing in the way of Sabina Grey's eternal happiness. And I gather that the entire female population of this town is concerned that Sabina is on the verge of becoming a spinster. Boy, you better get on with it and propose to Lucy before you have church ladies picketing the firehouse."

A bolt of emotional energy zapped Ross right in the chest and riveted him to his seat. He couldn't speak, move, react. He sat there like an electrocuted lump staring at his best friend.

If Sabina was on the verge of spinsterhood, it wasn't because of him. It was a situation entirely of her own making. She was drop-dead beautiful. All she had to do was crook her finger and guys would be falling all over her.

Just like in high school.

But she'd made it clear she was not in the market for a boyfriend.

The first week he'd returned to Last Chance, Ross had been astonished to discover that Sabina was still single. So he had screwed up his courage and asked her out for dinner, but she'd been too busy with the Chamber of Commerce. And then he'd asked her out to a movie, but she had something going with the Methodist Day Care Center. When she said no the third time—to drinks at Dot's Spot—the message had been crystal clear. And she'd underscored it a week later when she went out of her way to introduce him to her younger sister.

In the eighteen months that Ross had been dating Lucy, he'd gotten to know Sabina a whole lot better. She was a sweet person, but utterly uninterested in the opposite sex. She seemed to live a perfectly happy life hopping from one civic activity to another, the way she used to go through boyfriends in high school.

He'd watched her for a while. And every guy who ventured into her territory got shot down in flames. The idea of him being the roadblock to Sabina's happiness was ridiculous. If she wanted a husband, all she had to do was say yes.

"Don't give me that look," Matt said with a wiseass smirk on his face. "I know what you're thinking. In a minute you're going to serve up some firehouse mumbo jumbo about once burned twice shy. But I'm telling you, man, the women of this town have decided that your single days are over."

"Fear is useful. You wouldn't rush into a domestic situation without being cautious, would you? I certainly don't go rushing into a burning building without feeling some kind of fear. There are things in life that can hurt you. Marriage is one of them."

Ross had married for love at the age of twenty-seven. Five years later he found his wife cheating on him with one of his buddies. He wouldn't allow his gonads to blind him again.

"C'mon, Ross, marriage can be great with the right woman. Lucy's terrific. Besides, you've been dating her for a while."

"And?"

"You love her, right?"

"Yes." The answer was automatic. In fact, he and Lucy had grown comfortable together. He supposed that being comfortable was a sign. Maybe it was time for him to get off his butt and marry her.

"If you love her, the next step is marriage, right? So why not go get her a ring right now?"

"I'm not sure she wants a ring."

"Come on, Ross, every woman wants a ring."

Except Lucy didn't seem to be all that hot to get married. She wasn't like Betsy, his ex-wife. Betsy had taken Ross to look at engagement rings for months before he finally got up the nerve to ask for her hand. Lucy hadn't done anything like that. She hadn't hinted or demanded or any of the usual kinds of things.

Which made her perfect, actually. She was as cautious as he was. And kind of kick-ass in some ways. Lucy spent a lot of time down at the Dead Center Shooting Club. She could curse like a sailor. And she actually liked the taste of beer.

A guy could really adore Lucy. Which he did.

He especially liked the fact that she had a plan for her life. She'd insisted that they agree on a list of things that needed to be achieved before they could get married. Or even intimate. Most of the things on the list were Lucy's idea, but they all made sense. And they'd worked through every single one of them. He'd even taken some shooting lessons. And she'd agreed to get her CPR certification. So they shared interests.

There were only two major items left to be settled. She needed to finish her associate's degree. And he needed to save up enough for a down payment on a house.

So it was all good. Well, except the part about not having sex until they were married. That was, in his opinion, kind of an old-fashioned idea for a woman who had just turned thirty. But Momma had raised him up as a southern gentleman. And there were quite a few old-fashioned women in Allenberg County who frowned on premarital sex. So Lucy wasn't all that unusual for this neck of the woods.

And he liked her. And he liked her family. Which probably meant he should marry the girl. But he deeply

resented Miriam Randall meddling in his relationship
with Lucy Grey.

So he cleared his throat and came up with the best
excuse for not proposing that he could muster on short
notice. "You know, you're not the only person on the
Allenberg County payroll whose job might be in jeopardy.
Mayor LaFlore is giving County Executive Hayden a real
election challenge this November. So Hayden has been
making all kinds of promises about property tax reductions and balanced budgets. It would be stupid of me to
take on any new responsibilities until after October first.
Until then I don't have any guarantee that the department
will be fully funded for another year."

"Bummer." The corners of Matt's mouth turned down.

"Yeah, total bummer, because I've been saving up
for a down payment on one of those new houses they're
building off Route 321, you know the place—Jessamine
Manor. Lucy and I took a look at the model home, and you
should have seen the way she lit up. She wants to practice all that stuff she's learning in college about interior
design. Well, anyway, until this latest round of budget
cuts, I was thinking that I could afford that house. And
with a house, you know, it might be a good time to . . ." He
shrugged off the last part of his sentence. Just saying the
word "marriage" made the spit dry up in his mouth.

"Well," Matt said, "job or no job, you're in deep crap with
the female population of Last Chance if you don't ask Lucy
to marry you. You know how it is, Ross. Miriam can hand
out a lot of bogus mumbo jumbo, but every female in town
believes it like the words came down from God Almighty.
Those women don't give a rat's behind that you are about to
be downsized. They think you need to fish or cut bait."

• • •

Lucy Grey stood on the concrete walkway leading to the parking lot at Allenberg Community College. She dug her cell phone out of her purse and switched off airplane mode.

The phone immediately rang. Momma was on the line. So what else was new? Momma called almost every hour of the day.

Lucy heaved a weary sigh as she punched the talk button. "Hey, Momma, what's up?"

"Honey, you won't believe it. This morning Miriam Randall herself came into Last Chance Around and gave your sister some marital advice."

Lucy's mood brightened. "Oh, my goodness, what did she say?"

"Well, honey, it's simple. She said that Sabina's Prince Charming won't show up until we have you safely married off."

Just like that, Lucy's balloon popped. "What?"

"You heard me. We need to put our heads together and figure out a way to help Ross over his commitment issues. Honey, the time has come for you and your fireman to get hitched. It's not like I'm asking you to do something you don't want to do. You and Ross belong together.

"And now we know that once we get you married off, the way will be cleared for Sabina. Daddy and I want to give you a big, fancy wedding. Like a fairy princess. We'll have so much fun planning it. And all the while we'll be doing something wonderful for your big sister."

"You're joking, right?"

"I am not. Why would I joke?"

"You don't really believe that stuff about Miriam Randall, do you?"

"I most certainly do. She may be an Episcopalian, but I think her track record speaks for itself. And besides, Lucy Ann, you owe your sister this. She gave up her college experience to help me nurse you after the fire."

Oh, boy. It hadn't taken Momma more than a minute to start ladling on the guilt just like gravy on her pot roast. And Momma never stinted on gravy.

Of course, Lucy was perfectly capable of feeling guilty without Momma's help. Lucy knew exactly how much Sabina had given up after the fire. She was also well acquainted with Sabina's guilty conscience. So it was hardly news that Sabina wouldn't move on in her life until Lucy was settled with someone like Ross.

Lucy should marry him. He was a good man. A loyal guy. A gentleman who put up with her weird need to control everything. Ross would make the perfect husband and father and mate.

But he'd never actually swept her off her feet. Because, well, she'd kind of never let him. She was frightened of being swept off her feet. She didn't like feeling out of control. It took her back to that night when she'd been surrounded by the flames and knew that she was no match for a force of nature. The fire had scarred her in so many ways.

Which was why Ross was so safe. He was dependable, and easygoing, and happy to let her make all the plans.

"Lucy, honey, are you still there?" Momma sounded annoyed.

"I am."

"So are you going to do something about Ross or not?"

"I guess I should."

"Well, don't sound like you're going to a funeral. Once you get that engagement ring on your finger, we'll plan a trip to Atlanta and go looking for the wedding dress to end all wedding dresses, just like those people on *Say Yes to the Dress.*"

Uh-oh, that didn't sound like fun. Lucy didn't want to be dressed up like a doll. Besides, even if you put a pretty dress on her, she'd still have scars on her forehead, arms, and legs. She wondered, sourly, if anyone made wedding dresses with long sleeves anymore. It seemed like every bride was wearing strapless mermaid dresses these days. She didn't have a figure for a dress like that, not to mention the way that kind of neckline would expose her flaws.

"All right, Momma," she said, knowing that arguing with Momma was a waste of time. "I'll talk to Ross."

She said her good-byes and headed for her old Saturn sedan. It didn't take long before her phone rang again. She checked the ID: Maryanne Carpenter. No doubt Maryanne had heard the news. She sent the call directly to voice mail, only to have the phone ring again.

This time it was Jenny, Maryanne's cousin and Sabina's best friend. That call was also sent to voice mail. She was thinking about turning her phone back to airplane mode when it rang a third time.

This time the call was from Ross. She sat there in the driver's seat contemplating her future. She wanted to send this call to voice mail, too. But she couldn't do that. Not to Ross. He was such a sweet man.

She pressed the talk button. "Hey, sweetie."

"Hey." He had the deepest voice. She had to admit the guy was pretty much perfect in every way.

He hesitated for a long moment before he spoke again. "So, uh, I'm here at Jessamine Manor, you know the Webster Homes development out on Route 321? I'm looking at that model home you liked so much, and I was wondering... well, I wanted to know if you had a minute to come down here."

"You're looking at a model home?"

"Uh, well, actually I just signed papers and put down a few grand in earnest money. To be accurate, I just *bought* a home and I need your advice about carpets and appliances and upgrades... you know... stuff."

Good Lord, the house was one of the last items on their joint to-do list, right after her graduation from college. If he bought a house and she graduated, there wouldn't be anything left on that list, except sex and marriage. Maybe in that order or maybe the other way around.

Yikes. Her life had changed in a matter of hours just because Miriam Randall had walked into Last Chance Around and talked to Sabina.

Of course Ross would never, ever stand between Sabina and her happy ending. He was too much of a gentleman for that.

And of course, Lucy owed Sabina happiness. Big time. She couldn't say no.

So really, she didn't have a choice, did she? She was going to marry Ross Gardiner on someone else's time line.

And that bugged the crap out of her.

CHAPTER 2

Sabina arrived at the Kismet movie theater at seven-forty on Thursday morning, late for the Discover Last Chance Association monthly breakfast and business meeting. She slipped through the lobby and into the dining room, where virtually all of the Palmetto Avenue merchants were already digging into their omelets.

Sabina had stayed up way too late last night drinking cheap champagne, compliments of Momma, who'd rushed right out to the BI-LO for the wine and some steaks the minute she'd heard about Ross buying one of those houses out at Jessamine Manor.

Attendance at Momma's impromptu engagement celebration was mandatory. Unfortunately, champagne always gave Sabina a headache. And cheap champagne was the worst.

She sat down at a nearly empty table in the back, pulled a bottle of Excedrin out of her purse, and reached for the coffee thermos.

"Sabina? Sabina Grey? Is that you?" The voice was low, masculine, and kind of husky.

She looked up from the coffee she'd just poured and blinked her hungover eyes at the other occupant of the table. The guy was wearing the usual uniform for Chamber of Commerce meetings: blue suit, white shirt, red tie. But that's where the comparison ended. The suit looked hand-sewn, the shirt had French cuffs, the tie was definitely Hermès. She had a feeling that if she looked under the table he'd be wearing Italian leather shoes.

But she couldn't manage that, because he was staring at her with an unwavering gaze, out of a pair of ice blue eyes that were somewhat obscured by a pair of tortoiseshell glasses. Those eyes were oddly still, as if he could see nothing but her. "You have no idea who I am, do you?"

Busted. The pounding in her head was joined by a definite pounding in her chest. "I'm afraid I don't."

He leaned in kind of stiffly, his body straining forward. And even though an ocean of table separated them, his forward posture left her feeling slightly invaded.

He spoke again, in measured tones. "You and I went to the eighth-grade homecoming dance together. You dumped me there." The words were a condemnation, and yet they were delivered with little emotion.

She knew him now. Layton Webster.

Oh, good Lord.

She wanted to slide right under the table so he wouldn't see her red face. Or maybe she could get up and run on the high heels she took out of her closet every month for this meeting.

But of course she couldn't do either of those things. She was a thirty-five-year-old grown woman, not the cruel fourteen-year-old she had once been.

And boy howdy, Layton Webster had grown up nice.

Really nice. Who would have ever thought he'd turn out so well?

"Layton Webster," she said and screeched to a stop. What could she say that would make up for the way she had tormented him?

Layton Webster had been a dork in high school. But he'd been a smart dork. He'd gone off to MIT, and she remembered hearing some gossip about how he'd invented some kind of system or software for computer-generated animation that he'd sold to Disney Studios for millions.

"Uh," she said, her mouth as dry as the Sahara, "what brings you back to Last Chance? I heard you've been quite successful."

"Uncle Elias asked me if I'd help him develop a project management system for his construction business. With all the growth around here, he's got two housing developments in Allenberg County, and two more up north near Orangeburg. It interested me. I'm thinking I might be able to make this into an off-the-shelf software product that I could sell. As for this morning, Uncle Elias is busy, and he sent me here to see what y'all are getting up to."

There was something in the way he said "y'all" that kind of put Sabina off. And then there was the fact that he'd taken a seat here in the back of the room, at an empty table. Layton had always done that. He'd always set himself a little bit apart.

But then how could she blame him for that? He'd been the geeky kid in school. The one who didn't fit in. The loner. And she'd been cruel to him.

It was incredible how much penance she faced for the person she'd once been. And here was another opportunity for her to repair the damage she'd done.

"Layton," she said, looking him square in the eye, enduring that deeply unsettling stare of his. "I am mortified by what I did to you at the eighth-grade dance. It was cruel and nasty and wrong, on so many levels. I apologize from the deepest places in my heart. I am a different person from that spoiled little girl I used to be. Life has a way of changing people. So I do hope you will forgive me. And I'm not saying this because you've been a success. I'm saying it because I was wrong. I owe you something."

He leaned back and looked away, almost as if he didn't care about her apology or even the fact that she was sitting right there at the table with him. She couldn't blame him. And really, even if he did accept her apology she would still find a way to wallow in the guilt. Guilt was one of her weaknesses.

To her utter surprise, Layton's lips curled halfway, and he caught her gaze once again. "Sabina, I accept your apology. And if you really want to make it up to me, join me for drinks or dinner sometime."

Oh, boy. This could be really great, or it could be Layton's way of paying her back. It would serve her right if he invited her out to dinner and then stood her up.

On the other hand, this could actually be something important. It was almost spooky the way Layton had shown up the day after Ross proposed to Lucy. The day after Miriam showed up at the store. And she owed Layton a pleasant night out—or maybe an opportunity to stand her up.

She was mulling over the risks and rewards of accepting his invitation when Savannah Randall, the chair and founder of the Discover Last Chance Association, got up in front of the stage and welcomed everyone with a few announcements. DLCA had been founded for the express purpose of branding the town and building tourism. Last Chance had a few things going for it: a Bible-themed miniature golf course called Golfing for God, a converted bottling plant that provided studio space for working artists and artisans, and The Kismet, the movie palace that Savannah owned, which had just been recognized as a historic building by the State of South Carolina.

"I hope y'all enjoyed your omelets this morning," Savannah said. "Now I'd like to recognize Lark Chaikin, the chair of the program committee. She's got a terrific idea she wants to discuss."

Lark, the wife of Allenberg County's sheriff and an award-winning photographer, got up and started outlining plans for a town-wide fall festival that, unlike the summer Watermelon Festival, would focus exclusively on Last Chance. Lark's plan called for a parade, a sidewalk arts and crafts fair, a film festival of southern movies, and a Miniature Professional Golf Association tournament.

Lark revealed the logo for the event and outlined the publicity plans, which included regional newspapers and social media. She wanted every Palmetto Avenue merchant to display flyers and to incorporate the logo into their own marketing materials.

"We're going to need some volunteers," Lark said. "We especially need someone to coordinate the arts and crafts festival. We'll have the bottling plant studios open to the public, of course, but we would like to attract local crafters for booths on the sidewalk in order to create a street party feel for that Saturday. And I know it's probably bad form for me to call on someone publicly, but Sabina, I see you hiding there in the back row; we really need your expertise on this. We figure you know a lot of people who have crafts to sell, since a number of them rent stalls at Last Chance Around."

Oh, crap. For the second time that morning, she wanted to slink under the table. She didn't want to volunteer for this. She already had obligations to the Altar Guild, she was helping to organize the Christmas Bazaar, and she had picking trips scheduled, and Lucy's wedding coming up.

But on the other hand, what Lark had said about her was absolutely true. If anyone else in town tried to coordinate a craft sale, they would probably make a mess of it and tick off the local crafters. And if that happened, she'd never hear the end of it—from her friends or the crafters.

So either way, she was sunk.

She stood up, resigned. "I'm happy to volunteer," she lied.

"You're a sweetheart," Lark said.

Sabina sat down, utterly annoyed at herself. Why was she always the first one everyone asked to volunteer? Why did she never say no?

The meeting droned on while she drank her second cup of coffee and tried hard not to look at Layton. She failed utterly, and at one point he turned away from the speaker to give her a look that practically smoldered. Was he flirting?

Possibly.

He finally leaned in. "So, about drinks and dinner? How about tomorrow?"

Wow, the guy actually picked the one night she had free. This could be good or bad. She didn't know. Best not to agree to dinner. "Uh, why don't we meet for cocktails down at Dot's Spot tomorrow evening, say around six?"

He gave her that half grin that passed for a smile. She remembered that expression. As a boy, Layton Webster had worn that smirk like armor, as if to say that no one could touch him or hurt him. Although everyone tried, including herself.

This was her chance to atone for her sins. Besides, a girl could do a lot worse than having a couple of drinks with a guy who'd graduated from MIT and had a few million in the bank.

It would be utterly ironic if her Prince Charming turned out to be Layton Webster, wouldn't it? But stranger things had happened. And God moves in mysterious ways.

Ross closed up the firehouse and headed down the sidewalk toward Last Chance Around Antiques. He was feeling pretty good about himself.

He'd given this some thought the last two days. It was quite possible that Miriam Randall had hit the nail on the head about Lucy and her sister.

When Lucy got hurt in the fire, Sabina blamed herself for what happened. Over the years she'd become something of a mother hen when it came to her younger sister.

So maybe he could take the job of looking after Lucy off Sabina's hands. And then she could finally take that vacation she was always talking about. And maybe she'd get away from the Altar Guild and the book club and all the other groups that seemed to demand most of her time.

It made sense. Once Lucy was married, Sabina could get on with her life.

So it was good. And of course, it was nice to have the community behind him. A steady stream of neighbors and friends had stopped by the firehouse today to offer their congratulations. One of them, Angel Menendez, had come bearing a gift—a six-month-old Labrador-Dalmatian mix puppy.

Angel was always trying to find homes for strays, and this particular dog had been taken from an abusive environment several weeks ago. Angel figured, since the puppy was part Dalmatian, he belonged in a firehouse.

It was a case of love at first sight. The not-so-little guy was built more like a retriever than a Dalmatian, but he sure had black and white spots. His floppy ears were black, his muzzle was mostly white, and he had one exceptionally cute spot over his right eye.

Ross named him Sparky on sight, because he'd always wanted a firehouse dog with that name. And it seemed like a good time to commit to a dog. After all, he was now engaged and would soon have a mortgage payment.

A dog seemed like the next logical step. Like practicing for kids, or something.

Although the idea of kids was mildly terrifying.

He'd bought a collar, leash, dog bed, and some food from the hardware store. He'd made an appointment with the vet. And he was really excited about introducing Sparky to Lucy.

She was going to love him.

Ross and Sparky pushed through the double doors at Last Chance Around and were immediately greeted with enthusiasm.

"Oh, my goodness. He's adorable. When did you get him?" Sabina hopped down from her perch behind the checkout counter and made a beeline for the puppy. She squatted down and gave his head a scratch.

Sparky knew a friend when he saw one. He wagged his hind end so hard, Ross thought he might topple over. It wasn't long before Sabina was getting a bunch of dog kisses.

Which kind of lit up her face.

Man, she was one good-looking woman. Her black hair was a little straighter than Lucy's, and she had a tendency to wear it up in a ponytail that kind of swished from side to side when she walked. Her eyes were an intense cobalt blue that always made him feel as if she could see right through him. Sometimes it was nerve racking to stare Sabina in the eye.

And then there was her mouth.

It was pouty and kind of made for sin. Ross had had his share of teenaged fantasies about Sabina's mouth—like just about every guy at Davis High. Sabina was the captain of the cheerleading squad, the homecoming queen, and a member of the Watermelon Festival court of honor.

She was popular and built. Everyone lusted after her.

In high school she'd been rumored to be easy. Guys talked about her all the time. But Ross figured most of that was just guy talk. Even if she had gone through a whole passel of boyfriends. That didn't mean anything, except that she was picky.

Trying not to admire Sabina was like trying to stop the Edisto River from flowing to the sea. She was beautiful. There wasn't a guy in town who didn't look at her when she walked by.

But she was also about as untouchable as an ice queen. She wasn't interested in anyone, least of all him.

"Where's Lucy?" he asked.

Sabina stood up. "She's in the back, spray-painting her latest project." Sabina turned. "Hey, Lucy, Ross is here. And he's got a big surprise for you."

The door to Lucy's studio creaked open. "Did you call?" Lucy shouted.

"Yeah, Ross is here."

"Oh." Lucy's footsteps sounded down the aisle between the dealer stalls. She appeared a moment later, wearing an old paint-stained shirt that must have belonged to her daddy. As usual, she was wearing a pair of baggy jeans and black canvas lace-up sneakers with dirty white laces.

Her hair was down around her shoulders, hiding the scars on the side of her face. Blue paint that matched the smudge on her cheek and the speckles on her hands highlighted the curls on the right side of her head. She looked like a waif. Adorable and girlish.

Ross was a lucky man.

Sparky seemed to agree because he rushed Lucy, jumping up on her and knocking her back a few steps.

Uh-oh.

"What the heck is that?" She pushed Sparky down and then pointed at the dog like he was some kind of slug that Ross had dug up in the garden.

Sparky reacted immediately by hunkering down, his tail going between his legs. Clearly the dog had encountered a lot of disapproval in his short life.

"His name is Sparky. Angel brought him over to the firehouse as an engagement gift."

"Oh. Great." She rolled her eyes. "You didn't accept this gift, did you?"

"Well, yeah. I'm here with him, aren't I?"

"And you didn't call me?"

Oops. He should have called her. They hadn't discussed pets. And Lucy was big on discussing everything, which kind of made a lot of sense. It certainly avoided arguments. But it put the kibosh on surprises.

"Uh, well, Lucy, sweetie, I'm really sorry. I guess I should have talked to you. But look at him. He's adorable, and every firehouse needs a dog."

"Fine, he can live at the firehouse then because I'm not a dog person. I don't want to deal with dog hair, or the chewing, or the poop on the floor, or the damage they do to the furniture and the hardwood floors." Lucy's mouth pinched, and her eyebrows tilted in. Ross knew that look.

Lucy never got angry like Betsy used to. Lucy never threw stuff or yelled or anything like that, which was nice and calming. But that look on her face was enough to tell him he'd screwed up. If he'd just called her first and discussed the matter instead of surprising her, this would have gone much better.

Lucy didn't like surprises much. He had to remember that.

Unfortunately Sparky recognized Lucy's body language like an old pro. He assumed a completely submissive posture. It was kind of sad, really. Someone had done a number on this dog.

Ross squatted down and gave the puppy a reassuring pat on the head, while a completely surprising surge of stubbornness welled up inside him. Okay, he'd screwed up. But Ross was going to get his way this time.

If they were going to get married, then Lucy would have to meet him in the middle on this one thing.

"Sweetie. Look at him. He's been abused. And he needs a home or they're going to put him down." Ross straightened his shoulders and stood up. "I apologize for not talking to you first. But I'm not giving Sparky back to the animal shelter. I will solemnly promise you that I will make sure he's trained and behaves. And you will never have to walk him or.feed him or pick up his poop."

"I don't want a dog, Ross." Now she sounded whiny, and it kind of annoyed him. Although he understood where this was coming from. It was a control thing.

"You'll learn to love him. We're going to compromise on this. Just like we've compromised on other things. Like I've agreed to go with you to the shooting range once a week, even though I'm not that into it. You can agree to let me have a dog, even though you're not that into dogs."

"No." She turned, her curls whipping, and stalked back into her workroom.

"Wow," Sabina said when Lucy actually slammed the door to her workroom. "I've never seen her that ticked off. At least not recently."

Wow indeed. It wasn't like Lucy to stomp away from a discussion or slam doors like a teenager. She was always so rational about things. This whole marriage thing was scaring her. He could relate to the feeling.

"Give her time. She'll come around," Sabina said, patting his shoulder. Even through his polo shirt, his skin reacted to that tiny pressure as if her fingers had branded him. And when she moved her hand, he felt a keen sense of loss.

He needed to get out of here.

"If she wants to know, I'm going to the park to give Sparky some leash training." And with that, Ross left the store and headed down to the village green where Sparky, smart dog that he was, did his business in the bushes.

Lucy was acting like a spoiled child. This, too, was partially Sabina's fault. She and Momma had spoiled Lucy. But this time, Sabina needed to do something about it.

So she headed back to Lucy's workroom and opened the door without being invited. Since there was no lock on the door, it wasn't a good place for Lucy to hide out.

Lucy was standing there at her workbench staring into space. Thank goodness she wasn't crying or throwing stuff. But that wasn't Lucy's way.

"Uh, Luce, don't you think you were just a little bit harsh on Ross?"

"No." Lucy picked up a sizable chain and slammed it onto the top of the dresser she was distressing. So much for not throwing things.

"No? Honey, you scared that dog and you ruined Ross's day. What's come over you? And what's wrong with getting a dog? He's adorable. And it's clear Ross loves him."

"He didn't ask me."

Sabina understood. So much of Lucy's life had been completely out of her control. And Ross usually let her have her way. Which made for a happy relationship. But this time, Sabina was on Ross's side. It wasn't exactly the most comfortable place to be.

And she probably had no business interjecting herself into her sister's relationship. But she was going to say her piece anyway.

"Honey, he didn't ask you first because he wanted to surprise you."

"I don't like surprises. He knows that. We talk about everything. We have a *plan*."

"Right. And he decided to stray from your plan. Is that it?"

"Well...I don't want a dog."

"But he does. Can't you compromise?"

"No. This is important. Getting a dog is a big decision. And he knows me well enough to know that he should have discussed it with me first."

"Honey, that man has been running away from commitment ever since he came back here two years ago. And in the space of several days, he's bought a house, asked you to marry him, and committed to a dog. This is cause for celebration. Besides, you can't control everything, Lucy. It's not reasonable. And it's not fair to him. He has to be able to make some decisions on his own."

Lucy fluffed her dark hair forward. It was an old, old habit. When Lucy got out of her comfort zone she pulled her hair forward and tried to hide behind it. It was one of the things the fire had done to her.

And every time Lucy pulled her hair forward like that, it made Sabina's heart ache. "Honey, he loves you."

Lucy shrugged like a ticked-off teenager. Emphatically. She hauled off and whacked the dresser again.

Oh, boy, this was bad. "Honey, what's wrong? This is about more than the dog, isn't it?"

Lucy slammed the chain down again, so hard the dresser danced across the concrete floor. "Do I have to tell you everything?" she said in a tight voice. "Can't I keep some secrets?"

It was time for Sabina to retreat. "I'm sorry. I didn't mean to pry. I'm just saying that you hurt Ross a minute ago. And you should think about that."

Sabina turned away, a familiar and toxic mixture of anger and guilt gripping her gut, making her stomach cramp up.

"The only reason Ross asked me to marry him is because of you." Lucy said the words in a dead voice and yet it was as if she'd used a whip to lay open Sabina's back.

Sabina turned. "That's not true."

"Isn't it? He's been dragging his feet, and then Miriam Randall comes in here and tells the world that I'm standing in the way of your happiness."

This was exactly what Sabina feared would happen the moment Momma told the Altar Guild about Miriam's visit. Lucy had a right to be furious. No one could control the Altar Guild once they got hold of an issue.

The truly ironic thing about this horrible situation was that Miriam hadn't said anything remarkable, because Sabina had promised to look after Lucy on the night of the fire. It was Sabina's fault that Lucy was scarred. Sabina was supposed to babysit, but she'd gone out skinny-dipping with her friends instead.

Sabina would never be able to move on in her life until Lucy was settled and happy. Everyone in town already knew that. So what had changed?

Not one thing, except that Miriam Randall had opened her mouth and the church ladies of Last Chance had decided that it was time for Lucy and Ross to get hitched. Sometimes living in a small town could be a trial.

Sabina counted to five before speaking again. "Honey, the only reason to marry Ross is because you love him. If you don't love him, then don't marry him. Don't let Miriam Randall change your mind about things. But don't play with Ross, either. You hurt him a minute ago.

He came in here all happy, and you popped his balloon. Seems to me you need to apologize."

Sabina turned away and walked slowly to the front of the store. When she arrived at the sales counter, she couldn't manage to sit down. She wasn't going to stay here counting the minutes while Lucy stewed.

For once, Sabina was bone-weary of sitting around waiting on Lucy to figure things out.

So she pushed through the front doors and headed down the sidewalk, trying to shake off a sudden sense of deep dissatisfaction with her life. She'd been waiting for years, planning trips to places she knew, down deep, she'd never visit. Waiting for some magical moment when she could trust herself to leave Lucy.

She had done this to herself. Momma and Daddy had never blamed her for the fire. In fact, everyone agreed that if Sabina hadn't sneaked out that night, Sabina herself might have been killed or scarred. The fire had been intense, and it had started in Sabina's room.

Still, Sabina couldn't shake the guilt.

And here she was being blamed by the one person she loved more than anyone. The one person she'd devoted herself to.

It wasn't fair. But nothing in life was fair. Was it fair that Lucy had been burned in the fire? No.

She was near tears when she reached the park in front of City Hall. So the last person she wanted to see right at that moment was Ross Gardiner and his adorable dog, Sparky.

But there they were, right in her path. And there was no way to escape. Ross had already seen her and was waving halfheartedly.

"Are you okay?" he asked. Damn but he had a deep voice—the kind that was made to talk slow. When she found Mr. Right, she sure hoped he had a deep, slow voice like that.

And hazel eyes. And a square chin. And a tall, fire-fighter body. Yeah, she would order up one of those, please.

"I guess I'm in the doghouse too," she said. "For what it's worth, I told Lucy she was being unreasonable."

"Hey, Sabina, don't sweat it. This was my fault. I should have asked first," he said.

She resisted the urge to fuss at him. Lucy had worn her out. "Sometimes Lucy can be inflexible."

"Yeah, I know."

"That doesn't mean you have to bend around her. It means you have to soften her up a little. She's just scared."

"I know."

She looked up into his face. He was classically hand-some with a take-no-prisoners body. He was, in fact, exactly like the images of naked Greek statuary she'd seen during her online travel planning.

She pushed those images out of her mind. "We need to reassure Lucy," Sabina said.

This earned her a frown. "No, Sabina, *I* need to reas-sure her. And to tell you the truth, I'm trying to figure out how Lucy and I never got around to talking about dogs in the last year and a half. God knows we've talked about everything else. And I had a dog once."

"Did you?"

He nodded. "Yeah. I lost him in the divorce."

"Oh."

"Yeah. I guess maybe that's why we never talked about it. Painful subject."

"I can imagine."

"So you think I should take Sparky back to the shelter?" He sounded as earnest as an altar boy. And come to think about it, he had been an altar boy once—for the Episcopalians. Which probably explained why Ross was such a good man. Good down to his soul.

He would do anything to please Lucy. But she hoped, with all her heart, that he wouldn't take Sparky back to the pound.

"No. You need to keep him. He's perfect." She squatted down and gave the dog another good scratch behind his ears. He lapped it up, and her heart melted.

"Look, Ross," she said as she continued to pet the dog, "this is undoubtedly my fault. I always let Lucy get away with murder. And I'm afraid she's become good at manipulating us. So on this issue, you should hold your ground. You're a fireman. You need a Dalmatian. Lucy isn't going to break up with you over a dog." She finally turned her gaze up toward him.

He gave her a slow smile. The kind that sparked an iridescent fire in his hazel eyes. Good Lord, when he turned that smile on her, it was like staring right into the sun.

A girl could end up sunburned and blind if she stared too long.

Between the whining puppy, his own misgivings about the dog, and Lucy's angry silence, Ross found it impossible to sleep. He tossed and turned before he drifted off well past midnight.

And right after he'd closed his eyes, his beeper sounded, jolting him awake again. His digital bedside clock read 2:30 a.m. Within a dozen heartbeats, Ross hailed the county dispatcher on his emergency radio.

The fire was out on Route 321 at Jessamine Manor.

Adrenaline was already pumping through his system, and his training kicked in. He jumped into his clothes, which were laid out in case of an emergency. He made it to the station in two minutes flat. It took one minute more to jump into his turnout suit.

Four minutes later the E-One pumper/tanker was headed down the road with Dash Randall behind the wheel, Ross in the chief's seat, and Matt Jasper, Red Canaday, and Bubba Lockheart riding jump. Ross had a clipboard in hand with his Incident Commander checklist ready. The Last Chance Fire Department was likely to be first on the scene, which meant he would be in charge of this incident come hell or high water.

The fire's glow was visible a mile away. "This is going to be a big one," Dash shouted above the siren.

Ross nodded, his thoughts suddenly turning to a fire he'd fought in a new housing development out in Tacoma years ago. That fire had been big and dangerous, and set purposefully.

"When we get there, I want a reverse hose lay," he said to the guys in the jump seats. "But I don't want anyone going near that fire with personal lines, is that clear?"

"Sure," Matt said. "What's up?"

"Just a very bad gut feeling."

The Tacoma fire had been set with incendiary devices that used a metal accelerant, and the fire burned for hours as they struggled to turn off the natural gas lines. The memories prickled Ross's skin.

And his heart slammed against his ribs as they pulled into the access road for Jessamine Manor. Ross had been prepared to use a bolt cutter to get through the gate, but it was already thrown open and a big, white bedsheet had been draped over it.

The spray-painted slogan had been rendered in blood red paint. "You can't control what's wild," it said. It was signed "Earth First."

"What the hell?" Dash said. "Earth First? Who are they?"

"Eco-terrorists."

Matt let go of a string of profanity that he'd probably learned in the army.

"C'mon, Dash, let's get the hoses down," Ross said.

Dash motored through the open gate toward a fire that was probably the biggest thing any of the volunteers had ever seen. Seven nearly completed houses, including the one Ross had bought Wednesday, were burning. The flames threatened two more homes that were in the early stages of construction. There was no way to stop this fire at its source.

There were probably multiple sources fed by incendiaries. Ross opened a radio channel to the county dispatcher even before Dash maneuvered the pumper beside the hydrant closest to the fires.

"We need help," he said into the mic. "Seven homes are fully involved in fire. No likely casualties since the homes are unoccupied, but we need more than five firefighters and one cannon. And Sheryl, this fire looks like arson. It might be eco-terrorism. I've seen this before. Everyone responding should use extreme caution. You should probably call the Sheriff's Department and the Department of Public Works. We need to shut down any gas lines, and we need to do it now."

"Sending Station One and Three." The dispatcher's voice crackled over the static.

"You better send them all, Sheryl. And you might need to call in help from Bamberg."

Red, the hose man, jumped out of the pumper with a wrench in one hand as he started pulling out hose from the back of the truck. He wrapped the hose end around the hydrant and gave Dash a wave. Dash inched the truck forward toward the house at the end of the cul-de-sac. This maneuver would leave room behind the Last Chance pumper for the other fire companies that would soon be on their way.

Once he had the truck positioned, Ross took command and directed his team. He sent Dash to start working the pumps. Then he went through his incident checklist. Saving lives was always his first priority. In this case, the houses were still under construction and probably unoccupied. But more important, the fire was so big his team was unlikely to be able to control it with hand lines. He needed to darken it down fast, so when the additional fire companies came, they could get close enough with hand lines to secure the utilities and avoid a natural-gas-fed disaster.

So he directed Matt to man the deluge gun located above the pump panel. Within a minute Matt had a master stream of water trained on the roof of the last house on the cul-de-sac. The gun could put out a thousand gallons per minute. And Ross figured they would need more than one gun before the night was over.

While Matt and Dash were aiming the cannon, Ross helped Red and Bubba lay the reverse hose line from the Last Chance pumper back to the hydrant.

When Station One from Allenberg arrived minutes later, they were able to tap into the water fast, using Ross's pump instead of having to find another hydrant. Their cannon went to work, and by the time the Big Swamp station arrived, the firefighters were able to move in with hand lines.

Even so, it took all five county fire companies more than four hours to put out the fire, and they had to let four of the houses burn themselves out because they couldn't get close enough without putting lives in jeopardy. And even though one of those houses belonged to Ross, it was just an empty building. It could be replaced.

It wasn't quite sunrise when Ross found himself standing by the construction fence along with Sheriff Rhodes, County Executive Dennis Hayden, and Elias Webster, the president of Webster Homes.

The Sheriff's Department had set up a bank of arc lights for the firefighters. A point of some irritation for everyone, since Ross and the rest of the paid fire chiefs had been requesting a budget for arc lights for years. But right now, the sheriff's lights were trained on the bedsheet and its red slogan.

"I've called the FBI," Hayden said.

It was hard to tell if the sheriff was annoyed by this announcement. Stone Rhodes had the ability to mask his emotions better than anyone Ross had ever known. It should have been Sheriff Rhodes who made that call. And without question, the arrival of the FBI would probably cause him no end of headaches. But Hayden was a Republican and Rhodes was a Democrat. And these days everything seemed to come down to partisan bickering. There was an election less than two months away.

Even without the politics, Sheriff Rhodes was the kind of guy who hated anyone coming into his territory and making trouble. It wouldn't sit well with him to have some outside FBI agents taking over the investigation.

"So, Ross, you said you've seen this before?" the sheriff asked.

"Yeah, I was a firefighter in Tacoma when Earth First burned down those model green homes. You may have remembered the incident. It was all over the national news. They torched six, million-dollar homes."

"Yeah, I vaguely recall that. Did they catch the perpetrators?"

Ross shook his head. "No. They used something call

thermite to set those fires. They burned really hot and incinerated all the evidence."

"You think they used that stuff here?"

"I don't know, but those fires were pretty hot, Stone. And it's going to be impossible to tell one way or another. There's too much damage."

Sheriff Rhodes nodded. "I reckon they thought the development was too close to the swamp."

"The county approved our building permits, Sheriff. We went through a boatload of red tape and an environmental assessment to get them." Elias Webster was a small man with thin shoulders and a bushy mustache. He stood there wringing his hands, his eyes flicking back and forth like jumping beans. The guy looked panicked and guilty as hell.

Sheriff Rhodes nodded. "I know that, Elias, but not everyone was all that happy about it."

"We aren't harming the swamp. And besides, Allenberg County is the last place on earth I would expect to find Earth First people."

"Well, that's why we've called in the FBI," Hayden said. "We'll let them figure it out."

Elias crossed his arms and practically hugged himself. "I gotta go. I gotta call my insurance company. This is bad."

Ross took out his cell phone and snapped a photo of the bedsheet. He looked up at the sheriff and said in a low whisper, "Can I have a word in private with you?"

Stone Rhodes nodded.

"I see the guys have stowed all the hose," Ross said in a louder tone. "It's time for us to get some shut-eye." Ross nodded at Hayden and Webster, then he turned toward the Last Chance pumper engine. Stone walked with him.

"What's up?"

"I can't put my finger on it," Ross said. "Call it a gut feeling or something. This looks a lot like that fire up in Tacoma. Too much like it."

"What does that mean?"

"The slogan on that bedsheet is almost word-for-word the same. The same colored paint. Shoot, Stone, the spacing of the letters looks similar."

"Are you saying we have a copycat?"

"I don't know. Maybe. Earth First is pretty decentralized. The chances of two cells using the same slogans seems unlikely. This could be something else."

"You seem to know a lot about Earth First." The sheriff's eyebrow arched.

"I was there for those fires in Tacoma. I saw the damage. That was the biggest fire I ever encountered. And crap like that lives with you when you do what I do for a living."

The sheriff nodded but didn't say anything more.

"You know, Sheriff, this could be a lot of things besides terrorism. Someone in town might be mad about the changes and growth we've been having. Or it could be a simple case of economic arson. There's something a little off about Webster's reaction to this."

"You think Webster has issues?"

Ross shook his head. "I don't know. I'm just saying something doesn't feel right."

"I can't act on gut feelings," the sheriff said. "If you come up with anything concrete, let me know. Of course, by tomorrow we're going to have both the FBI and the ATF crawling up our butts. I'm so not looking forward to that."

• • •

ATF agent Zach Bailey leaned back in the single, ugly side chair in Ross's office, one foot cocked over his knee. He was a wiry guy in his early thirties, with military short dark hair, dressed in a gray suit, white shirt, colorless tie, and spit-shined wing tips. The bulge of his shoulder holster was evident. An American flag lapel pin completed the classic G-man profile.

Except that he had that hungry look in his brown eyes. Like he knew this arson was going to be his ticket out of the Columbia ATF office and on to bigger and more urban things. And like all ATF agents his grasp of the facts exceeded his understanding of them. What was it about ATF agents that made them so arrogant? Did the feds train that crap into them at the Federal Law Enforcement Training Center in Georgia?

"This is a classic case of eco-terrorism," Agent Bailey said. "We've set up a federal task force and detailed a few FBI agents as well as ATF and local law enforcement. County Executive Hayden wants all of the Allenberg County fire chiefs to cooperate with the federal authorities. I have only a few questions."

Of course they were setting up a task force. It was SOP. But this wasn't terrorism; it was arson. And Bailey was ATF, he should know this. The gung-ho FBI types maybe not so much. "Look, Agent Bailey, I—"

"You can call me Zach." He flashed a boyish grin. Man, did they teach them that grin at FLETC, too?

Ross ground his molars and managed to speak through his locked jaw. "Okay, *Zach*. I agree that the bedsheet makes this look like a terrorist act, but I have two problems with that scenario. First, this is East Nowhere, South

Carolina. We don't have terrorists here. And those houses weren't near any environmentally sensitive swampland."

Bailey shook his head, his face going grim. "Chief Gardiner, that's exactly the kind of attitude that led to the Oklahoma City bombing. You can have terrorists anywhere. And besides, Webster Homes had some issues getting their permits. They were required to do an environmental impact statement. So it's plausible that a disgruntled person might have taken things into their own hands."

Okay, so the guy had some evidence to support his case. But it was still ridiculous to think that eco-terrorism could strike such a small, sleepy town. Ross stretched his achy shoulders. "All right, I guess I agree that you have to investigate the possibility of terrorists. But really, Zach, it's kind of far-fetched in this community. Besides, I think you should compare those bedsheets we found last night with the ones Earth First strung up outside the fire they set in Tacoma, Washington, four years ago."

"Of course we're going to do that."

Ross refrained from rolling his eyes. Instead he turned his laptop computer toward Agent Bailey and pulled up the AP News photo that had been taken of Earth First's most notorious arson. "Do you see what I mean?"

Bailey frowned, missing the obvious. Typical.

"The sheets are almost identical," Ross explained. "Not just the words, but the spacing of them is almost the same. If this really were Earth First, the slogans would be different. Earth First is composed of anarchists. They don't have any central control. If you look at every arson they've perpetrated, the slogans are different every time. But not this time. Why?"

Zach looked up from the computer screen, his dark gaze narrowed. "Why does a small-town fire chief know so much about Earth First?"

Oh, brother. Twice now, law enforcement had given him that look. At least Stone didn't come right out and suggest that his knowledge made him a prime suspect. But then Zach Bailey was most definitely not Stone Rhodes.

"I guess I just put myself on your suspect list, huh?" Ross said, forcing a smile.

A muscle worked in Bailey's cheek, but he said nothing.

"If I'm not, then I ought to be. Let me run it down for you," Ross said, ticking off facts on his fingers. "I was on the Tacoma Fire Department when Earth First burned those luxury homes, which is how I know so much about them. And now I'm here, where they strike again. Funny how an Earth First arson followed me from Tacoma to this sleepy little town."

Ross paused for a moment, but Agent Bailey remained silent. So he continued to lay it all out for him. "If you follow the KISS principle, the theory that I'm a serial arsonist is way more likely than any eco-terrorist threat."

"I guess so," Bailey said.

"Look, all I'm saying is that if you want to do your job right, you'll have to jettison eco-terrorism as your first theory of the crime."

"Someone set those fires," Bailey said.

"That's right, and—"

The door flew open and slammed against the doorjamb as Lucy came striding into the office like she owned the place. "Hey—" Her greeting was cut short the moment she saw Agent Bailey.

And then her mouth kind of dropped open for a

moment and her eyes got wide. Ross wasn't sure what to make of Lucy's expression except that Lucy had a thing for guns. And Zach was clearly carrying one. He halfway expected her to ask Bailey about his weapon. And if she did that, they'd be there all day talking target shooting.

"Hey, Luce," he said, "I'd like you to meet ATF agent Zach Bailey. Zach this is my fiancée, Lucy Grey."

Agent Bailey hopped up from his chair and shook Lucy's hand. The guy held on for a little bit too long to suit Ross. It was almost the last straw. If Ross weren't a reasonable and calm sort of guy, he would pick Bailey up and drop-kick him to the curb outside his firehouse. He got up from his desk with the intent of making sure the guy let go.

The minute Ross stood, Agent Bailey dropped Lucy's hand and took a step backward.

Lucy turned toward Ross and opened her mouth to say something, but before the words came out Sparky scooted from under the desk and rushed Lucy the same way he'd done the day before. He really wanted to make friends, but unfortunately this time he left paw prints on her white pants.

"Oh, damn. Go away, you dog." She pushed Sparky down just as Ross grabbed his collar and told him to sit. The dog didn't obey. Sparky just panted and wagged his tail.

"Ross Gardiner, I came over here to have an adult conversation with you about the house and the dog. But how can I do that when that animal is jumping all over me? Let me make myself clear. That dog has to go."

She paused in order to draw breath, then continued her tirade. "And as for the house, I'm sorry that it burned down, but I think we should postpone the wedding until the house can be rebuilt."

"But Lucy, what about—"

"I think we should wait, Ross. You know our plan was to wait all along. And Sabina said something yesterday that made me think. We shouldn't be rushing off just because of something Miriam Randall said. Even if we had to wait a year for the house to be rebuilt, that wouldn't be the end of the world. It would put us right back on schedule the way we planned. Clearly this misunderstanding about the dog indicates that we need some more time."

She turned and headed out of the office.

Ross followed her, wondering if this meant he was going to be celibate for yet another year. He was smart enough not to ask that question out loud, though. Instead he said, "But what about Sabina?"

"What about her?"

"Well, you know."

Lucy turned. "Look, I love my sister, but I'm not rushing into something just because some senile old lady tells me I'm standing in the way of her happiness. We had a plan, and I think this fire may be a blessing in disguise."

"A blessing? When is a fire ever a blessing? How can you say that, especially after all you've been through?"

His thoughtless words didn't go over too well. Lucy pursed her lips. He knew this look. She wouldn't yell at him, but there was ice in that stare. So he shut his mouth and stood there, jamming his hands into his pockets as she turned and walked away.

When Lucy had slammed the main firehouse door behind her, Ross took his hands out of his pockets and walked back into his office. He was furious. With Lucy. With the ATF. With Sabina. With himself.

"Wow," Bailey said after a long moment.

Ross's fists curled of their own accord. He had to stifle the urge to pop the guy in his pretty-boy face. He looked down at Sparky and consciously relaxed his hands. "Sit," he commanded in a soft voice. And of course the dog did as he was told this time. "Good dog."

"So did I misunderstand something? Was one of those houses yours?" Bailey asked.

"Yeah, I put down a binder on it a couple of days ago."

"And it was supposed to be a wedding gift, huh?"

"No, it was more of a requirement before she said yes."

Bailey's forehead rumpled. "Guess I need to take you off my list of potential suspects." There was restrained humor in his voice, and Ross didn't like it one bit. The ATF agent was trying not to laugh at him.

"What exactly does that mean?" Ross spat out the words.

"It means that, if I were in your position and a woman like that wanted me to buy her a house before she said yes, I would definitely buy the house. Obviously you had a lot to lose if the place burned down."

CHAPTER 4

Sabina was surprised when Layton didn't cancel their date for drinks on Friday. With all the uproar over the fire at Jessamine Manor, it would have made sense. But he'd called at three that afternoon to confirm, so here she stood at the threshold of Dot's Spot in the middle of Friday happy hour with her hands kind of sweaty and her pulse rate definitely a little high.

Not that she was all that excited to be having drinks with Layton Webster. But it did strike her that it had been a long, long time since she'd had drinks with *anyone*. She'd put herself on a shelf some time ago, for reasons she couldn't even articulate. Maybe it was just that she'd been too busy to date. She had something going almost every day of the week, it seemed, what with the Altar Guild, helping out at the assisted living place, and running a business.

Layton sat at a booth on the opposite side of the bar. She squared her shoulders and tried to smile at him, but the smile kind of flopped. Probably because her mouth was trembling.

She needed to get a grip. But one look at him, dressed in a blue sport jacket and gray slacks with those gorgeous Italian loafers on his feet, and she knew that Layton had outgrown Last Chance. He was way out of her league, which was kind of humorous, actually, given that he'd once been the high-school dork.

It was always a bad sign when your date outdressed you. Her outfit—a pair of gray slacks and a teal twinset she'd gotten on sale at Belks—felt a little bit... What was the word? Dowdy? Small-town? Unsophisticated?

She slipped into the booth, thankful for the dim light. She could hide her nervousness and the fact that her outfit probably cost less than one of his shoes. He sure was getting the last laugh, wasn't he? Maybe that's all he wanted.

"So." Her voice came out like she was starving for oxygen, which was kind of true because she was so nervous she was practically hyperventilating. So when she managed to get her voice going again all she could say was, "I guess it's been a rough day for you."

He picked up his highball glass. It looked like scotch or bourbon on the rocks. "Uncle Elias is pretty upset. This whole eco-terrorism thing came from right out of the blue. And the insurance company is kind of on his back right at the moment."

"Hey, Sabina," Reba Burton said as she came up carrying a drink tray under her arm. Reba had been working Friday nights at Dot's for about a year now. The bar had started to draw a substantial crowd on Fridays because the Wild Horses performed there, and the band had gained an impressive following thanks to Clay Rhodes and his weekly radio show on WLST. "I haven't seen you here in ages, hon. How's life at Last Chance Around?" Reba blinked her overly made-up eyes.

"The same."

"Whatcha drinking?"

"I'll have a glass of your house Chardonnay."

"Coming right up."

Layton laughed when Reba left. "I never figured Dot Cox would serve Chardonnay in her place. The town's come a long way, hasn't it?"

Sabina nodded and tried to make eye contact, which was difficult. Layton sometimes stared, but often kept his eyes trained elsewhere. Sabina didn't know if he was happy to see her or just waiting to spring a trap. She tried to relax and talk about the town. It seemed like a safe topic. "Last Chance has changed a lot in the last few years. We all have Rocky Rhodes to thank for that. I guess she got the last laugh, too, huh?"

His wandering gaze returned and locked itself on her. What was it about that stare that made Sabina wary and drew her in at the same time? Layton had a certain amount of sex appeal, she'd give him that. His mouth twitched up into his ever-present smirk. "Sabina, I'm not here to make you feel bad."

"I guess that makes you a better person than me. I am so sorry for the way I behaved."

"You were fourteen. I've already forgiven you."

Sabina relaxed a little. He seemed earnest, with those avid blue eyes sparkling in the light from the votive candle on the table. "Thank you."

Reba returned with her wine, and she took a hearty gulp then got the conversation rolling with the news of the day. "So, do you really believe eco-terrorists burned down your uncle's houses?"

He shook his head no, but he said, "I think so." Which left Sabina wondering what he actually felt about the matter.

"It seems hard to believe that we'd have something like that in Last Chance."

"I saw the slogans on that bedsheet," Layton said. "And the damage to the houses was extensive. Allenberg fire coordinator Baako was out there with a bunch of FBI and ATF agents this morning. They seem to think the fires were started with explosive devices of some kind. That doesn't sound like your garden-variety arsonist."

So he really did believe it was terrorism. That was unsettling. "Your uncle must be beside himself," Sabina said.

"He's got insurance. If they agree to pay the claim. They're being hard-asses. And this will set him back, I'm afraid."

"I'm sorry."

"Let's talk about better things," Layton said. "I was kind of surprised to learn that you've been living here all these years. You never went to college? I seem to remember that you were a good student. You were the only girl in math club in eighth grade."

Which was exactly how she'd ended up inviting Layton to the eighth-grade dance. And then she'd let some of her girlfriends talk her into being cruel. And then she'd given up the math club because she wanted to be a cheerleader and she'd kind of gotten the message that cheerleaders never, ever hung around with geeks. Nor did they admit that they liked doing math.

She looked down at her wine for a long moment. She'd

been such an idiot teenager. And revisiting that time with Layton was the last thing she wanted to do. So she evaded. "Well, it turned out okay. I have a business I truly love."

"Selling junk?" He seemed truly surprised.

She tried not to judge him too harshly. Because, in fact, she did sell junk. But one person's junk was another person's treasure. And it was something she loved doing. So she leaned forward, perfectly happy to talk about her business. "You know, when I was real young, Momma would take me and Lucy on road trips, and we would stop at every old barn or junk shop along the way. I thought it was like going on a weekly treasure hunt. I started investing my allowance in things I liked. And then I started selling some of them on eBay. And when I started making real money at it, I decided it was probably my calling."

"And you never had any desire to leave this town?"

She shrugged one shoulder. "Once Lucy gets married, I'm going to take a European vacation."

He leaned in again. Her personal space contracted. "What does Lucy have to do with it?"

Damn. She'd walked right into that, hadn't she? "Layton, you know good and well what happened to Lucy our senior year. That's why I didn't go to college. I don't want to revisit the past. Let's just say that I feel a certain amount of responsibility for what happened. And I'd like to see her settled before I leave for an extended vacation."

Oh good grief, she'd done it again—ruined a perfectly romantic moment by talking about her younger sister. "I'm sorry," she said in a rush, trying to salvage the disastrous situation. "I don't like talking about the past. And I'm guessing you don't, either. You couldn't have been very happy growing up here."

This got no reaction from him. He didn't smile or smirk or nod his head or anything. It was as if the words passed him right by. "But *you* were happy." He said the words like a statement, not a question.

"I was, and then everything changed."

He nodded as if he understood. And Sabina wasn't sure where to take the conversation next. So she left the ball in his court. Then someone punched up a George Strait tune on the jukebox. It was only seven o'clock, two hours before the live music started. Layton knocked back the rest of his drink and put the glass down on the wood table. "Sabina Grey, I've been waiting decades for this. Would you like to dance with me?"

"Oh!" She had not anticipated this.

He smirked. "Trust me, I'm not really trying to relive the past. I'm trying to make a new memory. Maybe for both of us."

Good Lord, he really had grown up, hadn't he?

So she let him lead her to the dance floor. His hands were dry and surprisingly smooth for a guy. But then Layton worked with his mind, not his hands. No one else was dancing, of course, so they had the entire dance floor to themselves. Which was a little unnerving, since everyone watched them. And of course, the song was a waltz—kind of intimate and romantic.

She panicked for a moment. Did Layton know how to waltz? She remembered an awkward boy who had no sense of rhythm. If he didn't know how to waltz, they were going to be in big trouble. Because Sabina had only the most rudimentary idea of how to do this dance.

She worried for no reason at all. Somewhere along the line, the nerdy boy had taken dance lessons. Or maybe like the ugly duckling, he'd grown up and turned into a dancing swan.

He knew how to waltz. Even better, he knew how to lead. And he didn't try any cheap tricks like trying to pull her too close or anything like that.

He was, in a word, the perfect, waltzing gentleman.

Ross walked into Dot's with two intentions: a tall, cold beer and some good country music. But he didn't get far once he realized that Layton Webster had Sabina Grey in a death grip as he waltzed her around the dance floor. The guy looked like he was channeling a *Dancing with the Stars* contestant.

And speaking of stars, it sure looked like Sabina had them in her eyes. She was looking up at Layton with one of those sappy looks that women get sometimes.

Damn. Ross crossed his arms over his chest and swallowed down the visceral reaction.

He didn't like Layton Webster. The guy had been a creepy nerd growing up. And now he was a little too smooth to be real. Sabina deserved someone more genuine than *that guy* with his fancy shoes and monogrammed shirts.

Besides, as far as Ross was concerned, Layton's uncle Elias Webster was the prime suspect in last night's fire. Arson for profit was a much better theory of the crime than eco-terrorism. So naturally Ross didn't want Sabina having anything to do with the Websters right now. Not until he could satisfy himself that they weren't a bunch of crooks.

So when the dance ended, he followed Sabina and Layton back to their table and crashed their date. He was doing it for Sabina's own good, even if she did give him a get-lost eye roll the moment he sat himself down.

"Layton," Ross said. "It's been a long time. I didn't have a chance to say hey this morning when you were down at the scene talking to Agent Bailey."

"Ross, uh, what are you doing here?" Sabina gave his shin a swift kick under the table.

It stung, but he held his ground. "Just catching up with an old classmate," Ross said, leaning back in his chair, cocking up the bruised shin and giving it a quick massage. "How are you doing? It's been years."

"I've been good," Layton said in a mild-mannered voice. The guy leaned back in his seat, and for a moment he seemed to be looking anywhere but directly at Ross. But then Layton must have realized what his body language was saying because he stopped and looked Ross right in the eye.

He had a goofy smile on his lips, but there was nothing in those blue eyes. They were kind of dead, even if the candlelight flickered in them.

Wow. This guy wasn't wired right.

Ross immediately went into serve-and-protect mode. There was no way in hell he was letting Sabina spend any more time than was necessary with this dude. "So how's your uncle doing?" he asked.

"He's upset, as you can imagine. He's spent the day with the insurance company. Getting a payment from them is going to take some time since arson was involved. I gather they're sending an investigator." Layton's voice had changed slightly. The volume went up, and he was talking fast.

He was hiding something. Ross was sure of it. He moved in, his palms on the table, invading Layton's space. And yet the guy didn't look away. He held Ross's gaze with an unnatural steadiness that confirmed Ross's suspicions.

"Did your uncle get any warning at all from Earth First?" Ross asked.

"I don't know. Look, I only got here a few days ago. I don't really know what's going on with Uncle Elias. He's had some recent success, but he's never been what you'd call a business whiz."

"So what brings you back?"

"Didn't I just tell you that Uncle Elias isn't exactly the brightest bulb in the chandelier?" Layton's snotty tone was unmistakable. The little nerd had the audacity to look down on Ross, and probably every other person in Last Chance who had to work for a living.

"My uncle has been having trouble with project management issues," Layton continued. "I offered to help him with a new automated system so I've only just started my audit of his systems. I started day before yesterday. I've hardly scratched the surface."

"Anything odd turn up?"

Layton leaned forward, his face oddly unemotional considering the way Ross was pushing the envelope. "Are you interrogating me?"

"No, I'm just asking a few questions."

"But I'm not answering questions. Not from you, anyway. My uncle is cooperating with the ATF and the insurance company. So if you're suggesting that Uncle Elias set that fire for financial reasons, you're crazy. Didn't you see those bedsheets?"

Sabina touched Ross's shoulder, and heat flowed down his arms. "Ross, please," she said in that tone of voice that always made him want to do anything to please her. "I'm having drinks with a friend. I know you're upset about the house, but—"

"I'm not upset about the house." Ross blurted the words and immediately regretted them.

Sabina's expression telegraphed her shock. "How can you say that when you know how much Lucy wanted that house? She loved that house, and she wants a house before—"

"Well, it's clear y'all have some family issues to work out," Layton said, standing up. "And I'm not going to sit here while you discuss them."

Layton dropped a fifty-dollar bill on the table and marched toward the door. Lucy immediately tried to get up but Ross caught her by the wrist. "Don't go after him."

She tried to pull away, but he held her fast. "Ross, you're being an ass."

"You need help over there?" Dot called from behind the bar. It was amazing how Dot had a nose for conflict.

"Nope, we're fine," Ross said with a tight smile.

Dot gave him a sober look. "I certainly hope so, Ross. Otherwise your reputation for being a Boy Scout might be in jeopardy."

"Let me go," Sabina whispered.

"No. Sit down. I want you to hear something important about Layton Webster." He turned toward Dot. "Can you please get Sabina another glass of wine, and I'll have a longneck Bud."

Sabina sat down and pulled away from Ross, even though a small part of her didn't want to. Which was crazy, because Ross had just behaved like a complete jerk.

"I don't trust that guy. You're better off without him," Ross said.

"Oh, my…" She refrained from taking the Lord's

name in vain but she sure did want to. She wanted to spit in Ross's eye, too, but that would be unladylike. So she pushed her annoyance down deep inside and tried to behave like a grown-up. "Layton Webster has endured more than his share from the judgmental people in this town. We treated him like crap in high school. And you just did it again. I'm so disappointed in you."

Before he could respond, Reba came by with their drinks and saw the fifty-dollar bill on the table. "Uh, are these on the same tab?" Her gaze bounced from Ross to Sabina and back again.

Sabina picked up the money and handed it to Reba. "No, honey. Use this to cover the first round and then keep the change. Ross is paying for these drinks." She gave Ross the stink eye. "Since he ordered them."

Reba grinned. "Thanks, Sabina. That Mr. Webster sure is a high roller, ain't he?"

"Yeah, he sure is," Ross grumbled.

Ross picked up his beer and downed it in several long swallows. Sabina found herself watching his Adam's apple, trying to remain angry with him. Instead her anger morphed into something hotter and much more dangerous.

Damn.

"I need to go." Sabina made to get up.

Ross's hand shot out again and pulled her down. "Not yet. We need to talk."

She pulled her arm away. "About what?"

"About the fire. About Layton and his uncle."

"What about them?"

He hunkered his big shoulders over his empty beer bottle. His voice came out in a whisper so she had to cock her head to catch what he said. "There's this ATF dude in town who has convinced himself that we've got terrorists right here in Last Chance. But he's an idiot. The truth is, most arsons are for profit. So until I can eliminate Elias Webster, he's my top suspect. Since the fire happened only a few days after Layton showed up, Layton is also on my short list. And that makes both of them potentially dangerous. I don't want you hanging out with either of them. Is that clear?"

"Since when are you the boss of my life?" Sabina's words had an angry bite to them. She swallowed down her annoyance and spoke again, more calmly, "Besides, why would Layton Webster need to set a fire for insurance money? He's got millions in the bank."

"His uncle might need money. You heard what Layton said a minute ago. It sounds like his uncle has some business issues."

"Oh for goodness' sake." She grabbed the glass of wine she hadn't ordered and took several long swallows. She slammed it down on the table with more force than was entirely necessary. "Do you have any idea how long it's been since I've had a date with anyone? And you just chased off a guy worth millions."

His eyebrows rose as if he'd just now realized what he'd done. But there was almost no remorse in his expression. Even when he muttered the word, "Sorry," it came out lame.

She ought to slap his face. But not here with so many people watching. Besides, Ross was going to be her brother-in-law.

She broke eye contact and spoke to her wineglass. "Look, I know you bought that house because of what Miriam Randall said. And I'm sure Momma or Lucy or someone told you that you needed to do it for my sake. But that doesn't give you the right to decide what's best for me. Honestly, Ross, you need to get out of my personal life." Somewhere in the middle of this tirade she lost control of her voice. It cracked and wavered, and she was on the verge of sounding downright girlie.

"C'mon, Sabina, stop being so dramatic. Look at me."

She wanted to continue ranting at him. But if she did, she'd lose control and make a scene that everyone in town would be talking about tomorrow.

Plan B was to get up and run. But what was to stop Ross from grabbing her again? He was big and overpowering. And that would create even more gossip.

So she sat there, looking down, toying with the stem of her wineglass.

"Look at me, hon." There was so much kindness in his voice, it was hard not to be swayed by it.

She held out for another long moment before she looked up. And got lost.

If eyes were the windows to the soul, then Ross, for all he'd been a jerk tonight, had a shining, kind, good soul. In contrast, Layton's blue gaze hid as much as it revealed.

"The truth is," he said in that deep voice of his, "I may have bought that house earlier than Lucy and I planned. But I did it for Lucy, not for you. I love Lucy, and she wanted that house."

Of course he loved Lucy. It had been wrong of her to make him declare it out loud.

"I'm sorry. I didn't mean to lay a guilt trip on you. I guess I forgot that the world doesn't revolve around me."

She picked up her purse and was ready to make her getaway when he spoke again. "Hon, you are the least selfish person I know. You volunteer everywhere. You look after your folks and Lucy. You're a good person,

Sabina Grey, and I would never accuse you of being self-ish. I'm just saying that you need to move cautiously with Layton Webster."

"But you're upset about the house, aren't you? That's why you got so ticked off at Layton. It's not really about me. It's about the house and the arson."

"Of course it's about you, too. I don't like that guy."

"But I do like him. I mean, he's the first guy to ask me out in a long, long time. So back off, okay?"

His lips narrowed into a tight, disapproving line. Clearly he'd judged Layton and found him wanting. So be it. This would be one of those forbidden topics, like politics and religion. It was time to change the subject.

"So have you decided what you're doing with the dog?" she asked.

"The dog stays." He delivered this line with a stubborn thrust of his chin. He picked up his second beer and took a long sip.

Clearly the dog was another sore spot.

"I had to give up Kramer. I'm not giving up Sparky."

"Kramer?"

"The dog I had when I lived in Tacoma. Betsy named him. She was addicted to *Seinfeld* reruns. She got custody of him." Ross hung his head over his beer for a long moment. The picture of good ol' boy sorrow.

"You know Sparky might have gone over better if you'd told us all about Kramer."

"Yeah, well, I don't want to be one of those guys who sits around drinking beer talking about his ex." He let go of a short, cynical laugh. "Except here I am doing exactly that, like some cliché from a country song."

"Well, I don't think you're a cliché. And if you want to

talk about Kramer, I'm happy to listen." Sabina picked up the full glass of wine that Reba had brought when she'd replenished Ross's beer. She took a sip.

And that's how she ended up settling in at a table with Ross, listening to him talk about his first wife and how the woman had broken his heart and stolen his dog. It was precisely like one of those sad, country songs. And while Ross poured out his troubles, he drank way too much beer. And she tried, foolishly, to keep up with him.

By the time the Wild Horses started their first set, Ross and Sabina were feeling a little free. When Clay and Jane Rhodes started singing the romantic duet "I Was Born to Be Your Man," Ross asked Sabina if she wanted to dance. And of course, she said yes.

Sabina stopped thinking altogether when she found herself in Ross's arms, enveloped by his warmth and his hard chest, her nose buried against his shoulder. Good Lord, he smelled like some heady mixture of laundry detergent, beer, and firefighter. Something smoky lingered on his skin.

It wasn't until the song ended and they broke apart that she realized what she'd done, right in front of the big Friday-night crowd.

Not good.

"Uh, I gotta go," she said, without making eye contact. If she looked into his beautiful, smoky eyes she might lose it altogether. And that would be wicked and wrong.

Instead she turned her back on him and headed, a bit unsteadily, toward the door.

And this time, Ross didn't stop her.

CHAPTER 5

Ross stood in the middle of the dance floor absolutely shit-faced, watching Sabina make her escape. He might have staggered after her except that Dot Cox was suddenly right in front of him.

"That's it, Ross. I'm cutting you off."

The red-headed bartender stood there with her sparkly earrings swaying and her fists on her hips. She couldn't be more than five feet tall if she tried. But he didn't want to tangle with her. He'd seen Dot in action. She'd taken self-defense classes or something down at the community college.

"Time for you to go home."

He nodded and staggered a little to the right. Dot braced him before he could fall all the way over. "Honey, I reckon life has just handed you a big, fat bunch of trouble. But I promise you, things will look better the day after tomorrow. I can't promise tomorrow will be better because you're going to have one hellacious headache. And chances are, your future mother-in-law is going to be all over you for your un-gentlemanly behavior. And your fiancée is probably going to be annoyed that you were slow dancing with her sister. But it will pass. I promise."

He knew better than to nod. The room was kind of spinning.

"Now, I want you to sit right down here. I'm calling Damian to pick you up and take you home. You're in no shape to drive. And if there's a fire call this evening, Ross, I want you to stay home. You understand me?"

He nodded again, but since he was sitting down, he didn't fall over. Which was good, considering that people in the bar were watching this scene with avid interest.

The next morning Dot's predictions came true in spades. He had the mother of all headaches even before the mother of the bride showed up at his door. Henrietta Grey had the audacity to actually ring his bell at nine in the morning.

On a Saturday no less.

Thus proving that the Last Chance gossip mill worked even in the dead of night when those old biddies should have been tucked up in their beds.

He thought about not going to the door, but Henrietta shouted, "Ross Gardiner, I know you're at home so don't you pretend you aren't."

Hiding from Henrietta would only make a bad situation worse. So he rolled out of bed, stepped into a pair of jeans, pulled on a dirty T-shirt, and answered the door.

"Ross Gardiner, just what do you think you're doing?" Henrietta's high-pitched voice lanced his skull. He should have stood his ground at the doorway, but the pain in his head made him fall back a step, allowing Henrietta to push her way in.

Only to be greeted enthusiastically by Sparky, who had yet to learn when to protect his master from pissed-off future mothers-in-law.

Henrietta and the dog became instant friends.

"He needs a walk," Ross said, feeling guilty about the dog he'd kind of neglected last night. And Sabina whom he'd sort of abused. And Lucy whom he'd sort of cheated on. He snagged the dog's leash from a hook by the door and stepped into a pair of flip-flops. "I'll be back in a minute."

"Ross Gardiner, don't you use that dog as an excuse to avoid me, you hear?"

"No, ma'am, but—"

Sparky made a puddle on the floor.

"Oh," Henrietta said.

"Like I said, he needs to go out. Let me get some paper towels before that stains the floor."

He headed into the kitchen for the towels, and when he came back Henrietta and the dog were gone. He cleaned up the mess and hoped that maybe she wouldn't come back.

Losing the dog would be bad, though. He sank down into his sectional sofa—the one Lucy hated—and was just dozing off when Henrietta and Sparky returned.

"You should be ashamed of yourself," Henrietta said as she made herself comfortable in his kitchen. He had no idea what she was doing in there, but as long as she was in there and he was out here that was good.

She eventually returned to the living room. But bless her, she came with a mug of coffee and a couple of aspirin. Thank the Lord she didn't say anything as she handed off the coffee and painkillers.

She sat down at the other end of the sofa, where Sparky was all over her for attention. After a long moment she spoke again.

"Honey, I know you and Lucy had a fight yesterday about something. But I gotta tell you, even if you were angry at Lucy, it was unfair to take it out on Sabina. Sabina deserves better. We both know that, don't we?"

His pain redoubled. Only this time the ache was somewhere near his heart. Damn it. Why couldn't he just lose his fascination with Sabina? She wasn't interested in him. Hell, the only reason they ended up dancing last night was because they both had too much to drink.

He should have done something to make sure she got home safe last night. Instead he'd made an utter a-hole of himself.

"Yeah," he said. His voice sounded rusty. "I intend to apologize."

"You better." Henrietta stopped speaking for a moment and his hopes rose, only to be dashed again when she picked up where she'd left off.

"Layton Webster is worth millions. Sabina and he were friends in high school. And what with Miriam's prediction and all, you should have left her alone with him. But no, you had to pursue a fire investigation right in the middle of her date. And then you had to get her drunk and dance with her. Honestly, Ross, what were you thinking?"

Ross wasn't about to discuss his guilty conscience. Instead he took the offensive. "Henrietta, I don't think Sabina and Layton were ever really friends in high school."

"You're wrong, Ross. They were both in math club together, and she went to a dance with him once."

Ross frowned. He didn't remember Sabina at any dances with Layton. Sabina had been one of the most popular girls in high school. She didn't hang with nerds like Layton Webster. Or quirky soccer players like himself. She was the darling of the football team. The queen of the prom. The prettiest girl in the whole school. She had been out of Layton's league. Hell, she'd been out of Ross's league, too.

Which was part of what pissed him off about seeing her with Layton last night. What, besides his millions, made Layton so suddenly attractive? Why did she say yes to drinks with that guy when she'd been too busy two years ago to have a drink with him?

"I'm exasperated with you," Henrietta said.

"Yes, ma'am."

"So I'm here to tell you that you need to think about how you're going to put things to rights. For starters, you need to apologize to Layton."

"What? No, absolutely not." His head throbbed.

"Ross, you're being stubborn."

"No, I'm not. Until Elias Webster is cleared of the arson, I'm not going to do any such thing. And in my opinion, Sabina needs to stay away from that guy. He could be part of a conspiracy."

"Oh, for goodness' sake. You and your conspiracy theories. Why don't you just leave the investigation to the FBI?"

"You mean the ATF. And no, I'm not going to leave it up to the ATF, because the agent in charge is an idiot."

Henrietta folded her arms across her chest. "Well, at least you should apologize to Lucy for being seen slow dancing with her sister."

"Yeah, I should."

"And to Sabina for crashing the first date she's gone on in months, maybe in more than a year."

"Okay." He gnashed his teeth. Why was he so annoyed about that? Seeing her dancing with Layton Webster had unlocked something nasty inside him. Could it be envy? Boy, that was sick. Sabina was his future sister-in-law.

"And given the situation, I think it would be best if you thought about moving up the wedding date."

His heart flip-flopped. He didn't want to move up the wedding, but even more important was the fact that Lucy didn't want to, either. And whatever Lucy wanted, Lucy usually got. "Look, Henrietta, I think you need to talk to Lucy about that. She's the one who thinks we should wait until the house is rebuilt. She's the one who's mad at me because I adopted Sparky. I'm ready to tie the knot whenever Lucy wants. But right now I get the feeling she would rather wait."

"Really?"

Henrietta sounded so surprised that Ross suddenly realized that he'd kind of overplayed his hand. He wasn't actually all that red-hot to get married, either. "Well then," Henrietta said in a no-nonsense voice, "you and I will have to figure out some way to light a fire under Lucy's behind, won't we? Because Miriam was explicit in what she said. You and Lucy need to be settled. For Sabina's sake."

He gave Henrietta a rapidly sobering look. "We might not have much choice, you know. It might take months before the house can be rebuilt. And Lucy has it in her mind that we need a house before we can get married."

"I know all about your to-do list, son."

"You do? Lucy told you?"

"No, not exactly. But my only point is that the homes at Jessamine Manor aren't the only ones in Allenberg County."

"And the dog? Lucy's mad at me about the dog, too. She wants me to get rid of it."

Henrietta petted the animal. "You leave that problem to me. I'll persuade Lucy to give up her objections to the dog. Sparky is such a sweet puppy."

Why couldn't Lucy see what Henrietta and Sabina saw in the dog?

"I'll help you with Lucy. But I need you to promise me that you'll quit trying to discourage Sabina from dating Layton Webster. He can give Sabina everything she's ever wanted. The chance to travel the world and live in luxury. She deserves Layton Webster."

No she didn't. She deserved something better than Layton. But Ross was smart enough not to argue. Instead he carefully said, "Yes, ma'am." But he made no promises.

Sabina had the headache to end all headaches when she slipped the key into the front door at Last Chance Around and turned on the lights. She would have loved to sleep in this morning, but Saturdays and Sundays were their busiest days of the week.

She had just finished brewing the first pot of coffee back in Lucy's workroom when her sister came storming in with a big frown on her face. "What the hell happened last night?"

"Don't yell," Sabina said as she rubbed her forehead between her eyebrows. She poured herself a cup of coffee and took a little sip. Better.

"So it's true. You got sloppy drunk at Dot's Spot and danced a slow dance with Ross." Lucy stood with her legs apart and her arms behind her back. It was almost as if she were trying to restrain herself.

"Uh, yeah, I guess I did. But before we danced, Ross scared away my date and forced me to sit with him while he talked about you and his ex-wife."

"Forced you? Really? I have a hard time seeing Ross forcing anyone to do anything."

"Well, he was in a mood last night. I tried several times to get up and leave, but he clearly needed someone to talk to. Someone to pour out his sorrow to. It should have been you. But I was there and available." She couldn't hide the annoyance in her voice.

"Sorrow?" Lucy asked as if it had never occurred to her that Ross ever felt sorrow. Her hands came to rest on her hips.

Sabina pulled in a lungful of air and exhaled deeply. She did it again. And again. And then, instead of giving Lucy a piece of her mind, she turned her back on her sister and headed for the checkout counter.

"Sabina, don't you walk away from me, you hear?"

Right then Sabina wanted to tell Lucy she was acting like a spoiled child. But if Lucy was spoiled then it was halfway Sabina's fault. And why not? Lucy deserved to be spoiled.

"Sabina!" Lucy yelled like a tyrant or a drama queen.

To heck with sparing the rod and spoiling the child. Sabina stopped and turned. "Don't you yell at me. I mean it. You're behaving like an out-of-control brat."

Whoa! Sabina's sudden outburst stopped Lucy in her tracks. She stood there with her mouth agape. Sabina's face went hot and then cold. There had once been a time when she had never missed an opportunity to tell her pesky sister that she was a brat. But those days were long gone. She struggled for control. "I'm sorry I said that," Sabina said in a tight voice. "But before you start pointing your finger at me, maybe you should stop and find out the whole story. I was having drinks with Layton Webster. Ross came over and crashed my date and behaved like a jerk. He scared Layton away. Then he got drunk and talked about his ex-wife, who cheated on him. And Kramer."

"Kramer? Who is *that*, besides the weird guy on *Seinfeld* reruns?"

Sabina shook her head. Her still-pickled brains kind of rattled around. "I can't believe you guys talk about everything and he's never told you about Kramer. Kramer was his dog. I got the feeling that Kramer was like his best buddy. He took him fishing and hunting and man stuff like that. Ross's ex got custody of the dog, and he's really heartbroken over it."

Sabina turned and headed toward the checkout counter. Thank goodness Lucy didn't follow her. Because while she was annoyed at Ross and Lucy right at that moment, she was even more annoyed at herself.

Lucy had every right to be ticked off. Sabina should never have stayed and listened to Ross pour out his sorrows. She should never have had a second glass of wine. She should never have danced with her sister's fiancé. And she should never have called Lucy a brat.

Just then Momma came breezing through the front doors. "Girls," she shouted, her voice knifing through Sabina's pounding head, "I've just come from visiting Ross. Both of y'all should expect an apology. Probably after he gets over his headache."

"What?" Lucy's voice exploded like a Fourth of July rocket. "Momma, you did not go to Ross's house and talk to him this morning, did you?"

"I most certainly did. And he had a few things to say about you, young lady. Why on earth are you being so hard on him about Sparky? He wants that dog, and you should let him have it. The dog is going to spend most of its time at the firehouse anyway."

"See," Sabina said as she sat down behind the checkout counter, "I told you he's all torn up about the dog."

"Really?" Lucy sounded utterly mystified, proving that her sister wasn't a dog person. But maybe she could learn to be.

"Really," Momma said.

"Oh."

Momma put her arm around Lucy. "Honey, Ross was hurting last night, and he went looking for someone to talk to. Unfortunately, your sister got in the way of that. I don't think Sabina did one thing to bring this onto herself. For goodness' sake, Lucy, think about what Ross did to your sister's date."

Lucy nodded. "Yeah, I guess."

"You need to give in on the dog, honey," Momma said. "Ross Gardiner is the best husband material in town. He's ready to do anything to please you. Y'all need to get on with this wedding."

Lucy stood there quietly, her lip quivering. And every time Lucy blinked back tears, Sabina's guilt redoubled. It was true that she hadn't asked to hear Ross pour out his heart. But it was also the undeniable truth that she'd enjoyed that slow dance way more than she should have.

Sabina was about to open her mouth and make a full

confession followed by an apology, when Lucy shrugged Momma off. "I need to think about this," she said and hurried from the store.

"She'll be all right," Momma said in her infernally optimistic tone. "Give her an hour at the shooting range and she'll be right as rain."

Lucy walked down the sidewalk, her head down. Furious. Sabina had no reason to call her a brat. She hadn't done one thing last night except go home and watch TV by herself. And Momma needed to quit trying to run her life.

She felt trapped by the people who loved her best.

Tears sprang to her eyes, and her throat knotted up. She looked up from the sidewalk only to see Wilma Riley coming out of the post office. Oh, great, the last thing she needed right now was Wilma spouting her feminist BS. So Lucy ducked into the Wash-O-Rama, expecting it to be deserted this early on a Saturday morning.

But Agent Zach Bailey was sitting on the broken folding chair in the front by the dryers, looking decidedly out of place in his freshly pressed khakis and his navy ATF golf shirt. He looked up from a faded and dog-eared copy of *Cosmo*—the same copy that had been sitting up on the folding table for months. It was the issue with the headline "Your Ultimate Guide to Oral—for Both of You" in bright red type on the cover.

Lucy had never gotten up the nerve to read that article, not even hiding out in the Laundromat. Heaven knows just about every other single woman in Last Chance *had* read that article. Of course, Wilma Riley anonymously left those random copies of *Cosmo* at the Wash-O-Rama.

Wilma was on a mission to liberate every female in Allenberg County.

Agent Bailey obviously had no qualms about picking up feminist magazines. Or turning right to the article in question. And there was something soft and sinful about his mouth. It was open a bit, and she could almost see his tongue. And even though he didn't appear to be carrying his weapon today, Lucy's body still went hotter than the blacktop on Palmetto Avenue on a sunny day in August.

Oh, man. She wanted that mouth in a carnal way, which surprised her. Because carnal thoughts were scary. And besides, he was a complete stranger.

Who was obviously learning something from reading that article.

She rushed to the back of the Wash-O-Rama hoping the guy would just stay put and go back to reading the article on, well... you know.

But no. He didn't do that. He'd obviously noticed her distress. So he stood up and followed her. For which he kind of got points, given the subject matter of the article in question.

"Uh, can I help?" he asked. He sounded like he came from somewhere up north. But she didn't hold that against him. She sniffled and wiped her cheeks with both hands.

"No, I'm okay."

"Obviously not."

She sniffled again and willed her eyes to stop weeping but they were not following orders. "I'm just mad at my fiancé." Of all the words she could have blurted to this hot guy who probably had sex on his mind, why had she chosen those?

Short answer: Hot guys who read sexy articles in *Cosmo*

scared her. Zach Bailey didn't look like the kind of person she could control, precisely. And she liked being in control.

Which was sort of why she was so ticked off at Momma and Sabina right at this moment.

Agent Bailey pulled a handkerchief out of his carefully pressed khakis and offered it.

Wow. She hadn't expected that. And it made him seem a tiny bit less frightening. Obviously he was a gentleman. Only gentlemen carried monogrammed handkerchiefs, right? So she took it and dabbed at her eyes.

"Who carries a handkerchief these days?" she found herself asking.

He shrugged in a bashful sort of way that knocked her right off her feet. Figuratively.

He had white teeth that shone in his tan face. And dimples. And a square chin. He was movie-star gorgeous. And he sometimes carried both a handkerchief and a weapon—probably the standard-issue Glock.

Wow.

"My dad carries one, and I've always wanted to be like him. He was a cop on the Boston PD. He's retired now," he said.

She had a moment's confusion as to whether Agent Bailey was talking about handkerchiefs or handguns. It probably didn't matter. If his daddy was a cop he had packed heat, too.

"So what's with the tears, huh?" he asked.

"It's complicated," she said, reeling in her runaway emotions. "I mean, since the house burned down." She paused again, this time gathering her thoughts. "Actually it's more complicated even than that. It started getting complicated when I was thirteen."

"That far back, huh? Well, I've got plenty of time and nothing good to read. I'm happy to listen."

She almost choked. He had sure looked kind of riveted to that article when she'd first walked in.

"What are you doing here?" She asked as she looked around the shabby interior of the Wash-O-Rama. "Besides reading back issues of *Cosmo* that Wilma makes available from time to time?"

Was that a tiny blush? It was hard to see in all that beautiful tanned skin, but maybe his ears reddened. "Please give her my thanks for the magazine," he said. "And I, uh, had to leave Columbia unexpectedly and was kind of behind on my laundry. So I packed a suitcase of dirty clothes. I'm staying out at The Jonquil House for a few days, but they don't have laundry facilities for guests. So here I am."

"Reading *Cosmo*."

He laughed. It was a sweet and rich laugh, like sunlight on butterscotch. "Yeah. It was all that was available. And it looked more interesting than my emails. So what happened when you were thirteen that has you crying today?"

He leaned back on one of the washers. He seemed genuinely interested.

"Come on, Agent Bailey, you can see the scars. Don't pretend that you can't."

"Call me Zach." He tilted his head and frowned. "Oh, yeah, I guess now that you mention it. So what happened when you were thirteen?"

"My family's house burned to the ground. And I was caught inside." She looked down for a moment and expected him to say something like "I'm sorry." People always did that. They always pitied her.

But when a few moments passed without him saying a word, she looked up. Right into his deep brown eyes.

There wasn't any pity in them. In fact, his gaze shifted, taking in everything—her jeans, her t-shirt, her boobs. The guy was actually checking her out.

She tried to remember if Ross had ever checked her out that way. Well, of course he looked at her, but maybe not like Agent Bailey was looking right at the moment. Her face went hot.

And she started to babble. "Ever since the fire, my older sister has been treating me like I'm fragile or something. And my mother never misses an opportunity to remind me that my sister gave up a bunch of things for me. And my boyfriend is being impossible. And everyone in town is telling me what to do. And then the house at Jessamine Manor burned down, which was kind of scary. And Ross got a dog, and I don't like dogs."

Zach's gaze traveled back up to her face. "I do get it. It definitely sucks having the environmental Looney Tunes torch your dream house."

She blew her nose and then realized she couldn't give his handkerchief back in that condition. So she stuffed it in her pocket. "You know, Zach, I realize that you're all over the arson thing and all, but if you want to know the truth, I'm not all that upset about the house."

"No?"

She shook her head. "I was kind of planning to get the house and all that next year, after I finish my associate's degree in interior design. I figured Ross and I would get the house and get married then. But everything got moved up because of Sabina."

"Sabina?"

"My sister. It's complicated."

He hooked his thumbs into the pockets of his khakis and tilted his head. "I've got time. And I'm a good listener." He flashed one dark eyebrow.

Oh, boy, was he *flirting*? Kind of. Maybe.

No, not possible. A man that handsome would never look twice at someone like her, all scarred and everything. No, he was just being nice. Because he was a nice guy who carried a handkerchief and never ever wore pants that weren't pressed. She wondered if he ironed his jeans. Did he even own jeans?

She was suddenly dying to know. So she told him all about what Sabina had done at Dot's Spot, and what Miriam Randall had predicted, and what Momma expected of her, and how Ross was suddenly in a hot hurry to move up the wedding date. She had plenty of time to give Zach all the details. And it turned out he was a very good listener.

And when his laundry was done, she discovered that Zach Bailey wore white boxer briefs and liked them folded.

CHAPTER 6

By two o'clock on Saturday afternoon, Ross's headache was bearable enough to do something about the situation he'd created for himself. Henrietta had called him not more than fifteen minutes after she left his place to let him know that Lucy and Sabina had had a big fight.

Which was both stunning and troubling news, because he knew he'd been the cause of the rift. So he needed to do something truly heroic to rescue the situation.

He decided that giving Sparky back to the animal shelter was not heroic. But finding another home for Lucy—that would be.

So he cleaned himself up and hiked into town (since his truck was still parked at Dot's Spot) and strolled into Arlo Boyd's real estate office. He intended merely to schedule an appointment, but it turned out Arlo was actually there, instead of out showing properties to prospective buyers.

He found Arlo back in his office, finishing off a late lunch that looked like a pulled pork sandwich from the Kountry Kitchen. Ross's stomach growled, suggesting that he might actually be on his way to recovering from last night's stupidity.

Arlo was a big man who filled up his small office. He had once been a member of the 1991 state champion Davis High football team, and he was now a regular booster of Pop Warner football programs. His office walls were festooned with decades of team photos. Arlo was a friendly guy and a near celebrity in town. Which explained why he was pretty much the only real estate agent of any note in all of Allenberg County.

"Ross," he said, standing up and wiping a little grease from his mouth with a paper napkin, "I'm sorry to hear about what happened out at Jessamine Manor. I gather one of those new houses had your name on it."

Ross sat down in the facing chair. "Yeah, it's a bummer. And it looks like it's going to be months and months until they rebuild those homes. So that's why I'm here."

Arlo gave him a sober look. "Trying to get back into Lucy's good graces, huh?"

"What?"

Arlo shook his head. "Son, everyone knows about how you behaved last night at Dot's."

Ross's headache made a sudden reappearance, and he idly rubbed the space between his brows. It didn't help. "Yeah, well, so I'm here to do something heroic."

"Heroic?"

"You know, like buying flowers except much bigger. Lucy wants a house. So that's why I'm here. What's available that doesn't cost a zillion dollars?"

The real estate agent leaned back in his chair. "Well, that's the problem. There's a housing shortage in Allenberg County these days. Which is a good problem to have, if you know what I mean. DeBracy Limited has breathed new life into our economy. Did you hear they just landed a new contract and will be expanding?"

"Uh, no, I didn't."

"Well, that's the problem, see. We don't have much in the way of available homes for sale—not in any price range. I can check listings for you. What are you looking for?"

Ross rattled off a few requirements and a price range, and Arlo entered the parameters into his computer. The search came back with exactly *no* results.

"Okay, how about a little more money," Ross said, although he couldn't afford more.

Arlo searched again and the results were the same. "I'm telling you, Ross, there just aren't many houses for sale. It's a complete sellers' market. Just a week ago a couple came in here and actually wanted to see the old Smith house. They decided to pass on it, of course."

"The Smith house?"

"Yeah, you know that run-down Victorian at the intersection of Julia and Baruch."

Oh, yeah, he knew that house. Its backyard bumped up against a tiny brick ranch house his parents had once rented. Momma had always talked about how one day, when Daddy's ship came in, they would live in a big ol' house like the one owned by Miz Evelyn Smith, the old, unmarried neighbor lady. Unfortunately, Daddy's ship never came in. He'd worked his entire life as a handyman and janitor at the elementary school. And then he'd died of a heart attack. Five years ago Momma moved away to Atlanta to take care of Great-Aunt Beth.

But the idea of buying that house and restoring it, and then having Momma come visit, truly appealed to him.

He suddenly wanted the Smith house. It was a visceral thing.

"How much are they asking for that old place?"

"Not much." Arlo rattled off a price that was astonishingly low—no more than unimproved land, which was still a bargain in Allenberg County.

"So little?"

"The house is falling down. You'd have to tear it down and build a new one."

"I'd like to see it, Arlo. Momma always loved that house."

Arlo shook his head emphatically, as if to say that Ross had truly lost his mind. "It would need to be gutted from the inside out. All the plumbing and electrical would have to be replaced to bring it up to code. It's a money pit."

"Maybe not in a sellers' market, Arlo. I could probably flip that house and make a profit on it."

"Maybe, but you'd exhaust yourself. And do you have the money to renovate?"

That was a slight problem. But maybe he could float a construction loan or something. "I want to see it."

"No, you don't. There are dead rats in that place. I know Lucy, and this is not what she wants."

That got Ross's dander up. "I think I know my fiancée pretty well. She loves to restore old things. This will be the project to end all projects."

Ross could hardly temper his enthusiasm as he strode into the Last Chance Around Antique Mall in the late afternoon. He'd just come from looking at the Smith house, and while the place was an absolute pit inside, the bones of the house were sound.

It was a classic example of a Victorian farmhouse with

a hipped roof, opposing peaked gable, and two tall, corbeled brick chimneys. It had a wraparound veranda with a spindle railing and some truly beautiful, if weathered, fretwork above the bay windows. Inside, the oak floors seemed to be mostly intact. There were four fireplaces. The staircase balusters were hand-carved and ended in a graceful spiral at the newel post.

Momma had talked about that staircase for years. Old Miz Smith used to invite her over for sweet tea from time to time, since they shared a backyard. And Momma always said she wanted a house with a swirly newel post like that.

Of course there were problems with the house. The 1920s-vintage bathroom and the ancient kitchen were both complete gut jobs. Arlo was right about the wiring and the plumbing. It would have to be redone.

The house had been on the market for three years, and Miz Smith's nephew and sole heir had recently dropped the price again. The place was a steal. Ross could probably swing the purchase and a construction loan. He just needed to talk to the bank on Monday.

The antiques mall was kind of busy, it being a Saturday afternoon. Sabina was at the counter talking with a couple of customers who looked like they came from out of town.

The moment he laid eyes on her, his body went haywire. He stopped in his tracks, unable to move. She stole his breath.

What the heck? He was sober now, and lusting for his soon-to-be sister-in-law was not allowed. He loved *Lucy*. He was so over his infantile fascination with the cheerleader who had never given him the time of day.

Except, of course, Sabina had stopped being that shallow cheerleader years ago. The self-centered girl he remembered had been replaced by a sweet, mature woman with a big heart. Last night she'd proved that in spades. She'd listened to him pour out his soul without any judgment.

He was still trying to come to terms with the idea that the seriously beautiful Sabina Grey had actually spent the evening listening to him go on and on about his ex-wife, his broken heart, and his old dog, Kramer. The whole scenario was embarrassing.

And it didn't help that she looked pretty damn terrific this afternoon. She'd pulled her black hair into a ponytail that kind of swished when she turned her head. He loved her hair that way. It showed off her neck and ears, both of which sparked fantasies that he shouldn't have.

Uh-oh, he was in deep trouble. He needed to back away slowly. He tore his gaze away from Sabina and headed toward the back of the store, where Lucy could usually be found working on her various projects.

She never locked her workroom door. So he knocked and called her name and then opened it. But the room was dark.

Damn. Henrietta had told him that Lucy had left the store this morning in a huff. It looked like she was still ticked off. He made a quick survey of the various vendor stalls, but Lucy wasn't anywhere to be found.

He was so seriously in the doghouse.

By the time he returned to the front of the store, the customers were gone, and Sabina was standing there looking at him as if he'd dropped in from another planet.

The word "awkward" didn't even start to describe the way he felt. One part fatally attracted, one part guilty as hell.

"Hey Ross," she said, and damned if it didn't look as if she was blushing. There were fifteen different ways he could read that blush. So he chose to ignore it.

"Where's Lucy?" he asked.

Her blush seemed to deepen. "She's not here."

"Where is she?"

"Do I look like my sister's keeper?"

Uh-oh. Time to beat a hasty retreat. The sisters were definitely in the middle of a serious tiff. "No, ma'am. And I'm really sorry about last night." He headed toward the door.

"She's furious at me." Sabina's voice sounded wounded and sad somehow. Her tone halted his retreat.

He turned. "I'm sorry," he said. "Really. If you want to date Layton Webster, I won't stand in the way. And I promise I'm going to move heaven and earth to get Lucy to the altar, just as soon as I can."

She cocked her head. "Momma really did a number on you this morning, didn't she?"

"Uh, well, I guess. But she was right, and when Lucy hears about what I've got planned she's going to be excited."

"Please don't tell me you're going to elope because, while I understand your urge to just get it over with, Momma would have a conniption if you did that. You'd spend the rest of your life hearing about how you denied her the opportunity to plan the wedding to end all weddings."

He laughed in spite of himself. Sabina had a knack for drawing out his laughter. "Give me a little bit of credit, Sabina. I know better than to elope," he said. "I came here to talk about a new home for Lucy. I took a tour of the Smith house this afternoon with Arlo Boyd."

Sabina blinked a few times, and the color drained from her cheeks. "The Smith house? Really?"

He nodded. "Don't look at me that way. I know, it needs some work."

"Saying that the Smith house needs work is like saying Freddy Krueger could use a face transplant."

He almost laughed. "I know, but it's not a lost cause. And Lucy will love it. She can redo it to her heart's content, like she redoes all those old things."

Sabina's forehead rumpled. "Ross, I don't know. Lucy isn't as into old things as you think."

"Yeah, but if we bought it and fixed it up, it would be one of a kind instead of just another tract house. Fixed up, we could get it on the annual Garden Club Tour."

It was her time to laugh. "Since when do you even care about the annual Garden Club Tour?"

His face warmed. "Momma always said that house ought to be on the tour. I think it bothered Momma that Miz Smith didn't take care of the place the way it deserved."

"It always bothered me, too," Sabina said and looked away. Boy, she must be really hung over, because her complexion looked so pale it was practically blue.

"What's the matter?" he asked.

"Not a thing. I just have some work to do."

He stood there for a long moment not knowing what to say. He really *had* crossed the line last night. Damn. It was one thing to have Lucy annoyed with him. She'd spend a couple of hours out at the target range, and she'd be over it. But Sabina was different. Sabina was sensitive.

"I'm sorry," he said.

She looked up. "It's all right, Ross. I forgive you." But the look on her face said something different.

Sabina stared at the computer screen as Ross left, lost in memories she usually suppressed.

It was seventeen years ago on a May night, the Saturday before graduation. One of Daddy's business associates was giving a big dinner party up in Orangeburg, and Sabina was supposed to babysit Lucy.

But Momma and Daddy's dinner party was the same night that a group of Davis High seniors had planned an impromptu get-together down at the public dock on the Edisto River. All her friends were going, and besides, Lucy was thirteen and perfectly capable of being left alone for a couple of hours.

Sabina didn't have a car so she walked down to the high school to meet up with the designated drivers for the night. A group of four or five boys, all of them members of the football team, walked with her. They caught up with Ross on the way—right in front of the Smith house.

Even then the house was in bad shape. Miz Smith was a spinster, and she was probably ninety years old back then and confined to a wheelchair.

Alfie Roche, the idiot who played center for the Davis High Rebels and who had always wanted to be a quarterback, took one look at the old house and boasted that he could throw a rock through the upstairs window.

The guy was enormous, except for his head. Which probably explained why he was a tiny bit short on brains. Not to mention any kind of moral compass.

The really sad part was that the other guys—defensive linemen all—thought it was a terrific idea to throw rocks at Miz Smith's house. Not a one of them listened when Sabina tried to stop them. They just laughed at her. They seemed to think she might be impressed with their rock-throwing ability.

If Ross hadn't been there, the rocks would have been thrown.

But he had saved the day.

Compared with Alfie, Ross was a skinny kid. But he stood right in front of Alfie and got all up in his face. He told everyone how Miz Smith was a sad lady who sometimes invited his momma in for tea. He made every one of those big, stupid football players stop and think.

In that instant Ross became a hero as far as Sabina was concerned. And being young and romantic, she kind of fell in love with him right then. It took courage in Last Chance to stand up to anyone on the football team. Those players existed inside a culture where throwing rocks at an old lady's house was okay. They all felt entitled.

To whatever they wanted.

And sadly, Sabina had discovered that sometimes those boys felt entitled to her. They all expected to get right into her panties. They expected her to be easy, just because she was on the cheerleading squad. In truth, none of the girls on the squad were easy. But you'd never know it by the trash the guys talked.

Looking back, she'd spent most of her high-school years fending off unwanted passes from the entire football team. If she kissed a boy, he always wanted more. So she played hard to get, flitting from one boy to the next. Playing them off each other.

Which was all well and good until the football players started spreading filthy stories about her. It had never occurred to her to say or do anything about the harassment some of those players aimed in her direction. She wasn't brave or foolish enough to upset the apple cart known as high-school football. Not in this town. Not seventeen years ago. Things were changing when it came to that culture. But she'd gotten caught up in it when she was a teen. The hard truth was that she didn't want to give up her place on the cheerleading squad. And like any shallow teen, she had loved all the attention.

She wasn't a hero. Not like Ross.

And sadly, until he stood up to Alfie, Sabina had never noticed Ross. That night, out at the public dock, they'd gotten to know each other a little bit better. That's when she'd discovered that Ross was not only heroic but smart, and talented, and athletic. The University of Washington in Seattle had given Ross a *soccer scholarship*, making him the only student-athlete of her class to have been recruited by a Division I school.

A summer friendship might have blossomed between them, but the house burned down and Sabina's life was forever changed. She'd never talked to Ross about the night they spent out on the dock. It was ancient history, and memories of that night were best left in the past.

When the Smith house went up for sale a few years ago, she'd given serious thought to buying it and flipping it. Ross was right. It was a diamond in the rough.

And now Lucy would get to live there with a real-life, everyday hero. They'd be like George and Mary Bailey, the heroic characters in *It's a Wonderful Life*, who bought an old house and renovated it and filled it with love and kids.

Yeah. Sabina swallowed back the lump in her throat. Lucy was a really lucky girl.

She straightened her shoulders and keyed the word "Mallorca" into her search engine. Fabulous photographs of aqua blue water and white sand beaches filled her screen.

Much better.

Lucy's funk lasted much longer than Ross expected. In fact, by the time Saturday evening rolled around he was convinced his girlfriend was actively trying to avoid him.

She was known for turning her cell phone off when she didn't want to be bothered. But Ross couldn't find her sulking at the tiny, two-bedroom rental cottage she shared with Sabina, and she wasn't off with Henrietta planning the wedding of the century. She wasn't even hanging out with the guys at the Dead Center Shooting Club in Allenberg.

He couldn't remember a time when Lucy had been so angry with him. And deservedly so.

He figured it was a bad strategy to hang out on her front porch waiting for her to come home, especially since he had Sparky with him. And he was pretty sure Sparky was the epicenter of the problems between them.

So he retreated for the day and hung out with Bubba Lockheart in his basement man-cave, and watched the Carolina Gamecocks crush Clemson. Which was gratifying.

The next day he hauled his butt out of bed at an ungodly hour and cornered Lucy in her favorite pew of the First Methodist Church. He was not precisely a Methodist, but this was an emergency. So he squeezed himself next to her, forcing her momma, daddy, and Sabina to make room for him. He knew he'd done the right thing when he got a nod and a sweet smile from Henrietta.

Of course Lucy gave him a scowl. But he reckoned that church was a great place to confess his many sins and to find forgiveness from his beloved.

He settled himself and leaned toward her. "I wouldn't have to resort to these tricks if you'd just answer your phone," he whispered as he pulled a hymnal out of the rack on the back of the pew and started searching for the hymns of the day.

"I suppose I should be glad you're here, since you almost never come to church anymore," she murmured. She tossed her head, and her dark curls bounced. She was really cute. Not as drop-dead gorgeous as her sister, but really, really cute. She stuck her nose up in the air.

"Yes, you should be glad. And I apologize for being a jerk."

She turned and gave him a flirty little pout. The ice was melting between them. They settled in for the services.

Which were incredibly boring. He kind of wished he could be like Lucy's daddy, Earl, who turned down his hearing aid and took a nap during Reverend Lake's long-winded sermon. Earl even got away with it. Henrietta only elbowed him once, when he started to snore.

Ross figured he had earned some points for enduring that sermon without sleeping. Even so, Lucy was determined to make him work for his forgiveness. When services ended, she managed to escape quickly and went to work helping the Altar Guild ladies put out food and coffee during the fellowship hour.

So he waited patiently and finally caught up to her in the church's kitchen about forty-five minutes later, when the doughnuts and coffee were beginning to run out and people were moving on to their Sunday activities, which mostly involved watching the Carolina Panthers who were playing the Redskins.

"We need to talk," he said.

"Yes, we do." That cute nose of hers was still up in the air.

Betsy used to strike that pose sometimes, like she was a princess and it was his job to put her up on a pedestal or something. Lucy not so much, so her behavior was a big, red flag.

Lucy deserved an apology.

"Look, sweetie, I'm sorry for my behavior down at Dot's Spot on Friday. I got completely toasted and treated your sister without any respect. She tried to put me in line, and eventually it took Dottie herself to cut me off. So don't blame Sabina for what happened. It was all my fault."

"Uh-huh. And . . . ?"

Wow. He was going to have to grovel this time. "And I'm going to make it up to you."

"You are? How?" Was that a tiny curl at the corner of her mouth? Maybe. He warmed to his task. She was so going to love what he had to tell her about the Smith house.

"I went to see Arlo Boyd yesterday about finding another house."

Her eyebrows lowered. "But I liked the one we bought already."

"Yeah, I know, but it burned to the ground, and it could be a long time before Webster Homes rebuilds. So I was looking at other houses."

"Without me?" Her tone of voice sounded anything but happy and excited.

Oh, boy. "I just thought I'd make a survey of what was available. And sweetie, we could get the Smith house for a song. You know, that old Victorian down on Baruch..."

He stopped speaking. The look on her face said it all: She knew the house and she apparently shared Arlo Boyd's opinion of it.

"You don't like the Smith house?" he asked.

"It's falling down."

"We could fix it up. You could practice being an interior designer."

"That house needs more than interior design, Ross. It needs to be bulldozed."

He knew right then that he'd miscalculated. Apparently Lucy had no imagination when it came to the Smith house, even though she was gifted at turning old furniture into new reimagined pieces.

He was a complete dolt when it came to women. They were mysterious and unfathomable and he always seemed to be inserting his feet into his mouth.

Just then Henrietta came breezing into the kitchen with Reverend Lake in tow. "Y'all, I have the most wonderful news," she said in her screechy voice. No wonder Mr. Grey needed a hearing aid. His wife had worn out his hearing years ago.

Ross braced himself. There was a wicked gleam in Henrietta's eyes, and he'd learned that, once his future mother-in-law had an idea about something, she was kind of like a dog with a bone. And besides, he needed her interruption of this important conversation like he needed a root canal.

Lucy also stiffened.

Henrietta wasn't good at reading body language because she breezed ahead. "Tell them, Tim."

The minister cleared his throat. "Well, I just told your mother that the church is definitely available on October eighteenth for a wedding, and we've got the date all blocked out for you. I'll want to schedule a time to talk to you both before the ceremony, of course."

"Isn't that exciting?" Henrietta squealed. "It's perfect. I already checked with the VFW hall and that's the only weekend they have free for a while. So it's all settled. The wedding date is October eighteenth."

Ross and Lucy stood there silent for a couple of beats.

And then Lucy put her hands on her hips, shot her mother a look that could kill, and said, "Momma, that's the weekend after the Fall Festival. Oh, my God, it's only like a month away. We can't plan a wedding in a month. And besides, where am I going to live?" Lucy's voice could reach the upper registers, too, especially when she was upset. Clearly this news didn't bring his future bride any joy.

And in truth, it was a bit startling to himself.

"Lucy Ann, I am not letting any grass grow under your feet on this. Just think about your sister and her happiness. And besides, you have nothing to worry about. Your marriage has been blessed by Miriam Randall, and I have complete faith in Ross. He'll find you another house. And if not, y'all can live in his apartment for a while. It's not the end of the world."

Lucy turned toward Ross. "Oh, my goodness, you went out house hunting because Momma asked you to?"

He opened his mouth to respond but Lucy put up her hand palm outward. "Don't. I know you did. When are the two of you going to consult me about these plans? Don't I have a say in them?"

"Of course you do," Ross and Henrietta said more or less simultaneously.

"All right, then," Lucy said, ticking items off on her fingers. "Here's what I think. First, I'm not wild about moving into your bachelor pad. Second, I'm not moving into the Smith house unless you have the money to make it more than merely habitable. I had my heart set on a modern home. And third, Momma, you need to take a big step back."

"The Smith house?" Henrietta asked, ignoring the last part of Lucy's speech.

"I was looking at it yesterday," Ross said. "It's in rough shape but I promise I'll fix it up. I'll make it a show place."

Henrietta beamed in his direction. "Oh, Ross, that's wonderful."

Lucy scowled at him.

This wasn't going well. Both Henrietta and Lucy liked to be in control of things. So naturally this was a disaster waiting to happen. A guy could get seriously wounded standing in the crossfire.

But he knew which team he was playing for. It was time to rescue his intended. "Uh, Henrietta, if Lucy doesn't want to get married on October eighteenth or live in the Smith house then maybe we should—"

"Don't be silly, Ross," Henrietta said. She turned toward Lucy. "Sweetheart, everything will work out. Restoring the

Smith house is a wonderful idea. And don't you worry about planning the wedding on short notice, either. Your daddy has already booked tickets for you and me and Sabina to go to Atlanta next week. We'll get our dresses and have a wonderful time shopping. How about that?"

"But Momma, it's my wedding and—"

"I'm not listing to another word from you. You're being silly. You know we have to do this for Sabina, don't you? She's never going to find happiness until you and Ross are married. Y'all know that's true, don't you? Miriam Randall is always right about these things."

Henrietta had her back to the door. So she didn't see Sabina when she came into the kitchen carrying the empty coffee urn. Sabina stopped, her eyes glued to her mother's back. Her face went white and then red. She looked up at Ross, and their gazes collided.

She needed his help.

Maybe it was time for him to take control.

He took Lucy by the shoulders. "Sweetie, I love you. I want to marry you. It doesn't matter what Miriam Randall says about anything. The important thing is that I care about you. So let's just do it, okay?"

She looked into his eyes. He couldn't tell if she was about to laugh or cry. So he gave her a little peck on the mouth. "C'mon, we've been planning this for long enough. Let's quit stalling."

She nodded and rolled her eyes in a truly adorable fashion.

"Okay, so here's the plan," he said in his fire commander voice. "You and your mother and sister concentrate on the wedding, and I'll put all my energy into buying that old house and getting it ready. I promise you it will be a showcase when I'm done, and you can help me design the interior spaces. And maybe if I work really hard, I can have it partially finished so, on our wedding night, I can carry you over the threshold."

Elsie Campbell, who had been watching this scene play out, let go of a gigantic sigh. "Isn't that romantic?" she said to the other members of the Altar Guild. "It's like that old Christmas movie. You know the one, where they get married and move into the old house that's practically falling down."

"*It's a Wonderful Life*," Sabina said. She put the coffee urn down with more force than was necessary and then she turned her back on all of them and headed for the kitchen door.

Henrietta followed after her older daughter. "Sabina, what's the matter? Where are you going? We need to get packed. We're all going to Atlanta for the week."

Sabina turned and stared at her mother as if Henrietta had just escaped from the loony bin. "Momma, I have a business to run. I'm planning to go up to Florence for an estate sale tomorrow. I've been planning that trip for two weeks. There's a mahogany dining table I want to bid on. Besides, I have to be at the store today, and on Tuesday I promised to help out at the senior center for a little while, and then I have to organize the craft fair. I can't just pick up and go to Atlanta for a week. You and Lucy pick out a dress for me. You know my dress size, and we can get alterations done here if necessary." She turned and walked away.

Sabina was in deep, deep doo-doo now. It was bad having Momma go manic on the wedding plans, but to spout her thoughts to the entire Altar Guild made it way worse. Sabina's humiliation was as deep and wide as the Grand Canyon.

She probably ought to go to Atlanta with them, but it would mean closing the store on one of her busiest days, not to mention having to renege on a promise she'd made to help out on Tuesday. And then there was the craft fair, which she hadn't actually volunteered for, but she certainly hadn't said no.

So really, she had to stay home.

She checked her watch. It was almost noon, and she needed to get going and open up the store. Sunday afternoons were almost as busy as Saturdays.

She was still looking down at her watch as she hurried out of the church's front door and stumbled, quite literally, into Layton Webster.

He caught her before she could fall flat on her face. His hands found her shoulders and stuck there even after she steadied. She was wearing a sleeveless dress so the skin-to-skin contact was kind of surprising. And nerve racking.

"Layton." Her voice came out tinny and awkward, while her innards flip-flopped like a bass on a fishing line. Her body seemed to think she might have an adolescent crush on Layton. She wasn't sure her brain agreed.

He launched a wide commercial smile, like he was advertising toothpaste or something. The grin was too perfect. Just like the Armani sport jacket and the Hermès tie and the Gucci shoes.

"I was looking for you," he said.

"For me?" She stifled the urge to look over her shoulder. At any moment, other members of the Altar Guild would be coming through this door. She was about to give them something else to talk about.

Which was embarrassing. On the other hand, having the Altar Guild speculating that she and Layton were an item was a whole lot better than being pitied for her nonexistent love life. So she decided that having Layton looking for her was most definitely a good thing.

"You sound surprised. Why? I know you're a Methodist. And this is Sunday. I figured I might have a shot at finding you here."

"Oh, yeah, I guess."

"I just came from across the street." He nodded toward Christ Church, where the Episcopalians were creating a traffic jam getting out of their parking lot.

"Oh." This was pathetic. She was reduced to monosyllables. Why was that? Did she have issues with guys who knew how to wear fine tailored sport coats? No. She didn't. In fact, she liked it. A lot.

"I wanted to apologize for Friday night. I shouldn't have let Ross get under my skin." Layton gave her the same direct stare that had lured her in on Friday night.

"I don't blame you for leaving," she said, hitching up her shoulder bag in a successful attempt to get him to take his hands off. "In fact, walking away was probably the right thing to do. I should have slapped his face and walked away, too."

Now that his hands and arms were free, he crossed them as if he was just the tiniest bit nervous himself. Sabina felt so much better knowing that. Layton Webster, millionaire, had sought her out. He was concerned and apologetic. He was *for real*.

He dropped his arms, as if he knew the whole folded-arm

thing was sending bad messages. Instead he gave her another one of those big, wide, commercial smiles. "So I know it's kind of late notice, but I was wondering if you'd like to take a drive in the country, maybe find a nice place to have dinner."

Oh, boy. Opportunity was knocking at her door, and she was otherwise engaged. This happened often in her life. "I can't, Layton. It's Sunday, and while I know that there are some Baptists in this town who think it's a sin to work on Sunday, the truth is Sunday afternoons are one of my busiest times at Last Chance Around."

"Oh." He sounded so disappointed.

"But I have tomorrow off. I was planning to drive up to Florence for a tag sale. You want to join me?" She couldn't quite explain why these words popped out of her mouth, except that it occurred to her that the last few times any single man had asked her out, she'd been busy.

It didn't seem possible but Layton's smile widened even further. "I'd be happy to come with you. What time should I pick you up?"

Ross closed up the firehouse during his Monday lunch hour and headed over to Jessamine Manor. Zach Bailey and a team of ATF people were combing through the wreckage, no doubt trying to understand where and how the fires had started.

Ross suppressed the urge to find out if Agent Bailey had changed his mind about the motive for the crime. There wasn't any point. As far as Ross could tell the feds were all over the arson as an act of terrorism, and they were like a bunch of junkyard dogs. They weren't giving up on that theory no matter what anyone in town had to say about it.

Ross wasn't the only one who was skeptical about the presence of eco-terrorists in Allenberg County. Sheriff Rhodes had given Ross a call early that morning to discuss the situation. The sheriff wanted Ross's opinion about other possible scenarios, and Ross hadn't been shy expressing his opinions.

Ross forced himself to turn away. He hadn't come out here to pick a fight with Zach Bailey. He'd come on the much more mundane errand of seeing about getting his earnest money back.

He headed into the model home, which, luckily for Webster Homes, had not been torched. Surprisingly, Donnie Simmons, Webster Homes' top salesman, had shown up for work today. It was semi-encouraging. As if Webster was saying he wasn't going to go down without a fight.

So maybe Elias Webster wasn't an arsonist. If this wasn't a case of arson for profit, then who burned the houses down? The idea that there might be some sicko-crazy serial arsonist in town was disturbing. And in Ross's view about as unlikely as the eco-terrorists.

"Hey, Donnie," Ross said as he stepped into the garage portion of the model home, which had been turned into an office. A few days ago, Ross and Lucy had spent several hours in this room selecting flooring and cabinet upgrades for their dream home. Man, if Ross ever got his hands on the a-hole who torched his house, he would...

"Ross." Donnie nodded, looking decidedly somber. Which was pretty unusual, because Donnie was a natural-born salesman who always had a grin on his face.

"I reckon you're here to find out about getting your money back, huh?" Donnie asked.

"Yes, I am."

Donnie looked away shaking his head. "Man, Ross, I'm really sorry, but Webster Homes isn't giving refunds."

"What do you mean? We had a contract, and—"

Donnie held up his hands. "Look, you'll get your money eventually. Maybe. But right now we're not giving any money back to anyone. For one thing, we've got the feds all over us, and for another, the insurance company has launched an investigation."

Donnie pointed through the window to the ATF agents combing through the wreckage. "Those guys might think this disaster was a terrorist act, but the insurance company wants to make sure this is not a case of insurance fraud."

Well hallelujah, sort of. At least someone beside the sheriff was thinking straight. But just because the insurance people were being cautious didn't mean Webster Homes got to sit on Ross's money.

He opened his mouth to protest, but Donnie interrupted before he could speak. "Look, I know, Ross. It's ridiculous. You have a contract that says the company will deliver a home by such and such a date at which point you'll go to closing. But right now, the company isn't issuing refunds. If you want that money back, you'll probably have to sue. And if the insurance company refuses to pay for the damages, it won't matter because the company will be bankrupt.

"So my best advice is for you to sit tight until the dust settles. We'll get back to building that dream house that you and Lucy want. I'll stake my life on it."

Damn, damn, damn. Ross wanted to yell at the guy but there wasn't any point. In fact, he should have realized that Webster Homes would be hanging on to his money.

"Sorry, man. You're not the only person who is upset by this. You can always talk to a lawyer. But I know Elias Webster; he didn't burn down these houses. He's a good man. He builds a good product. I've never seen that man cut a corner or not deliver as promised."

Ross didn't trust himself to speak. He was likely to start ranting. So he simply turned and marched out to his truck.

Well, that was that. Either Lucy gave in and agreed to move into his apartment while they waited for the "dust to settle," or they postponed the wedding. Unless, of course, he could get a sizable construction loan for the Smith house. The house was so cheap he could probably swing the purchase price in cash, even with the hit his reserves had just taken. But if he couldn't qualify for a construction loan, then all bets were off.

He turned toward Sparky, who was sitting in the passenger's side of his Dodge Ram. "Sparky, my momma always used to say that there ain't no ill wind doesn't blow some kind of good. And it's the truth. I think we'll need to take a visit to the bank this afternoon."

He was about to climb up into the truck when ATF agent Bailey sauntered up. Boy and howdy, this guy was the absolute last person on the face of the planet Ross wanted to talk to.

"I saw your truck," Bailey said, his tone and his ready-for-action stance somewhat challenging.

"I'm not here to interfere," Ross said. "I came to get my money back for that house." He pointed to the blackened remains. "We were about a month away from closing."

"Yeah, I know, and I heard a lot more about it when I ran into your girlfriend at the Laundromat."

What the hell was Lucy doing at the Laundromat? She and Sabina rented a little salt box of a cottage on Dogwood Avenue, but it had a washer and a dryer. "When exactly was this?"

"On Saturday. Man, she was furious with you."

What? He'd spent a good part of Saturday afternoon looking for Lucy, and she'd been at the Laundromat? With Agent Bailey? Telling him all about their private stuff? He turned away and opened the truck's door before he said or did something stupid to Agent Bailey, like wring his neck. Sparky gave a happy little *wuf*.

"It sure sounds like she's got a big case of cold feet," Agent Bailey said in a tone that could only be called snide.

Ross's emotions churned, and memories played through his mind of that afternoon when he'd caught Betsy and Eric together. He jettisoned the idea of getting into his truck. Instead he turned, faced Bailey, and leveled the stoniest stare he could muster. "My fiancée has gone off to Atlanta to look at wedding dresses. So I don't think she has cold feet. And you should mind your own business."

"Uh, well, actually I was minding my business when she came into the Laundromat and started telling me her life story."

"She what?"

"She was upset. I listened. And I almost wish I hadn't."

"Well, fine, you can just go f—" He was about to say something truly obscene but he ground his back teeth together.

"No, you don't understand," Bailey said in the mildest of tones. "Lucy told me all about that fire when she was thirteen."

"Yeah, so?"

"Well, maybe she shouldn't have. The fact that Lucy seems to be associated with two major fires is something of a problem. You know, a coincidence."

"Oh, come on, man, you don't—"

"I don't like coincidences," Bailey said in a firm but quiet voice. "So I'm telling you right now that I went back and looked over the newspaper reports of the fire seventeen years ago. There was some question as to whether it was accidental. In fact, the man who had your job back then was certain arson was involved. But there wasn't much evidence left since the house burned to the ground."

Ross turned and got right up into Agent Bailey's face. And since Ross was taller, it was satisfying to look down at the jerk. "What are you suggesting?"

"I'm not suggesting anything. I'm just pointing out a coincidence. The kind of coincidence you should be concerned about as the fire chief for this jurisdiction."

"Are you saying someone has it out for Lucy?"

"Maybe. Or maybe there's another explanation."

"Look, if you're suggesting that Lucy is some kind of serial arsonist you must be smoking something. She was badly burned in that fire seventeen years ago. She spent years recovering from her injuries. In fact, in a lot of ways, she hasn't fully recovered and probably never will. If you want to go investigate something, maybe you should start with Elias Webster and his creepy nephew Layton."

Bailey didn't seem intimidated. "You think we aren't looking at Elias Webster? Come on, Chief, give us some credit. We're investigating every possible lead and ruling nothing out. I'm pretty sure Lucy isn't involved. But you should know that I had to report the conversation to my team and my superiors. Just like I reported the conversation we had on Friday. And they want me to investigate both of you further."

Bailey gave Ross a little nod then turned and walked away.

Ross took a step toward Bailey's back, intent on drop-kicking the guy into next week. But his phone took that exact moment to buzz. That little vibration in his pocket stopped him from making matters much, much worse.

He pulled the phone from his jeans. Henrietta. He punched the talk button. "Hey," he said.

"Honey, I need a favor from you."

He was afraid to ask what. And he sure wasn't about to tell his future mother-in-law that he couldn't get his earnest money back. Or that Lucy was under investigation. In fact, he decided right on the spot not to say one word about anything. The less the females in his life knew about his problems, the better.

"Are you there, honey?"

"Uh-huh."

"I was wondering if you could check in on Sabina. She hasn't been answering her cell phone, and she was supposed to go off to a tag sale today, and she was going with Layton Webster."

"What?" Every atom in Ross's body reacted to this news.

"You heard me. And while I'm delighted to see that she's caught a man with deep pockets, I'm a bit concerned. It's not like Sabina to turn off her cell phone. Lucy might do that sort of thing, but not Sabina, you know?"

Yeah, he did know. And after what Agent Bailey had just said, he suddenly felt as if the world were closing in. Damn it all, Last Chance wasn't a place that had problems with terrorists or arsonists. And the people in his life shouldn't be in jeopardy.

"No worries, Henrietta, I'll check in with her."

"Thanks."

"How's Lucy?" he asked. It was kind of sad that, for the last couple of days, he'd heard more from Henrietta than from his intended bride. Did Lucy really have cold feet? Had she done more than talk to Agent Bailey?

These thoughts were beneath him. Betsy had shaken his trust, but he refused to let his ex-wife's behavior ruin the rest of his life.

"Oh, Lucy's fine," Henrietta said into his ear. But there was something in the way she said the words that told Ross that Lucy wasn't fine at all.

CHAPTER 8

Sabina pulled her van into the driveway of the tiny cottage she rented on Dogwood Avenue at about six-fifteen, just as the sun was hitting the horizon. She turned in the driver's seat and gave Layton a big smile, which he returned in gigantic fashion. He brushed back the dishwater blond cowlick from his forehead in a boyish gesture that told Sabina he was nervous about what came next. She was nervous, too.

She had already decided that it would be best not to invite him in. She wasn't ready for that, yet. Even though they'd had a terrific time together at the tag sale and then at a barbecue place for an early dinner on the way back home.

But a good-night kiss would be nice. It had been a heck of a long time since she'd kissed a man over the age of ten and under the age of forty-five.

He started to lean in, but the Ford Motor Company had put a gigantic console in between the seats. Maybe if they had taken his BMW, this would have worked out. But a 720i is not a good car to take on a picking trip.

She pretended not to notice the way he'd moved toward her, and instead she opened her door and hopped down onto the drive. He left the van and strolled in her direction. She could read his intent in his body and his face.

Good. They were on the same page, apparently. Their bodies met. She snaked her arms around his neck. He put his hands on her hips.

She'd kissed a few boys in high school, it was true, but that had been half a lifetime ago. And in truth, she hadn't much liked any of the boys she'd kissed.

So she expected great things from this kiss. Layton wasn't anything like those jerks from her past. Besides, there was a chance, if you believed Miriam Randall, that Layton Webster was the man of her dreams.

Layton moved in. And his mouth was soft and okay. His kissing technique seemed pretty good. In fact, there wasn't one thing awful about kissing Layton.

But the earth didn't shake beneath her feet.

If he was her soulmate, wasn't the earth supposed to shake? Or bells chime? Or something?

She didn't know for certain. And it was kind of disappointing to think that this was as good as it was going to get. So she let the kiss go on for a while in the hope that something would happen.

He smelled of expensive aftershave. It was sweet, not at all hot or smoky.

Good Lord. She was comparing him with Ross. No. No, no, no, no.

She stepped back and stifled the urge to wipe her mouth. Not because his kiss had been wet or sloppy. But because she was kind of horrified at herself.

He let go without any complaint, for which he earned

points. "Um," she started and didn't exactly know where to go.

"Can I come in?" His bright blue eyes had dilated and darkened with desire.

Of course he wanted more. They always did.

"Uh, well," she stammered, "It's late and I—"

"I'd like to come in."

Damn. Damn. Damn. The profanity that she couldn't say out loud was sprinting through her brain.

"Layton, I had a very nice time today. Thanks for dinner and for helping me manhandle that dresser I bought into the van. But I'm…well, you could say I'm old-fashioned or something. I'm not ready yet to take the next step in this relationship."

He cocked his head. "So there's a relationship?"

Wow, he wanted a relationship? She'd never really been in one, which was kind of pitiful for someone her age. Maybe it was time. "Of course."

"You know, Sabina, I never really thought of you as being old-fashioned."

"No?"

His already focused gaze narrowed in an uncomfortable way. "You were a cheerleader. From my perspective, it looked as if you had one boyfriend after another."

Wow. Was he like those football players, too? Did he think he was entitled? Or was it just the cheerleader stereotype? Why was it so amazing to the male gender that she, a former cheerleader, was a good girl?

Maybe she shouldn't have worked so hard to be good. Look where being a good girl had gotten her. Thirty-five and still a virgin. She almost jettisoned her plan to keep this to a good-night kiss. But there was that noticeable lack of bells and whistles when she kissed him. It seemed to her that there ought to be bells and whistles.

So she straightened her shoulders and stared him in the eye. "Well, Layton, I'm not a cheerleader now. I'm a grown woman and I'm not ready to become intimate with you after only one date. I've had a lovely time, but I'm tired, and I think it would be best for us to call it a day."

Henrietta was not exaggerating. Ross called Sabina five times, and she didn't pick up once. So at about six o'clock, he decided to run down to her house just to make sure she wasn't home alone and incapacitated.

Or something worse.

The sun was just starting to set when he parked his pickup in front of a white BMW 7 Series that he suspected belonged to Layton Webster. He had just killed the engine when Sabina's van pulled into the drive. He should have departed the scene right then, but he hesitated.

And that's how he got a curbside view of the kiss.

Awkward.

How many times had he watched Sabina flirt with guys in the lunchroom? Too many to count. And every time she batted an eyelash at one of those big, stupid football players, a deep adolescent yearning would come over him.

Why couldn't she see through those guys? They were all wrong for her. And Layton Webster was wrong, too.

Of course it was immature to judge Layton by high-school standards. The guy wasn't the geek he'd been. And everyone in town was talking about how much money he'd made with his computer programs. He was loaded. He drove a BMW, for goodness' sake. That car probably cost more than eighty grand.

Any woman in her right mind would find a reason to kiss Layton Webster.

Not that Sabina was a gold digger. But she wasn't dumb, either.

Was it the money that made Layton so attractive? Had she been turning down dates with guys all these years because they weren't rich? Or maybe Layton had some other hidden talent.

Like kissing.

Because Sabina sure did seem to be enjoying Layton's mouth. And old Miz Curran was sitting right out on her porch next door taking in the view. Oh yeah, Miz Curran was riveted to the action taking place in the driveway next door.

Boy, the church ladies would be all over this development like a cheap suit. He should get the hell out of here, but he had the hardest time making his fingers turn the key in the ignition.

Ross had expected Layton to follow Sabina into her house. But after the kiss, they talked for a couple of minutes, and then Layton headed for his fancy car.

It looked like old Miz Curran wouldn't have to report on any hanky-panky taking place right there within the city limits.

Sabina stood in the drive watching Layton as he peeled away from the curb at a ridiculous rate of speed for this quiet neighborhood. It was just after Layton's dramatic departure that Sabina's gaze shifted toward the truck where Ross and his new sidekick, Sparky, were sitting like a couple of church lady spies.

"Oh boy, Sparky, we're in trouble now," he said to the dog. The dog wagged his tail and gave Ross a big doggy smile.

"Ross Gardiner, are you spying on me?" Sabina strode forward, her arms swinging like she meant business. She stopped moving right by the driver's side window.

He had no other option but to roll it down. "Uh, no, not spying. I was worried about you." The words felt right in his mouth and in his heart.

"You were worried?"

"Yeah, I called you five times today, and you didn't answer once."

"Oh?" Her expression softened.

"Don't tell me you let your cell phone battery die. That's always Lucy's excuse when she's dodging my calls."

She smoothed back her hair, the gesture almost defensive as color rose to her cheeks. "Uh, um, well, I'm not sure. I haven't checked my phone to see if it's lost its charge," she said.

Crap. She was totally infatuated with Layton Webster. Something deep stirred in the pit of Ross's stomach. It wasn't a pleasant feeling. And there wasn't a damn thing he could do about it, either.

So he needlessly cleared his throat. "The truth is I came over because your mother asked me to check in with you to make sure you were okay. The whole town is talking about how you and Layton went off together."

"Well, everyone can just go to the devil." She turned and headed toward her van.

Oh, boy.

Ross snapped a leash on Sparky's collar, and the two of them climbed down from the truck and followed her. "Sabina, c'mon. Your momma is happy you have a boyfriend. She's just upset that you didn't go with them to Atlanta, and then you didn't pick up her calls."

She yanked open the van's passenger door and snagged her purse. Then she closed the door with a savage jerk. "Layton is *not* my boyfriend."

"Could have fooled me," he said. "And kissing him in public like that kind of confirms that you guys have a thing going." He nodded to the house next door where Ida Curran was still watching, even though the sun was fading into twilight. No doubt the scene was way more entertaining than anything on television right at the moment.

"Hey, Miz Curran." Ross waved.

"Stop it. Right now." Sabina spoke through her clenched teeth.

"No, I'm not going to stop. Sabina, this reminds me of the times in high school when you used to tease all the boys in the lunchroom."

Damn, he didn't mean to say that. It just sort of popped out of his mouth. But it was the truth. He'd had a crush on Sabina and built her up into a paragon of virtue in his mind. He flat-out hated the way she flirted with the idiot football players in the lunchroom.

"Oh, my God, not you, too. For the record, Ross, I am *not* a slut." She pressed the lock button on her keys and then headed toward the front door of her house. Her movements telegraphed more than mere annoyance.

He followed, and when she yanked the door open, he and Sparky scooted inside before she could lodge any protests.

"I didn't call you a slut, Sabina. What happened? Did Layton call you a slut?" Something ugly and mean churned in his gut. Good thing geeky Layton wasn't around, because Ross was ready to mash the guy flat.

She headed across the living room and into the kitchen.

He followed after her. She yanked open the refrigerator and pulled out a can of Diet Dr Pepper. She popped the top with a jerk and took a couple of long swallows.

Her neck was exposed, and there had always been something about Sabina's long, graceful neck. Heat flowed through him. No. No. This was all wrong. He needed to get the heck out of here.

"Look," she said slamming the can down on the counter, "I was a cheerleader, but that doesn't mean I *did* the football team." She made air quotes around the word "did." "In fact, I was not terribly popular with those idiots because I wouldn't *put out*." More air quotes.

What the hell was he supposed to say to that? He didn't want to know about her sex life. Except he did want to know. And besides, this confession eased his mind about a lot of things.

"Uh, Sabina, I'm really, really sorry I said that. I'm an idiot. I don't have stereotypical views of cheerleaders. I never thought you were a slut. Never. I know firsthand how picky you are about guys and dating and all that. So I guess I'm just wondering about you and Layton. I mean, well, uh…" He stopped speaking. He was digging himself to China. He gave Sparky's leash a little flick. "C'mon, Sparky. We should go." He turned toward the door.

"You better not call my momma and tell her about what you saw."

He turned back, irked now. "Sabina, by tomorrow morning the whole universe is going to know you kissed Layton Webster. In fact, I'll bet you a nickel that Miz Curran is already on the phone to the Baptist gossip tree, and it's only a matter of time before it makes its way to Elsie and the Methodists. When Ida Curran is your next-door neighbor, it's probably wise not to do any kissing in the front yard."

Sabina sagged back against the counter, her shoulders drooping. "Oh, brother."

"Yeah, well, why don't you just call your momma yourself." He turned to go and then stopped. Suddenly needing to get this thing off his chest. "And Sabina, I don't like Layton Webster. I think you could do better."

She stood there blinking at him, the color kind of draining from her face. And now, even though he wanted to go, his feet felt like they'd been encased in cement. He was stuck there, lost in the look Sabina gave him.

"Why do you say that? Everyone else thinks he's a great catch," she whispered.

He had no answer. Because if he started talking, what might come out would be all wrong. Heck, he had to accept the fact that maybe what he didn't like about Layton was just that Sabina had said yes to him, when she'd turned Ross down flat.

He'd made a serious, deep dive into jealousy these last few years. He knew it when he felt it. But feeling jealous of Layton Webster was all wrong. Sabina was his future sister-in-law. Not his girlfriend.

He would have gone right then, but Sabina squatted down to give Sparky a little head scratch that turned into a puppy love fest.

After a long moment, she said, "Maybe I can do better than Layton Webster. But a woman my age doesn't have so many choices." Her voice was low and shaky. She kept her focus on the dog.

What was he supposed to say now? He'd never been good at emotional moments. And he'd be utterly destroyed if Sabina started to cry. He stood there watching Sparky bestow doggy kisses and finally decided that, when in doubt, it was always best to apologize a second or third time.

"I'm sorry," he said. "I shouldn't have yelled at you. I was worried when you didn't answer the phone, and I've had a really, really bad day, but that's no reason to take it out on you. Your private life is really none of my business."

She looked up at him then, her face a mask of pain and uncertainty. He wanted to kiss that look away. "I'm sorry, too," she said. "What was so bad about today?"

"I tried to get my earnest money back from Webster Homes, but they aren't making refunds until the insurance money comes in. If it comes in. And when I went down to the bank to talk with Ryan Polk about construction loans, he pretty much told me that I'd have to come up with more equity. I could buy the Smith house for cash but he refuses to see the value in the property. I couldn't get a big enough line of credit to do the renovations that need to be done."

The muscles in his shoulder and back eased. It felt better to tell someone. Lucy had been incommunicado for most of the day, busy picking out the wedding dress to end all wedding dresses.

Sabina stood up and opened the fridge again. A moment later she pressed a longneck Bud into his hand. "How much do you need?" she asked, leaning back on the opposite counter in the small kitchen.

He told her the amount, then took a long pull on the beer. As the bitter, cold taste filled his mouth, he promised himself that he wasn't going to drink away his sorrows tonight.

"I can help," Sabina said.

He carefully put the bottle on the counter. "I can't let you do that, Sabina. It's a lot of—"

"I have the money. I've been saving for years."

"But that money is for your big trip."

She shook her head and looked up at the ceiling with a little eye roll before she returned her gaze. "Last week Miriam Randall came into Last Chance Around and told me I needed to get Lucy settled before I could find happiness for myself. Maybe this is what Miriam calls 'the Lord's plan.' I have the money."

"I won't take it."

"Oh, come on, Ross, don't be proud. It would be my pleasure to give you the money."

"I'm not taking money from you. If you want to give me a loan, okay, I'll consider that. Or we could just write up a temporary business arrangement or something and buy the Smith house together. And then you can charge me rent or something until the loan is paid off."

"Why do you have to make it so complicated?"

"Because I'm not taking your vacation money. I know how you've been saving. And I know you'll never take that vacation until Lucy is settled. I don't really understand why you feel that way, but I'm smart enough to know that I'll never change your mind."

"Come on, Ross, you were there the night of the fire. You know why."

He nodded. "Yeah, I guess. All the more reason you should take your money and go to France or wherever it is you want to go."

She bit her lip in clear exasperation. "Are you finished telling me how to live my life now?"

"No." He shook his head. "I'm not telling you how to live your life. I'm just saying that you should go and enjoy yourself." *Maybe find that perfect guy.* But he didn't say that part. That part kind of stuck in his throat.

"Okay, if you won't take a gift, then you and I will go down to talk to Ryan Polk tomorrow and see about buying the Smith house together. And then we'll hire a contractor and get that place turned into a dream house so that you and Lucy can move in shortly after the wedding." She stuck out her hand, like she expected him to shake on a deal.

He stood there for the longest moment, looking down at Sabina's hand. A part of him didn't want to make this deal, but a part of him wanted to end the limbo he'd been living in.

And that part was bigger and stronger. So he took her hand in his, jolted by the soft warmth of her palm. "It's a deal."

Several beers later, Sabina finally convinced Ross that it would be simpler, all the way around, for him to buy the house for cash and let her figure out how to pay for the renovations. Then, once the house was fixed up, Ross could get a traditional mortgage and pay Sabina back with interest. And since this was all in the family, so to speak, she refused to draw up any papers. Papers would have complicated everything.

Once the agreement was made, things moved fast, probably because Ross was paying cash.

So on Thursday afternoon, with keys and deed in hand, Sabina, Ross, and Sparky stepped up onto the house's veranda. They planned to inspect the place, making notes for the crew of firefighters who were coming to help with cleanup and demolition on Saturday and Sunday. Sabina also wanted to pick through the trash and junk that had been left behind. You never knew when you might find something of value.

Lucy should have been there for this moment, but she

was still in Atlanta shopping for dresses. And really, it was probably for the best, because the closer you got to the Smith house the more it resembled a shack. It would be better if Lucy saw the place after it had been cleaned up a little bit.

Nevertheless, Sabina was acutely aware of Lucy's absence as Ross slipped the key into the lock on the front door. She stood right behind him, holding Sparky's leash and watching the fabric of Ross's blue plaid shirt stretch across his shoulders. The shifting pattern across the muscles of his back practically mesmerized her. It would be so easy to pretend that they were the newlyweds, just embarking on a wonderful adventure.

Not good.

Sabina forced herself to look away. She studied the gap-toothed railing on the porch and tried to imagine what the wraparound veranda would look like once it had been repaired and given a fresh coat of paint.

She failed. Not because she lacked imagination, but because the heat coming off Ross's body distracted her.

He belongs to Lucy. You introduced them. Remember?

She repeated this phrase like a Tibetan monk seeking transcendence. Unfortunately this particular mantra didn't lead to enlightenment. It just ramped up the guilty feelings that had been unleashed last Friday at Dot's.

She needed to forget that dance with Ross and concentrate on Layton and his kiss. Layton was definitely interested in her. Layton was loaded. Layton was smarter than your average guy. And she had a dinner date with Layton on Saturday. He was taking her to a nice restaurant in Columbia.

"Okay, brace yourself," Ross said. "The place is really dirty and kind of disgusting and smells really bad."

"It's all right. I'm not squeamish."

He opened the door. Dust and mildew greeted her like an old friend. Sabina knew this odor. She encountered it whenever she picked through junk looking for discarded treasures.

The foyer was grimy and disgusting. Papers tilted in big stacks. Rat poop littered the floor. Wallpaper hung in tatters, dust covered every surface, and old curtains rotted from the rods in the front parlor.

"By the looks of it, old Miz Smith was a hoarder," Sabina said.

"Apparently. Although when Momma came to tea twenty years ago, she didn't say anything about hoarding. She said the house was a little shabby, but not dirty."

"Yes, but I heard that she suffered from dementia in her last few years. It was kind of sad. She didn't have anyone to look after her."

"Where was her nephew?"

It was exactly the kind of question Ross would ask. It would never occur to Ross to neglect a family member. He was always calling his momma who lived in Atlanta with his aunt. If his mother needed anything, he was on it.

Sadly Miz Smith hadn't had anyone like that. "I don't think he cared very much," Sabina said.

Ross shook his head. "Poor lady." The pity in his voice knocked her sideways. The more she got to know Ross, the more she realized that his momma had done an excellent job of turning him into a paragon of southern manhood. He always held doors. He always helped little old ladies. And he regularly saved lives.

Whoa, step back, girl.

She turned away, inhaling the dusty, musty scent

as she studied the magnificent central stairway with its hand-turned spindle work and spiral newel post.

"Lucy is going to love this place. When we're done, it's going to be one of the finest houses in town. You're doing a good thing bringing it back to life." She spoke in a hushed tone as if she were standing in a grand cathedral. A little shiver worked its way down her spine. Maybe Miz Smith was watching them from heaven.

Or maybe she haunted the place. Right now the Smith house looked like the proverbial haunted house.

Ross took out a heavy-duty, fireman-issue flashlight. He set off into the front room, where he muscled open several windows—a display of male strength that made Sabina's mouth go dry.

While Sabina picked through fifteen-year-old magazines, Ross settled Sparky down on a long lead with a water dish out in the shade of the backyard where he wouldn't get into trouble. Then he fired up a gas generator to run a heavy-duty fan, which he set in the open window.

"That should draw some air through the place. We'll leave the door open, too. It's hot in here." He dusted off his hands. "Let's explore."

They made their way through the mess in the front parlor to the kitchen, which was in even worse shape. The cabinets were 1970s vintage. The appliances were avocado green. Cracked linoleum covered the original hardwood floors.

"It's pretty bad in here," Ross said. "I think we'll get the guys to demo this room first."

"Good plan."

"There's a back staircase," he said, leading the way to a narrow stairway that ran from the kitchen up to the second story.

They followed it up and took in the three bedrooms and a disgusting bath that smelled of sewer gas. Piles of junk littered every room, and Sabina rolled up her sleeves and started picking through it. She didn't find anything worth keeping.

"Are you going to examine every piece of trash?" he asked.

Sabina gave him a tolerant smile. "This is what I do for a living. And besides, you might find something incredibly valuable. You never know."

"Right." He stepped into the hallway and pulled down the attic stairs. "Wanna take a look up here?"

"Absolutely."

He went first.

Which gave her a really great view of his jean-clad butt. In fact, it was an almost intimate view as they climbed the ladder. And this, in turn, explained why she was practically hyperventilating when they arrived in the attic.

The afternoon sun poured through the grimy panes of two round attic windows set into the ends of the gable. The sunlight danced in the motes of dust and shone over a floor that was mostly exposed joists, except for a little portion right next to the trapdoor where plywood sheets had been laid down.

The temperature under the old tin roof had to be up in the mid-eighties. "Wooee, it's toasty up here," Ross said as he picked his way over the dusty plywood to the closest window. He had to bang on it a couple of times, but the pane eventually swiveled, letting in just enough breeze to swirl the dust. Which in turn clogged Sabina's throat and made her cough a couple of times.

"We're going to need insulation up here," Ross said,

using the back of his hand to wipe the sweat from his brow. He started examining the rafters like an engineer, making notes in a small hard-bound notebook that he pulled from the back pocket of his jeans.

Sabina forced herself to look away, out into the corners of the dimly lit room.

Pay dirt. Shoved into one of the corners under the rafters stood four or five battered cardboard boxes and, in their midst, a wood-and-canvas wardrobe trunk.

Sabina headed in that direction. The dust on the cardboard boxes was so thick it felt gritty under her hands. She left slightly damp handprints as she moved them aside. A quick peek inside told her that one of the boxes contained 1950s-era Christmas ornaments—the kind that sold well at Last Chance Around. The other contained 78 rpm records that would definitely interest online collectors.

"I told you I'd find something of value in the trash," she said with a grin.

Ross chuckled. She looked over her shoulder at him.

The corners of his mouth dropped the moment she looked his way, but the smile in his eyes deepened. The sun backlit him and cast a halo around his sweat-dampened hair, lighting up the brown with fiery highlights. He was beautiful, with a lean athletic body, his shirtsleeves rolled up to expose forearms with ropy muscles. But her gaze got stuck when she got to his mouth, which had softened. Strong chemistry coursed through her veins, making her pulse race.

"You should see yourself," he said, his voice low. Sultry.

"What, is my hair a mess?" She patted back the ponytail. Wisps of hair had definitely escaped. She pulled out the rubber band and smoothed it all back.

"You've got dirt on your nose."

She rubbed.

"Nope, still there, a little to the left."

She rubbed some more.

"That's got it." His mouth quirked.

She looked away. Wow, it was *hot* up here. Or maybe her hormones had just gone haywire.

She turned her attention back to the trunk and tried to get it open. But it was too heavy for her. She would have to call him over. She hesitated for a moment. Proximity wasn't such a good idea, with her mind on forbidden things. But her curiosity about the trunk overpowered her caution.

"There's an old wardrobe trunk over here," she said, turning to look over her shoulder again. "I need your help getting it open. It's early-twentieth-century vintage. Nineteen forties, I think. It could be filled with treasure."

That got a laugh as he walked up behind her, his boots sounding hollow on the plywood. He leaned over, inadvertently invading her space. She twisted the key in the brass fitting, and he applied the muscle needed to pry the two sides apart.

"Holy gee," Ross said, "is that a wedding dress?" He stood up and moved away, but the heat still came off his body in waves.

"Uh, maybe. And a veil. Oh, my gosh, it's gorgeous." She lifted the frothy garment that hung on the left side of the trunk. It was definitely a veil. Probably made from silk, given the excellent condition of the netting and lace. She held it up toward the sunlight. It was 1920s vintage or thereabouts. It had a Juliet cap complete with ruching across the top. And the veil had lace and seed pearls at its fingertip length.

"You think this was Miz Smith's wedding dress?" Ross asked.

Sabina looked back at the wardrobe. A silk, bias-cut gown hung on a padded hanger, and behind it, a man's suit of traditional morning clothes.

"Wow," Sabina said. "It makes you wonder, you know, because Miz Smith never married."

"You think she was left at the altar?"

"I don't know. Maybe her fiancé passed away, like that Dickens character, you know, the one in *Great Expectations*."

"Miss Havisham."

"Yeah," she said in a hushed voice, as if she were afraid to disturb the ghosts that might reside in this old house. And then she did something absolutely unthinkable. She pulled the ponytail rubber from her hair and settled the veil's Juliet cap on her head. The silk whispered in her ears as she adjusted it. She stood. "What do you think?"

Ross stared at her, his Adam's apple bobbing as he swallowed. But he didn't say anything. His lips remained tightly sealed, which, upon reflection, was probably quite wise of him. Then he turned away and started opening the drawers on the right side of the wardrobe trunk.

He grunted. "What the—"

"What?"

"It's a top hat." He pulled the flattened hat out of the drawer. With a flick of his thumbs, he popped it open. The gray silk was intact and not even faded since it had been sitting all these years in a dark trunk.

He put the hat on his head and stood up. The hat was small for his head, which gave it a rakish angle. "What do you think?" he asked, dusty sunlight sparkling in his eyes.

"Very Fred Astaire."

And for just an instant, Sabina wished that he were Fred Astaire and they were dancing again. Not at Dot's Spot, but someplace classy and definitely art deco.

She must have telegraphed something of her thoughts. Because time kind of stopped for a long, sultry moment.

And then Ross stepped toward her and raised his hand, as if he were about to lift the veil away from her face. But instead he asked, "May I have this dance?"

She gazed at his hand for an instant, a warning tugging at her conscience. She ignored it.

Maybe it was the veil. Or perhaps the shaft of light streaming through the ocular window. But when she put her hand in his, it seemed as if she had been transported to a grand cathedral somewhere. And suddenly her mind filled with that verse from the Song of Solomon that Momma had just mentioned a few days before. The one about quenching the flame of love. The one Lucy wanted read at her wedding.

That should have been enough to make her pull away, but she didn't. Instead, she felt as if she were about to combust right there, especially when he drew her forward and encircled her waist with his right hand. She touched his shoulder, registering soft, worn shirt over hard muscle. He gave her a half turn, and it was enough to make her light-headed and weak in the knees.

How long did they dance like that, turning slow circles in the dust? She didn't know. She was lost in the experience. And they might never have stopped, if it hadn't been for the all-too-familiar voice sounding from the attic stairs.

"Yoo-hoo. Are y'all up there? Y'all left the door open so I just invited myself in. My goodness, but this house is a wreck. What are y'all—Oh! Oh! Good Lord."

And Elsie Campbell, chair of the Methodist Altar Guild, was rendered momentarily speechless as she stood on the attic stairs staring at Sabina and Ross playing dress-up as a bride and groom.

Ross was lost. Lost in Sabina's touch. Lost in the look in her eyes behind that amazing veil. Lost in a rush of lust so strong that his skin practically itched with longing.

He wanted her touch. He wanted his hands buried in that mass of unruly hair. He wanted this dance to go on forever.

So when Elsie hollered "Yoo-hoo," it took him a moment to get his bearings. And even when she popped her head up through the attic door, it took him a moment to process the situation. It was like waking up from an incredibly sexy dream.

But when Sabina pulled away from him and then snatched the veil off her head, reality kind of dropped on him like an atom bomb.

Oh, crap.

He ripped the top hat from his head and set it on top of the wardrobe. That didn't exactly get rid of the incriminating evidence, but at least he didn't try to hide the hat behind his back like Sabina did with the veil.

"Oh, Elsie, hi—" Sabina's hand-in-the-cookie-jar tone telegraphed her guilt.

Elsie climbed the rest of the way into the attic. Silently. Which was both eerie and unheard of.

"We found an old wardrobe filled with wedding stuff," he said into the embarrassing quiet. "Do you think Miz Smith was left at the altar?"

"Wedding stuff?" Elsie's gaze ricocheted from Ross

to Sabina and back again. For an instant she looked like a spectator at a Ping-Pong match.

"Uh, yeah." Sabina gestured wildly, bringing the wedding veil out from behind her back, where it hadn't been effectively hidden anyway. "We found a veil and a dress and a top hat."

"Obviously." Elsie's usually cheery voice sounded as ominous as a big, black thundercloud.

Time to escape. Ross figured that, if Elsie was going to read anyone the riot act, it would be Sabina. And while he knew it wasn't heroic for him to abandon his future sister-in-law, he was going to do it anyway. He wasn't a fool. He knew when to retreat from a dangerous situation.

He would have to hope that Sabina would smooth things over. Besides, she wasn't the guilty one. She may have put on the veil and mentioned Fred Astaire, but she wasn't the one who initiated the dancing.

It had been him. All him. And it was the second time he'd put her in a bad situation. If he allowed Elsie to interrogate him, he might confess to having a totally inappropriate yearning for his fiancée's sister. And that would make him a jerk of the highest caliber.

"I think I'll just take this box of Christmas ornaments down to your van, Sabina," he said in a falsely bright voice. He picked up the dusty box and headed for the attic ladder. "Excuse me, ladies."

He took three steps toward the ladder without mishap. But the fourth step, onto a previously un-trod-upon plywood board, proved the killer.

The wood beneath his boot didn't crack. It was too rotten for that. It just sort of crumbled and gave way. And his foot went plunging through the floor and then through the lath and plaster beneath. The box of ornaments went flying as he let go, in order to catch himself on the joist before all of him slipped through the hole and ended up on the floor below.

Ornaments scattered and broke. Elsie and Sabina both gave girlie gasps. And it crossed his mind that this was what happened to guys who took the coward's way out.

"Oh, my God. Are you all right?" Sabina rushed to his side like an angel and grabbed him by one arm.

"Uh, no. I just almost fell through the floor. I reckon we need to add dry rot to our list of problems with this old house." He looked up at her, his skin on fire where she touched him. A part of him wanted her to back away, but another part—his dangling legs—was glad she had hold of him. Although if he let go of the joist now and took her hand, he'd probably pull her down with him.

"I'm good. You can let go now."

She hesitated for an instant. Their gazes met like flint and steel.

"Let go, Sabina. I'm fine." His voice came out cool and controlled. Good.

She let go. He pushed himself up on the joist.

"Oh, God, I was so worried." Sabina threw her arms around him and was hugging on him like she cared. Which of course she did because she was his future sister-in-law. But this hug was not a sisterly hug. And she didn't even seem to care that Elsie Campbell was watching and probably taking notes.

He gently pushed her away. "I'm fine. I'm just glad that I didn't try to tap-dance on that board when I was doing my Fred Astaire impression."

"You can tap-dance?" Elsie asked.

"I can," he said. "Momma had me in dance lessons for the longest time. You'd be surprised how much the dancing helped with my soccer." He turned and beat a hasty retreat.

Behind him, he heard Elsie say. "So he was imitating Fred Astaire?"

"He was," Sabina answered.

"And what were you doing? Trying to be Ginger Rogers in a wedding veil?"

"C'mon, Elsie, I put on the veil first. I couldn't resist. It's in perfect shape. I was just playing dress-up and thinking how great Lucy would look in this veil. And then Ross found the top hat and I told him he looked like Fred Astaire and he decided to bust a move."

"Uh-huh."

"Honestly, that's all this was."

Elsie wasn't buying it.

Which was funny, really. Because Sabina was telling the truth. At least as Sabina knew it. But Ross knew better.

The truth went way deeper.

He had a jones for his fiancée's sister.

When they made it down the attic ladder, Elsie handed Ross a coconut cake in celebration of his new house and then retreated in a hot hurry. No doubt she was anxious to get out an email blast to the members of the Altar Guild.

Ross took the cake, secure in its Tupperware carrier, into the kitchen where he proceeded to go silent while immersing himself in his list making. It was a typical male reaction.

And Sabina, being a complete coward, was happy he didn't want to have a conversation about what had just happened. There were some conversations that two people never needed to have.

Ever.

So she hightailed it upstairs to look through the mostly useless junk in the bedrooms. The separation was definitely a good thing, even if it meant their stories weren't exactly coordinated. Then again, having coordinated stories would make them look guilty.

And they weren't guilty of anything really.

Twenty minutes later, Sabina's cell phone rang. It was her best friend, Jenny Raintree. And since Jenny was a member of the Altar Guild, it was a lead pipe cinch that she had been a recipient of any email blast Elsie might have sent out.

Sabina sent the call to voice mail.

Jenny called again ten minutes later. So did Maryanne Carpenter. And then Momma.

This was bad.

So Sabina pulled a page from Lucy's book of tricks and switched her phone to airplane mode. She sat in the middle of the upstairs master bedroom and composed her thoughts. She was going to tell the truth.

She had tried on the veil. He had put on the top hat. And then he had done an impression of Fred Astaire. That was the long and short of it.

Not.

Okay, so there had been a lot of hot and heavy glances and more chemistry than she'd learned in general science class back in the tenth grade. But so what? They hadn't done anything wrong.

Exactly.

She wasn't going to beat herself up about this. So she continued to sort through trash for the next hour until almost six-thirty, when the light began to fade. Since they had yet to turn on the electricity, it was time to quit.

Aside from the stuff in the attic, which had probably been overlooked by Miz Smith's kin, there wasn't much here but old papers and trash.

She clumped down the stairs, making as much noise as a herd of elephants. She wanted to give Ross warning of her approach. She poked her head into the gloomy kitchen, where he was measuring walls with a metal measuring tape.

"I'm going home," she said without preamble. "It's too dark to do anything more today. There isn't anything of value in the bedrooms. You can have your firemen buddies haul all that stuff to the dump. But once you stabilize the floor in the attic, I want those boxes and that steamer trunk."

"Okay." He looked at her over his shoulder. "See you tomorrow?"

Wow. Was it her imagination or had he suddenly become more handsome and appealing? Yes, it was her imagination. Fueled by her hormones. She was in such trouble.

"Uh, maybe. You've got your crew coming in to clean. I'm happy to write checks."

The spark in his eye faded. Did he know she had just lied? She wanted to be there for every step of this renovation. But of course, that was wrong. This was Ross and Lucy's house.

"Ross," Sabina said in a voice that almost rasped, "Lucy comes home tomorrow. She's the one you need to consult about the design decisions. That's what she's studying in school. I'm satisfied there isn't any junk here that I want for the shop, except the wardrobe, the box of records, and any of the ornaments that survived your fall."

And with that she turned and headed for her car.

She didn't turn her phone back on. She needed a little time to brace for the onslaught, which was surely coming.

But she didn't expect it to reach her front door that evening. At eight-fifteen someone rang her doorbell. She peeked through the peephole: Jenny Raintree looking stern and concerned. Sabina opened the door.

"What in the Sam Hill are you thinking?" Jenny said before she even took a step into Sabina's living room.

"Uh, what are you talking about?" When confronted, it was often best to feign ignorance. This didn't work on Jenny because she had once been a high-school teacher so she knew every adolescent trick in the book. The fact that Sabina was down to trying adolescent tricks was a warning sign, pure and simple.

Jenny walked into the middle of Sabina's tiny living room, turned, and glared. "Honey, you've just told the biggest whopper I've ever heard." To punctuate this point, she gestured with her hands about a yard apart.

"Whopper? What whopper?"

"The one about how you're pining away for a husband."

"When did I say that?"

"When you dressed up like a bride and apparently threw yourself at Ross."

"Is that what Elsie's saying?"

"Yeah, she says you took one look at some old wedding veil and were so overcome with longing, you poor dear, that you had to play dress-up. And that Ross, dear boy that he is, made pretend with you because he has such a big heart."

"Wow. I'm kind of amazed myself." Sabina collapsed on the couch with a sigh.

"Okay, so what really happened?"

"Between me and Ross? Nothing. Well, sort of. I mean I'm helping him financially so he can fix up the Smith house for Lucy. We were picking through the junk left in the attic and we found an old wardrobe with a top hat and a wedding veil in it. He put on the hat and I told him he looked like Fred Astaire and he decided to dance. With me. Enter Elsie bearing a coconut cake."

"And you were wearing the veil while you danced?"

"Yeah. I put it on because ... I don't know. It was beautiful. You would have, too."

Jenny sat down on an old wooden trunk that served as a coffee table. This allowed her to get right up into Sabina's face. "Except that you have a thing for Ross. We both know this. So don't you lie to me."

"Yeah, but Ross—" She bit off the words. She was about to say that Ross didn't have a thing for her. But for the first time, it occurred to her that maybe that wasn't true.

Wow.

She'd been telling herself that Ross loved Lucy. And all indications were that he did. But that was not the vibe he sent this afternoon. Or last Friday.

"Oh, good Lord." Jenny buried her face in her hands, the portrait of a best friend who has just discovered a truth best left unspoken.

After a long, discouraging silence, Jenny looked up. "What are you going to do about this?"

"I'm not going to do anything."

"Lucy's going to hear about this."

"My guess is that she already has. Momma called. I didn't talk to her. That was about the time I decided to turn off my cell phone."

"Oh, Sabina." Jenny didn't seem to be able to find the words to continue.

"Look, it's fine. I'll tell Lucy the truth."

"The truth?"

"I didn't make a play for him. I didn't encourage him.

He didn't encourage me. We didn't flirt. And we certainly didn't kiss or anything like that." She ticked these items off on her fingers. "Jenny, it was entirely innocent. We found some old clothes, and we danced. For about thirty seconds."

"And you lusted in your heart."

"That's beside the point."

"And he lusted in his heart, too."

Sabina shrugged. "Maybe not. Maybe it was my imagination. It's not like we discussed it. You know the subject is sort of taboo. Cheating on your fiancée with her sister ranks right up there with, I don't know, things you shouldn't even think about. You know?"

Jenny leaned forward and took Sabina's hands in hers. "Honey, I don't know where the gossip is going to go on this. I'm hoping people will just say that you're a little crazy because of Miriam's marital forecast or something stupid like that. But you know how it can be. Remember what happened when Pastor Tim came to dinner? Oh, my goodness, it was awful."

"Yeah, I remember. And I owe you one. This is my payback for setting you up on that date." Sabina stood up. "I think we need some wine."

"This isn't funny, Sabina."

"I know," she said, escaping into her tiny kitchen.

"I think you need to have your head examined." Jenny followed her.

"That would cost too much. Wine is cheaper." Sabina yanked open a drawer and started searching for a corkscrew.

"Sabina! You're avoiding the truth. Turn around and look at me, darn it."

Sabina turned and looked. Jenny had a gleam in her

eye that could cut through steel. "I think you're jealous of Lucy."

Sabina almost stepped back, Jenny's accusation was that strong. "I *am not*." She folded her arms across her chest.

Jenny's sharp gaze softened. "I know you believe that, Sabina. But that's not what it looks like. And I'm afraid people are going to say this about you. And that's why you need to keep your distance from Ross."

"It will be hard. He's a member of the family. Practically. And we're working on the house together."

"It's not your place to work on that house. You can pay the bills. But it's Lucy's house."

Sabina nodded. She had slipped again. She needed to remember that the Smith house would never be hers. And neither would Ross.

Okay, so maybe for once in her life she was jealous of Lucy. In some ways, that could be considered a minor miracle. Lucy was the one with scars. Lucy was the one who had nearly died. Lucy was the one who'd lived a difficult life. Who would ever be jealous of Lucy?

Jenny continued, "I know you don't want my opinion on your social life, honey, but a few more dates with Layton would make all of this blow right over."

"What?"

"You heard me. The Altar Guild wants to see you with Layton Webster, and Lucy with Ross. And to tell you the truth, I think Layton would be a great catch."

She wanted to argue with Jenny. She wanted to point out that Layton's kisses didn't do anything for her, while all she had to do was touch Ross to unleash a torrent of hormones.

But of course, she couldn't explain this to anyone, not even her best friend, because her feelings for Ross were wrong. And besides, it was a huge mistake to trust anything that made her hormones go out of control like that.

So maybe she ought to focus on Layton. It would be the mature and correct thing to do. And it would make everyone happy.

Sabina dreaded the first organizational meeting of Discover Last Chance's craft fair subcommittee. It was scheduled for five-thirty on Friday evening—almost twenty-four hours after Elsie had discovered her playing bride and groom with Ross.

No doubt the first half hour of the meeting would be occupied with a humiliating Q&A session. The citizens of Last Chance considered it perfectly normal to concern themselves with their neighbors' business. This was part of the charm of small-town life.

It was charming until you became the center of attention.

At least the committee wasn't big. There were only five members. Teri Summers from Last Chance Bloomers, Pat Canaday, owner of the Knit & Stitch, Olivia Devin, a local quilter, Carly Perez, a local artist, and Wilma Riley, a woman who never saw a committee she didn't like.

Wilma was going to be a problem. She never failed to express her opinions about everything—usually with all the tact of a New York cabdriver.

And predictably, Wilma got things started as they all took their seats around a big mahogany dining table in Sabina's stall at the antiques mall. "Sabina," she said in her raspy voice, "you know you're going to have to tell us what really happened last night. I cannot, for the life of me, imagine that you are so desperate for a husband, you dressed up as a bride in order to throw yourself at Ross."

Sabina's face flamed. "C'mon, Wilma, can we please just focus on—"

"No, we need to get this out in the open because what Elsie said is just ridiculous. You have never struck me as particularly man-crazy. In fact, I think you and I are cut from the same cloth, so to speak. I always thought you were smart enough to realize that marriage isn't a panacea. So I'm thinking Elsie's story is just part of the usual insanity that occurs whenever old, senile Miriam Randall opens her mouth."

It was a well-known fact that Wilma looked down on Miriam. Wilma had a dim view of marriage in general, and Miriam seemed to think the Lord spent most of His time thinking up ways to match people up for life.

It was a definite clash of philosophies.

Sabina sat at the head of the table and scanned the faces of her committee. The women around the table were awaiting a more reasonable and believable explanation than the one Elsie had supplied. If Sabina tried to avoid this topic of conversation, censure and endless gossip would follow.

The gossip would destroy Lucy. And she couldn't allow that, especially since nothing had really happened between herself and Ross. But still, getting caught twice in the arms of her sister's fiancé was going to require a lot of explaining.

"There's nothing to explain," she said firmly. Denial of everything seemed wise at this point. Then she retold her prepared story about how it had all been an innocent and spontaneous moment sparked by an old steamer trunk.

She watched them, hoping they would buy it. And then Pat Canaday, bless her heart, said, "You think that wedding dress belonged to old Miz Smith?" Sabina wanted to give the proprietor of the Knit & Stitch a big hug for that question.

"There was a wedding dress in the trunk and a suit of morning clothes. I didn't have time to look at everything in the drawers before Ross fell through the floor," Sabina said.

"Wouldn't it be cool if Lucy could wear that dress?" Carly said. Carly was into recycling just about everything. She had a studio over at the old bottling plant where she welded together sculptures made of mostly trash.

"What's Lucy going to do with the dress she's bought? I heard from Henrietta that she shelled out more than five thousand dollars," Teri said. "I only know this because she called me yesterday and wanted to discuss the floral arrangements. I declare she's going whole hog for your sister's wedding. There isn't going to be any left for you, honey." Teri winked.

"I think I'll elope when I find Mr. Right," Sabina said. "Now can we—"

"Maybe you've already found him." This came from Olivia Devin.

Sabina's face went hot, and her hands started to sweat. Oh, boy, here it came. She braced herself for an onslaught, but then Olivia continued. "So when are you going out with Layton again?"

It was as if someone had released a band around her chest. "Uh, well, we're going out for dinner tomorrow night."

"You won't need to worry about how much your momma spends on Lucy's dress, honey," Wilma said. "Not if you land Layton. I don't think much of marriage, but if you are determined to get married, I think marrying a rich man beats marrying a poor one every day of the week."

"I think you should wear the vintage dress." Carly folded her arms across her front and leaned them on the table, the gesture a bit defensive. Some of the "critics" in town had suggested that her art was on the tacky side.

"Okay, y'all, enough about me and my love life. We need to talk about the craft fair."

Wilma let go of a long, audible sigh. "I just have one question. Are we choosing the artisans for the craft fair or is this going to be a free-for-all? Because if we let Myrtle Smith in with her tacky jewelry boxes, I won't be participating."

Pat gave Wilma a murderous look, but the daggers in Pat's gaze didn't faze Wilma one whit. Nothing much phased Wilma. Pat turned in her chair. "I think it would be a mistake to get picky over vendors. At least in the first year." Her look said it all. She wanted Sabina to take sides.

Which Sabina didn't want to do. Pat and Wilma had some kind of ancient history that had something to do with a man that neither of them had married. But the residue of that conflict was absolutely toxic.

Sabina rolled her neck to ease the tension and then spoke in her soft, southern girl voice. "Y'all, why don't we see how many crafters sign up for this before we talk about limiting who can participate?"

"Myrtle will be the first one in with her application, you mark my words." Wilma actually pointed her finger at Sabina—a gesture that definitely put her off. Wilma was a good woman, and she was single-handedly improving the sex lives of the women of Last Chance by leaving copies of *Cosmo* at the Wash-O-Rama. But she could be a pain in the rear sometimes.

Pat wasn't about to let Wilma score any points. She leaned forward with a squinty-eyed look. "Some people like Myrtle's boxes."

Sabina cast her glance around the rest of the committee. They *all* had their arms folded across their chests. Boy, this was not auspicious.

"All right, let's just put that item aside for a moment. We have a lot to do." Sabina started passing out papers with a map of Palmetto Avenue that had an area marked off for the craft fair.

"And I think we need to keep this as simple as possible. We'll make it first-come, first-served as far as renting spaces—"

She had to put her palm up to hush Wilma. "It's my turn to talk now," she said, giving the older woman a hard stare. Wilma pushed back from the table, the last one of the group to fold her arms. In a minute World War III was going to break out.

"C'mon, y'all, I don't think we want to get into the business of judging people's crafts. Sorry, Wilma, but we don't. And I, for one, don't have the time, seeing as Momma is determined to have Lucy's wedding on October eighteenth, which is just a week after the festival. And we can't tell Myrtle she's not invited. Every member of First Baptist Church would be offended if we did that."

A muscle ticked along Wilma's jaw. Sabina had a good idea what Wilma was thinking. She didn't have much good to say about anyone who was a Baptist, either.

"So this is what we're going to do," Sabina said in her best assertive-businesswoman voice. "I think we should provide each applicant a space and require them to bring their own table and chairs. As you can see from the hand-out, I'm suggesting that we designate sidewalk space from the bottling plant down Palmetto to the Cut 'n Curl. I checked with Savannah and Lark, and they've okayed that layout and are working with the Last Chance police to make sure there are no safety issues with blocking off the street for the event.

"If everything checks out, we'll have room for fifty vendors. Our expenses will be limited to some printing for the flyers. The rest will be free because we're going to use social media. So our goal is to clear two thousand dollars on this. DLCA is going to give half of our proceeds to support the Last Chance independent library."

Sabina continued to speak for a few more minutes, outlining her plan for outreach to crafters, as well as what volunteer functions they would need the day of the event.

When she was finished, everyone looked down at her map and up at her. There was an awkward silence, and then Teri said, "Well, shoot, looks like you have it all figured out, Sabina. I'm trying to figure out what you need a committee for."

Sabina refrained from telling them that she hadn't wanted or asked for a committee—or the responsibility for organizing the craft fair in the first place. Savannah and Lark had foisted it off on her, and she didn't feel as if she could tell them no.

She tried to invest her voice with earnest appreciation. "We need all y'all because our marketing depends on word of mouth and social media. So y'all need to be tweeting and posting on Facebook. That's especially important for those of us with businesses on Palmetto Avenue. We'll need to get every business engaged in promotion. Oh, and Molly Wolfe has already created the Facebook page for the event, so I just need to give her the information about registering for the craft fair and we're pretty much done with that part of it. All we have to do is share and talk it up to our friends. And we'll need to work together on the day of the event, of course."

They all nodded.

"So are y'all good with this?"

For a moment she thought Wilma might say something, but thankfully she kept her trap closed.

"All right, that was easy. I hope—"

Just then Lucy came blustering into the shop like she'd been blown there by a hurricane. Her gaze fixed on Sabina. "What are you doing?" Lucy demanded, her stance wide and her hands clenched into fists.

"Having a meeting of the DLCA craft fair committee?" Sabina's inflection went up in question like she was uncertain of this fact, even though it was obvious.

"Is it true that you gave money to Ross so that he could buy the Smith house?"

The heads of the committee members turned in unison awaiting Sabina's reply. The boredom had completely disappeared from their faces.

Of course she hadn't expected to be called out for floating Ross a loan. Having her head handed to her for dancing with Ross a second time seemed more appropriate.

Lucy should be jealous. She had every right to be furious. But maybe not about her giving Ross a loan.

"Uh, well, yeah, I did offer to help him out. I thought it would be okay with you, especially after what you said last Sunday about being okay with him buying the Smith house and renovating it. Are you sure you're not upset with me about something else?"

"Oh, for goodness' sake, I heard what Elsie was saying about you and it's ridiculous. You didn't throw yourself at Ross. But I am flabbergasted to come home from Atlanta and find out that Ross came to you for money to buy that house and you just gave it to him. What about your vacation?"

Sabina didn't know what to say. She'd been dreading this moment when Lucy came back from Atlanta. She had expected accusations. She had expected tears. She had expected something way different from this.

"My vacation can wait. And believe me, when he's finished with the renovations, you'll have a home worthy of the garden tour. It will be the home of your dreams."

"Which house are we talking about?" Carly asked. Carly was a Yankee from Connecticut, and she didn't really understand the mores of a situation like this. If she'd been a proper southern girl, she'd have kept her mouth shut now and gotten all the details on the gossip vine later.

"The Smith house," Lucy and Sabina said in unison.

"Which house is that one?"

"It's the old, broken-down house where Julia Street dead-ends at Baruch Street," Olivia supplied.

Lucy and Sabina glared at the members of the committee in unison. Pat leaned toward Carly and said, "Be quiet, hon. Let them work it out for themselves."

Lucy and Sabina faced off again.

"Oh, for goodness' sake," Lucy said. "First Momma wants to go into hock for this wedding by buying me a gown that costs too much. And now you're spending your vacation money. And all because Miriam Randall said what she said. I wish you'd just go take the vacation you're always talking about. I don't deserve your money, and I hate that everyone keeps telling me that I'm standing in the way of your happiness. How do you expect me to feel about that?"

Lucy's big green eyes glazed over with unshed tears, so of course Sabina's heart melted. "Oh, honey, you're not standing in the way of my happiness. And you deserve the best the world has to give. I don't care about my vacation, if it means helping out Ross. He's a member of the family. And family comes first. Besides, it's only a loan, and Ross is going to pay me back. We have an agreement."

"You do? A written agreement?"

"Well, no. But he's going to be my brother-in-law. I don't need a written agreement."

"But don't you see, every time something happens in my life, there you are smoothing the way forward. For once, I was going to stand on my own two feet. Ross and I had a plan." The tears spilled over.

"But the plans changed when the house at Jessamine Manor burned down."

"Oh, Sabina, you just don't get it." She abruptly stopped speaking as she wiped tears from her cheeks. And then her hands covered her mouth as if she was trying to hold in a sob. She stood there for a moment, seemingly paralyzed. Then she turned and ran from the store, leaving Sabina mystified.

Lucy hurried from Last Chance Around, struggling to keep the tears from overwhelming her. Sabina should not have to spend her vacation money on a house.

Sabina was always sacrificing herself for Lucy. No doubt this is why Miriam Randall stopped by the store with her odd advice. It made sense that Sabina would only quit putting Lucy first if Lucy had been "handed off" to someone else.

Which was an irksome way to look at marriage, really.

Even worse, this brouhaha over the Smith house suggested that Sabina might continue to hold herself accountable for Lucy's life even *after* she got married. It suggested that there was no end to Sabina's guilt.

A guilt that Lucy had never asked for.

And a day didn't go by without someone in town reminding her that she owed her sister for all the things Sabina had given up. The debt kept growing, year by year.

Lucy was grateful for her sister and those sacrifices that Sabina had made after the fire. But it wasn't easy to stand by and let Sabina wreck her own life in her utterly misguided mission to make up for that night when the house burned down.

Sabina needed to get over it. The fire was never her fault.

But how could Lucy possibly help her sister understand that no amount of self-sacrifice would change the past? And how could she in good conscience let Sabina throw away her savings on this stupid house? She hurried down the sidewalk, heading in the general direction of the public parking lot, behind City Hall. She needed to hide out for a little at the shooting range until she could get her emotions back in check. Then she needed to explain things to Ross.

She was so busy thinking through what she would say to her fiancé that she ran headlong into a barrier that knocked her back, both physically and emotionally.

She looked up. The barrier had arms and legs and wore khakis with a cleaner's press in them.

"Whoa. Lucy. You should look—" Zach stopped speaking. "Are you crying again?" Zach's voice was as rich and sweet as butterscotch. He was carrying today, and the bulge under his arm was noticeable.

"Actually, I was trying hard not to cry," she said in a firm voice. "But unfortunately, you've once again caught me on a bad day."

"Who are you angry with this time?" Zach asked.

Wow, how did he know she was angry and not sad? She looked into those big brown eyes of his. Perceptive eyes. And darned if she didn't want to tell him the whole truth and nothing but.

Of course she couldn't do that. He was an ATF agent. He would not be amused by the truth.

"My family is being a pain in the butt."

His mouth cocked. "That's what families are for."

"Right." She let go of a sigh. He had some long eyelashes for a dude. His glance seemed suddenly reserved. And yet there was nothing reserved about the way he continued to keep his hands on Lucy's shoulders.

The moment stretched out awkwardly. Should she tell him to move his hands? Should she shrug? What should she say?

"So, do you ever go out to the firing range?" The words kind of showed up on their own accord. She needed to say something or that moment might have stretched to infinity and beyond.

He blinked. "Uh."

"You know, for target practice."

"I'm required to."

She really should shrug off his touch. But his hands felt nice, kind of. Sort of reassuring or something. "There's a real nice practice range over in Allenberg. I was just heading there. It's a great way to blow off steam when the family gets annoying."

Oh, good grief, had she just invited him to the target range? She needed to go. Now.

His eyebrows lowered. "You have a weapon?"

She started to babble. "Uh-huh. Daddy got me into shooting when I was about fifteen. It helped some with my rehab, but mostly it was a distraction. I made it all the way through the Winchester/NRA marksmanship qualification program."

He cocked his head. She mirrored his movement. "Are you inviting me out for a challenge?" he asked.

Challenge? Wow. That hadn't actually been on her mind at all. "No, I was just... Well, to be honest I'm really curious about your Glock."

Oh, no. She was spinning out of control, and she didn't

even know why. Agent Bailey just made her brain kind of short out or something.

"Are you, now?" His eyes got a little darker.

"Yeah, I guess." She finally managed a shrug.

He dropped his hands from her shoulders. And it was kind of funny how she suddenly felt naked. What the heck was she doing, anyway? She should be sitting down with Ross and trying her best to make him understand how she felt about taking Sabina's money.

But that was one conversation she really wanted to avoid. At least until she was in a calmer frame of mind.

"Uh, look, I gotta go." She tried to step around him.

"To the firing range?" he asked.

"I was sort of heading there."

"Really?"

"What? Don't you believe it when I say I've got a gun and know how to use it?"

He didn't say a word, but his crooked smile was a challenge.

The Dead Center Shooting Club occupied a nondescript industrial building on Route 78 between Last Chance and Allenberg. You had to be a member to shoot there, and Daddy was one of the founding members.

Lucy had officially become a member when she turned eighteen.

The place was deserted in the middle of a working day. She took Zach into the range, a concrete structure with retractable targets that could accommodate rifle practice at one hundred feet.

"You shoot a .45?" he asked when she got her Smith & Wesson 1911 Mil-Spec out of its storage case.

"Not every woman wants a .38 snub nose. So are you carrying a Glock?"

His deep brown eyes turned wickedly sharp as he pulled his service weapon from the shoulder holster. "You know what's standard issue for ATF agents, huh?"

She nodded. "I'm shooting a bigger caliber than you are," she said as she donned her ear and eye protection. She set a target at fifty feet, loaded a magazine, and started shooting. For a while, she was in another world. She stopped when she needed to reload and took a look at Zach, who was shooting in the next stall.

He was a sight to behold. All that coiled male energy, the sharp focused look, the chiseled features. Wow! Talk about eye candy.

Why couldn't Ross enjoy shooting that way?

The errant thought sent guilt and annoyance through her. If she loved Ross she had to accept that he hated guns and violence. He was an EMT and had to deal with gun-shot victims right up close and personal. He would never let her keep a gun in the house, not even for personal protection.

So it was natural that she'd end up feasting her eyes on Zach. It was natural for her to pine away for something she could never have.

Zach finished and pulled in his target. He looked over at her, a quick smile softening his features. "How'd you do?" He held up his target—they were using the bull's-eye type. He'd put all but one of his shots right dead center. And she kind of liked that little tone of male pride in his voice.

She pulled in her own target, held it up, and grinned.

"Man, you're good," he said.

"I've spent hours and hours here. Daddy brought me right after my first skin grafts healed. He had this idea that it would give me control or something. There was a time, right after the fire, when I felt completely out of control. It worked. I've also won a couple of shooting matches along the way."

He shook his head. "You're a puzzle, aren't you? An interior designer with a gun."

"Those things are not mutually exclusive, you know."

"I guess not. Just unusual. So, does your boyfriend the fireman shoot?"

She glowered at him. "He's tried it. He comes out here to please me. But he's not that into it." Jeez, why was she telling Zach her life story. And besides, Ross was a good guy. He tried to make her happy.

Zach cocked his head. "You and he are having a hard time right at the moment, aren't you?"

She turned and started packing up her gun. "Don't tell me you've heard all that stupid gossip about him and my sister."

"I have."

"Well, don't believe it."

He didn't say anything, and that bothered her. She took off her ear and eye protection and slipped the gun back into its padded case. When she turned to look at Zach, he was standing there, hands on hips, with a sober and probing stare on his face.

"What?"

"I do believe it," he said.

"What? The gossip about Ross and Sabina?"

"Yeah. I believe it. I think you and Ross are both looking for a way out."

Whoa, wait one sec. She wasn't looking for a way out. She just wanted to go slow. And she sure as shooting didn't want Sabina to use her vacation money to renovate the Smith house. But she wasn't going to explain all that to him.

"You don't know me," she said instead.

"I know you better than you think." He crossed the concrete floor until he stood right beside her, his maleness invading her space like nobody's business. And she had to admit that all that sexual energy was having an impact. A nice impact. The sort of impact she ought not to be feeling.

"I'm going to prove it to you," he said in a low, deep, dirty-sex kind of voice.

He took her by the shoulders and kissed her. It wasn't a nice kiss. Or a sweet kiss. Or a peck-on-the-cheek kiss. It was a full-body experience that involved hands and legs and lips and necks and lasted for a long, long time.

And when it was done, she wanted more.

But she wasn't going to get it. Because Zach stepped back and said, "See what I mean?"

Lucy slapped his face and told him to leave.

Which he did, but not before giving her a sultry look that scorched her insides.

Given the gossip in town, Sabina decided to make a big deal out of her forthcoming date with Layton. He was planning to take her all the way to Columbia for a "dinner you'll never forget."

She didn't tell anyone she would have been just as happy going to the Red Hot Pig Place. Instead, she gushed about Layton and the mystery restaurant whenever she had a spare moment.

This had the effect of arming Momma, who was more than a little affronted by Elsie's insinuations. Momma had convinced herself that a second wedding was soon to be had. So Momma gossiped all over town about the upcoming dinner date and managed to remind everyone that Ida Curran had seen Sabina laying a big, fat, juicy kiss on Layton Webster a few days before Sabina allegedly "threw herself" at Ross.

By midday Saturday, the tide of public opinion began to swing Momma's way.

Unfortunately, Momma believed her own propaganda. Which explained why Momma scheduled Sabina for a manicure and hair appointment at the Cut 'n Curl, and even offered to cover the front desk at Last Chance Around on a busy Saturday.

And once Sabina got to the Cut 'n Curl, Ruby Rhodes, the proprietor, and several of her customers (members of Christ Episcopal, where Layton worshiped) wanted to know where Layton was taking her, what she planned to wear, and every other little detail about their "romance." Sabina had no other choice but to feed the gossip machine with a pack of gigantic lies.

And then she added fuel to the fire by wearing the little black chiffon cocktail dress that she'd bought last year for the Animal Rescue Council's black-tie auction. She even made a point of waving to Ida Curran on her way out the door.

Layton told her she looked like a million bucks. And she liked being complimented. She definitely enjoyed riding in the expensive luxury of his BMW, and listening to the equally impressive sound system. He played Bach's *Well-Tempered Clavier* for the entire forty-five miles. The music was surprisingly soulless. It sounded like piano scales.

The surprise restaurant turned out to be Saluda's, a place near the University of South Carolina. The restaurant occupied a converted VFW officers' club and had a big mahogany bar in the dining room. The tablecloths were the whitest of linen, and the glassware was crystal. The place exuded class.

Layton made a great show of ordering their wine, selecting a bottle of Pinot Noir that cost a hundred dollars.

And then he presumptuously ordered their entrées.

And that's where he lost Sabina. She was completely capable of ordering for herself. But Layton didn't ask her opinion before he ordered the biggest and most expensive steaks on the menu. And she wasn't a big red meat fan.

She thought about bursting his bubble, but decided it was way too early in the relationship to make him feel bad about something so unimportant. He would learn over time. For now, she would just enjoy the feeling of being with a man who wanted to impress her and who treated her like a special lady.

That was pretty exciting, actually.

When the sommelier poured the wine and left them alone, Layton leaned forward with that avid look of his. "So you've been the subject of town gossip, I hear."

She squared her shoulders. "Layton, we've both been the subject of gossip."

"So I've heard." A tight curl at the corner of his mouth might have been a smile, but it did nothing to soften his mouth. Nor did the smile reach his eyes. He always seemed to be hiding behind his horn-rimmed glasses.

He reached across the pristine white tablecloth and

snagged her hand. His palm was dry and not nearly as soft as she expected. There wasn't anything objectionable about his hand. So why did she feel slightly trapped?

Comparisons flew through her mind. She needed to stop. Ross belonged to someone else.

She tried to relax her shoulders, then she consciously turned her hand palm up in a gesture of submission. It seemed to please him.

But it didn't please her. She eyed their joined hands. His hand was kind of pale against the white cloth. Not brown or muscular like...

Stop!

"So what's up with the arson investigation?" she asked, because she wanted to change the subject and this was the first thing that came to mind.

He released her hand and leaned back, his face sobering. "Let's not talk about that, okay?"

She dropped her hand into her lap where it didn't run the risk of being trapped again. "Oh, I'm sorry," she said. "Let's make a deal. I won't talk about Earth First and eco-terrorists if you won't mention the stupid stuff Elsie Campbell has been saying about me and my future brother-in-law."

He leaned in again. "So there's no truth to that rumor?"

"Absolutely not." She managed to sound affronted. But she wasn't sure he bought her lie. She was no good at lying even though she had been practicing it a lot the last few days.

"But you were caught dancing," he said, his head cocked.

"Oh, come on. Ross put on a top hat and did a Fred Astaire impression."

"Really?"

"Yeah. He told me he took tap-dancing lessons as a kid."

Layton chuckled. There was something cool and controlled about his laugh. "I guess he was almost as big a geek as me when he was a kid."

She didn't say anything in response because to confirm his comment was to admit that she had never really noticed Ross until that night when he'd stood up to the idiots on the football team. And the fact that she hadn't paid much attention to Ross in high school was a condemnation of her own self and the shallow and often mean crowd she'd hung with.

She looked away from Layton and took a sip of the wine. It was drier than the Mojave Desert and made her mouth pucker.

"So," Layton said, "I was thinking about the stuff you told me about your business last weekend."

She turned toward him. He was leaning back and had a somewhat distracted look on his face. Like he had settled on this conversation but, since it wasn't about him, it wasn't nearly as interesting.

"What about my business?"

"Well, it's not exactly making fistfuls of money, is it?"

"No, but it pays the bills. And I enjoy it."

"I can see that." He paused for a moment, his gaze fixed on her in an odd, unmoving way. "Anyway," he continued, looking away, "I had a conversation with your friend Jenny Raintree. She praised your talents as an interior decorator. I gather you had a hand in the renovations made to The Jonquil House bed-and-breakfast."

Heat rose up her cheeks. She deserved this from Jenny. Last year, Sabina had worked her butt off to match Jenny up with the new minister in town. Sabina's efforts had flopped. Spectacularly. She could only hope that this dinner with Layton didn't end as ignominiously as the dinner Sabina had arranged between Jenny and Pastor Tim.

Oh, boy.

"Uh, well, I didn't decorate The Jonquil House. I only helped Jenny find some antiques. We went to a few auctions together. But it was mostly her vision. She wanted to restore the place and find historically accurate pieces." She took a big gulp of bitter wine and looked down at the sterile whiteness of the tablecloth.

"I can help you, Sabina," Layton said in a light tone, as if he had missed everything she'd just said about being happy with her business.

She looked up. "I don't need a fancy computer system for what I do, Layton."

"I didn't offer to build you one. I have something better in mind. You see, Uncle Elias has several projects under way in Orangeburg and Allenberg Counties. The homes at Heritage Oaks out on Route 78 east of Allenberg will be considerably more upscale than the ones at Jessamine Manor. The model home is ready to be staged and decorated.

"But unfortunately, our usual decorator has decided to part ways with us. I don't know all the details of why, but we're looking for an interior decorator and stager. It's a good opportunity."

"You're offering me a job?" It was her time to lean back. Didn't he realize that she was an independent businesswoman? She didn't want a job.

"Well, sort of. It's not a permanent position. But I was thinking it would help put you in touch with a new class of wealthy clients."

She turned on her southern girl charm. "Layton, honey, that's so sweet of you. I'm truly flattered. But I'm not an interior designer or stager. If you're looking for someone to do that for you, you might want to talk to Lucy. She's been studying interior design. In fact, it would be sweet of you if you'd think about hiring her. She wants to do this sort of work in the worst way."

"Your sister? You're sure you're not interested?"

"Honestly, it would mean so much to me if you would talk to Lucy about this. This could help her get her business off the ground. And getting Lucy launched in business will be good for me, too. Since I deal in antiques."

"Oh. Well. I'll pop by the store in the next few days and see if she's interested."

Sabina put her hands back on the table. "Thank you."

He cocked his head, his gaze narrowing. "You truly love your sister more than anyone, don't you?"

"More than anyone? I don't know. I love all of my family. But I guess it's true that I feel responsible for her in some ways. I should have been there the night of the fire."

"Yes, you should have," he said.

The words jangled in her head as she processed them. No one had ever agreed with her. She must have said these words a million times since that terrible night, and everyone, including her parents—who should have been furious with her—had insisted that it was a lucky thing that she'd disobeyed and gone out swimming with her friends. Otherwise she might have been burned just like Lucy.

The fire had been hot and sudden. The fire department had never determined the cause, except that it had started in Sabina's room. The leading theory was that the electric heater in her bedroom had shorted and caused the blaze. But it had been summertime, so the idea of something going wrong with the heater had always seemed far-fetched.

In any case, Sabina wasn't used to having people agree with her on this point. And instead of feeling good about Layton's words, they annoyed her profoundly.

He'd put her on the spot, hadn't he? He'd called her guilt into question. He'd made her face the truth. And the truth was so unpleasant.

Just then, the waiter returned with their gigantic, bloody steaks. One look at all that meat lying on the plate turned Sabina's stomach. But the food had the benefit of changing the subject.

She managed to choke down a couple of bites while Layton talked about his uncle's business failures and his own business triumphs—a subject he never tired of talking about.

And when he dropped her off that evening and moved in for his good-night kiss, the bells and whistles remained elusive.

CHAPTER 12

Lucy put the finishing touches on the old dresser she'd been working on. The 1940s French provincial reproduction had once looked kind of moldy and dated. But now it had been transformed into a piece of farmhouse chic. The bright blue distressed paint made it one of a kind.

In fact, she already had a buyer—one of the newcomers to town, the wife of a deBracy Ltd. vice president. Leslie had bought several items from her over the last few months. This one would definitely help retire some of Lucy's student debt.

It was almost quitting time on Sunday. She needed to clean up and get over to the house so that Ross could give her a tour of what he'd been working on. She was less than enthusiastic.

Which was her own fault. She'd utterly capitulated on the Smith house renovation. Ross wanted this house more than he had wanted just about anything, except for the dog. And given that he'd been such a good sport about a lot of things—her to-do list, her rules about sex before marriage, and his unfailing attempts to show interest in her shooting—he deserved to get what he wanted.

Besides, after she'd kissed Agent Bailey, Lucy was no longer of a mind to pick fights with Ross. It was truly amazing how guilt could change one's perspective.

And it looked as if Sabina didn't really need her vacation money. She definitely had something going with Layton Webster. Just knowing that Sabina might be on the cusp of finding happiness lightened Lucy's heart.

It was quiet in the store. Joe McDonald, who sold old Confederate memorabilia in his stall, was minding the front counter.

Lucy was cleaning her hands with some denatured alcohol when Layton Webster, himself, poked his head into her workshop.

She gave him a big, warm smile. This guy just might end up being her brother-in-law. And maybe he'd take Sabina on a monthlong cruise somewhere exotic and give her her heart's desire. "Hey, Layton, Sabina's not here. She went to pick up some old stuff from the Smith house."

"Oh, that's all right, I actually came to speak with you." He sauntered into her space as if he owned it. He certainly had something commanding about him. "I was talking to Sabina on Saturday, and she says you might be interested in a job offer."

"A job offer?"

He leaned back against her workbench, apparently unconcerned about getting dirt on his Ralph Lauren sweater while he explained all about how his uncle Elias was looking for a designer and stager for the model home at Heritage Oaks.

This had Sabina's fingerprints all over it. And Lucy was seriously thinking about refusing the job, but then he mentioned the fee. It was real money. And it represented a kind of independence that she yearned for.

She threw her arms around his neck. "Yes. Yes. Yes. Yes. I don't even need to think about it. Layton, thank you so much. This means the world to me."

His little smile—the one he kept on his face most of the time—blossomed into a big, wide grin full of teeth. "It's my pleasure."

She was about to ask him a few more questions about the job but they were rudely interrupted when Zach Bailey came strolling into her workroom. He wasn't dressed for work today, it being Sunday, but he had a crease pressed into his blue jeans. And the polo shirt showed off his biceps and a lot of tanned arm and neck.

And of course, the moment he arrived her hormones when into hyperdrive.

After their last encounter, Agent Bailey should have had the good sense to keep his distance. But maybe the guy didn't know what a slap to the face meant.

"Lucy, can I speak with you . . ." Zach glared at Layton, who glared right back. "Privately?"

Layton remained where he was, leaning back on the workbench and giving the impression that he wasn't in any hurry to go anywhere. This had trouble written all over it. What if Layton told Sabina that Zach had come looking for her? Zach had no business being here or talking with her. About anything. And boy, there was an avid look in Layton's eye.

"Why don't we take a little walk?" Lucy said to Zach. "I'll be right back, Layton, and we can talk more about the job."

"I'll be here," he said, that goofy grin never leaving his lips.

She and Zach left Last Chance Around via the back door that led to the parking lot. "Why are you here?" She turned and put her fists on her hips. "Layton Webster is my sister's boyfriend. If he tells her that you came here looking for me..." Her voice trailed off as a whole list of bad consequences ran through her head.

"I'm here to apologize." He paused a moment as tension mounted. "I shouldn't have gone target shooting with you. And I sure shouldn't have stepped over the line."

For some reason, this apology—as much as it was deserved—left her feeling slightly bereft. Of course it had been a big mistake for them to go out shooting together. And it had been a big mistake for them to kiss. But that didn't change the fact that his kiss was proving difficult to forget. Still, she needed to forget it.

"Thank you, Zach. I accept your apology."

They stood there staring at each other. A small part of her—the one governed by her hormones—wanted to walk right up to him and get a few more kisses.

Luckily her brain was in control.

He managed one of his crooked smiles. Then he shook his head. "Man, I have lost my perspective when it comes to you. You know that? I'm going to have to take myself off this case."

"Because of the..." She couldn't say the word "kiss." If she said it aloud, it would be like acknowledging that she'd actually betrayed Ross.

"Look, Luce, I've got one thing to say. Dump that guy. You don't love him. From what I can tell, you've let a bunch of meddling small-town people convince you that marrying him's the right thing to do."

She gritted her teeth. "And if I dump him, what then? Am I supposed to run away with you?"

His big brown eyes narrowed. "The thought had crossed my mind."

"I don't know you. I don't know anything about you. I've been dating Ross for almost two years."

"And obviously the romance has faded."

He was so sure of himself. His posture, with legs apart and shoulders square, was over-the-top cocky.

Her girl parts were totally down with the idea of running away with him. In fact, the idea of running away from Sabina and Momma was almost as seductive as running away from Ross.

But her brain was still in charge, thank goodness.

"Go away," she said. "I don't need you telling me what to do or how to think or what to feel. I've got a boatload of people who think they have the right to order my life to meet their expectations. And believe me, Agent Bailey, you are the last guy on that list of people."

He nodded. "Suit yourself." He dug into the pocket of his jeans and pulled out his business card. Then he took two steps forward—the heat of his body warmed her skin.

He leaned in as he handed her the card and whispered in her ear, "If you need someone, give me a call."

Shivers attacked her spine, and her legs felt as if they might melt and dump her in a heap on the blacktop. He didn't draw back for a long moment, and she stood there inhaling his scent and his warmth. Then he planted a soft, hot, devastating kiss on her cheek, and she groaned out loud.

An instant later he was gone, walking away while Lucy watched, wondering if she'd just made a tragic mistake.

It was a good thing the Carolina Panthers were playing the Atlanta Falcons on *Sunday Night Football*, because that meant Ross's volunteer firefighters were free during the day to help him tear down the Smith house's plaster-and-lath walls and clear the place of debris.

By five o'clock the job was done and the crew had gone home for Sunday-afternoon beers and barbecue. Ross remained behind, standing in the shell of the kitchen staring at the hundred-year-old knob-and-tube electrical wiring that would have to be ripped out. Lucy would be joining him here in half an hour.

After Lucy busted up the Fall Festival craft committee meeting, she'd gone off to the shooting range and thought things over. The range always calmed her down.

Afterward, she'd stopped by Ross's apartment with a big hug, a few kisses, and a huge apology for her behavior. She capitulated on the issue of Sparky, after admitting that the arson, Miriam Randall's forecast, and her mother's over-the-top wedding plans had stressed her out. And then they'd had a mature, grown-up conversation about the Smith house.

She wasn't angry about him buying the place.

She was upset that he'd used Sabina's vacation money. When Ross put Lucy's mind at ease by making a solemn promise that Sabina's money would be paid back with interest, she stood down.

They talked a lot about Sabina on Friday night. And they were in complete agreement that Sabina needed to get over the past and move on with her life. Unlike Lucy, he was not, however, all that keen on Sabina moving forward with Layton Webster. But he kept that opinion to himself. He was clearly a minority of one on that subject.

He was thinking about Sabina and measuring for the kitchen cabinets when a voice called from the front foyer. "Is anyone home?"

"Lucy, is that you? I'm back here in the kitchen." He checked his watch. For once his bride was early.

"Uh, it's not Lucy. She's just finishing up that dresser she's refurbishing for one of her clients. She told me to tell you that she'll be along shortly." Sabina entered the kitchen, her gaze wide. "I see y'all have been busy."

Oh, man. Ross hadn't seen Sabina since Thursday, when Elsie had caught them dancing up in the attic. And of course he'd spent the intervening days having long, meaningful conversations with Lucy, while simultaneously telling himself that the dance in the attic hadn't meant a thing.

Which was a bald-faced lie. His whole body knew it the moment Sabina stepped into the room.

She wore a pair of faded blue jeans that clung to her hips and butt like they were part of her. Her green tank top looked like something she might have found at a tag sale. The slippery, clingy fabric was covered in Oriental flowers, and it was almost see-through.

Not to mention that it exposed her shoulders, which had freckles on them. As usual, Sabina had pulled her hair back into a ponytail. And as usual, wisps of hair had escaped around her face. He wanted to cross the room, pull that damn rubber band out of her hair, and bury his hands and his nose in all those amazing curls.

Oh yeah, and his hands itched to touch her breasts

through that silky fabric. Which is why he balled them into fists and jammed them into his pockets. Then he pretended that his feet were set into concrete.

A man could get hurt by lust like this.

And that didn't even count the damage his feelings for Sabina might do to Lucy or Henrietta or even the folks in Last Chance who were all invested in him marrying Lucy.

He didn't want to feel this way.

About anyone.

Lust like this was just crazy. It made a man do stupid things, and he had been there and done that. He much preferred the cool, calm feeling he had for Lucy and her lists.

Sabina stood there staring at him for a moment, her lips soft and parted. The afternoon sun coming through the dusty window lit up her hair. Her voice sounded squeaky when she started talking, and she stammered, which was not like her at all.

"Uh...I...uh. I got a call from Bubba Lockheart. I gather y'all moved the trunk down from the attic?"

"Oh, yeah, you came for the trunk." He had the twin sensations of being relieved and disappointed at the same time.

She nodded.

"It's in the living room. Let me get the hand truck." He hurried out onto the back porch, snagged the dolly, and wheeled it into the living room.

Sabina was waiting for him.

"So, did you search through it? What else is inside?" She tilted her head, and for an instant she resembled a little kid on Christmas morning, so excited to be unwrapping a present.

"Uh, no. We were kind of busy today." He kept his

words sharp and short. He shoved the dolly under the trunk and tilted it back. Then he wheeled it all the way out to the porch and down a makeshift ramp that had been set up over the front steps. Sabina followed him and opened the tailgate of her van.

"Can you lift it yourself or do you need help?" she asked.

"I can do it." He wanted her to leave. Fast. But the trunk was awkward and he almost tilted it sideways when he tried to lift it. Before he could stop her, Sabina bent down and grabbed one of the handles and helped.

Together they got it up into the van. But in the process they ended up side by side and their shoulders touched.

He'd never been burned by a fire. He was practically religious about keeping his gear in top-notch form. But that touch scalded him. It would have been normal to jump back from all that heat. After all, he'd been trained to know the danger of uncontrolled fires.

But his training went right out the window, along with his common sense. Instead of running like hell, he turned toward her. She looked up at him, the fire dancing in her eyes. Oh, man, this was so wrong.

And so right.

"Ross," she whispered, her voice so damn sultry.

His mind told him to stop. But his heart had a completely different idea. His heart had been waiting decades to kiss Sabina Grey. And there she was, right in reach, and her mouth looked so ready to be kissed that he couldn't help himself.

He leaned down and pressed his mouth to her lips, and even though this wasn't exactly the hands-on, bodies-pressed-together, hot-and-heavy kiss he'd once fantasized about, the heat of the moment still swept through him.

He wanted to pull her close. He wanted to explore her mouth a little deeper. He wanted to do a lot more than dance with her.

But Sabina pushed back.

"We can't do this." Her look was stunningly sober.

"Right," he said on a deep exhalation. "Right." He repeated the word because his mind had sort of checked out for a moment. "I'm sorry."

She didn't accept his apology. She just gave him one of those female looks that were so hard to decipher. This one was pretty badass.

And then she backed away, ran to the driver's side of the van, and took off, sending the gravel on the driveway flying.

Ross just stood there, mouth and body tingling, as he watched her taillights fade into the distance.

Sabina had started to wonder if there would ever be bells and whistles in her life.

And now she knew.

Unfortunately, hearing bells peal when kissing your sister's boyfriend ranked right up there with adultery and other deadly sins.

So Sabina drove like a crazy woman, down Route 321 and off into the middle of nowhere. She couldn't go home. She couldn't face Lucy. Or Momma.

Or anyone.

Not even her good friends like Jenny or Maryanne or Annie Jasper.

What was she going to do?

She pulled the van to the side of the road, not far from the public landing along the Edisto River, and sat there reliving the feel of Ross's lips and the heat of his body until she recognized how dangerous even thinking about him had become.

Had she given Ross the wrong idea when she offered the loan? Did he think she was looking for something hot and temporary with him?

She didn't see Ross as the kind of guy who played around on his girlfriend. Especially not after listening to him pour out his sorrow that night at Dot's. His wife had been unfaithful to him, and he was still torn up about that. She'd heard the pain in his voice that night.

So if he kissed her ... then ...

Oh, boy.

Sabina should have slapped his face or something. But no, she had just stood there, enjoying the hell out of that kiss.

She needed to go on her vacation now.

Unfortunately, she had a craft fair to organize, a sister to marry off, and a house renovation to pay for. So a monthlong escape was not in the cards.

But she could go picking. There was an estate sale tomorrow up in Fayetteville, North Carolina. She could go up there and stay at her favorite B&B and leave Lucy and Ross to themselves. And maybe that would send Ross the right message.

She was mulling over this plan when her phone rang. It was uncanny how quickly people managed to find her when the serious crap went down. She yanked the phone out of her purse, ready to send Momma to voice mail, only to discover that the caller was Layton Webster.

No-bells-or-whistles Layton.

She stared at the phone for a couple of seconds. Maybe

Layton was the answer to her prayers. Bells and whistles notwithstanding, the guy was prime husband material.

What was not to like about him? Chemistry was dangerous, especially since this forbidden desire had put Sabina in the position of hurting her sister.

So Sabina pressed the talk button. "Hey, Layton, what's up?"

"Not much. I was just talking to Lucy, and I'm pleased that she's accepted the job."

"Oh, that's wonderful news."

"And I was wondering if you wanted to go to dinner with me tomorrow night."

"Oh, well, uh, to tell you the truth, I was thinking about getting the heck out of Dodge before someone volunteers me for another committee, or Momma ropes me into helping her select the boutonnieres for the groomsmen."

"Another picking trip?"

"I was planning to go up to Fayetteville, spend the night at a B and B up there, and then take my time coming home. I've got a couple of regular suppliers out in the boonies of Columbus County, you know, old codgers with barns chock-full of junk."

She imagined Layton picking his way through a dusty barn, rife with cobwebs, wearing one of his hand-tailored suits. The image wouldn't compute. All she managed to see was Ross, wearing a plaid shirt and work boots.

That mental image was a warning sign pure and simple.

Which is probably why she opened her mouth and said, "Hey, Layton, you want to come with me?" It struck her the moment the words left her mouth that going away with Layton for a couple of days would have tongues wagging all over Last Chance.

Which might not be a bad thing considering the current situation. It would certainly hide the inconvenient and troubling truth that she had the hots for her sister's fiancé. And it might discourage Ross.

She held her breath, waiting for Layton's response. When it came, it kind of knocked her back. "Are you suggesting something naughty, Miz Sabina?" he drawled.

Uh-oh, she hadn't thought this through, had she? She wasn't ready. Not with Layton, anyway. Not yet.

Awkward.

She let the moment spin out for a bit while she collected her thoughts. She needed to get the ground rules right, or this trip could be worse than what she was trying to escape.

"No, not naughty," she said. "I'm suggesting separate rooms. But I would enjoy your company on the road. And I would love to see you picking through a dusty old barn."

"That doesn't sound like fun, Sabina."

"It does to me. So can you get away? Or do you have to work tomorrow and Tuesday?"

"Well, as it turns out, I don't have to work tomorrow. Since Uncle Elias is not actually paying me, I can set my own hours. And besides, the insurance investigators are all over him right at the moment. So getting out of town seems like a good idea."

"The insurance investigators? I thought it was eco-terrorists who set the fire."

"I did, too, but I've been informed that an insurance investigation is pretty much standard in all arson cases. Uncle Elias would probably just as soon I stay away from the office for a few days, even though, to tell you the truth, the old guy could use my help. But he's rejected all my offers. So let him deal with his own problems. A trip to beautiful Fayetteville with beautiful you sounds way better to me."

Boy, he really didn't have much respect for his uncle, did he? Last night he'd spent much of the evening telling Sabina all the ways his uncle was a failure in business. It must be pretty hard for someone like Layton. He was incredibly bright, and he saw things others didn't. All those years ago in math club, he'd run rings around everyone. Of course, the kids resented it because Layton knew he was smarter than most people. And he'd never been afraid to boast about it. Layton was not a humble man.

On the other hand, his brain had made him millions so he was entitled to have a high opinion about himself. Everyone else did. And he was also entitled to have his own family issues, just like everyone else.

"All right then," she said, casting the die. "I'll pick you up at seven tomorrow morning. Are you staying at your uncle's house?"

"Oh, it's all right. You don't need to pick me up. I'll drive over to your place in the morning. I'll bring coffee and doughnuts."

CHAPTER
13

The news that Sabina had left town with Layton was all over town by ten o'clock Monday morning. Ross heard all about it from Clay Rhodes at the hardware store, where Ross had gone for a new blade for his reciprocating saw.

Apparently Ida Curran had seen it all: Layton bringing coffee and doughnuts. Layton planting a hot kiss on Sabina's mouth. Layton putting an overnight bag into the back of Sabina's van.

Miz Curran had even taken a picture of Layton's BMW 720i parked right outside Sabina's house and emailed it to all the ladies of the Baptist Women's League, some of whom shared it with the Episcopalian Ladies' Auxiliary, who in turn clued in the Methodist Altar Guild.

And when Henrietta heard the news—rather late as it turned out—Lucy confirmed it all. Much to everyone's collective delight.

Except for Ross, of course. He didn't like Layton Webster. And he had the feeling Sabina had run off with

Layton because of that forbidden kiss they'd shared on Sunday evening.

He should never have kissed Sabina. He'd broken a sacred trust with Lucy. It had been the same kind of irresponsible and thoughtless act that Betsy had done to him at the end of their marriage. Guilt consumed him.

But even more toxic was the fear that he'd put Sabina in a terrible position. He was deeply worried about Sabina and her relationship with Layton, and he couldn't say for certain whether his fears were real, or just the product of jealousy.

He'd crossed a line.

A deep, dark depression settled over him. His intended bride didn't love the house he wanted to restore, but her sister did. His intended bride didn't love his dog, but her sister did. His intended bride wanted to wait to become intimate, but her sister...

No, he was not going to think about the way Sabina had responded to his kiss. Madness lay in that direction. He knew how lust could fog up a man's rational mind.

Of course, not thinking about Sabina was taking all his attention. So he didn't hear the outer firehouse door open and was kind of surprised when someone tapped on the door frame of his office.

He looked up. Tiana Baako, the fire and emergency response coordinator for Allenberg County, stood at the threshold wearing high heels and dressed like she was headed straight for church. Tiana had no experience firefighting; nor was she an EMT. She had a master's degree in public administration.

A near-lethal dose of adrenaline hit Ross's system. Tiana didn't ever come calling in person. If she wanted to speak with one of Allenberg's paid firefighters, she usually issued a summons.

"Hey," she said, a phony smile curving her lips. She wore a dark-colored lipstick. It made her expression seem particularly sinister. "Can I come in?"

He waved toward the molded plastic chair, which had probably been in the firehouse since 1960. It was the only office side chair Ross had ever had. It was old, but clean. Firemen were meticulous about their equipment.

Nevertheless, Tiana eyeballed the chair for a moment before she settled herself in it. She leaned back, as if she didn't want to get too close to him.

"I reckon you know why I'm here," she said. The smile had vanished.

He sat in his creaky old chair for a good thirty seconds while his brain slowly processed the fact that Allenberg County was about to fire him.

Tiana cocked her head from side to side and rolled her shoulders. She wasn't enjoying this conversation.

"So, how many of the other chiefs are being let go?"

She folded her arms over her breasts. The gesture so defensive. "All of them."

"All of them?"

She nodded. "Me too."

He leaned back. "What the hell."

She looked away for a moment. "I don't know how we got to this place, Ross. All I know is that, when the county council finished debating the budget in closed session last Friday, they decided that we didn't need any paid firefighters. They're converting all fire and emergency services to volunteer only."

"Are they crazy?"

"Yes." She gave him a hard look. "They are crazy. I'm afraid our county government has been taken over by a bunch of Tea Party extremists. And for the record, I told Executive Hayden he was nuts. And you don't even want to know the words that were spoken between Dennis Hayden and Sheriff Rhodes. They want the sheriff to reduce his force by thirty percent."

"Why?"

"To give everyone a break on their property taxes."

"Good grief."

"I'm sorry, Ross. Your employment with the county ends as of this Friday."

"So fast?"

"An election is coming."

"Right. And Hayden thinks this will help him beat Kamaria LaFlore?"

"I guess so. Why he thinks he needs it is beyond me. As near as I can tell, he's way ahead in all the polls. Maybe he just believes his own rhetoric. I can't tell you how his mind works."

Tiana stood up with a deep sigh that communicated her disgust for the situation and her role in it. "I was directed by County Executive Hayden to let you know that he expects and hopes that you'll stay on as a volunteer chief."

"He expects me to stay on?"

"He does." She nodded. She was as upset as Ross about this turn of events. He could see it in her eyes.

"Well, you can just tell Dennis Hayden he can go straight to hell."

"I will do that. You should know that all the other fire chiefs have sent similarly worded messages. Heaven help us if we have another fire like that one down at Jessamine

Manor. And I wonder how people will feel about their tax breaks when they don't get speedy emergency services."

She stood and headed for the door.

"Tiana," he called after her.

She turned with an expectant look on her face.

"I didn't mean what I just said. Oh, well, I hope Kamaria defeats Dennis Hayden this November and sends his political career into the garbage. But you know, and he knows, that none of us is going to walk away."

"He's expecting it."

"Which is maddening. Because in this day and age, you can't really provide emergency services with a completely volunteer force. You know that."

"I do. But he doesn't care. He's counting on you and all the other chiefs to do the caring."

She turned and walked away, shaking her head.

Ross's worst-case scenario had just presented itself.

He no longer had the time or the money to waste on all of the high-end improvements Lucy wanted to make to the Smith house. He'd have to throw himself into the project and flip it fast. The profit from the sale might be all he had to live on until he could find another job.

He had no illusions that Kamaria LaFlore, the current mayor of Last Chance and the Democratic candidate for the county exec's position, would win the election and restore the fire department.

So as of Friday, there were no paying firefighter jobs anywhere in Allenberg County, and that meant he and Lucy were going to have to leave Last Chance.

Sabina couldn't remember the last time she'd had so much fun on a picking trip. Layton was good company, even if she remained a little uncertain about his touches and kisses. He also got a little bored at the estate sale, but he amused himself by stepping out of the auction house and making phone calls.

She ended up not buying anything at the auction, which was a big disappointment. But that was the nature of picking for a living. Sometimes big buyers from the city showed up with deep pockets. Of course Layton, sweetie that he was, offered to buy the mahogany table she wanted, but she managed to make him understand that the entire point of her business was buying items at low prices and then reselling them.

Besides, she wasn't about to start taking money from Layton.

She was happy to let him take her to dinner, though. But this time she chose the restaurant—the Hilltop House, one of Fayetteville's landmarks. The restaurant occupied a house that was built in 1910, and she loved the old charm of the place. Sabina never missed an opportunity to dine there whenever she came up this way for auctions.

They were just reviewing the menu when Sabina's cell phone rang. Layton's cell phone had been ringing on and off all day, and she hadn't complained once about it. But when Sabina's phone buzzed, he gave her a funny look, as if he resented the intrusion. She pulled the offending electronic device from her purse.

Lucy was on the line. And some second sense, or maybe just sisterly devotion, took over. "I'm sorry, Layton. I need to take this." She punched the talk button.

"What's up?"

"Oh, Sabina, I'm so glad you answered my call. Ross lost his job." Lucy's voice wavered. "He's so upset. And

Momma won't listen to reason. We need to postpone the wedding, and you're the only one who can talk sense to her. Honestly, this thing with Miriam Randall saying that I'm standing in the way of your happiness has gotten way out of hand."

Sabina glanced at Layton. He glowered back. "Uh, Lucy, honey, I'm in the middle of a fancy restaurant having dinner with Layton. I will call you back when I get a minute. In the meantime, I suggest you support and comfort Ross." And with that, Sabina did something that she rarely did. She hung up on her sister and then put her phone into airplane mode.

Really. For all Lucy took her to task about the Smith house and pitched her little tizzy about wanting to be independent, it was a sad fact of life that, whenever anything bad happened, everyone seemed to look toward Sabina to fix it.

And she was tired of fixing stuff for Lucy.

She gave Layton a slightly forced smile. "I'm sorry. It's the usual family drama."

He cocked his head. "Has something happened to Ross?"

Was it her imagination or did Layton seem pleased by the idea that something might have happened to Ross? Well, she couldn't actually blame him for that after the way Ross had behaved that night at Dot's.

"Lucy said he lost his job."

"Really?" Layton seemed genuinely surprised.

"I don't know the details. But the county council has been on this crazy austerity kick for some time. They closed the Last Chance branch of the Allenberg Library, shut down the animal shelter, and Ross has been concerned about the budget for fire and rescue."

"They canned the fire chief? After the fire at Jessamine Manor?"

"Apparently. Do you want me to call Lucy and get the details?"

He shook his head. "No, not right now. Later maybe. Uncle Elias won't be happy about this."

"He won't be alone. Although I suspect people will be thrilled when County Executive Hayden delivers a reduction in property taxes."

She picked up her menu and studied it while she processed the fact that she'd hung up on Lucy. She had never done that. Well, maybe not never, but certainly not recently.

"I think we should have the chateaubriand for two," Layton said, breaking into her thoughts.

She dropped the menu and studied him. Of course he wanted to buy the most expensive thing on the menu. But this time Sabina needed to let him know her preferences. And besides, he needed to understand that buying the most expensive item didn't actually impress her much.

"I would prefer the salmon," she said in her best impression of a sweet southern belle.

"But the chateaubriand sounds delicious. You don't need to watch your pennies tonight. I'm buying." He gave her one of his little half grins. "And besides, you don't need to lose weight. I like women with a little meat on their bones."

She ground her back teeth together. She wasn't sure his last comment was a compliment. But she let it go. It was more important to make him understand that she didn't like red meat. "I'm not trying to watch my calorie or fat intake. The truth is, I'm not a big fan of beef."

He stared at her from behind his horn-rimmed glasses as if she'd been dropped there by aliens. "You don't like steak?"

"No. I would prefer the salmon. And I'm not counting my pennies, either. It's just what I would prefer."

"Whatever." He leaned back and hid behind the menu. For the next five minutes, he said not a single word. It was almost as if he was pouting or something.

She allowed him to pout, and then to pick the wine, which he did, but not without offending the waiter. He apparently wasn't all that impressed with the Hilltop House's wine cellar. Of course, Hilltop House wasn't located in a big city like Saluda's. It was a nice restaurant not too far from Fort Bragg. As far as Sabina could tell, the wine list was just fine for this patch of North Carolina.

They settled into their meal, and Layton got over his funk. He spent much of the meal talking about his business as if it was the absolute height of scintillating conversation. Every time Sabina tried to talk about the auction or the farms they were going to visit on Tuesday, he found a way to steer the conversation back to himself.

He really did have an ego the size of Alaska.

But just when she had reached her saturation point, he stopped and shook his head. "I'm sorry, I've been rude, haven't I? I get to talking about what I do and I'm slightly obsessed."

"It's all right. I love my job, too, and it's not for everyone. I have a feeling you didn't bring any dirty jeans to go picking through junk tomorrow."

"Dirty jeans?"

"It's all right," she said in a tolerant voice. "You can make phone calls. I'll do the picking."

He ordered cappuccinos, which she didn't want. Coffee this late in the evening kept her awake.

Then he moved his chair a little closer to her, the smirk back on his face. The expression on his face reminded her of the geeky boy he'd been. Back in school, he used to walk around with that goofy look no matter what the bullies did to him.

Maybe his overly pleasant mask was for protection. If only she'd understood that when she was fourteen.

"So," he said, "Ross has lost his job. I guess that means he's going to have to leave Last Chance, huh?"

"Why do you say that?"

"Because he's a firefighter. I get the feeling he likes his job."

"I guess you have a point."

"So that means Lucy will be moving away."

The thought bowled her over. The idea of Lucy moving away seemed completely wrong. And of course, she'd hate to see Ross leave town, now that he'd returned. But then again, maybe this was a cloud with a silver lining. If Ross moved away, she wouldn't be tempted to ever kiss him again.

"Unless Ross finds another job nearby," Layton said.

"Doing what?" she asked.

"I think I might have a solution. It turns out that Uncle Elias just fired his private security company because of their failure to protect Jessamine Manor. He doesn't take my advice on everything, but in this instance I've convinced him to bring security in house so we can have complete control. Ross would make an excellent security guard. He could give us pointers on protecting our developments from arsonists."

Layton was a sweet and generous man, even if he was a little bit self-absorbed and socially awkward. So he probably didn't even understand how this offer might offend Ross. Ross was a certified EMT, had an engineering degree from University of Washington, and had been a firefighter for years. He was way overqualified to become a night watchman.

But she didn't say any of that. It wasn't her place. "Layton, that's so kind of you. Maybe with your help, Lucy and Ross won't have to postpone the wedding."

That seemed to please him, and Sabina thought the evening was headed for a nice, happy conclusion. But she had a rude awakening when they got back to the B&B.

No sooner had they gotten out of the car and begun walking down the inn's upstairs hallway than Layton made a move on her. This time the kiss was considerably more demanding. He pressed her up against her room door, his body all over hers.

There wasn't one thing about the kiss that excited her, and when he touched her breast, she felt positively violated.

She pushed him back. He resisted for a moment until she gave him a no-nonsense shove. "Layton, please," she said.

He must have come to his senses because he finally let her go. But the look in his bright blue eyes frightened her. "Come on, Sabina, don't play shy," he said.

"I'm not playing shy." She had to fight the urge to wipe her mouth with the back of her hand.

He shook his head. "Don't play games. I know what kind of woman you are. Everyone knows."

This statement confused her to no end. "What kind of woman am I, Layton?" She was angry now.

"You slept your way through the entire football team. So what gives now?"

"I did not." She drew herself up. "I hate it when people try to pin that old, shopworn stereotype on me. Just because every member of the defensive line tried to score with me doesn't mean I let them. I told you, before we came on this trip, that we'd be sleeping in separate bedrooms. Don't ruin it now." She crossed her arms over her breasts in the hope that her body language would give him a hint.

But he wasn't good at reading body language, apparently. His ice blue stare practically froze her in place. "You didn't do the football team?" he asked.

"Good Lord, Layton, is that the kind of question you ask a lady you're interested in?" She turned and jammed her key in her door. She hoped to God he didn't try to force his way in. She was prepared to scream if he did.

"Sabina, please, I'm sorry. It's just that you're so beautiful and—" His voice sounded like a pitiful whine.

She turned. That infernal smirk was back on his face. How did he expect her to read that expression?

"I'm sorry. I overstepped my bounds," he said. "I just thought, with what I've done for Lucy and Ross, you'd realize how serious I am about you."

Damn. The guy was keeping score. That was a little scary. And sadly, it made him a whole lot like those idiots on the football team. They all thought that they could buy their way into her panties. She remembered Alfie Roche having a conniption because she wouldn't let him cop a feel after he bought her a milk shake at the Kountry Kitchen.

She hadn't even asked him to buy that milk shake, either.

It was depressing. In her whole life, she'd never dated

one single guy who didn't think she came at a truly cheap price. Even Layton Webster, who had millions in the bank.

"Layton, I am not a slut. Don't treat me like one." She turned and slammed the door in his face.

Sparky gave a happy *wuf* and took off across the weedy yard, like a true watchdog. Ross looked up from the wisteria vine he'd been trying to dig up. His intended bride and his new puppy dog were locked in a staring contest.

"Hush," Ross commanded. And Sparky sat like he knew what was expected of him.

Lucy, on the other hand, stood on the back porch hugging herself like she was scared to death of the dog.

"I'm taking the job with Webster Homes," Lucy announced. "And I think you should take the security job." She eyed the dog. "You could take Sparky with you on foot patrol."

The stand-off between his dog and future wife did nothing to improve Ross's mood. He looked down and vented his fury on the stubborn vine. He gave the thing a couple of whacks with his pickax and imagined he was taking a swing at Layton Webster.

Man, he sure did resent that guy. He resented the way the guy was worming his way into the Grey family. He resented the way the guy flashed his money around town. He resented the way the guy had kissed Sabina. And he resented the job offer, too.

If Webster Homes wanted to help him out, they'd return his earnest money, not give him a stupid minimum-wage job.

What was the deal with Layton, anyway? Was Ross the only person who thought there was something off about him?

"Are you listening?" Lucy asked.

Man. How many times had Betsy asked that question? Ross hated those three little words.

He dropped the pickax and looked up at Lucy. "Yeah, I'm listening. But I'm not a security guard. I'm sorry, sweetie, but I'm not." He stripped off his work gloves. "I'm a fireman. It's what I do and who I am. There are jobs available in Atlanta and Charlotte. I've been searching online and I've already sent in résumés to four or five departments."

"But in the meantime, you don't have any income." Were those tears in her eyes? Lucy never cried, and she'd been like a waterworks for a couple of weeks. What was up with her, anyway?

There wasn't ever going to be a satisfactory answer to that question. Women were a complete mystery. He didn't understand them. He never had and never would.

He crossed the weedy yard and gave Sparky a little pat on his head. "Good boy. But Lucy isn't the bad guy. If you're going to live up to your Dalmatian ancestors, you need to learn who the enemy is."

Sparky thumped his tail and gave Ross an adorable look. Ross turned toward Lucy. "You know, sweetie, if we went to Atlanta, you wouldn't have Sabina and Henrietta in your hair all the time. And you might have more success as a stager and designer."

"I didn't say I was opposed to moving, Ross. I only pointed out that you need income." She gave him one of her big-eyed looks. The kind that always melted him. And he felt himself melting, sort of, but for some reason, Lucy's big-eyed look was losing its potency.

Her lip quivered when she spoke again. "Sabina said

you could make money flipping this house. And I was thinking that the logical thing to do is for you to work on the house, put sweat equity into it, and then work part-time at night. We could make ends meet."

"And put off the wedding?"

Her shoulders rose a bit. It wasn't quite a shrug, and she probably didn't even want him to see that small tell. But the gesture was so eloquent. "Momma's already sent out the invitations."

Wow, Henrietta wasn't letting the grass grow under her feet, was she? "I didn't know that." His chest constricted.

"Yeah, she did."

He pushed his fear to the side. Everyone said he was commitment-phobic since his divorce. It was true. Getting married was scary. But Lucy was sweet. He needed to remember that. He reached out and tucked a stray lock behind her cute little ear.

She almost immediately pulled the hair forward again. The gesture made his heart ache. Didn't she know she was cute? Didn't she realize that the scars were nothing?

He decided to capitulate, because that was usually the best course of action. It would make her happy and maybe she'd stop with the tears. The tears really upset him. If Lucy was crying like this, it had to mean she was tense. And having Henrietta for a mother could make anyone anxious.

He cupped her cheek. Affection spilled through him. "Sweetheart, I don't want you to get all stressed out. We're going to be fine. We'll get married, and you can live in my apartment for a while. You can decorate the place any way you want."

"I can throw out that old couch you love so much?"

He closed his eyes. He hated to part with that couch. It had belonged to his mother, and it was comfy. He exhaled and opened his eyes. "Yeah."

An up-to-no-good smile softened her mouth, and he wanted to give her a hug and protect her from herself and the world. This was real love. This kind of love would last a lifetime. Unlike the overwhelming desire he felt for Sabina, which would definitely ignite a conflagration that would burn itself down to smoke and ash.

He opened his arms. "Come here, sweetie. I'm tired of being angry."

"Me too."

She walked into his arms, and he held her tight. It was nice. She was small and needed him, and he liked taking care of her. "It's all going to work out."

Sparky clearly agreed because the dog came up onto the porch and leaned into them like he wanted to be part of the family.

Unfortunately, Lucy wasn't down with that. She kind of shoved the dog aside. "Sparky!"

The dog looked up adoringly, but Lucy was blind. Instead she turned toward Ross. "So you'll take the job? Give it a few months. You never know what might happen. Daddy was saying that Mayor LaFlore is furious with the county about the fire department. She's all over town telling folks this will compromise their safety."

"It will."

"Maybe they'll change their minds. Maybe she'll win the election in November and restore the money for the fire department."

He seriously doubted that. "Lucy, have you considered that moving away from your family might be a good thing? I know we both love this town, but I can see how Sabina and Henrietta have upset you."

This earned him a genuine smile. "You know, Ross, I think you may be the only person who actually gets this. I'm open to moving away if you need to find a job. But as for getting Sabina out of my hair, well, things have definitely changed now that Layton's on the scene. She's going to move away when she marries Layton."

"Whoa, wait a sec. Has Layton proposed to your sister?" He stepped back a pace, still holding Lucy's shoulders as toxic, angry, jealous emotions spilled through him.

Sparky sensed the change and barked a couple of times until Lucy glared at him. "Hush up," she said, then turned back to Ross. "You need to take that dog to puppy obedience classes."

"I will. I promise. Did Layton propose?"

Lucy shook her head. "Not yet. But he will. He's obviously the man Miriam Randall predicted for my sister. And I'm happy to see Sabina with someone. Finally. I'm starting to see that our getting married might clear the way for her, just like Miriam said. The truth is, I owe Sabina more than I can ever repay."

CHAPTER 14

Ross figured there was some truth to the old adage about having a happy wife and a happy life. The minute he gave in on the part-time security guard issue, Lucy's funk disappeared. In fact, for a whole week, Lucy was happier than he'd seen her in a long, long time. She had lists of fabrics she needed for curtains at the model home. She had lists of furniture stores to visit. She had lists of colors and paint swatches and a whole bunch of other stuff. This was the in-charge woman he'd grown to know and admire.

Of course she and Sparky didn't have the best of relationships. But she was making an effort, and he was certain that she'd come around. So long as Ross could break the puppy of chewing on things that didn't belong to him. The dog had destroyed Ross's only pair of dress shoes. Heaven help the pooch if he ever got into Lucy's shoe collection.

And since the dog liked to chew, Ross had come to the conclusion that the best way to keep Sparky out of trouble was to keep him close. So Ross brought him to work every night. No one at Webster Homes seemed to care, and since

Dalmatians had been bred as watchdogs, it seemed like a smart move, even if Sparky wasn't exactly all Dalmatian.

Heritage Oaks was going to be an exclusive neighborhood. Construction on the high-end model home had been completed a week ago, and Lucy had jumped in with both feet, decorating and staging the place. Webster planned to open Heritage Oaks for home sales next Saturday.

None of the fifteen homes in the development were more than foundations. Each one sat on an acre, and the entire complex stood miles away from any ecologically sensitive land. So eco-terrorists were probably not a big threat. Nevertheless, Layton Webster had gone out of his way to impress upon Ross that eco-terrorists were the company's main worry.

Eco-terrorists notwithstanding, the work of guarding the place was beyond boring. It involved driving around the development a couple of times each night and checking the security fence hourly. In three days of working there, the only living thing Ross had apprehended was a possum trying to get into the Dumpster at the work site next door to the model home.

And he actually hadn't apprehended the possum. Sparky had sounded the alarm way before Ross figured out that the disturbance was nothing more than a food bandit. And the minute Sparky barked, the possum took off. Ross got a glimpse of the ugly critter streaking through the beam of his flashlight.

Sparky wanted to give chase, but Ross had a firm grip on the dog's lead.

When he wasn't driving around the development, Ross hung out in the model home, where he kept the coffee machine working. On Wednesday at about two in the morning, Ross had just brewed himself a cup when Sparky started growling and pawing at the wood trim around the French doors that led from the kitchen onto a deck. Ross figured the nighttime food bandit had returned.

"Stop it, Sparky," he said, but the dog was in no mood to behave. Ross turned off the lights and peered through the doors. He didn't see anything, but the dog was definitely putting up the alarm.

He fumbled in the dark and managed to get Sparky's lead hooked onto his collar, then grabbed his flashlight and stepped out onto the back deck. He aimed his beam at the Dumpster. Sure enough, a flash of white and a pair of eerie, glowing eyes told him he had a critter to contend with.

The dog wuffed and growled. The possum took off across the backyard, and Sparky strained at his collar. With a sudden, almost audible snap, the leash let go.

Damn it. In all that fumbling in the dark, he must not have attached the leash securely. Sparky raced after the possum, showing the world that he was as much a hunting dog as a watchdog.

A stream of cuss words left Ross's mouth as he ran down the back stairs and out into the dark night. "Sparky, you come back here," he shouted.

And then, out in the darkness, Sparky let go of a different kind of bark—the kind that made the hair on the back of Ross's neck rise. The sudden rush of adrenaline tingled all the way down his backbone.

What the hell?

He headed toward the sound, flashlight scanning the distance. A movement in the shadows. The shape of a human wearing black.

Ross reversed the direction of the light. Searching. There was nothing. Was he imagining things? If someone was out there, they had just made it to the drainage ditch at the edge of the property.

He slowed his steps, not certain that he wanted to come face-to-face with anyone out here in the dark. His gut told him he was in mortal danger, and he always listened to his gut. It had saved his life a time or two in the middle of fires that were about to go out of control.

He reached for his cell phone, intent on calling in some backup from the Sheriff's Department. But before he could dial the number, the night exploded with orange light.

Ross went airborne.

And right before he blacked out, he felt searing heat on the back of his neck.

Sabina's cell phone jolted her awake at 3:00 a.m. This couldn't be good. One glance at the phone confirmed the worst. It was Annie Jasper, one of the nurses down at the clinic.

Adrenaline hit Sabina's bloodstream, making her hands tremble as she touched the talk button. "Tell me it's not Daddy with a heart attack."

"It's not your daddy, Sabina," Annie said. "I'm trying to get hold of Lucy. Do you know where she is?"

"Lucy? She's here. I think."

"There's been a problem down at that new development."

"Heritage Oaks?"

"Yeah. Ross has been hurt."

If her hands had been shaking before, they were beyond her control now. Her heart took off at a mile a minute, too. "Oh my God, how bad is it?"

"He's got a concussion and a bunch of bruises. He's really lucky. He was almost blown to smithereens."

"What happened?" Sabina got out of bed and headed down the hall to Lucy's room.

"Some kind of explosion blew up the model home. Matt told me that they've got firefighters from Bamberg helping to put out the fire. It looks like more eco-terrorism. This wasn't an accident, Sabina. Someone intentionally blew up that house." Annie's voice wavered.

"Hang on. Let me get Lucy."

She banged on Lucy's bedroom door and opened it. "Lucy, did you put your cell phone in airplane mode again?"

"What?" Lucy sat up in bed, her hair a big, messy tangle around her face.

"Here." She thrust the cell phone in Lucy's face. "It's Annie on the phone. Ross has been hurt doing that night watchman job you insisted he take."

Sabina regretted the words the moment they left her mouth. This disaster wasn't Lucy's fault.

This was Sabina's fault, pure and simple. She should never have encouraged Layton to offer Ross that job. She should never have invited Layton to join her for that weekend getaway. She should have stayed far, far away from the guy.

But of course, she hadn't done any of those things. And even worse, she'd encouraged Layton for all the wrong reasons. She'd used him to cover up her own dangerous and forbidden feelings.

This was nothing but karmic payback.

Lucy hated hospitals. And even though the Last Chance clinic was hardly a hospital, the antiseptic smell of the place, coupled with the flashing lights from the

Sheriff's Department vehicles and Last Chance ambulance, almost paralyzed her. She could hardly bring herself to enter the building.

Thank the Lord Momma was with her and took her by the arm and practically dragged her into the clinic. The treatment area was like an emergency room with beds lined up, separated by curtains. Ross was in one of those beds.

He was conscious. But he had a gash along his hairline that had been stitched up, his arms sported multiple scrapes and bruises, and his lower lip was swollen and bloody. He looked like he'd just gone ten rounds with Mike Tyson.

Momma pushed her in his direction, but it felt as if she were wearing cement shoes. Each step toward him took a gigantic effort. Her heart was pumping like she'd just run a 5K race. She didn't know what to say or do.

She didn't want him to be hurt.

She managed to make it to the side of his bed and was heartened to see him open his eyes.

"Hey," he said. His deep voice sounded rough.

"Hey," she answered back. She didn't know what else to say.

That was okay because he closed his eyes again and didn't seem like he was all that interested in talking. Which was sort of like him, actually.

Momma took over, the way she always did. "Oh, my goodness, Ross, you are a sight for sore eyes. What in the world happened out there?"

He opened his eyes and squinted. "Huh?" He reached one bruised hand up to his ear. "Can't hear. Explosion."

"Oh, you poor man. Who in the world would do such a thing? And where is the doctor?" Momma turned and strode off, obviously more than happy to take charge.

Ross managed a grotesque smile. "I'm good. Sparky saved me." Then he closed his eyes again. His rumpled brow belied his words. He looked like he was in pain.

Lucy grabbed the safety bar along the bedside in a death grip. She wondered if she should hold his hand, but the hand closest to hers was all banged up and kind of swollen. So maybe not.

A moment later Momma returned with Doc Cooper in tow.

"Ross, honey, they're sending you up to Orangeburg," she said in that voice she always used when Daddy turned his hearing aid down. "Doc wants you to have an MRI."

Ross opened his eyes and squinted at Momma. Clearly Momma's technique had made it through his compromised hearing.

The doctor took over. "You've got a concussion," he said, getting right up in Ross's face so he could hear and understand. "And I'll bet you have one hell of a headache. But I can't give you anything for it. You'll just have to tough it out. You're an EMT, you know how head injuries can be. Do you understand?"

Ross gave him a little nod.

Doc Cooper patted his shoulder. "Good. Some of the volunteers from the Last Chance Fire Department insisted on being the ones to take you up to the hospital. They're all worried about their chief. They're coming right now to get you."

Doc turned and sure enough here came Dash Randall and Bubba Lockheart wheeling an ambulance gurney. Matt Jasper brought up the rear, and for once he didn't have Rex with him. Instead he was holding Sparky's leash.

Sparky took one look at Ross and began to wuf. Matt put his hand on the dog's head and said a couple of quiet words and the dog sat and stopped barking. But Sparky's big brown eyes locked on his master, and anyone could see that the dog would go the extra mile to protect Ross.

Lucy wasn't particularly a dog person, but in that instant her heart softened a bit.

Matt gave Lucy a big smile. "Ross says Sparky is the hero of the day," he said. "He got Ross out of the house before the explosion. And when we arrived on the scene he was right there waiting for us. He led us right to where Ross was."

"Where was he?" Henrietta asked.

"In the drainage ditch behind the house. I gather he got that far before the place blew."

"What in the Sam Hill blew that place up?" Doc asked.

Matt shook his head. "We don't know yet. It wasn't natural gas; those houses are all electric. Someone blew that model home up on purpose, though. There were bed-sheets up on the fence. Just like at Jessamine Manor."

Ross tried to push himself up off the bed, but Dash was right there. "Whoa there, cowboy, you stay put. We'll get you on the gurney."

"The ATF is crawling all over the scene," Bubba said. "I just don't get it. Those houses were being built on land that old man Nelson used to plant soybeans on. There is nothing ecologically valuable about it."

Matt handed Lucy the leash. She took it because she didn't know what else to do, but it was ridiculous for her to be taking care of the dog. He might be a hero, and her heart may have softened toward him, but she was still not a dog person.

Ten minutes later Ross was all loaded up and the ambulance pulled out of the clinic's parking lot, headed for Orangeburg.

"He'll be fine," Momma said, giving Lucy's shoulder a motherly pat. "C'mon, let's go home. I just gave Sabina and Daddy a status update, and they're making omelets for us. We'll eat some breakfast and head up to Orangeburg afterward. Sabina said she'd take care of Sparky for you."

And wasn't that just like Sabina. But of course, her sister hadn't minced words this morning, had she? Ross had almost died.

And it was her fault.

She and Momma were headed toward the parking lot when Zach Bailey pulled up in his gray Ford Focus. He unfolded from the driver's side with a sinuous grace that made the spit dry up in Lucy's mouth. Oh, boy, Zach was the last person on the face of the planet she wanted to see right now.

Wasn't she already guilty enough? God was rubbing her nose in it this morning, wasn't He?

"Lucy," he said in his sweet, butterscotch voice, "I was hoping to talk to Ross. I gather he's the only witness to what happened tonight."

"You're too late. Doc Cooper just sent him up to the hospital in Orangeburg for tests. He's got head injuries." Momma managed to sound dramatic.

"Damn." Zach stabbed his fingers through his hair. The motion gave Lucy a glimpse of that Glock he carried. The gun was such a turn-on.

"I heard the explosion was set off by terrorists. Is that really true?" Momma sounded frightened, which had to be a first. Momma was the original steel magnolia.

"I'm not at liberty to say." Zach's gaze shifted from Lucy to Momma and back again. "I need to talk to you, Lucy."

Panic jumped up her spine. "About what?"

"About your job at Webster Homes."

"What about it?"

His gaze shifted to the dog and over to Momma.

"Honey, I'll take Sparky for a minute. You talk to Agent Bailey. We need to get to the bottom of this. Honestly, I nearly 'bout died myself of a heart attack when I heard how close Ross came to losing his life tonight."

Momma took Sparky's leash, and the next thing Lucy knew she was being herded toward the clinic's waiting room. It wasn't a terribly private place, but the waiting room happened to be deserted at this early hour of the morning.

She halfway expected Zach to go into his lover-boy routine, but this time he was all business. He started firing questions at her.

"When did you leave work yesterday evening?"

"About six. Just as Ross was coming on shift."

"Did you see him?"

"Of course I saw him. I gave him a kiss, and I told him I'd see him tomorrow . . . uh today, I mean."

Zach's gaze narrowed, as if her stammering over the time made her guilty of something terrible. Sweat suddenly dampened her palms.

"Were you painting anything at the house yesterday?" he asked.

She frowned. "No. I wasn't painting anything. I was working in the upstairs, staging the bedrooms. Why?"

He didn't respond to her question. He just kept firing off his own. He wanted to know what time she arrived at work, who she spoke with, who had been in and out of the house, and when they'd been there. Not to mention all the things she had done that day, what parts of the house she'd been in, and if she'd seen anything amiss.

She felt like one of those innocent suspects on a *Law and Order* rerun who has been dragged into a tiny, sterile room and had a light shined in their eyes. He was treating her like she was guilty of something terrible.

Which, actually, wasn't that far from the truth. She hadn't blown up Heritage Oaks, but she was guilty of a lot of other stupid things.

"Okay, so tell me about your relationship with Ross," Zach finally asked.

"C'mon, let's not go there again, okay?"

That stopped him. His eyes softened a little. "Lucy, this is not about what happened at the shooting range. This is suddenly serious business." He paused for a moment. "The truth is, I should probably tell my superiors about what happened at the shooting range. The state of your relationship with Ross is no longer a matter for my speculation. It's a matter for thorough investigation."

"You wouldn't."

"I might have to."

"Are you threatening me?"

"Lucy, if I tell them about what happened between us, it will probably cost me my job. I crossed the line that day. I don't want to tell them about it. But I will if it means catching the slimeball who did this tonight."

She stood up. "Okay, I understand. But I don't see how my relationship with Ross has any bearing whatsoever on this case. Ross and I are engaged. We're in love. We're getting married in a couple of weeks. And that's the beginning and end of it."

"But you want to postpone the wedding, don't you? And don't deny it because I've heard you say it out loud several times. Is Ross being difficult about that?"

"No. My mother is being difficult. Ross is almost never difficult. About anything. Except maybe his dog. There is absolutely nothing wrong with my relationship with Ross Gardiner."

Zach stood up and got right up in her face. And damn it all, he still managed to trigger a deep, sexual longing in her. But he wasn't a friend. She had to remember that. Even though she still had his card in her wallet and had taken it out several times, just to look at the number.

"Lucy," he said in that soft, deep voice, "don't you lie to me. I can see right through you."

And of course he could. So she had no other option but to turn and walk away.

Everyone in the family went up to the hospital except Sabina. She told them it was all right. Someone had to open the store and take care of the dog. But even though she had made the offer to stay behind, she still resented being left out.

And every moment waiting on Lucy or Momma to call with news was an agony.

She wanted to rush right up to the hospital and hold Ross's hand. She wanted to take care of him. She wanted to bake him a casserole and take him a bouquet of get-well balloons. But of course, that was Lucy's job.

She was in trouble—the kind of trouble she didn't know how to escape without ruining her relationship with every person she loved.

Possibly even Ross.

Who she didn't love, exactly. It was more a case of run-away lust. And didn't it say in the Bible that lust was a sin? It certainly felt like a sin today.

The afternoon dragged on as she sat at the checkout counter at Last Chance Around processing applications for the craft fair that was only ten days away. She needed a distraction in the worst way.

Layton Webster was not what she had in mind. He came into the store like he owned the world, wearing his ever-present smirk. Today it seemed out of place. Ross had almost died doing a job for Webster Homes. It wasn't a day for smiling, or smirking, or grinning.

"Hey," he said as he strolled up to the checkout counter and leaned his hip into it. He looked as if he'd just come off the green at an exclusive country club. The Rolex on his wrist made a definite fashion statement. So did the Maui Jim prescription sunglasses.

"Hey, Layton," she said in a neutral tone as she tried to think up ways to get him to leave. She hated those sunglasses. It was bad enough the way he hid behind his regular glasses, but these were like an impenetrable mask.

"So where are the flowers I sent?"

He'd been sending flowers every day for three days running, and she'd pitched them all into the trash. She should have told him the truth, but there was something about her southern upbringing that stopped her. Besides, she had been cruel to him once; there was no reason to be cruel now. Just firm.

"I sent them on to the hospital. To brighten Ross's room."

This was obviously not the right thing to say. Layton's chin firmed, and she got the distinct impression that she might have been better off telling him the truth.

"Are you free for dinner tonight?" he asked.

Was he insane? "No, I'm not free. I'm dog-sitting, and I might drive up to the hospital to see Ross, assuming he stays overnight." Of course she ought to stay away from the hospital. But she was weak. Sparky would be fine left alone for a few hours, wouldn't he?

As if thinking about him was enough to rouse him, Sparky, who had been snoozing at her feet, stood up and began to strain at his leash. He gave a few determined barks before his hackles rose and he started growling.

The snarls were aimed at Layton.

"Hush," Sabina said, giving the leash a little snap. Sparky sat, but he didn't relax.

She looked up at Layton. "He's kind of protective," she said, her face growing hot. Was it possible that the dog was smarter about Layton than she was, or was Sparky just picking up on her uncertain vibes about the guy?

Layton's smirk disappeared, replaced by a hard, unreadable expression. He gazed a moment at the dog, his face going stiff and hard. Then he abruptly turned his back on them and strolled down the main aisle between the vendors' stalls. His sudden disengagement went beyond rudeness. But that was Layton. He'd never had good social skills. And no doubt, he'd never been much of an animal lover, either.

Which was kind of a red flag, wasn't it?

She wanted to ask him if anyone from Webster Homes had gone up to Orangeburg to talk to Ross. She wanted to know if they were going to help Ross with his medical bills. She wanted to know if Layton was even remotely concerned about what had happened to Lucy's boyfriend.

But she didn't say anything. Instead she crossed her arms over her chest and tried to keep all the negative words and thoughts inside. She had grown into a polite southern woman, and sometimes that could be a trial.

Layton took his time window shopping. She watched

him as he moved slowly from stall to stall. He seemed to know she was watching and he clearly enjoyed being the center of attention.

Sabina had just about decided to go back to her paperwork when Layton lost interest in browsing and returned to the sales counter. He immediately bent forward over the counter in a way that made Sabina back up a step.

Sparky stood up again and growled.

Layton gave the dog a withering look, and Sparky sat down again with a little, uncomfortable whine.

Then Layton's mouth quirked at the corners, as if that smirk was trying to return. "Your place isn't with Ross Gardiner. You know that, don't you?"

Could Layton read her mind or was her growing affection for Ross that obvious? She opted to say nothing to his taunt.

"Don't you?" His voice cut like a sharp paring knife right through her core.

"He's going to be my brother-in-law. I should be with Lucy and my family tonight."

"You have a thing for Ross Gardiner, don't you? All that gossip in town is true."

"It is not." She drew herself up and forced herself to take a step forward. Sparky whined. Layton didn't back up.

"How can I believe you?" he asked, his eyes hidden by the dark lenses. "You're a good liar, Sabina Grey."

"Good Lord, Layton, Ross is my sister's boyfriend, and he was almost killed last night. It would be wrong for me to go out to dinner with anyone tonight. Just like it was wrong for me to dump you at the eighth-grade dance. And it was wrong for me to leave Lucy alone all those years ago on the night of the fire. I've learned from my mistakes. Have you?"

His mouth quivered again, but his smirk didn't fully return. "I would be very unhappy if I discovered that the town gossips are right about you and Ross. Up until right now, you've led me to believe that those rumors aren't true. But..."

Good grief, the guy was acting like they had some kind of understanding, when she'd been trying to let him know that she wasn't all that into him. But he hadn't gotten the message, had he?

Maybe she needed to jettison the polite southern woman and borrow a page from Sparky's book. Growling might be the only thing he understood. "Get out," she said, all pretense at southern hospitality evaporating.

"What?"

"You heard me. Get out of here. I have nothing to say to you. And I think we should stop seeing each other." It wasn't the way she had wanted to let him down, but he had pushed too many of her buttons for her to let him down easy. He deserved to be dropped like a rock.

He stepped back, a mild and stiff expression on his face. "You'll change your mind when the truth comes out."

"What truth?"

His smirk returned, but he didn't say a word. He merely turned and strode from the store.

The moment he was gone, Sparky laid down and resumed his nap. Sparky, it would appear, was a better judge of character than most of the humans in Last Chance.

CHAPTER
15

The doctors poked, prodded, x-rayed, and scanned Ross. Now they were just observing him. Which explained why the law descended upon his hospital room with their questions.

Sheriff Rhodes beat the ATF through the door, which was comforting and not at all surprising. Sheriff Rhodes might have been elected to his job, but the guy was a cop first and foremost. He threw his Stetson on the visitor's chair, just vacated by Henrietta, who had not been all that keen on leaving Ross alone.

"So I hear you have a pretty big bump on the head," the sheriff said.

Ross nodded. It was a mistake. His head pounded, and his stomach roiled. He'd been feeling dizzy and nauseated all day. He hated for Lucy and Henrietta to see him like this, not that Lucy had spent all that much time holding his hand. Lucy had gone AWOL an hour and a half ago, apparently lost forever in the hospital cafeteria.

"So what do you remember?" Sheriff Rhodes asked.

"Not much," Ross said, his voice vibrating through his skull. He recounted his story as succinctly as he could. Which didn't mean much. Everything that happened from the moment he opened the back door to the point where Sparky awakened him in the ditch seemed dreamlike. He wasn't at all certain whether he'd really seen someone back there by the drainage ditch or if his mind had supplied that information. Either way it had been dark, and there was no way he could identify the person he thought he might have seen.

Even after Sparky found him and revived him by licking his face, Ross's memories were sketchy. He didn't remember being sent to the clinic or anything Doc Cooper had said or done. Henrietta told him what had happened, but his mind was a blank until he woke up here in the hospital, happy to be alive.

Once Ross told his story, the sheriff began firing off questions about what had happened before the fire. He wanted to know how Ross had ended up working for Webster Homes in the first place, given the fact that they hadn't returned his earnest money. And then the sheriff started in on a bunch of questions about Lucy.

When it came to Lucy, the questions started getting a little strange, like whether she'd been painting anything in the house and, if so, what color.

"What gives, Sheriff? Lucy had nothing to do with this."

Sheriff Rhodes had a granite face that never gave anything away. The utter passivity of his expression told Ross that the authorities were working up some kind of theory about the crime.

Ross pulled himself up in the bed even though his

head twinged with every movement. "Don't tell me the idiots from the ATF think Lucy is guilty of something."

Stone continued to stare at him, deadpan. "She spent time in the house, therefore she is a person of interest, just like you."

"Oh, come on, Sheriff," Ross said, "Lucy didn't set that fire to murder me. That's insanity. I might be a little light-headed, but I remember the heat from the blast. That fire had to be set with some kind of incendiary device that burns really hot. What do they say it was? Thermite? Lucy wouldn't have a clue how to set an incendiary like that."

The sheriff's impassive mask twitched a tiny bit. "Do me a favor, son, don't use that word when Agent Bailey and his boss come in here to grill you."

"Agent Bailey has a boss?"

"Yeah. His name is Wyatt, and he's a royal pain in the rear. Unlike Bailey, he's sure these fires have nothing to do with terrorism. And when he used that word 'thermite,' I had to ask him to define it."

"It's a metallic incendiary that uses—"

"I got the explanation," Stone interrupted. "And I suppose you should know about that kind of thing, being a firefighter and all. But just keep your mouth shut, okay? Let him bring it up."

"What are you saying, Stone? Does the ATF think I set the fire?"

"They have several theories of the crime. And in some twisted way, Agent Wyatt thinks you might have motive. After all, you've been downsized."

"Huh?"

"In this particular scenario, they have theorized that

you set the fires in order to make the fire department look important and necessary. They think you may have been responsible for the fires in Tacoma, too."

The throbbing in Ross's head intensified. He rubbed a particularly painful spot between his eyes. "You know this is ridiculous. I didn't set any fires. And Lucy is not a murderer or fire setter. Why would she have burned down the house we bought at Jessamine Manor? And that's not even considering the fact that Lucy is pretty much terrified of fire."

"I know. There are holes in their theories. But I have to take them seriously because you know how it goes. I have to chase down every lead. As for you being a fire setter, I'm pretty sure that idea came from someone in Dennis Hayden's office."

"Why?"

Sheriff Rhodes's face remained impassive, but there was a spark of something in his bright green eyes. "The county executive is taking a load of crap for the cutbacks to fire, police, and emergency services. I heard that the latest internal polls show Mayor LaFlore closing the gap on Hayden. If they can somehow suggest that these recent fires were intentionally set by one of the Allenberg County firefighters... Well, that kind of changes the nature of the debate."

"Stone, I didn't set that fire."

"I'm inclined to believe you."

"Neither did Lucy."

Stone shrugged. "Maybe not, but there's one additional thing you need to consider. There is gossip all over town about how you and Sabina are having a hot and heavy affair. That gives Lucy motive."

A boatload of guilt descended on Ross. He'd definitely crossed the line with Sabina when he'd kissed her. But Sabina had pushed him away, like she always did. There wasn't anything between them.

And the gossip was just that. If Lucy had been jealous or hurt by what folks were saying, she would have said something. Instead she'd just dismissed it as silly talk from a bunch of busybodies.

"Good grief, Stone, it's gossip."

"I know that. But don't forget that Lucy also had opportunity. And Lucy was the one who talked you into taking that job. You need to understand that the circumstantial evidence looks bad right now."

Ross collapsed back onto the pillow, his head screaming in pain. He closed his eyes. This wasn't happening.

The sheriff gave him a little squeeze on the shoulder. "Look, Ross, I've just broken with every standard police practice to tell you that Dennis Hayden has decided to make you a scapegoat. I don't like politics. And I sure as hell don't like the feds coming in here helping Dennis Hayden win his election by pointing fingers at my neighbors and friends. I don't think for one minute you're guilty of anything except maybe having an affair with the wrong woman."

"I have not had an affair with anyone."

"I'm glad to hear that. In the meantime, maybe for Lucy's sake, you better put up a united front and nip the gossip in the bud."

After her argument with Layton, Sabina decided it would be best, all the way around, to stay away from Ross. So she avoided the hospital on Thursday night. And even on Friday, when Ross came home, she kept herself busy by helping the Altar Guild with their Friday-night senior supper. She was determined to let Lucy and Momma look after him.

It took amazing willpower to stay away. Sabina likened it to sitting in the same room with a plate of Momma's homemade peanut butter and raisin cookies and not eating a single one. She persevered. But only because she loved her sister more than she loved any other person on the face of the planet.

Momma helped, too, because she put herself in charge of Ross's full recovery. She organized a squadron of Methodist ladies to bring casseroles, walk the dog, and randomly check up on him. So Sabina knew Ross was well cared for, even though Lucy, who should have been the one doing the organizing, seemed kind of clueless about her role as a future wife. Lucy continued to attend her classes at the community college, and every day she put in a few hours back in her workroom at the store. She gave lip service to her concerns for Ross, but it was hard for Sabina not to judge.

But maybe that was because, if she were in Lucy's shoes, she would have stayed at Ross's side, holding his hand, walking Sparky for him, and making the casseroles herself.

Unfortunately, Sabina couldn't avoid Ross forever, especially since she was going to be the maid of honor at his wedding. So when Momma insisted that the family get together for a barbecue dinner on Sunday afternoon to discuss wedding plans, there was no escaping, even if Sunday was one of the busier days at the antiques mall.

Sabina got one of the vendors to mind the store and arrived a little after three in the afternoon on a glorious

Indian summer day. She headed out to the patio, where Daddy had fired up the grill. Momma and Lucy were sitting at the table poring over checklists. Ross was sitting in a lounge chair beside Daddy, watching the outside television that Momma and Daddy had installed last year. The Panthers game was on. They were losing to the Cowboys by fourteen points.

It was a few days since the Heritage Oaks fire. Ross's bruises had turned various shades of green and yellow, and the stitches along his hairline seemed to be healing. He looked so at ease in his madras shorts, faded golf shirt, and flip-flops.

Biblical lust—the kind Reverend Lake sermonized about—seized her innards. She'd never understood what the minister meant until this moment. Biblical lust was like free falling.

She wanted to rush right over to Ross and give him a big hug, and a whole lot more than that. But she stayed rooted to the patio pavers while the yearning within her deepened.

And then Ross looked up, and their gazes met and held. The moment became utterly carnal.

This was wrong. And so terribly confusing.

Sabina had to quell the urge to turn and run like a coon with a hound on her tail.

Unfortunately, Momma cut off her only avenue of escape by materializing beside her with a glass of sweet tea in hand. "We've been waiting on you," she said in that tone of voice that telegraphed her displeasure. Dinner had been scheduled for two. So Sabina was an hour late.

"I was busy working at the store," Sabina lied. In truth, she'd driven the entire length and breadth of Allenberg

County trying to decide what to do about her inappropriate desire for her future brother-in-law.

"I declare, honey," Momma said, "you need to remember that the Lord made Sundays as a day of rest."

"Yes, ma'am," she said, and then clamped her lips together.

As she moved toward the table, she became uncomfortably aware of Ross's gaze following her. She glanced at him.

Oh, boy. He had totally mastered the smoldering look.

This was a problem. It was one thing for her to be consumed by inappropriate lust. But it was quite another to discover that the lust was returned. She hadn't made it up in her mind. She wasn't alone in her inappropriate feelings.

Ross had been the one who'd initiated the dancing at Dot's. He'd been the one who'd initiated that wonderful, romantic moment up in the attic. And of course, Ross had been the one to initiate the kiss that day when Sabina had picked up the steamer trunk.

Sabina may have lusted in her heart for a long time, but Ross had acted on it.

The enormity of the situation tumbled down onto her like the proverbial ton of bricks. Lucy deserved to be with someone who loved her, a man who would look at her the way Ross was looking at Sabina right now.

She pulled her gaze away, her heart doing a tap dance inside her chest. What should she do? She couldn't sit here and plan a wedding knowing that Lucy deserved someone better.

And yet how could she broach this subject without destroying her relationship with all the people she loved, especially her little sister?

She sat down at the table like a zombie, hardly paying any attention to the discussion Lucy and Momma were having about the catering and seating arrangements—the main items on one of Lucy's to-do lists. Lucy had four or five lists, including the ones labeled "Out-of-Town Guests," "Moving Lucy into Ross's Apartment," and "Choosing the Tuxedos for the Groomsmen and Father-of-the-Bride."

It looked like they would be at this until late into the evening unless Sabina or Ross put a stop to it.

Sabina endured the discussion for a good fifteen minutes. And with each tick of the clock it felt as if someone were slowly tightening a garrote around her neck. Her hands started to tingle. The spit dried up in her mouth.

This was *wrong*. And if Ross wouldn't stop it, maybe she needed to.

"Uh, Momma, Lucy, I need to say something." Her voice came out hoarse.

Momma stopped in midsentence. "Oh, honey, if it's about how you and Layton have cooled off, I already know."

Sabina didn't want to even guess at how Momma was privy to the conversation she'd had with Layton on Thursday. Although it was a mystery how Momma could be so connected to what was going on in her daughters' lives and still miss the most important facts.

"Uh, Momma, no, that's not what I need to talk about. I have something I need to confess."

When she got to that word, Ross hopped up from his lounge chair, a frown on his face. It occurred to her that maybe she should have discussed this with him before forging ahead with her confession. After all, he was going to be blamed.

But then they both were guilty of feelings they shouldn't

be having. And for Lucy's sake, the truth needed to be brought out into the open and discussed before Lucy made a terrible mistake.

But the look on Ross's face put a chill into Sabina's plans. Had she misread him? Did he not share her feelings? Or was he a cad?

It was hard to believe that Ross was a cad. He had always struck Lucy as the kind of guy who would give you his left arm if you needed him. He cared about people. He saved lives on a regular basis. In so many ways, he was a local hero.

But he was cheating on Lucy. Maybe not in fact, but in his heart. And Lucy deserved better.

Sabina had just opened her mouth, trying to find the right words to broach this difficult and confusing subject, when the doorbell rang.

Talk about being saved by the bell. It was a cliché, but it was probably a darn good thing.

"Oh, I wonder who that could be?" Momma said and hopped up. "I'll just go check, y'all carry on." She gave Sabina's shoulder a little squeeze as she passed. "Honey, don't fret yourself. I know all about you and Layton. And if that's not the issue and it's something to do with the dress we bought you in Atlanta, it's all right. You can go up to Belks and pick anything you want, so long as it's not black."

Sabina didn't know whether to laugh or cry or scream. But once again, the doorbell saved her. It rang as if someone was in an all-fired hurry to gain admittance. "Hold that thought, hon," Momma said and scooted through the patio doors.

That left Sabina and Ross standing there staring at

each other, while Lucy continued to rearrange the reception seating chart using slips of paper with the names of various aunts and uncles on them.

Ross's eyes had gone wide and dark. *Don't do this*, he mouthed without making a sound. He shook his head. The message was clear.

Her heart lurched in her chest. Oh holy hell, she'd been completely wrong about him. She'd built this infatuation up in her mind, like her vacation fantasies. And he was a guy like every other guy who thought they could get a little from her, without having to pay any price.

So what else was new?

A commotion drew her attention toward the patio doors. "You can't do this," Momma screeched. A moment later Sheriff Rhodes, accompanied by a deputy sheriff and a guy wearing an ATF windbreaker, stepped out onto the patio.

"Lucy Ann Grey?" Sheriff Rhodes said.

Lucy looked up, her face a picture of confusion. "Uh, what?"

"You're under arrest for the crime of arson. You'll have to come with us." And then he began to read Lucy's Miranda rights as he took her by the arm and slapped on a pair of handcuffs.

Lucy frowned at the ATF guy. "Where's Agent Bailey?" she asked.

"He's been taken off the case," the agent said. "I'm sure you know why. I'm Agent Tony Wyatt."

"Stone, c'mon, we talked about this," Ross said. "Lucy is no arsonist."

"We have evidence that says otherwise," Agent Wyatt said.

Lucy crumbled into a mass of tears. "How did you figure it out?"

Ross stood rooted to the flagstone of Henrietta's patio. Had Lucy just confessed to burning down the Heritage Oaks model home?

Damn.

"Lucy, keep your mouth shut," he said as the sheriff's deputy hauled her away. "We'll get you a lawyer."

The headache Ross had been battling for the last few days made a sudden reappearance, especially when he found himself looking right into Sabina's wide, confused stare. Oh, man, she had some kind of witchy power over him.

"We need to get Lucy a lawyer, now." Ross turned toward Earl, who seemed to be the only other person left on the scene who wasn't in tears.

"Already on it." Earl had clearly turned on his hearing aid. He had a cell phone pressed to his ear. "I'm calling Eugene Hanks. He's not a criminal attorney, but he's local, and he can put us in touch with one. In the meantime, we need to see about making bail for her, too. I'm not about to let my baby spend the night in jail."

Henrietta, her eyes glittering, grabbed Ross by the upper arm. "You and Sabina go on down to the county building. Earl and I will follow. There has to be some kind of mistake. Why would she burn down that house? She knew you were there. Why would she do such a thing?"

Why indeed?

It wasn't long before Ross found himself motoring down Route 78 in the direction of Allenberg with Sabina riding shotgun. They hadn't said one word in the last five minutes, and the silence had become charged and difficult. She sat with her back rigid and her hands tight clasped in her lap. She gave the impression of a clockwork toy whose spring had been fully wound. In a moment, she was likely to jump into frantic action.

And Ross was at a complete loss as to how to raise the issue he needed to discuss. They needed to get their stories straight. Right now.

"She's going to be okay," Ross said. "But they've got some crazy-ass idea that she's jealous enough to have attempted murder. Stone warned me about this a couple of days ago, but I thought that once Lucy and I were married things would just settle down. We both know Lucy didn't set any fires." Ross wanted to believe these words, but he couldn't square them with what Lucy had said right as Stone was handcuffing her.

Had Lucy set that fire? Was she insanely jealous?

Guilt consumed him. And Sabina's silence condemned him.

He couldn't let things stand like this any longer. He considered his words carefully before he spoke. "Look, about what happened before the cops showed up."

He paused, hoping for some kind of reaction. He got none.

"You were about to tell your mother and sister about that kiss, weren't you?"

She said nothing.

"Okay, Sabina, I admit it. I'm a coward. I didn't want Lucy to know about that."

Sabina turned in her seat and gave him a look that screamed *ticked-off female.* "Of course you didn't. But she deserves better."

"Yeah, she does." He paused for a moment before continuing. "Look, I apologize. I got way out of line that day. And maybe Lucy does need to know about it...eventually. But not now."

She folded her arms across her chest and said nothing.

He went on the offensive. "The important thing is for us to rally around Lucy. They think she did this in a jealous rage. So the less we say about what happened, the better. We both know that the kiss wasn't important."

She didn't say anything to this, either.

When he pulled into the parking lot at the county building and killed the engine, she finally spoke. "I'm glad to hear that what happened wasn't important to you. To be honest, I thought there was something happening between us. But I guess I was wrong."

She opened her door and jumped down from the truck. But she didn't slam the door in his face. Instead her voice got hard-edged and angry. "I swear, Ross Gardiner, you should be drawn and quartered. Did you think you could dally with me while you were planning to marry Lucy? Or did you think we'd have some kind of crazy three-way going? Or what?" Sabina's voice wavered.

Oh, boy, she was furious. And he actually understood why, which had to be a first for him. Women were mysterious, but Sabina was being utterly frank. She may have run away from his kiss, but not because it was unimportant. That kiss was important. To both of them.

Sabina wanted him. How the hell had he missed that important fact? It changed everything.

CHAPTER 16

It was like being thrown body and soul into some horrible film noir retrospective. Except that everything was in living color and the man across the table was someone Lucy had known forever.

Sheriff Rhodes had taken off his Stetson but it left a mark on his forehead. His military-short hair was turning gray. And his eyes were unreadable. He'd been the Last Chance chief of police before he'd run for sheriff, and right up until this moment Sheriff Rhodes had always made her feel safe whenever she'd seen him making his rounds in his police cruiser.

But now that she found herself on the opposite side of an interrogation table, she noticed something dark and dangerous in the depths of his gaze. You didn't want to mess with Stone Rhodes when it came to the health and safety of the citizens of Allenberg County.

And that's when the tears filled up her eyes. Because the idea that she could be considered a threat to anyone's health and safety undid her. But maybe this needed to happen.

He handed her a tissue. She didn't bother to dab her eyes. She just tried to frame the words that should have been spoken years and years ago. Instead her throat closed up and she was on the verge of bawling her eyes out.

"Lucy, I need you to focus." The sheriff's voice seemed filled with kindness. No doubt he was playing the good cop. Although the only cop she really wanted to see right at this moment was Zach, but he was nowhere to be found.

She sniffled back her tears.

"I want to help you, Lucy," the sheriff said. "But I can't do that alone. I need you to be honest with me, okay?"

She nodded.

"So let's start with the bedsheet. Where did you get it?"

"What?" She looked up, blinking through her tear-streaked vision. "What bedsheet?"

"The one you put on the fence outside Heritage Oaks."

"I didn't put any bedsheet on the fence. I put bed-sheets on the beds that afternoon. I was staging the master bedroom."

"Lucy, you need to be honest with me. We found the spray can that you used. It's got your fingerprints on it."

Lucy opened her mouth, and nothing came out. They thought she'd set the fire at Heritage Oaks? Why would she do that? She'd been staging that model home. It had been her big opportunity. And the rooms were coming together so beautifully.

"I didn't set the fire at Heritage Oaks."

The sheriff cocked his head. "Lucy, you practically confessed when we arrested you."

"I did no such thing. What did I say?"

"You asked Agent Wyatt how he figured it out. What we really want to know is where you got the thermite."

She blinked. She had no idea what thermite was.

"Uh, Stone, there's been a big mistake."

"I don't think so. It would go better for you if you were honest. Were you trying to kill Ross? Was that it?"

"Kill Ross? Are you insane? He's my fiancé. I love him."

"Do you?"

She stared up into Sheriff Rhodes's sober green gaze. And for a moment, she wondered if she truly loved Ross or whether she was just comfortable and safe with him. But either way, Ross was an important person in her life. "I'm not a killer. And why would I, of all people, try to subject someone to death by fire. Oh, my God, I can't..." Her heart started pounding, and the memories of that horrible night returned to her. The fire was terrifying. The smoke clogged her lungs, the heat burned her skin, and the fire nearly killed her.

"Lucy?"

She squeezed her eyes shut and did the deep breathing exercises she always used before target practice. She hated it when memories of the fire invaded this way.

"About what you said?" the sheriff pressed.

She opened her eyes, her body shivering. "I can explain what I said."

"Okay. I'm listening."

Lucy forced the words through her trembling jaw. "I didn't burn anything down, except for my family's home."

"What?" For an instant the sheriff's granite features showed a boatload of emotion.

She hesitated, mustering her strength, and then the words came rushing out like a river that had broken the walls of a dam. "I started a fire in a metal trash can in Sabina's room. I was angry at her, and I just wanted to hurt her. I burned the stupid diary that she was always writing in. You see, she was supposed to stay home and watch movies with me that night, but instead she went off with Alfie Roche. He was such an idiot; I didn't even know why she liked him.

"Anyway, I wanted her to get into trouble, or something. I don't know. It was stupid, and I was thirteen. So I burned the diary and it set off the smoke alarm, which was scary. So I disconnected the smoke alarm, and then I poured some water on the fire in the can. I wanted Sabina to find the ashes, you know, kind of like Jo March finds her burned book in *Little Women*. Which is where I got the stupid idea, if you want to know. I left the can in her room and went to bed. But I never reconnected the smoke alarm.

"And that's where the fire started, in Sabina's room. I guess I didn't pour enough water on the fire or something. Honest, I didn't want the house to burn down. And I sure didn't want to end up burned myself.

"And then I was in the hospital and they had me on those drugs. They put me into a coma for a long time. And when I woke up, they told me the fire started in the electric heater in Sabina's room. And I left that trash can right next to the heater. I knew they were wrong about how the fire started. But it was convenient to go with the flow, you know? I was just thirteen and scared to death. And then, before I knew what had happened, Sabina had decided not to go to college, and I was kind of stuck. I just couldn't tell the truth after that.

"But I swear I didn't ever set any other fires. I don't like fire, Sheriff. You ask my daddy. I don't even like to light the gas grill. I learned a terrible lesson about fire that night."

Lucy's voice gave way, and the tears overtook her.

So of course, Zach came bursting into the room. He always seemed to make an appearance when she was at her emotional worst. No doubt Zach had been watching her confession through the one-way mirror.

How humiliating.

"I'll take over," he said to the sheriff, who didn't seem at all amused that his interrogation had been interrupted.

"I don't think so," the sheriff said in a don't-mess-with-me tone.

"Agent Bailey, you are officially off this case." The other ATF agent, the one who had been there when Lucy was arrested, came strolling into the interrogation room. He was older than Zach and had a hungry look in his eyes. He stared Zach right in the face. He was none too pleased. "You need to go back to Columbia. We'll deal with you later."

Zach turned. "Lucy, I'm so sorry." He left the room.

"I'll take over," the other agent said.

Sheriff Rhodes didn't cede his territory. "This is still my investigation, Agent Wyatt."

"I could bring federal terrorist charges, you know, and take you off this case entirely."

"Go ahead. Make my day." Stone folded his kick-ass arms over his kick-ass chest.

Just then Daniel Jessup, Eugene Hanks's new, young partner, strolled into the room. "Gentlemen, I've been officially retained to represent Lucy. This interrogation is finished."

He turned toward Lucy. "Your daddy sent me, and he told me to tell you that he loves you and knows you're completely innocent."

• • •

Sabina escaped to Last Chance Around on Monday morning. The store was closed on Mondays, but she had plenty of craft-fair-related work to keep her busy and to keep her mind off her sister's incarceration.

Lucy was scheduled to be arraigned this morning. Sabina wanted nothing more than to be in the courtroom, but Lucy and her attorney, Daniel Jessup, didn't want her there.

He had explained that Lucy was on the edge of a massive emotional breakdown and that Sabina's presence was a bad idea. Which was a stunner, because the fire wasn't Lucy's fault. It never would have happened if Sabina had stayed home that night. All these years, and she'd been right in believing that she bore the responsibility for Lucy's scars.

And now she bore the responsibility for Lucy's incarceration. Her behavior over the last few weeks had led to gossip. And the gossip had led to this problem. And all for a guy who didn't think the kiss was important.

Of course it was hard to remain angry at Ross, even if he had hurt her on Sunday. Especially since he seemed to be under suspicion along with Lucy.

Daniel said the case against Lucy was rife with political overtones. The fact that Lucy was Ross's girlfriend and both of them worked at Webster Homes made it easy for the county prosecutor, Avery Denholm, to announce that Ross was a person of interest in the case. He'd even been quoted this morning in the *Orangeburg Times and Democrat* saying that he thought there was a possibility that Lucy and Ross set the fires together, in order to convince the county to increase spending on fire services. Or perhaps Ross just wanted to play the hero. Denholm had announced to the world that Ross had been a member of the Tacoma Fire Department at the time of the eco-terrorist attacks several years ago.

Lucy was under arrest, and Ross's good name was under attack. So there was a ton of stuff on Sabina's mind and conscience when a knock came at the front door. She found Sheriff Rhodes standing outside with a couple of deputies behind him.

"Sheriff?"

He nodded, but his expression remained utterly impassive. "Hey, Sabina, I've got a warrant here. We need to search the premises. And when we're done here, I'm afraid we have to search your house as well." He handed her two documents filled with a lot of scary legal language.

She let them in, her heart suddenly drumming in her chest. The deputies fanned out and started searching the store from the back to the front. Sheriff Rhodes stayed put, looking grim and determined.

"I'm afraid I need to ask you some questions," he said.

"Uh, Sheriff, before I answer, I think I should call Daniel Jessup."

His mouth flattened in a clear display of impatience. "You can do that, Sabina, but if you won't cooperate, I can compel you to. Don't make me do that. Just tell me the truth. Hell, after what Lucy told me yesterday about that fire all those years ago, it seems to me that you'd want the truth."

"The truth?" Sudden anger sprung up. "The truth is, I should have been home the night of the fire seventeen years ago. That's the truth. And Lucy is so scared of fire it's ridiculous for anyone to think she could set one on purpose."

"We have a can of spray paint with Lucy's fingerprints

on it that was left at the scene. It looks like a match for the paint on the bedsheets."

Good Lord. This was bad. She needed to provide an alternative explanation. "Sheriff, you know as well as I do that anyone could have taken a can from Lucy's workroom at the back of the store. She never locks the place. You can ask your deputies. It's not locked now."

"Okay, fair enough. Can you think of anyone who went into the workroom?"

She folded her arms across her chest. It was unnerving to find herself at odds with Stone Rhodes. He was the good guy. "Sheriff, people come in and out of the store all the time. I don't have surveillance cameras. Heck, your own brother was in here a few days ago looking for a new headboard for that house he and Jane are updating. He was at Charity Rangel's booth for almost an hour mulling over his purchase. And Charity's stall is right next to the workroom. Your own brother could have taken that paint."

"All right. I have another question: What's going on between your sister and Agent Bailey?"

"My sister and— Stone Rhodes, what in the world are you suggesting?"

"Agent Bailey took himself off the case, Sabina. And from what I gather, it was because he crossed the line with Lucy at some point."

"Stone, I don't know that I ever even met Agent Bailey. Does Ross know this?"

Stone gave her an ironic look. "What do you think?"

That shut her up.

"And what about you and Ross?" he asked.

"What about us?" Her heart gave a guilty twist in her chest.

"Do you want me to recount the gossip around town?" Stone asked.

"What gossip?" It was hard to play dumb, especially when her face was getting hotter by the minute.

"The gossip about how you and Ross danced together at Dot's Spot. That story Elsie Campbell told about catching you dancing again in the attic of the Smith house. What about that?"

Sheriff Rhodes had already noted her suddenly red face. "Oh, come on, that was nothing," she lied.

"I don't think so."

Sabina was the worst liar in the universe, and Stone Rhodes had been trained to catch people in their lies. But she wasn't about to make a molehill into a mountain because she had experienced hot flashes when she danced with Ross, or because she almost melted when they kissed.

Ross had been clear last night. The kiss had meant nothing. It was unimportant. Sabina had blown the kiss up into something that wasn't there.

Ross might be a jerk and a cad, but he wasn't an arsonist. And neither was Lucy. So Sabina raised her chin and looked right at the sheriff and tried not to let her eyes wander to the left or right. "There's nothing between me and Ross Gardiner."

The sheriff was about to ask another question when he was interrupted by one of the deputies who called from the general vicinity of Lucy's workroom. "Sheriff, you better come back here."

Sabina followed Sheriff Rhodes as he headed down the aisle. They arrived at the door of the workroom, where one of his deputies stopped her from entering.

The sheriff said a string of cuss words that would have

shocked his momma, and then he asked, "Is that what I think it is?"

The deputy, wearing latex gloves and shining his flashlight at a can on the worktable like one of those characters from *CSI*, shook his head. "I don't know, but the can says thermite ignition mix."

"Tag it and bag it. We'll take it back to the lab for analysis." Sheriff Rhodes turned back toward Sabina. Was that surprise in the sheriff's eyes? He usually kept his emotions well masked.

She looked past him to Lucy's workbench. The deputies were putting what looked like a can of varnish into a plastic bag. In a million years, Sabina would never have noticed anything strange about a can like that, sitting on the workbench, surrounded by dozens of other paint cans.

"What exactly is thermite?" she asked.

Stone shook his head, and his shoulders sagged a tiny bit. "It's a mixture of metals used to ignite incendiary devices," he said. "Sabina, it's going to be a long afternoon. We're going to have to take the store and your house apart, inch by inch."

Sabina tried not to cry, but it was impossible. She sat on the tiny love seat in the tiny living room of her tiny cottage with tears streaming down her cheeks. The place looked like it had been subject to a home invasion.

The police had scoured the house, taking everything out of every drawer and cabinet in every room, including Sabina's bedroom. They'd stripped the beds of their linens and even opened up the box springs, looking for evidence. They'd carted off Lucy's computer and several other items from her room in big plastic bags and cardboard boxes.

They touched everything.

She was just working up the energy to start the cleanup when Momma called. Sabina's heart took another wild flight. In her misery over the police search, she had almost forgotten that a court in Allenberg was deciding where Lucy would be living for the next few months.

"Hey," Sabina said, her hands shaking.

"It's good news, honey," Momma's voice sounded high pitched and emotional but oddly reassuring. "They've let her out on bail, and the judge had some words with Avery Denholm, who wanted to set her bail at more than a million dollars. Daniel says they don't have much in the way of real evidence. Anyone could have taken that spray can from Lucy's workroom."

"Momma." Sabina's voice shook as badly as her hands.

"Honey, what is it?"

"The police have been all over the store and the house, tearing everything apart. They took her computer and a lot of stuff from Lucy's room. And they found something in the workroom."

"What?"

"Some chemical or something. They said it was the stuff she used to set the fire."

"Good Lord." Momma's voice almost pierced Sabina's eardrum.

"You can't let her come home. It's a mess here. It's completely torn up."

"Actually I was calling to tell you that we aren't going to bring her home. She's going to stay with Daddy and me. Because, well, it looks like the press thinks this is a story worth reporting on. There were reporters from Columbia at the courthouse, and by the time we left court a crew from WIS TV had set up shop."

"Oh, no."

"I'm afraid the media has gotten ahold of this. Daniel said I should call you because, by now, the press probably has Lucy's home address. Don't be surprised if they darken your door."

"How's she doing?"

"I don't know. She seems completely stricken by all of this attention. But most of all, she keeps telling me how sorry she is about setting that fire all those years ago. Honestly, Sabina, doesn't she understand that she's forgiven for that?"

"It was my fault, Momma. It always has been."

"Honey, it's water under the bridge. Y'all both survived and grew from it, and I love you both. I think you need to come over and give her a chance to apologize. Honestly, I think she needs it. But we won't be home for a while. We're all gathering at Daniel's office to talk about what comes next and to map out a plan in case the media really gets out of hand. But I think it would be good if you joined us for dinner."

"All right. I'll be there. In the meantime, I'm going to clean up this mess. And tell Daniel that the police found something important in Lucy's workroom. He needs to get on that right away."

"I will."

Momma hung up, and Sabina immediately peered through the front windows. So far there was neither hide nor hair of any media on her front lawn. She couldn't imagine having reporters camping out in her minuscule yard. Although, no doubt, Ida Curran would be out in hers fixing them sweet tea and running her mouth.

She headed into Lucy's room and started cleaning up the mess. About half an hour later the doorbell rang.

Boy, that hadn't taken long, had it?

She didn't go to the door. The press could just take a long walk off a short pier as far as she was concerned.

Her unwanted visitor gave up on the bell and started banging on the door. Sabina was on the cusp of serious fear when a familiar voice yelled, "Darn it, Sabina, I know you're in there. Don't make me stand out here hollering like some hillbilly. Ida is watching."

Jenny. Oh, God bless her.

Sabina hurried to the door and let in her best friend. Jenny took one look at the mess in the living room and started cussing like a sailor with the hives. Sabina had never heard half the words she said. No doubt she'd learned all those words from her new husband, who was renowned for his mastery of profanity.

"Who did this?" Sabina asked.

"The police."

"Shut up! Damian? Really?" Jenny said, referring to the chief of the two-man Last Chance police force.

"No, Sheriff Rhodes and his deputies." Sabina's voice wobbled. It was one thing to have a bad guy violate your space, but when the guy doing it was Stone Rhodes, the violation went so much deeper.

Jenny wasted no time in taking Sabina into her arms and giving her the kind of unconditional hug that only a best friend could. And it was a good thing, too, because three minutes later the doorbell rang again.

And this time it really was a reporter.

They ignored him, even though he rang the doorbell incessantly for the next few hours. By the time Jenny and Sabina had put the house back together, a whole gaggle of reporters had shown up, some of them bearing satellite dishes, klieg lights, and microphones.

And then Momma called and told her that CNN had just parked a truck outside of her house, and Daddy was going to come get Sabina for tonight's dinner since he could pull the car right into the garage. And Daniel's assistant said that CNN was now running stories that featured a new graphic with the word "HOAX" stamped over a photo of the bedsheet.

Sabina refused to turn on the television. She knew exactly how this would go. It was only a matter of days before various people who knew nothing about nothing started speculating about what had happened here. Was it really homegrown terrorism, or merely a crazy serial arsonist? What kind of monster was Lucy Grey? Or maybe the fire was her way of getting back at her boyfriend, the firefighter, who was having an affair with her sister. Or better yet, forget the sister; the fires were set by firefighters themselves, determined not to have their budgets cut. Lucy was just the fall girl.

Oh, boy. Nothing brought people out like love triangles involving sisters and the possibility of real, domestic terrorism.

Any way you sliced or diced it, people on the right and the left and in the middle had something they could say about what had happened. It didn't even matter what the actual truth was. The cable news networks had twenty-four hours they had to fill up, and this story was a doozy.

CHAPTER 17

Oh, my goodness," Jenny said from her station by the front window. She was peeking at the group of reporters on Sabina's front lawn as she sipped a glass of Chardonnay.

"Don't tell me Ida's out there talking to them."

"No, it's good."

"Good? How could anything involving the media be good?"

"Layton is out there talking to them."

"What?"

Sabina jumped up from the easy chair and joined Jenny at the window. Sure enough, Layton Webster, dressed for success (and media interviews) in another one of his dark, Italian-made suits, stood on the sidewalk right by his BMW with the klieg lights reflecting in his Coke-bottle glasses and lighting up his sandy blond hair.

"Oh, my God, we need to turn on the TV," Jenny said.

"No, we don't."

"But he's come to your rescue."

Possibly. But knowing Layton, he could just as easily

be throwing her under the bus. And after their last few encounters, anything Layton did to help Sabina would be totaled up on his scoreboard. Eventually she'd have to pay him back. And she knew how that game worked.

"Oh, my God, he's coming up the walk. I'll just make a quick exit out the back door. I love you." Jenny gave Sabina a quick hug, picked up her wineglass, and dropped it in the sink on her way out the back door.

No sooner had the screen door slammed than the door-bell rang.

Sabina couldn't exactly stand him up in front of all those cameras, could she? So she opened the door.

"Layton, what are you doing here?" she said as she let him in.

"Rescuing you, darlin'." He gave her one of his ice-cold smiles. The kind that never reached his eyes. She couldn't help but think about Ross and the way his eyes always crinkled up at the corners whenever he was even the slightest bit amused.

The comparison left her hollow and guilty. "That may be debatable. You know, Lucy's attorney might not want us to be seen together."

"Why not?"

She shrugged. "I don't know. Your development burned, and it looks like my sister is responsible."

His facsimile of a smile seemed to broaden. How did he do that? If you didn't know him, you wouldn't real-ize the expression on his face was a complete sham. And besides, he shouldn't be grinning at all.

"Do you think your sister is guilty?" he asked.

"No, of course not."

"Well then, neither do I." He strolled into her kitchen,

glanced at her sink, and picked up Jenny's wineglass. "Who was here?" he asked, his tone aggressively possessive.

"Jenny Raintree. She came to help me put the place back together."

He frowned.

"The cops tore it apart searching for evidence."

"Did they find any?" He seemed suddenly avid, his eyes lit up behind the glasses.

She decided Layton didn't need to know what they found. "I have no clue. They carted off her computer and stuff, but I doubt there's much there."

He nodded. "So I thought I would whisk you away from this freak show on your front lawn. How about an early dinner at the Pig Place?"

Finally, a restaurant that didn't have five stars. But of course, he was entirely overdressed for the Pig Place. Thank goodness she had a previous engagement.

"Sorry, Layton, I can't make it to the Pig Place tonight. I'm having dinner with the family at Momma's."

"Oh, well, that's entirely understandable. I hope my little interview with the press helps you out."

"What did you say?"

"I told them there was no truth to those rumors about you and Ross. I told them you and I were intimate, and that I arranged for Lucy and Ross's jobs because of my relationship with you."

Sabina's stomach turned. His statement seemed so innocent, and yet it contained an implicit threat. Sadly, Sabina was willing to let Layton manipulate her if it meant Lucy might have an easier time defending herself. So she played innocent. "Thanks, Layton. I really appreciate it. But now I think you should go."

"Let me help you, Sabina. You won't regret it. Why don't we leave the house together? Those reporters are going to be all over you with questions, but it will be a good visual with the two of us walking arm in arm. And I'll drive you over to your mother's place."

Daddy was supposed to pick her up, but she had to admit that Layton was making a lot of sense. It would help for the press to see her with her so-called boyfriend.

So she agreed. And Layton behaved like a true gentleman.

"We need to postpone the wedding." Lucy sat at the conference table in Eugene Hanks's office and gave Ross a tear-filled stink eye.

A part of Ross—the self-centered guy part who was a little scared of marriage—wanted desperately to walk away. But that would be cowardly. And stupid.

Any indication that the rumors about him and Sabina were true could lend credence to the current theory of the crime—that Lucy was ticked off at Ross and tried to kill him.

And since law enforcement now had hard evidence in the form of a can of spray paint and some thermite, the prosecutor was going full bore after Lucy. She was in terrible trouble, especially after she confessed to setting the fire that had scarred her.

Ross knew precisely what he needed to do to save Lucy. He needed to marry the girl. Marrying Lucy, no matter what, was the heroic thing to do. She needed him right now, and he was more than happy to take care of her.

"The wedding is going on as planned. Maybe we should invite CNN," he said.

Daniel chuckled. "That's the spirit, Ross. I think it's really important for all y'all to show the media that you're normal, upstanding, churchgoing folks. We also need to get out the message that Avery Denholm is ambitious and ruthless and is more interested in the media exposure than seeking justice.

"Now, this new development with the can of thermite is a problem. But if they don't find Lucy's fingerprints on that can, then they don't have much of a case. I can put reasonable doubt in any juror's mind about this. Y'all just remember that. And you'll win the public relations war by being the cute young couple that you are."

Lucy pushed back from the table. "This is my life you're laughing about."

Ross stood up, too. "No one's laughing, sweetie. But the wedding needs to go on as planned. You see that, don't you?"

Her lip quivered, and the endless stream of tears continued to dribble down her cheeks. "I don't understand why you still want to go through with it," she said. "I set that fire all those years ago, and I've been lying about it ever since. How can you want to be with me? They say I tried to murder you. Aren't you afraid of me?"

"Lucy, don't be dramatic. I know you're innocent. And I want to be with you because I care about you." He knew the moment these words left his mouth that they missed the mark. They were honest. He did care about her. But he should have said the L-word.

She must have noticed the omission, because his words did nothing to sway her. She savagely shook her head. "No. We're not getting married."

"But Lucy—"

"You heard me. The engagement is over. I'm breaking up with you."

"But you can't—"

"I can, and I—"

"Lucy." Daniel's voice was calm and deep. "Ross is right, you know. Y'all getting married would be good for public relations."

"Public relations? Do you think that's a good reason to get married?"

"It might be, if it means the difference between you spending the next few decades in prison or being free to live the life you want to live."

"I shouldn't have to get married for public relations. I'm innocent of this crime." She looked from Earl to Henrietta to Daniel and then right at Ross. "Someone is framing me. That can of paint and that stuff they found in the workroom—I don't know anything about that. Ross, who would want to frame me?"

"I don't know."

Her tearful look changed into something more like a glower. "I keep thinking about this. No one in this town knows bubkes about thermite. Except you, Ross."

"What? You think I tried to frame you?" His voice broke.

"I don't know what to think. I don't understand what's happening. But Daniel told me all about this other theory. There are people who say you set the fire because you lost your job and wanted to make a point about the need for emergency services. I don't want to believe that, Ross. I really, really don't. But I'm so confused right now. I don't know who to trust. And if I have doubts about you, how can I marry you?"

• • •

Lucy needed to stop crying. Crying was for sissies, and she wasn't a sissy. She'd learned to deal with excruciating pain. She'd learned to accept her scarred face, arms, and legs. She'd learned how to shoot a gun.

She was a strong woman, if not an entirely honest one. But she'd been honest about one thing. She had not torched the homes at Heritage Oaks. She hoped with all her heart that what Daniel had told her about Ross wasn't true, either.

But until she could figure things out she was calling off the wedding.

Of course, Momma harangued her the whole way home from Daniel Jessup's office. Thank goodness Last Chance wasn't such a big town so it didn't take long to get from one place to another, otherwise Momma might have damaged Lucy's hearing the way she'd done Daddy's.

When they finally pulled into the garage, Lucy had had enough. "It's my life and if I want to break up with Ross Gardiner, it's no one's business but mine."

She got out of the car and used her own key to let herself into the house. The garage door led right into Momma's kitchen, where she ran smack-dab into Sabina, who had obviously let her own self in and had taken the liberty of starting dinner for the family. The odor of baked ham and butter beans filled the air.

Lucy's forward motion came to an abrupt halt, and all the words she'd wanted to spill a moment ago dried up in her mouth. She braced herself, ready to receive Sabina's fury. She was past ready to be penalized for the one fire she truly had set. It was only fitting that Sabina be the one to hand out the punishment.

Everything slowed down. Her life hung on this moment, this turning point. She didn't know what she had expected, but certainly not her sister flinging her arms wide in a clear invitation for a hug. Nor did she expect Sabina to break down in her own flood of tears.

"Lucy," Sabina said, her lips trembling almost as hard as her voice, "I can't believe I was so careless. I almost lost you. Don't you know that you are more precious to me than anyone?"

"What?" Lucy stood there, completely confused. "I burned your diary. I lied. I burned down the whole freaking house."

Sabina took two steps and pulled Lucy into the warm cocoon of her arms. "I know. But you wouldn't have done it if I'd stayed home and made popcorn and watched *Titanic* with you for the umpteenth time. Instead I spent the night with a bunch of high-school football players, most of whom grew up to become losers and idiots. You told me that night that Alfie Roche was a jerk. And you were right. If you've been hauling around a lot of guilt over that fire, honey, you need to lose it now. Because that fire was an accident. And the accident happened because I wasn't where I was supposed to be."

Sabina squeezed her tight and then let her go. She pulled a couple of paper towels from the rack and handed one to Lucy. "Now we need to quit bawling about this, okay? And concentrate on your defense and your wedding, in that order."

"There isn't going to be a wedding," Momma said, sounding more angry than upset. She and Daddy had come through the door and witnessed the entire scene.

"What?" Sabina said.

"Lucy has broken up with Ross," Daddy said. The disapproval in his voice was unmistakable. He headed into the adjoining family room and turned on the local news. When Daddy escaped into the family room, you knew good and well he was fed up with the females in his life.

Momma stayed in the kitchen and turned toward Lucy. "If you push Ross Gardiner away, you will be the stupidest female ever, and I didn't raise any stupid daughters. You hear me?"

"You broke up with Ross?" Sabina asked. It was funny, but this time Sabina didn't seem at all surprised. She kind of stiffened and cocked her head to one side. "Why?" she asked.

"Lucy seems to think he borrowed a can of spray paint from her workbench," Momma said.

"You think he's framing you? Really?" Sabina asked, incredulity lacing her words.

Lucy shook her head. "No, I don't think he'd frame me. But it's possible he borrowed a can of paint with my fingerprints on it."

"Oh, my God. Ross would never set a fire, Lucy. Don't you know that?"

Lucy opened her mouth and was about to explain her reasoning one more time, when she was interrupted by Daddy. He hollered from the family room, and his tone of voice preempted everything.

"Sabina Elizabeth Grey, since when are you and that Webster guy engaged?"

The reporters on Sabina's front yard apparently didn't believe in camping out overnight. By eleven o'clock, when Daddy dropped her off, the coast was more or less clear.

"Honey," Daddy said before she opened the door to escape, "there's just one thing I want to know. Do you love him?"

For a moment Sabina thought Daddy might be talking about Ross. And the crazy thing about it was that she almost answered yes, before she realized he was talking about Layton.

"No."

"Then why are you getting engaged?"

"I told you before, we're not getting engaged, Daddy. I can only assume that he told that lie to the press in order to help Lucy. And I suppose he did me a favor. But I do surely wish the man had given me some warning."

"Well, I reckon I admire him for protecting both you and Lucy. And your mother says he's very well off."

"Daddy, leave the matchmaking to Momma and her friends in the Altar Guild."

He chuckled. "That's what I'm afraid of, to tell you the truth." His voice was low and worried.

"What is it?"

He carelessly ran his big, daddy hands over the steering wheel of his Pathfinder SUV, clearly gathering his thoughts. That was the thing about Daddy: He never said much, but when he did talk, you needed to listen.

"I kind of feel like your mother is pushing you girls into relationships that might not be right for either one of you. I like Ross. I admire him. I don't for a minute think he set any fires. He's a good man, and I'd be honored to have him as a son-in-law. But I don't think Lucy loves him. Her behavior today confirmed it for me. And to be honest, I don't think Ross loves her back. And as for Layton Webster, well, I admire his success, but I can't admire a man who tells the world he's engaged to a woman when he hasn't bought her a ring."

"I'm sure, if I asked for a ring, I'd get one that was too big for my hand."

"And that, right there, is the problem, you see?"

She saw this particular problem without difficulty. "Daddy, don't you worry. I'm not in love with Layton. There are facets of his personality that I don't even like. I'm not about to marry a man I don't like."

"Not even to save Lucy?" Daddy turned and looked her right in the eye.

"What do you mean?"

"Just this. I get the feeling that Ross is ready to marry Lucy in order to save her. And Layton is out there fibbing to the media in order to save you and Lucy. And you, my sweet baby girl, would do just about anything for your little sister. And I admire all of you for your selflessness. I do. But Lucy's got a point. It's time for Lucy to save her own self. And to be honest, baby, it's time for you to start living your life and stop blaming yourself for what happened seventeen years ago."

"But it was my fault, Daddy. Don't you see—"

"Even though you think I don't hear much, I heard what you said to Lucy tonight. You told her it was an accident. And that's what it was. Sure, you should have been there, but if your mother and I had been paying more attention, we would have realized that asking you to give up a big party a few days before graduation wasn't fair to you. We could have hired a sitter. Or—and this might surprise you—we could have simply trusted Lucy. She was thirteen. Last Chance is a small town. She should have been perfectly capable of taking care of her own self that night."

Daddy's words stunned Sabina. In all the years since the fire, she and Daddy had never had a discussion like this. They'd been too busy rebuilding Lucy's ego. Him with his guns, and her with her motherly care.

"Now give me a kiss," he ordered in his daddy voice.

Sabina leaned over and kissed his rough cheek and got a little hug. "Y'all are all going to be fine. I feel it. I've prayed over it. And I know the good Lord is going to look after everyone in this family. But I want you to think about what you do, baby. Of course I want you to help your sister any way you can, but don't ruin your life. For once, you need to be just a tad more selfish."

He gave her another quick kiss. "Now skeddadle, doodlebug. Your momma's going to be worried if I'm gone too long."

Her daddy's words churned in Sabina's mind and left her sleepless. After a couple of hours of tossing and turning, she put on a pair of yoga pants and a sweatshirt and went out for a walk.

Last Chance in the wee hours of the morning was kind of ghostly. The sidewalks weren't exactly rolled up, but close enough. The one stoplight in town kept cycling from red to green, but there were no cars coming in any direction. The only lights still burning were the ever-glowing neon signs from Dot's Spot.

Sabina walked for a long time without thinking about her destination, her thoughts filled with Lucy and all the things she'd done for her little sister. Her gifts had come from the heart, but she could see the truth in what Daddy had said. Maybe she had smothered Lucy a little bit. Maybe she had put her own life on hold.

And ironically, wasn't that the message Miriam Randall had handed to her that morning almost a month ago?

Her mind may not have directed her feet, but somehow she ended up standing on the sidewalk right in front of the Smith house. Her parents' house—rebuilt seventeen years ago—stood a couple of blocks down Julia Street.

A clear autumn sky arced above her, a nearly full moon casting a soft blue glow over the newly trimmed landscape. Lumber and building supplies sat in the yard, covered with tarps. The peeling paint was gone, leaving the siding weathered and gray and ready for paint. And there, in the dark, sitting on the porch steps was Ross Gardiner, with his trusty sidekick Sparky snoozing on the ground by his feet.

"Evening." His low voice carried over the chorus of October crickets, their song slowed down with the cool autumn night. Sparky raised his head and gave his own soft greeting.

She should go.

She wanted to stay.

She hung there poised for flight, something primal and needy rising up in her. It fed on the moonlight and the big, wide, starry sky, making her feel incredibly alive. This was a moment made for romance.

"So I guess congratulations are in order," he said.

His words had the same effect as a bucket of cold water being dumped on her head.

She could tell him the truth about Layton—how his engagement announcement was a sham, designed to save Lucy from the gallows. But maybe it would be better if Ross believed it. CNN was just waiting to bury the family's reputation, and this was not the time to hand them any shovels.

She turned, without saying a word, and headed back in the direction of her cottage.

"No, Sabina, wait." Ross got up and followed her, the dog trotting at his heels.

Damn. Damn. Damn.

He caught up with her at the corner. There was no point in running. He would follow.

He looked down at her, the moon sparkling seductively in his eyes. "I've had a rough day today. Lucy thinks I set that fire. And now I hear that you're marrying Layton. I'm wondering if you decided to do that because of the stupid stuff I said on Sunday when we were driving to the county building."

Oh, crap. She didn't want to have this conversation. But there was no point running away from it, either. "I'm not marrying Layton Webster. He just told CNN that story in a lame attempt to save me and Lucy."

"Thank God." His voice was as soft as the moonlight that spilled down over them, promising romance and maybe something more.

"Go home, Ross," she said, resisting the tug of the moon and the man. "We shouldn't be seen together. Especially not in the middle of the night."

She turned and headed down the street.

"I wish I had a home to go to," he said to her back.

She stopped and turned. He and Sparky stood under a streetlamp, looking slightly forlorn. Her heart ached for him, but she wasn't going to give in to this temptation, even if the way was almost cleared for her. Lucy had broken up with him.

"You have the Smith house," she said, and turned away again, her heart pounding in her chest.

"You know," he said to her back, "what people are saying about us is true."

She turned then. She wanted to deny it, but suddenly the words dried up in her throat.

He took a step in her direction. "I thought, for the longest time, that it was just me feeling things for you that would never be reciprocated. But after what you said on Sunday, I'm not sure that's true."

"What did I say? All I remember is you saying that what happened between us wasn't important."

"I'm a coward. I was trying to cover my ass. And you were ticked at me, and ready to tell the world I cheated on Lucy. And I was worried that Lucy might actually have set that fire in some kind of jealous rage. But I know now that's not what happened. She didn't set that fire. It's kind of ironic, what she said to me today, about how she can't trust me. She has good reason not to."

"What possible reason is that?"

"Because I am guilty of having feelings for you. Your kiss meant a lot to me, Sabina. More than it should have. And on Sunday, when you said something about how you might have feelings for me—well, that threw me for a loop. It made me hope for something I never dared hope for."

They stood there, gazes locked. And they might never have moved if it hadn't been for Sparky, who managed to wrap his leash around their legs.

And then, like a couple of magnets, the distance closed in a big, hot hurry. And his lips came down on hers. The kiss was everything she had ever dreamed of. There were bells. There were whistles. And Ross's body, hard and hot against her own. His kiss tugged at the secret places inside her like the moon pulls the tide.

She needed to touch him. Her hands found their way under the back of his T-shirt, to glide over the warm bumps and ridges of his backbone. His hands reciprocated. And she groaned with delight, right out loud.

He deepened the kiss, and it was as if they were dancing again. She following his lead, until the kiss swept her away breathless and aching.

She wanted more.

She wanted all of him.

Right now.

And she was about to suggest that they go back to the Smith house when he drew back, the moonlight glinting in his eyes. Her heart pounded in her ears, and her breasts practically ached for his touch.

"Oh Christ," he swore. "We can't do this, can we?"

"What?"

He looked down at the dog, who was happily wagging his tail. "Damn it, Sparky, what have you done?" He carefully unwound the leash and stepped back. "Sabina, we can't do this. Not now, anyway."

Her heart rate was slowing, and rationality was returning. Daddy had told her to be selfish. But could she be that selfish? If she allowed herself to fall for Ross it would be tantamount to giving CNN and the rest of the news hounds a shovel that they'd use to bury her reputation, and Ross's. Not to mention that it would thoroughly destroy Lucy's defense.

"No," she whispered, "I guess we can't."

CHAPTER 18

Ross's life was in a shambles.

It wasn't easy being dumped by another girlfriend. It called into question his ability to sustain a real relationship with anyone. And he was worried about Lucy, even though he was obsessed by Sabina. Which made him a complete jerk. He wasn't happy with himself.

So he spent fourteen-hour days at the Smith house doing a lot of the reno work himself to save money. But every time he needed to purchase something, he had to call Sabina. And it slayed him every damn time.

The conversations were always short and polite. She always approved the purchase. No one could find fault with what they said. But there was so much left unspoken.

In the meantime, Dennis Hayden was on a mission to kill Ross's reputation. The county executive had made so many public statements about Ross and Lucy that a large percentage of the cable news audience probably believed Ross was the one who put Lucy up to torching Heritage Oaks.

With his character assassinated this way, Ross would never find another firefighting job again.

And then there was Layton Webster, who, according to the rumor mill, dropped by Sabina's store every day with a bouquet of flowers. Layton never failed to chat up the reporters who hung out on Palmetto Avenue between Daniel Jessup's office and Last Chance Around. Layton made it on the evening news a couple of times, posies in hand, talking about how much he cared about Lucy's sister.

Layton was so photogenic and persuasive that some of the crazy church ladies in town had even suggested that Sabina and Layton take over the wedding that had been planned for Lucy and Ross.

After three days of this, a deep, dark depression invaded. Ross holed up in his apartment, turned off his cell phone, and went into hermit mode.

Unfortunately, no one in Last Chance was ever allowed to become a hermit. Which explained why Ross's doorbell rang at zero-dark-thirty on Saturday morning.

And the doorbell woke up Sparky. And seeing as Sparky had become very protective of him, the dog started barking. And the barking woke Ross from his extended sleep.

Since he wasn't expecting anyone, and had been hiding out from everyone, the early-morning intrusion was more than merely unwelcome.

It pissed him off.

He rolled out of bed and stomped his way to the door where Sparky was standing at attention. Ross grabbed the dog's collar, even though it would have served the nosy reporter right if he let Sparky out and scared the crap out of him.

But he didn't need a lawsuit on top of all his other

problems. So he decided just to tell the idiot in explicitly graphic terms exactly where he could shove his questions.

But the wind left his sails the moment he yanked open the door.

The volunteer members of the Last Chance Fire Department had gathered on his doorstep, with Dash Randall standing right in front. Sparky's tail immediately started wagging. The dog knew friends when he saw them.

"Why aren't you up and ready?" Dash asked in a tone he'd probably learned from one of his baseball coaches.

"Ready for what?"

Dash took a step forward. Ross backpedaled. "The parade."

"The parade?"

"Yeah, the Fall Festival parade. And, Chief, you know the SOP for every parade this town holds. The E-One pumper always brings up the rear. And the chief always rides in the jump seat and waves." He looked down at Sparky. "And so does our fire dog." Dash crossed his arms. He managed to look really badass when he did that.

"But—"

"But what?" he asked, taking another step into Ross's living room.

"Dash, you know what—"

"I know nothing, except that you are the chief of the Last Chance Fire Department. And it doesn't matter to any of us whether you get paid or not. None of us gets paid, but we're still members of the team. And if you think any of us believes for one minute that you set that fire at Heritage Oaks, then you're an idiot. We saw you that night. You were hurt. Bad. And I gotta believe that, if you decided to blow something up, you would set the fuse long enough not to have your head nearly torn off."

Dash smiled.

The guys behind him smiled.

Sparky turned around and smiled, too. In addition to wagging his tail and looking like he wanted to ride on the fire engine real bad.

"Guys, look, I can't. People would probably throw rotten tomatoes at me."

Dash actually rolled his baby blue eyes. The disgust on his face was almost humiliating. "You know, Ross, you have underestimated the goodwill of the citizens of Last Chance, South Carolina. We may be a bunch of gossips and busybodies but the stuff you've been hearing on CNN didn't come from the folks in town. I'm pretty sure all that crap came from Dennis Hayden and Avery Denholm and all those idiots in the county government. They are not our friends, are they?"

The guys behind him shook their heads and said no in unison.

"You didn't set any fires," Dash continued. "Lucy Grey didn't set any fires. And as near as I can see, we'd all be better off if Sheriff Rhodes had been left to his own devices on this. You know and I know that the ATF screwed this up and played right into Hayden's hands. Folks are ticked off about the fire department cutbacks. And it's kind of fun to watch this backfire on Dennis Hayden. By attacking you and Lucy, Hayden's just shifting the blame. That's all it is, and everyone with half a brain knows it."

Bubba Lockheart took up the arguments when Dash ran out of words. "Lillian Bray has organized picket lines down at the City Hall this morning. Hayden is scheduled to make some kind of welcome speech right before the Wild Horses kick off the day's entertainment. Rachel's planning to carry a sign." He grinned, clearly proud of his wife.

"I heard Mayor LaFlore is going to say something about fire and emergency services," Matt Jasper said. "The town council had an emergency meeting last night, and there is some talk about the town picking up the cost of the chief's position. And if you weren't so busy hiding out here or over at the Smith house, you might be aware of all this."

"No one's throwing tomatoes, Ross. At least no one local. Your presence is required." Dash stepped forward, took Ross by the shoulders, and turned him around. "Now go shower and shave. You're starting to look like a hillbilly."

Kamaria LaFlore, mayor of Last Chance and the Democratic candidate for county executive, stood in the foyer of Momma's home with Daniel Jessup and Daddy on either side.

"Are you ready?" the mayor asked Lucy, her big brown eyes calm and kind in her round face.

Lucy shook her head. She didn't want to show her face in public, especially not on the reviewing platform during the Fall Festival parade.

Daniel gave her a reassuring smile. "You'll be fine."

"I don't think so. Those people think I'm an arsonist and a potential murderer."

"You are neither of those things," Mayor LaFlore said.

"Why do you believe me?" Lucy asked.

"Because all the county prosecutor has is circumstantial evidence. And his so-called smoking gun is a can of thermite that could have been put in your workroom by anyone. And the fact that it has no fingerprints on it is mighty suspicious."

"So you really believe that someone in the county government is trying to frame me?" Lucy asked. It was a crazy, scary question.

"I don't know anything except that someone who knows how to manipulate the media went to great lengths to get CNN all over this story. And it's mighty convenient for Hayden's reelection to have the fire chief's girlfriend charged with arson."

"I can't believe this is happening in America," Lucy said, near tears once again.

Kamaria gave Lucy's shoulder a squeeze. "Stay with me, honey. The witch hunt Dennis Hayden has unleashed needs to stop, now. I need you up there on the stage with me so I can publicly support you and send a message to the community about fire and emergency services. Not to mention the absurdity of these charges that have been leveled against you."

"We talked about this, remember?" Daniel said in his always calm voice. "Avery Denholm knows he doesn't have much of a case against you or Ross. So it's incumbent upon us to take the PR narrative back. This will give the cable news people something else to chew over for a few days."

"And then we can pray that some real news happens and they all leave town," Daddy said with authority.

It was always good when Daddy spoke in an authoritative voice. And since Momma had taken to her bed with a four-day migraine, Sabina was busy running today's craft fair, and Lucy had dumped Ross, Daddy was the only one who was there for her.

Unless you counted her attorney and the mayor of Last Chance.

She took a big-girl breath and screwed up her courage. "Okay, let's do this thing." ·

. An hour later Lucy found herself up on the reviewing platform in front of City Hall, standing next to Mayor LaFlore. Below her on the village green, a group of women and high-school kids led by Lillian Bray, the chair of the Christ Church Ladies' Auxiliary, were carrying picket signs that said "Chief ·Gardiner Is Our Hero" and "Vote Against Fire and Rescue Cuts."

At a table nearby, volunteers from the local Democratic party were handing out campaign buttons that said "Free Lucy Grey, Vote LaFlore." And of course, the cable news channels were covering it all from every angle.

She stood beside the mayor, not five feet from Dennis Hayden who kept giving her dirty looks. She tried not to give any back to him and instead concentrated on the parade. The high-school marching band played "When the Saints Go Marching In" as they passed. The kids from Dash Randall's riding school did rope tricks. The Shriners made everyone laugh with their go-karts.

And finally, bringing up the rear, came the Last Chance Fire Department pumper. Two big American flags had been affixed to the front bumper. Bubba Lockheart was behind the wheel, but Ross and Sparky rode up on top while the rest of the force, wearing their navy blue polo shirts and blue pants, stood on the running boards at the back.

Oh, boy, Ross was a sight for sore eyes. She didn't realize how much she had missed him until right this moment, seeing him riding up there on the jump seat. Lucy even had to admit that Sparky looked like he belonged right there with him. The picket signs called him a hero. And he looked like one up there.

He'd always been good to her. He'd patiently worked through every item on her to-do list and hadn't complained even once. What had come over her a few days ago? How could she have listened to the garbage that Dennis Hayden or the media was spewing? Of course Ross didn't set any fires. And he hadn't borrowed any paint from her workroom. In fact, Ross might be the only person in town she could fully trust.

Just like that her confusion lifted and remorse filled her to overflowing. What had she done?

Short answer: She'd spent way too much time fantasizing about Zach Bailey coming to her rescue, when the hero of her dreams was right there in front of her. In truth, Zach was probably going to testify against her in court.

Oh, boy, she was a first-class idiot. How could she not have seen the truth? Hadn't Miriam Randall, herself, suggested that Ross was the man for her?

A strange, powerful urge came over Lucy. It wasn't too late. She could change her fate. She just needed to seize the day.

So she elbowed her way past Mayor LaFlore and half a dozen other dignitaries so she could stand right at the front of the viewing platform as the fire truck rolled by.

And when the truck drew near, she hollered his name.

He was busy looking in the other direction, and there was so much noise that he hadn't heard her. So she snatched up the microphone that had been set up for the upcoming political speeches.

Feedback screeched, and everyone turned, including

the cable news cameras that had been trained on the pick-
eters in front of the stage.

"Ross, Ross Gardiner," she yelled again, heedless of
the protesting mic.

He turned. Sparky turned, too, and wagged his tail.
Then Bubba stopped the pumper right there in the middle
of the street.

She hadn't intended to say anything today. She hadn't
even wanted to be here, with the cameras trained on her.
But suddenly, seeing Ross bravely riding that truck did
something to her.

She could trust this man. He would never, ever let her
down. He'd stand by her through thick and thin, just like
Daddy stood by Momma.

"Ross Gardiner," she hollered again. "Will you marry
me?"

Sabina and Jenny Raintree manned the craft fair vendor check-in booth, which had been set up near City Hall
and the reviewing stand. It had been a long morning, but
the parade was almost over.

The Last Chance Fire Department pumper finally
made it down the length of Palmetto Avenue with Ross
riding on the jump seat waving to everyone like he didn't
have a care in the world. Sparky was right at his side.

Boy howdy, he even looked heroic up there: square-
jawed, clear-eyed, and brave. The perfect October sun lit
up the red highlights in his brown hair, which ruffled in
the slight breeze.

For an instant Sabina's heart soared. He was magnificent. But she couldn't publicly acknowledge her feelings.
They had decided not to be seen together until the situa-

tion with Lucy was resolved. So she swallowed back all her emotions and refrained from waving.

But Ross caught sight of her anyway. His gaze stayed on her so long that he had to crane his neck as the truck moved down the street.

The longing in his glance awakened her body. If she could fly, she would have risen from her place and gone to him. She wanted him that much.

Just then feedback screeched through the PA system and then a voice called out Ross's name. Sabina knew that voice.

"Uh-oh," Jenny said. "What in the world is Lucy doing up there?"

Lucy called Ross's name again, and his head swiveled toward the reviewing stand. In fact, everyone on the green stopped what they were doing and turned in that direction.

"Ross Gardiner, will you marry me?" Lucy hollered into the mic.

If someone had taken a baseball bat to Sabina's stomach the impact wouldn't have knocked her back the way Lucy's words did.

Bubba Lockheart stopped the pumper. The crowd hushed. And Ross, hero that he was, nodded his head and said, "I will."

A roar came up from the crowd. And Jenny's hand came down on Sabina's shoulder. "Just remember that Miriam Randall had a hand in this, and be happy that your sister found her soulmate."

Soulmate? Really? No.

Lucy had ambushed Ross, right there in front of the cameras. What was he supposed to do? Say no?

Of course he said yes.

But did he love her?

Did Lucy love him back?

Fury coursed through Sabina. This largely unknown emotion weakened her knees and made her tremble all over. She wanted to storm right up to that microphone and tell Lucy that she needed to quit playing games with Ross.

And with her.

She wanted to wail to the world that Lucy had stolen the best years of her life.

But wait. How could she do that? Besides Lucy hadn't stolen anything. Sabina had *given away* those years.

"C'mon," Jenny said. "It's showtime. You need to put a smile on your face and be happy for Lucy. And just remember that Miz Miriam promised your soulmate would show up, just as soon as you got Lucy to the altar."

She wanted to believe in Miriam Randall, but she had lost her faith. How could this match be right, given the way Ross had kissed her a few nights ago?

To hell with Miriam Randall. Sabina needed to stop this wedding from happening.

She pushed her friend away and took a couple of steps forward. And then she looked around her, at the people carrying signs calling Ross a hero. At the people wearing pins in support of Lucy.

If she told them what had happened that night on the sidewalk. If she told them how she felt the night Ross danced with her at Dot's. If she told them about the heat of his kisses.

They would lose faith in their local hero.

And she knew, right then, that Jenny was right. She could do only one thing. Get out of the way of her sister and let the marriage happen.

And wasn't that precisely what Miriam Randall had told her to do?

It was amazing how quickly Momma got over her migraine. And Daniel Jessup was delighted with the way Lucy's public declaration of commitment went viral on YouTube. He told her that it would be tough to find anyone willing to believe she had burned down Heritage Oaks in order to murder Ross.

Besides, the prosecutor's case was falling apart. They had a weak case against Lucy for the Heritage Oaks fire, and no evidence whatsoever to tie her to the fire at Jessamine Manor. So it was a relief when Daniel reported back that the ATF had reopened its investigation, and Agent Bailey was back on the job hunting down additional leads. Daniel was confident that the charges against Lucy would eventually be dropped.

And then, two days before the wedding, something happened in the Middle East, and the cable news networks were off to the next big story. Allenberg County went back to being a sleepy place where not much ever happened and no one in the wide world was all that interested anyway.

When Lucy's wedding day finally arrived, Momma got

her up at the crack of dawn and dragged her off to the Cut 'n Curl. And the whole way there she babbled about how Lucy needed to wear her hair up and off her neck.

Which was the last thing Lucy was ever going to do. No one wanted to see her scars. And while the veil might hide them during the ceremony, she didn't intend to wear the veil for the entire day. Momma had hired a legion of photographers and videographers for the big day. Lucy wasn't about to let them record her imperfections for future viewing.

No, she was going to have Ruby make the most of her naturally curly hair. She would wear it down over her shoulders to hide her neck.

For once, Momma was not going to get her way.

It might only be eight in the morning, but the Cut 'n Curl was already crowded when they arrived. In fact, Ruby Rhodes, the proprietor of the shop, was so busy that she'd had to stagger the appointments for the members of the wedding party and the mother of the groom. Ross's mother, Grace Gardiner, was scheduled later in the morning. Meanwhile Sabina was off running errands at the florists and checking in with the caterers.

So it came as no particular surprise to find Jane Rhodes, Ruby's daughter-in-law, at the manicure table, working on Miriam Randall's nails, while Savannah Randall was having her hair styled. But it did come as an utter shock when, instead of being warmly greeted as she always was at the Cut 'n Curl, Miriam Randall looked up from her manicure, gave Lucy the stink eye from behind her upturned eyeglasses, and said in an ungracious tone, "Girl, you are not seriously planning on marrying that man, are you?"

All activity in the shop came to a sudden stop as the women turned to stare at Miriam. Savannah in particular looked practically stricken as she turned toward her aunt. Her face went ghost white. "Aunt Mim, please, I thought we'd agreed that it was not appropriate at this late date to talk about this issue."

"Humph." The old lady scowled at her niece. "Honey, if you're going to take things over, you have to be assertive. And sometimes you have to deliver unpleasant news." Miriam looked surprisingly well groomed today. Her hair was coiled neatly, and her eyes looked bright and sharp.

"Miriam, if you feel like delivering unpleasant news, I would be most obliged if you wouldn't do it in my shop. It's bad for business." Ruby turned toward Lucy and said in a hoarse whisper, "Don't you give Miriam no nevermind. We all know she isn't really herself these days."

Ruby's big grin lit up the beauty shop, but it did nothing to quell the sudden unease in Lucy's gut. Marrying Ross was the sensible thing to do, even if she had reasonable doubt. Even if her heart refused to forget those few moments she'd spent in Zach Bailey's arms.

But it was one thing to have a few doubts and quite another to have Miriam Randall point one of her knobby fingers at her and challenge her about Ross.

And until this moment, Lucy had seriously thought that Miriam Randall, matchmaker extraordinaire, had given her blessing to the match between Ross and herself.

"I may not be myself, Ruby," Miriam said as she struggled to her feet, "but I know what I know. And Lucy, honey, you can't marry that man. It's all wrong."

"Oh, goodness," Momma gasped, right before she collapsed. Good thing Ruby was quick or Momma would have ended up falling right on her face.

"Henrietta?" Ruby said firmly, as she lowered the

swooning mother of the bride into one of the refurbished
Queen Anne chairs that Ruby had purchased at Last
Chance Around. "Someone get a glass of water."

Jane hopped up to do Ruby's bidding while Ruby
checked Momma over.

Meanwhile Lucy stood there rooted to the floor, her
heart running a road race in her chest. "Momma?"

Henrietta's eyes opened up. "Goodness," she said
again, "I thought I heard Miriam say—"

"You heard me right, Henrietta. And I'm sorry, but
I told your daughter the truth a good six weeks ago. And
while I do understand the political and legal reasons for this
wedding, I can't stand by and let it happen on my watch."

"Aunt Mim, please, don't do this," Savannah said.

"What in the Sam Hill is going on?" Ruby said in her
no-nonsense, take-charge voice. Lucy had heard her talk
to her sons in that tone, including Sheriff Rhodes. And it
was amazing the way Ruby kept her boys in line.

Savannah stood up from the stylist chair, took Lucy by
the arm, and guided her to the other Queen Anne chair
in the small reception area. "Honey, you need to sit down
and listen. And I want to make it clear that I didn't want
to raise this issue. But now that Aunt Mim has opened her
mouth, I have no other choice."

"What are you talking about?" Momma's voice had
reached the upper registers, and everyone winced.

"I think a terrible mistake is about to happen." Savannah's voice was grave.

"Mistake?" Momma squeaked.

Despite Savannah's best efforts to take over the situation, Miriam was determined to have her say. "This could
have been avoided, you know. If you'd just taken what I

told you seriously, young woman, we wouldn't have had to make this intervention."

What? Now Lucy was confused. "Uh, Miz Miriam, you never gave me any advice. I would have remembered it if you had. You spoke with Sabina."

"I did not. I spoke to you."

"Miz Miriam, I'm really sorry, but you didn't ever speak with me. You spoke to Sabina in the store. Momma came in for the end of it, I think. I was in class that day you went to the store."

Miriam's gaze clouded over. "Oh, dear," she said in a voice suddenly old and frail. "I was sure I spoke with you."

"Was it about six weeks ago—right before the fire at Jessamine Manor?" Lucy asked.

"Oh, I don't rightly remember exactly. But the feeling came on me real strong, and I just dropped what I was doing and walked down to Last Chance Around and gave you a talking-to, you know."

"Uh-huh, and what did you say?"

"Well, I told you that your soulmate would arrive just as soon as you helped your sister see the truth. I told you, under no circumstances was it right for you to marry anyone before your sister was settled."

Time hung suspended for a moment as Lucy processed this incredible piece of news.

Momma piped up. "But Miz Miriam, I was there for the tail end of that conversation. You spoke with Sabina. We've been working under the assumption that you wanted us to light a fire under Ross's behind, if you'll pardon the use of that term. Seems like there have been too many fires in town the last few weeks."

"Oh, dear," Miriam said again and then plopped back

down into the chair by the manicure station. "Goodness, I could have sworn I spoke with you, Lucy."

Savannah exhaled as if she were breathing out all the troubles in the world. That sigh said it all. Miriam Randall's days of matchmaking were officially over. Savannah turned her gaze on Lucy. "I'm really, really sorry about this. I didn't know we would run into you here, but I guess I should have. Sometimes Aunt Mim is right. The Lord has His way of making things turn out right.

"Anyway, you see, I've been wrestling with this problem all week, honey. And I just didn't feel like it was my place to tell you what to do or to give you advice. Especially given your legal situation and the way this town has been overrun with reporters the last few weeks. But I have strong feelings about this."

"Whoa, wait one sec," Ruby said. "Since when do you get feelings about matrimonial matters?"

"Since she was knee-high to a grasshopper," Miriam said. "I've always known she had the same knack I do. But she needs to learn how to get up in people's faces, you know. She doesn't take this thing seriously. But it's time."

"What?" Everyone in the salon asked this question more or less simultaneously.

"Ah, well, this is sort of awkward, y'all," Savannah said. "But I guess I've known for a while that Ross wasn't your soulmate. I never said anything because, you know, Ross didn't seem like he was in an all-fired hurry to get married. And then there was all that gossip about him and Sabina, which I took to mean that things were moving in the right direction. I've been so busy with the Fall Festival that I haven't really been paying much attention to things, you know. And Aunt Mim is forgetful, and y'all, her eyesight is going.

"Of course she knew that Ross wasn't the one for you, too. But we never like to come right out and tell someone not to marry a particular person. That's sort of rude. It's way better if people discover that on their own. We just point folks in the right direction."

"Which is what I did." Miriam crossed her arms over her chest.

"Which is what she *thought* she did."

"Well, I can see how anyone could make that mistake, Miriam," Ruby said kindly. "Sabina and Lucy are like peas in a pod."

"Except for their eye color," Momma said, helpfully. "And Lucy's hair is curlier."

"It is," Ruby said.

"Uh, can we not talk about my hair, please," Lucy said, her voice almost trembling with the shivers that were running up and down her backbone. It was a wonder she hadn't fainted just like Momma.

"Well, anyway," Savannah said. "At this late date, I told Aunt Mim that we needed to keep our mouths shut. And I thought we were in agreement. But I guess it's hard to muzzle Miriam."

"Well, I'll be," Ruby said. "Maybe Elsie Campbell wasn't exaggerating about Sabina and Ross up in the attic of that old house."

"You know, y'all," Savannah said, "I never realized until this week that having this knack for seeing things is a terrible responsibility. I mean, you and Ross seem happy together. Where do I get off telling you that he might not be the right one for you? So I know I should have come by and talked to y'all before this. But I didn't know which way to go."

"I nagged her," Miriam added. "She's almost as stubborn as her husband about some things."

"Wait just one minute. Are y'all saying that Ross should be marrying Sabina?" Momma sounded angry now. "Because if you're suggesting that Sabina has been sneaking around with Ross, I'm not sure I like that innuendo. I thought we had put an end to that kind of talk."

"No, Henrietta, I'm not suggesting that Sabina has been sneaking around with Ross. But I am suggesting that it would be a mistake for Lucy to marry him."

"Well, thank you very much for your advice, but I don't see where you get to tell any of us what to do or say. Come on, Lucy, we're leaving. There's a perfectly fine beauty shop in Orangeburg where we can get our hair done without people messing with our private lives. And besides, you are determined to wear your hair down, so you don't even need much in the way of styling."

And with that Momma stood up, grabbed Lucy by the arm, and marched them both right out of the Cut 'n Curl.

Saturday morning had been more than merely hectic. Momma had dumped a boatload of errands on Sabina, and she gladly accepted them all. She'd come to the conclusion that staying busy was the best way to block out her unwarranted and forbidden feelings about the groom.

Who had been careful to keep his distance this last week. You could say a lot of things about Ross, but he was a good guy. He had agreed in public to marry Lucy, and he was prepared to carry out his promise.

Sabina understood now what Miriam had meant all those weeks ago. So she worked hard to get out of Ross and Lucy's way and to be as helpful as possible to Momma.

She picked up the flowers at the florist's in Allenberg. She checked in at the VFW hall to make sure that the cake was delivered and the centerpieces were done correctly. She picked up Mrs. Gardiner at Ross's apartment and took her to the beauty shop.

And that's where the day unraveled.

"Oh, Sabina, I declare," Ruby said the minute she and Mrs. Gardiner stepped into the shop. "I thought y'all would opt to go up to Orangeburg after what happened this morning."

"What happened?" A rush of adrenaline surged through Sabina. "Did Momma and Lucy have a big fight over her hair? Momma wanted her to wear it up, and you know Lucy is never going to agree to anything like that."

To say that Ruby looked surprised would be an understatement. Her jaw dropped, and her eyes widened. "Y'all don't know?"

"Uh, no. I've been running errands for Momma all morning."

"I've been with Ross," Mrs. Gardiner said.

"Oh, my. Uh, well, never you mind. Come on in, y'all."

Ruby turned away and gave Jane, the manicurist, a meaningful look and a little eye roll as if she was telling Jane to keep her mouth shut.

"Hey, y'all." Jane gave them her big, sweet smile.

"All right, what happened?" Sabina said.

Ruby and Jane exchanged glances, and then Ruby spoke again. "Honey, I'm afraid one of my other customers said something this morning that set your mother and sister off. They stormed out of the shop. I'm surprised they didn't call you and tell you about it."

"Who?" Sabina crossed her arms. After the showing of support Lucy and Ross had gotten last weekend, she couldn't imagine who might say something ugly at the beauty shop. Even Lillian Bray was on Ross and Lucy's side, which was saying something right there.

"I'm afraid it was Savannah Randall."

"Savannah? Really? Wow, that surprises me."

"Yes, well, it surprised me, too. But look, y'all are here, and there's apparently going to be a wedding, so we need to get both of you all dolled up."

And boy, Ruby wasn't kidding about that. When Ruby and Jane were finished with Sabina, she'd been transformed. Ruby put her hair up into a beautiful chignon with tendrils that looked as if they'd escaped on their own. Jane gave her a French manicure, and then she'd insisted on doing her makeup, too.

Ruby and Jane made Sabina feel as if she were the bride and not merely the maid of honor. They were obviously feeling guilty about whatever had happened earlier in the morning. But neither one of them was willing to explain in too great a detail what exactly had gone down.

In the end, Sabina enjoyed being pampered. Not to mention that Ruby and Jane made her look like a million bucks.

Mrs. Gardiner had brought her dress with her so they changed at Sabina's house and then headed for the church. Sabina handed Mrs. Gardiner off to Ross, who looked good enough to eat in his tuxedo. She didn't stop to enjoy the view, and he didn't look her in the eye, which was both good and bad.

Good, because if he had looked she probably would have blushed or burst into tears or something. Looking Ross in the eye was always awkward and intense these days.

Bad, because she kind of wanted him to look. The pink chiffon bridesmaid dress with the sweetheart neckline looked like it had been tailored especially for her. Momma was a lot of things, but she sure had a good eye when it came to picking out dresses.

Of course, in this instance maybe the dress should have come with a bright scarlet A embroidered somewhere. Because whenever she looked at the groom, her face heated, her heart took flight, and her girl parts made themselves known.

She might not have actually committed adultery, but she sure contemplated it every time she crossed Ross's path. This led to several existential questions:

Could you commit adultery with a guy who wasn't married yet?

And did it count as adultery if all you ever did was kiss him?

With an open mouth?

She didn't want to entertain any of these thoughts on her sister's wedding day. So she hurried away toward the little room right off the narthex where brides waited for that moment when Ella Miles, the organist at First Methodist for the last thirty years, struck up the wedding march.

She let herself into the little room. Momma stood on one side looking miserable. Her mascara was already running, and her nose looked red. Sabina had expected Momma to cry buckets, but not until the ceremony actually started.

Otherwise, she looked great. She'd poured her curvy body into a gorgeous champagne lace sheath dress and a little jacket with three-quarter-length sleeves. The dress accentuated her figure and was probably a little sexy for mother-of-the-bride attire, and her hairdo was a little over the top, confirming that Momma had not given her head over to Ruby Rhodes for styling this morning.

Lucy stood at the other side of the room, as far away from the mirrors as possible. She'd obviously won the battle with Momma, because her hair was down, and whoever had styled it had sprayed a gallon of something to hold the waves in place. It looked a little plastic.

The hair notwithstanding, Lucy also looked terrific. The Jenny Packham wedding dress fit her perfectly. Its simple A-line silhouette emphasized Lucy's slender figure. The ivory chiffon flowed as she walked. And best of all, it covered her arms and back with beaded fabric that hid as much as it revealed. She looked incredible.

But not radiant. In fact, her complexion was closer to sickly green.

"Oh, my goodness, Sabina, you look beautiful." Momma's voice trembled.

"Uh, well, I let Jane and Ruby do their thing."

Momma and Lucy shared a glance.

"What in the Sam Hill happened at the Cut 'n Curl this morning? Ruby told me that Savannah said something ugly and y'all left. I can't imagine Savannah Randall being ugly to anyone."

Momma and Lucy shared another glance.

"What?"

Momma gave a shrug that was anything but nonchalant. "It was just vicious gossip is all. Lucy and I are not going to repeat it."

"Was it about me?"

Neither one of them said a word, confirming the worst. She was about to press the point when Daddy strolled through the door wearing a rented tux that didn't fit him all that well. His blue eyes lit up when he looked at Momma. Clearly he had no problems with her big hair and tight dress. "Honey, I've been told that it's time for me to escort you to the front of the church." He turned and gave Lucy one of those soft-eyed Daddy looks. "Angel, your groom is waiting for you. I'll be back in just a moment, and we'll get this rodeo started."

Momma took Daddy's arm, and the two of them headed for the door. Just before she left the room, Momma looked over her shoulder at Lucy. "You'll be fine, honey. Just take a big breath."

When the door closed, Lucy took that big breath and then burst into tears.

These were not joyful tears. They weren't nervous tears. In fact, the word "tears" didn't quite convey the depths of the sobs that suddenly racked Lucy's body.

"What?" Sabina hurried to her sister's side.

"I can't do this," she bawled as she reached back for the zipper of her dress. She managed to get it down.

"Uh, wait, Luce, are you leaving Ross at the altar?"

She didn't say a word. She just wiggled out of the beautiful dress and left it like a puddle on the floor. She reached for a tote bag sitting in the corner and pulled out a bright pink T-shirt with the words "Keep Calm and Carry a Gun" across the front. She paired it with wrinkled jeans.

"Honey, what's going on?" Sabina asked as her heart began to pound.

When she had the jeans fastened, Lucy looked up at Sabina. "You can borrow the dress, if you want. It would probably make Ross's day if you marched down the aisle instead of me."

Uh-oh. "Uh, Lucy, uh—"

She put up a hand. "You don't have to say anything. I

know you and Ross haven't done anything to be ashamed of. But there's been a terrible mistake and I'm not going to compound it. You've given up so much of your life because of me, I'm not going to make you give up your soulmate."

"What are you talking about?"

"Miz Miriam. She made a terrible mistake. She thought she was talking to me, not you, when she came in the store that time. So the thing is, you're supposed to get married before I even find my soulmate. And today at the beauty shop, Savannah all but told us that Ross is the one for you."

She picked up the tote. "I'm taking the back way out. You can wear the dress, or you can just tell everyone that I've changed my mind. It's your choice either way. But in the meantime I'm getting out of here."

"Wait, Lucy, you can't leave Allenberg County. They'll send a bounty hunter after you. You'd be jumping bail."

"I don't care. I didn't do anything wrong. But if I marry Ross, it will be the biggest mistake I ever made. He's a good man, Sabina. I guess I love him in my way, but when Miz Miriam told me that he wasn't my soulmate, I knew she was telling me the truth. Momma says Miriam is senile and I should just ignore her, but I can't. And besides, Savannah isn't senile, and she was saying the same thing as Miriam. They both told me not to marry Ross."

Lucy stepped up to Sabina and threw her arms around her. "I love you, Sabina. I would do anything for you. And it's time I paid you back. If you care about Ross, this is your time to show it."

Ross stood in the front of the church, Matt Jasper beside him. He couldn't swallow. His heart felt like a jackhammer in his chest.

This was not how he'd felt the first time around. The first time he'd been besotted. He'd stood at the front of that church with complete certainty that he'd found his life mate. And Betsy had looked like a dream that day.

Right, maybe a guy was smart to have sweaty hands on his wedding day. This was some scary stuff.

Ella Miles started playing something by Bach. He couldn't remember the name of the piece. Earl escorted Momma and Henrietta to their places in the front pews. In a moment the music was going to change from Bach to the wedding march.

And of course, Sabina would be coming down the aisle, and he'd have to try pretty hard not to watch her. He was supposed to watch Lucy.

Damn. How the hell had he ended up here?

The music changed, and the door to the narthex opened. And there was Sabina.

But she wasn't carrying a bouquet. And she wasn't walking slowly in time to the ponderous music.

No, she barreled through those doors and marched in a two-step right up to the front of the sanctuary. And all that time, she refused to meet his gaze.

When she got to the front of the room, she turned and looked out at the congregation. It was just beginning to dawn on all assembled that this wedding had hit a major snag. His pulse should have climbed into the stratosphere at this point, but instead it steadied and calmed. A profound sense of relief washed through him.

"Noooooo." Henrietta got up from her spot in the front pew. "Sabina Grey, what have you done?"

"I haven't done one thing, Momma. I'm sure you think

I should have handcuffed the bride before she made an escape. But I couldn't do that to my sister."

A gasp went through the congregation.

Sabina frowned for a moment and then continued in rapid-fire fashion, "Uh, well, um, that was probably a poor choice of words given the situation. Maybe it would be better to say that Lucy had a change of heart." She stopped, turned, and looked at Ross. "Oh, and she told me to tell you that she thinks you're a wonderful man, but that Miriam Randall told her this morning that you are not her soulmate."

Another gasp went through the congregation, just as heat and desire flooded through Ross. He wasn't sure he believed in Miriam Randall and her marital forecasts, but he was willing to kiss the old woman the next time he saw her.

"Damn that woman," Henrietta said.

Reverend Lake, who had been standing there waiting to officiate at the nuptials, cleared his throat, then spoke in a sonorous tone. "Henrietta, I know you're upset, but I will remind you that we're standing in the sanctuary." He gave her a censorious look. Henrietta glared right back.

Just then, Earl Grey came jogging down the aisle huffing and puffing as if he'd run a race. "I looked for her everywhere outside. She's disappeared. I can't imagine she got very far unless she had someone helping her."

"Oh, goodness." Henrietta collapsed into her seat in the front pew and started to cry. Earl hurried to her side.

Sabina took charge. "So there you have it. There isn't going to be a wedding. However, we still have the VFW hall booked, and we have food and adult beverages. So y'all come on by and we'll have a party anyway."

Daddy had almost captured Lucy out in the church's parking lot. But she dove into a stand of azaleas by the playground that would have been terrific camouflage in the spring when they bloomed pink, but in October not so much. Lucy prayed like mad that her pink shirt wouldn't give her away.

God must have been listening because Daddy walked right by her and didn't see her. When he went back into the church, she hightailed it down Palmetto Avenue.

It was the moment of truth. Four hours ago, when she'd gone to the ladies' room at the beauty shop up in Orangeburg, she'd made a desperate phone call and left a desperate message. She had no idea if that message had been received.

She hurried down the alleyway and into the parking lot behind the Wash-O-Rama, her heart hammering in expectation. But there were only two trucks parked out there. One belonged to Roy Burdett. It had a dent in its front from an accident he'd been in a few months ago. The other truck was a classic 1950-something Ford pickup that belonged to Simon Wolfe.

Neither Roy nor Simon was going to rescue her.

Not that she wanted a knight in shining armor or anything. But she desperately needed a ride. Because the crap was probably hitting the fan big time down at the Methodist church, and there would probably be people who wanted to do her in for what she'd just done to Ross.

Not to mention the fact that her attorneys were crapping their pants, and she'd probably made an enemy out of Mayor LaFlore.

She stood there, gasping for air, her life practically flashing in front of her eyes. And then a gray Ford Focus entered the lot and pulled right up to her. The window rolled down.

And there he was, wearing a pair of jeans with a crease in them, a pair of mirrored sunglasses, and a T-shirt that sported a picture of a long gun and the words "I Think the Shotgun Speaks for Itself."

"Hi," he said. "Wanna go for a ride?"

She didn't think twice. She dropped her gym bag in the backseat and hopped in.

"You came." Her voice sounded thin and shaky.

His mouth twitched. "I told you, babe. All you have to do is call. Guess you decided the fireman wasn't your type after all, huh?"

She leaned back against the headrest. "It's a long, long story. And there's likely to be an angry crowd after me at any moment. So if I could run away now, it would be great."

"You can't leave Allenberg County, you know that?"

She was momentarily worried that he might have come to give her a lecture on the dangers of bail jumping. But instead of giving her any more crap, he pulled the car out of the parking lot and headed east on Route 78. She wasn't a fugitive from justice quite yet. The county line was miles and miles up the road.

"So you want to tell me what went down?" he asked.

"No, not really. It's all kind of crazy to tell you the truth."

"I don't doubt it."

"Why do you say that?"

"Because you're involved."

"You have entirely the wrong idea about me. I'm a sane, stable, list-making kind of girl."

"Uh-huh." He didn't sound convinced.

"I am, really."

"That totally explains why you've just left your fiancé at the church and you're contemplating jumping bail."

She heaved an enormous sigh. "Zach, are you going to testify against me?"

He laughed. "After the crap you just pulled, I don't need to testify."

"Oh, yeah, I guess." She looked over at him. It didn't seem possible but his jaw was every bit as square as Ross's. "Just tell me, if I hadn't pulled this crap, would you have testified?"

"I don't think the case is ever going to get to trial, Lucy."

"No?"

He shook his head. "No. And I don't think marrying Ross Gardiner is going to be necessary for your defense, either."

"You believe in me? Really?"

"I had to investigate you. But I didn't ever doubt you. Of course, Wyatt jumped the gun when we found your fingerprints on that spray can. And I'm sorry about that. He's kind of ambitious."

"So what now?" Lucy said. "Someone tried to set me up."

Zach nodded. "I know. That's why I'm glad you called. I'm going to keep you safe."

"Where are you taking me?"

"To the Magnolia Inn, which is right at the county line, so that you're not officially jumping bail. You'll be safe there for a while. And then I'm going to go follow up a lead."

"You have a lead?"

"I do." He grinned in her direction. "And when I'm done with my business, I'll come back with some dinner and we can catch a movie or something on the cable TV."

She found herself grinning back even though she had this feeling that they weren't going to be watching a whole lot of television once he got back.

God bless the volunteers of the Last Chance Fire Department. They closed ranks around their chief, hustled him from the First Methodist Church, and took him to some undisclosed location, where, presumably, they got him rip-roaring drunk.

Daddy took Momma in hand and dragged her out of the church, presumably home where he probably gave her a sleeping pill.

Which left Sabina and Grace Gardiner to play hostess to whoever decided to avail themselves of the free food and drink at the VFW hall. A surprising number of friends and family actually showed up. Cousin Sally on Daddy's side and her husband, Sidney, actually danced when the band started playing.

On the whole though, it was a pretty miserable party.

A few hours later Sabina pulled into the parking lot at the Edisto Pines Apartments to drop Mrs. Gardiner off at Ross's place.

"Thank you so much for coming to the VFW hall with me. I'm so sorry about what happened," Sabina said.

Grace turned in the passenger's seat. "I wish you would stop that."

"What?"

"Apologizing. First of all, it wasn't your fault that Lucy ran. Second, I'm glad she did it."

"You are? Ross is probably devastated."

She chuckled. "I doubt it."

"You doubt it?"

She reached over and took Sabina's hand. "I need to tell you something. I've kept my mouth closed for a long, long time. And I'm sure Ross would be embarrassed or something if he knew I ever said one word to you. But girl, my boy has had a crush on you since he was thirteen."

"What?"

Grace's eyes got all soft as she talked. "You know my husband wasn't a wealthy man. And I guess Ross was never really one of the popular kids. He played soccer. And he was always so shy as a boy. But his daddy and I both knew he was carrying a torch for the cheerleader who lived a few streets over. And I believe he convinced himself that he wasn't good enough for you.

"Maybe that's why he was willing to settle for your sister. So you see, I'm not at all unhappy that this wedding didn't happen. He made a terrible mistake with his first wife. And I've been so afraid that he was about to over-react to that and settle for something less than his heart's desire. So when you looked him in the eye and told him that Miriam Randall, herself, knew that Lucy wasn't his soulmate, well, I had to stifle a grin. It wasn't a big deal going to the party and drinking a glass of champagne." She had Ross's smile.

"Oh, boy."

"You can say that again."

"Mrs. Gardiner—Grace—I was such a stupid idiot in high school."

"We all were. Don't beat yourself up over it."

"I knew Ross, but I didn't *know* him. And then that night when the house caught fire, he did something that made me see him for the first time. We were all standing outside the Smith house. And Alfie Roche wanted to throw rocks through the window. And he stood up to him. Alfie had to have outweighed him by fifty pounds, but Ross got right up in his face and used words instead of his fists. I...well, I don't know. I thought he was someone I wanted to know that night. But then the fire happened and that changed everything."

"How do you feel about Ross now? Do you still want to get to know him better?"

Her face warmed. "I do."

"So that gossip I've heard about, it's true?"

"Well, yes and no. I mean we did dance up in the attic."

"I heard you found Evelyn Smith's wedding dress."

"So that dress in the trunk belonged to Miz Smith?"

"It did. She was supposed to marry a man name Hubert back in 1925. But I gather he ran off with some woman named Mabel who was a bank teller or something. He just left her standing there in the church. She never got over being left that way. I used to come to tea and she would tell me the story of how Hubert ran away with Mabel every time. So you can imagine how I felt when I heard the gossip last evening about you and Ross up in that attic wearing Evelyn's bridal veil. Elsie Campbell herself told me what she saw. And I knew how Ross felt about you.

"Last night I tossed and turned. And this morning,

before you picked me up, I almost took Ross aside and asked him mother-to-son if he truly loved Lucy or if he was just playing the hero and protecting her. But I knew it was already too late. My son is too much of a gentleman to ever leave Lucy standing at the altar. And I'm pretty sure the two of you never cheated on Lucy, either. But I bet you both thought about it."

Whoa, it was one thing to harbor a secret fascination with someone and quite another to be called out on it. It was a good thing that dusk had settled and it was dark in the car, otherwise Mrs. Gardiner would be able to see the blush on her face.

"You don't have to answer that. I can see the truth in the way you look at Ross. And the way he looks at you. Any fool can see it if they're looking for it. So if Miriam Randall has given you some kind of blessing, you need to act on it. In fact, you have my blessing to act on it. And I can't think of a better time than now."

There was something incredibly satisfying about driving screws into Sheetrock. The drill and the screw made a ripping sound that echoed through the empty house.

Through the lonely house. Not even Sparky was here. Dash had offered to dog-sit for the duration of the honeymoon. So Sparky was out at Dash's farm hanging with the horses for a few days.

He could have had the guys over for a Sheetrock-hanging party, but he didn't feel like enduring their pity. He'd had to endure a boatload of it this afternoon. The guys had taken him to Bubba Lockheart's basement man-cave where they plied him with Budweiser and forced him to watch the Florida State Gators trample the Carolina

Gamecocks. By the end of the afternoon, it was fair to say that everyone ended up drowning their misery in Bud.

So he was not exactly sober. But he wasn't really drunk, either. He probably shouldn't be here alone playing with power tools, but the idea of going home and facing his mother was more than he could bear. She would be sweet and understanding.

And he didn't want anyone to be sweet and understanding. Besides, it was kind of hard to mess up hanging Sheetrock. He could always mud over his worst mistakes. And screwing in screws suited his mood.

The noise also drowned out the sound of Sabina walking into the upstairs master bedroom where he was working. God alone only knew how long she'd been standing there when he got the oddest prickling sensation up his back.

She was still wearing that incredible pink dress that showed off her breasts. And her hair was still piled on top of her head, but tendrils of it were kind of falling down around her ears. His hands itched to take out the hairpins. And strangely enough, she didn't look as if she'd shed a single tear today. No runny mascara. No red nose. No nothing like that.

She looked good. And hot.

"Did Miriam talk to you? Do you know what happened?" she asked.

He shook his head. "What do you mean? What happened is that Lucy left me standing at the altar, which is kind of humiliating." Although he wasn't feeling humiliated. But maybe his pride was a little jerked around.

Maybe if he was sober, he'd be pissed off at Lucy. She'd played him for a fool. Several different times.

"Well, here's what I've pieced together," Sabina said, breaking into his thoughts. "Apparently when Miriam came into the store that time, she thought she was talking to Lucy, not me. So when she told me that I needed to get out of my sister's way, she actually meant that Lucy needed to get out of my way. And when she said that thing about a fish not being able to see the water, I think what she meant was that sometimes the thing you're looking hardest to find is just right there in plain view."

Oh, crap. His heart started beating so hard he could hear it in his ears. He was a little buzzed from the beer, but that didn't account for the sudden strange, rubbery feeling he was getting in his knees.

"And then your momma told me that you had a crush on me when you were in high school. Did you?"

Oh, crap. She'd been talking to Momma. "Uh, well, um..."

Sabina's mouth turned up in a devilish grin. "You did have a crush on me, didn't you? But here's a secret. When you stood up to Alfie Roche that time, I realized you were a bona fide southern gentleman and probably real hero material. I might have developed a reciprocating crush. But I never did get the chance because..."

"Because of the fire."

She nodded. "Yeah."

"Sabina, when I came back two years ago, I asked you out on a date—several times—and you always had something else to do. I mean, a guy gets the message when a woman isn't interested. And then you pushed Lucy at me."

She nodded. "I know I did that. Because all these years, I've been looking after Lucy, and I've always felt this huge responsibility for her. And I told myself that I wasn't going to leave town or get married or, heck, live my life until I was sure Lucy was taken care of. And the minute you came back to town, I knew that you were the perfect guy to care for my sister. I knew that because of the way you stood up to Alfie that time. And the thing is, you never saw her scars."

"They aren't that noticeable."

"They are to some guys."

He shrugged. "Stupid guys. Your sister is a beautiful woman."

"See, I loved you all the more for thinking that."

He stood there blinking at her, something deep in his chest pulling him forward. He put down the drill and moved to stand in front of her. "You're beautiful, too. And I've discovered, these last couple of years, that you're not just some shallow cheerleader with a pretty face and a curvy body. Sabina Grey, you are a wonderful woman. You would go to the ends of the earth for the people you care about. You give of yourself every day. You volunteer for everything. And the more I've gotten to know you, the more I can see that you aren't the person I once thought you were. And, well…" He suddenly couldn't say the words he wanted to say.

He didn't trust those words.

And it was too soon after Lucy and maybe too soon after Betsy. The last few weeks kind of confirmed that he wasn't entirely over the catastrophe of his first marriage.

But that didn't stop him from wanting Sabina. And he wasn't misreading that look in her eye. And he'd had just enough beer to be willing to throw caution to the wind.

So he touched her cheek, and fire blazed through his fingertips and up his arm and right into his belly. It was scary how one touch could ignite such an inferno.

He knew better than to play with fire, but he couldn't help himself. He deepened the touch, cupping her cheek and then pulling Sabina up into a kiss so hot that it scorched his insides. That's when he lost whatever fear he had of the fire that raged between them. He embraced it. He welcomed it. And he used his hands and his tongue and his whole body to fan those flames into a conflagration.

Sabina had sought Ross out with only one thing on her mind. And in truth, she'd walked into that room feeling a little small and nervous. She'd spent a lifetime pushing guys away. She'd protected her virtue with single-minded, and probably misguided, determination.

So the idea of seducing anyone, much less her sister's ex-fiancé, daunted her. She had no experience. She had no idea how to get what she wanted.

But apparently she had secret talents. Or maybe Ross was just primed and ready after what had happened today. And after all, he'd shown incredible restraint over the last few weeks.

He might have stumbled over his words of love, but he'd gotten the message across. So when he touched her, when his lips found hers, it was as if he embraced more than her body. He brought her body to life and unlocked a soul-deep part of her that she didn't know existed.

His touch changed her. She reveled at the way he had awakened her body, the secret aches, the mysterious flow. And when he unzipped her dress and let the chiffon float to the floor she had no doubts about what was coming next.

Where had her modesty gone? She stood naked before him, lost in the crazy, aroused look in his eyes. And then it occurred to her that seeing him naked would be fun. So she grabbed a fistful of his T-shirt and helped pull it over his head. It wasn't the first time she'd ever seen his chest, but it was certainly the first time she had ever dared to touch it.

There wasn't anything soft about his chest, except for the skin that stretched over the bones and sinew and hard muscle. His skin was warm and utterly intoxicating. She couldn't resist running her hands over his abs and down to the placket of his jeans.

Such scary fun—like that adrenaline rush she always got as a kid when the big guys on the cheer squad tossed her into the air. She felt almost weightless as she undid the button. And then he helped her shuck those jeans right off, and he was standing there nude and erect and utterly gorgeous.

It seemed like they stood facing each other for an eternity, just enjoying the view. The beat of his pulse at the nape of his neck matched hers precisely—wild and fast and kind of erratic.

And then all that looking wasn't enough. It became necessary to touch, and the touch set her flying, even as he picked her up and gently laid her down on a twin mattress he'd hauled into the room. It wasn't exactly a wedding bower, or a beautiful bed.

But it was softer than the wood floor, and it astonished her just how badly she wanted to get horizontal.

If she thought he'd aroused her before, she had another think coming. The man had some talented hands, so when the big moment came, she was kind of ready. Well, she thought she was ready.

But it hurt. And she stiffened slightly.

He stopped. His brow lowered, his eyes dark, wide, aroused. "No," he whispered in a hoarse voice.

"No what?" she said, the sudden pain of her lost virginity receding fast. A primal need to move her hips replaced it.

"Don't tell me this is your first time, please?"

"Would you stop if I did?"

He didn't say anything. He just kept staring at her, as if this one thing was a huge barrier between them. But really, now that it was done, it wasn't such a big deal at all.

"Don't stop," she said firmly, and then wiggled her hips.

That did it. He forgot about his qualms. And she discovered something new and amazing and proceeded to lose herself in that primitive and essential and utterly mysterious thing that couldn't really be explained.

This, oh this, was what she'd saved herself for.

Zach didn't come back until almost eight that night. So Lucy spent a lot of time alone inside the shabby motel room worrying about everything.

She worried about Ross. And Sabina. And Momma. And Daddy. And she worried about Zach, more than she wanted to admit.

Terrible scenarios captured her imagination. What if Zach never came back? What if she were found guilty of something she hadn't done? What if...

But then Zach opened the door and she was all over him with a gigantic hug before he took two steps into the motel room.

He laughed. "Happy to see me or just hungry?" He gave her a hot kiss on her cheek.

"I was so worried about you."

"Sorry it took so long. But I have good news and pizza. You must be hungry."

For the first time, she noticed that he was carrying a pizza box and a bottle of wine, which explained why he wasn't hugging her back. And that was a shame, because she really wanted him to hug her back.

"Let go, Lucy. I'm fine."

She reluctantly stepped back. "You brought wine, too?"

"Champagne." He held up the bottle. It looked expensive.

It struck her that drinking champagne with Zach on this night of all nights, which was supposed to be her wedding night, might be tacky. Of course she was already at the Magnolia Inn, the main no-tell motel in the county. And she'd left her fiancé at the altar. So she'd probably already crossed the tasteless line.

But still, she didn't feel like celebrating anything. In truth, she was scared.

Zach put the pizza down on the table at the front of the room. "We have something to celebrate."

"We do?"

He began to unwrap the wire from the wine's cork. He popped it and managed not to spill any, a move that won him points. He poured some wine in the paper water cups the hotel had supplied. "Lucy my dear, you are off the hook."

"What?"

"About three hours ago, the sheriff of Orangeburg County arrested a man named Terry Keller and charged him with the arson at Jessamine Manor. I'm expecting the Allenberg prosecutor to drop his case against you, maybe as early as tomorrow, but certainly by Monday." He handed her a cup. "Drink up. You're practically a free woman."

She didn't drink. She suddenly had a million questions. "Who is Terry Keller?"

"He's a guy who sent several threats to Elias Webster over the years. Apparently Keller claims that Webster sold him a home that was defective in some way. They went to court over it, and Webster won the case, but Keller kept up his harassment. Turns out your ex-boyfriend was right about one thing—this isn't eco-terrorism. But it's not arson for profit, either. This is a simple case of revenge."

"Do you have evidence?"

He nodded. "Keller is a welder."

"So?"

"He has access to the metals that are used to make thermite. That fact, coupled with the nature of the mail threats he made, enabled me to convinced my superior that we should check him out. We got a search warrant and hit pay dirt."

"What did you find?"

"The makings of thermite in his basement. We found evidence linking him to the first fire—the one at Jessamine Manor."

He gave her a completely self-satisfied smile. He was definitely on the cocky side, but she liked that about him. Unfortunately his news didn't completely warm her heart.

"What's the matter?" he asked, his smile never wavering. "Drink your champagne."

She put the wine on the table. "Do you have evidence linking him to the second fire—the one that almost killed Ross? Someone set me up to take the blame for that fire. And I don't know this Terry guy. Why would he frame me for the fire at Heritage Oaks?"

Zach stood there, the smile fading from his mouth. "We'll find the evidence to convict this slimebag, babe. You don't have to worry."

But she was worried. Something didn't add up. "Don't tell me what to feel, Zach. That would make you just like everyone else in my family."

His big brown eyes softened. It was hard to look into them without feeling as if Zach understood exactly what she was feeling. "I'm sorry. I didn't mean it that way." He put his wine down as well. "I just meant that I would keep you safe, no matter what happens. And I'm pretty sure we have the right perp this time."

She folded her arms. "I'm happy you caught the guy who burned down my house, but if he wasn't the one who framed me for the second fire, and you don't have any evidence connecting him to the fire at Heritage Oaks, then how can you be so sure both fires were set by the same person?"

He stood there blinking at her, his expression changing. "I guess I can't."

"Look, Zach, Mayor LaFlore seems to think that Dennis Hayden set me up as the fall girl for the fire at Heritage Oaks. She's certain he orchestrated all of that for political reasons to make me and Ross look bad. If it's true, then you guys should be investigating Executive Hayden for abuse of power. And if it's not true, then isn't it possible that someone else set the second fire?"

"Lucy." Zach said her name softly as he stepped toward her. "It's okay. You're safe with me. I'm sure we'll find some connection between this slimeball we just arrested and the second fire. And if we don't, I promise you I will find the a-hole who planted that can of thermite in your workroom. And when I do, I will send him away for a long, long time."

He caressed her cheek and leaned down for a soft, deep, intimate kiss that was worlds apart from the one he'd given her that time at the shooting range. This kiss spoke a language that her heart understood. She was safe with him, forever, no matter what.

CHAPTER
21

The room was pitch dark when Ross's pager sounded. He woke with a jolt, momentarily disoriented, until Sabina stirred beside him on the lumpy, single mattress with an old sleeping bag thrown over them.

"Is that a fire?" she asked in a husky, sex-kitten kind of voice.

Which was sort of ironic because she wasn't a sex kitten. She was a virgin.

That thought, and the incessant buzzing of his pager, finally jolted him fully awake.

He grabbed the pager and started searching in the dark for the floor lamp that was the only lighting in the half-finished room.

"Gotta go," he said, as he turned on the light and jumped into his clothes. He didn't look at Sabina or even give her a kiss before he was out of there, taking the steps down to the main level two at a time. Guilt made an appearance. But his feelings were new and fragile; he needed time to figure things out.

Because he'd done it again. He'd fallen in love after just one night.

But then again, he'd known Sabina for years, hadn't he?

He shook these thoughts out of his mind and focused on his job. He was going to have to use one of the old turnout suits, since his was at home instead of in his car. He'd left the suit at home because the car was filled with luggage for the honeymoon.

Boy, that was awkward. Lucy's stuff was still in the back of his car.

He was moving slow, and he knew it. Probably because he hadn't had much sleep and had consumed one too many beers yesterday. So he was the last one to arrive at the firehouse. The guys were about to leave without him.

"We didn't expect you to show up. Are you sober?" Dash asked.

"I am."

"You don't have your gear," Matt said.

"I was at the Smith house when I got the page. The gear is at home because . . . Well, you know."

"Give the guy a break. He was supposed to be on his honeymoon tonight," Bubba said.

Ross ignored the friendly ribbing and grabbed the spare turnout suit. The boys were never going to find out that he'd spent his honeymoon night with Sabina on a twin mattress on the floor of the Smith house.

Or that she'd been a virgin.

He'd never been anyone's first lover. Ever.

It was humbling.

And too damn complicated to think about right now.

"What have we got?" he asked.

"A brush fire way out of town on old man Nelson's farm," Dash said.

Ross jumped into the chief's seat and started pulling on the turnout suit. Dash drove like a maniac, and they made it to the Nelson farm in seven minutes flat, which had to be some kind of record since the farm was at the far edge of their service area. The fire had started in a brush pile at the corner of the property, well away from the barn where George Nelson kept his milk cows.

By the time they arrived, George had all but put the fire out with a garden hose. But the smell of kerosene hung in the air.

"Someone set this fire on purpose," George said as Ross jumped down from the pumper.

Ross nodded. "Did you see anything?"

"Uh-huh. One of my cows just dropped a calf so I was up in the barn with Doc Polk most of the night. She's the one who saw the flare when the fire started. I got to the barn door in time to see someone dressed in black running down the road. It was a man of about middle height. I couldn't tell you what race or hair color. It was too far away. But he got into a light-colored sedan. I can't tell you what make it was, either. But I'd say it was white or light gray. He headed back toward Last Chance at a pretty good clip."

Just then a sheriff's deputy rolled up to the scene, and George repeated his story. The deputy put out a BOLO and questioned Doc Polk, whose eyewitness account was just about the same. White or gray sedan, make unknown, tags unknown. Yeah, it was all kind of vague.

After another ten minutes, the guys were done stirring ashes and putting out hot spots. It was annoying when someone pulled a prank like this. The guys were all ticked off as they headed back into town at a much more leisurely pace.

And to think this is what pulled him out of bed where he was naked with a really hot woman. Who, if he knew Sabina, would probably get herself up and go home.

On account of the fact that Lucy was still not out of the woods.

Damn.

Sabina decided not to wait for Ross to come back. She might have his mother's blessing but Last Chance was still a small town. And bless her heart, Lucy was still facing an endless list of problems. It wouldn't help Lucy if Avery Denholm, the county prosecutor, ever found out that Sabina had seduced Ross Gardiner on what was supposed to be his wedding night.

So she put on her fancy dress, left off the high heels, and negotiated the nearly pitch black staircase without a flashlight. Her eyes were fixed on the stair treads. Her thoughts were a million miles away, wondering if Ross was facing danger or saving a life. Wondering where Lucy had gotten to. Hoping both of them were safe.

She didn't see the threat until it came at her from out of the dark corner of the foyer. Someone who reeked of kerosene grabbed her from behind and put his smelly hand over her mouth.

She almost gagged as she simultaneously tried to elbow her way free. But the man was much stronger than she was. He dragged her through the front parlor and around to the room that had once been the kitchen. He snapped on a small electric lantern that he'd hung on a nail protruding from one of the open wall studs. A straight-backed chair stood in the middle of the otherwise empty room. A roll of duct tape sat in the chair's seat.

She was dead if she let him get her to the chair. So she redoubled her efforts to get away. She tried to bite his hand and may have gotten him. He swore at her, but still got a piece of tape over her mouth. The minute that tape landed, she started to panic. The tape obscured one of her nostrils in addition to her mouth. It was hard to breathe.

The panic didn't help her any. And it didn't recede when her attacker nearly broke her arms twisting them back so he could bind her at the wrists with more tape. Her feet were all that was left. And she kicked for all she was worth. She even landed one right in his groin area as he tried to push her down into the chair.

For a moment, she thought she might have a chance to get away. But the guy had a high pain threshold, or her kick must have glanced off his thigh. Either way, he redoubled his efforts, and within a matter of moments he had her completely subdued.

When the struggle ended, she finally looked up at him in the eerie blue glow of the LED lantern. Layton Webster. Good Lord.

"It's really a shame," he said, his eyes kind of wide and strange behind his glasses, his breath coming in gusts from the exertion of the brief fight. "I thought you had changed, Sabina. You fooled me, didn't you? I bought all that sweet crap about not being ready for intimacy. But it was just another one of your games, wasn't it?"

She couldn't answer him. But did it even matter? Layton was perfectly capable of carrying on a one-sided conversation. Her misgivings about him, stemming all the way back to eighth grade, tumbled through her mind.

He'd never been quite right. But she'd never figured him for crazy.

Then again, didn't they say psychopaths had a way of gaining people's trust?

Well, she was guilty of trusting him, up to a point. But he'd sure pulled the wool over the eyes of all those match-making busybodies in town. And hadn't she played right into that scenario for her own selfish reasons?

She was in mortal danger. Layton planned to rape her, or maybe worse. And she could do nothing. She struggled against the tape that bound her like the threads in a spider's web.

She was prey.

"You could have had me, Sabina," he said. "You could have had me in eighth grade, but you chose to humiliate me instead. You could have had me now. I was willing to overlook your slutty behavior in high school. I thought you'd learned a lesson. I thought my initial punishment had changed you. But it didn't, did it?"

What on earth was he talking about? He paced back and forth, his voice becoming more and more strident. And then he stopped and glared at her. "I will have to punish you again, I'm afraid."

He stopped and looked away for a moment. "If only you'd learned your lesson the first time." He said these words almost as if he were sorry or something. What was all this talk about punishment? When had he punished her?

He turned his gaze back on her, and she must have responded to him in some way because he seemed to realize that she needed further clarification, and Layton had always been willing to clarify things—*ad infinitum.* "It's so ironic, isn't it? All these years Lucy blamed herself for that fire, when she wasn't to blame at all.

"I was at your house that night. I used to watch you sometimes. But that night I saw Lucy burn something in your trash can. And that gave me an idea. So when she went to sleep, I jimmied open the window and, well, I used some paper and matches by your bedroom curtains. I didn't think I'd hurt Lucy. I figured she'd be awakened by the smoke detector.

"I admit I got a little scared when she was hurt. And then I realized my mistake. It would have been far more effective if I'd scarred you. If you were scarred, no one would look at you or lust after you. Maybe if you were scarred, you would have learned your lesson.

"Oh, well," he said on a gusty sigh, "At least I saved you from that life you wanted. You never got to be a cheerleader at Clemson. You never had the chance to sleep your way through another football team. You should thank me for saving you from all that sin.

"To be honest I thought of you often over the years. I kept tabs on you, but I didn't want to come here until I was ready. And then Uncle Elias invited me back with his pathetic little project. I really thought I had changed you. I dared to think that you and I could be happy, even if you were a slut, once.

"And then someone did me a huge favor by burning down those houses at Jessamine Manor. I have no idea who that person was, but I could see how I could use that disaster to my advantage. I helped your sister any way I could. I knew she was the key.

"But I was so wrong. I'm ashamed to say it. All that time you piously supported your sister, and dated me like you cared, and what were you doing? Banging the fireman on the side.

"I couldn't let that go on, could I? I had to put a stop to it. I decided to set another fire. It's pretty thrilling, actually, especially when you use technology to get it done. So much more fun than the first fire I set with the paper and matches.

"It's just unfortunate that Ross brought that stupid dog to Heritage Oaks that night. I still can't believe Uncle Elias allowed it. If it weren't for that dog, Ross would have been eliminated. And Lucy would be facing murder charges. Just imagine how you would have turned to me if that were the case?"

He paused a moment, clearly lost in some grotesque fantasy.

"But the dog ruined it all. And then you had to go screw that man."

Good Lord, had he been watching her every move over the last few weeks? Had he been down here plotting his revenge while she and Ross were . . .

And then she remembered that Ross had been called away for an emergency. And Layton smelled of kerosene or something like that. What had he done? Oh, God, was Ross okay?

"So I'm afraid this time the punishment is death. I'm sorry," Layton said into her frantic thoughts. "I thought I could teach you a lesson, but you're hopeless. And I won't sully myself with a slut. There's no honorable way out of our engagement for me unless you die. And of course, the authorities will have plenty of evidence to convict Lucy of the crime."

He smiled. It was like looking right into the face of the devil.

"I'm afraid it's going to hurt. But the fire will purge your sins."

Good Lord, he planned to burn her to death.

Her heart pummeled her rib cage, her struggle against the tape becoming frantic. There was no escape. She was going to die.

She stopped struggling and started praying. Of course she asked God to save her, but that seemed unlikely. So she asked for forgiveness. If she'd been a kinder person in her youth, maybe she wouldn't have ended up here.

And then she asked God to protect Lucy and Ross. She tried not to cry, but the tears filled her eyes when she thought about what she and Ross had shared last night. He'd left so quickly, running off to an emergency like a hero. There hadn't been any time to talk about what happened between them. He had said no words of love.

Nor had she.

But maybe their bodies had spoken. Maybe he would know that she loved him. She just wished she'd gotten the chance to say it out loud.

"You can cry, sweetheart, but it won't affect me. I have to move quickly now. Before Ross comes back. The timing is important. I want him to know that you're burning in here. It will be exquisitely painful for him, don't you think? And imagine when he discovers that Lucy did the deed."

Ross would be back. Her heart took flight at that. It was something to cling to. Something to hope for.

"I thought about knocking you out before I start the fire, but it turns out that's hard to do unless you set up an intravenous line, and I doubt I could do that properly. And chloroform doesn't work unless it's administered continuously. They never tell you that on TV. And besides, chloroform might kill you."

Did he even know what he was saying? Did it matter if she died from some drug or if she burned? Apparently, in his fevered mind, it did.

"It's clear that God needs you to experience the pain." He gave her another one of his monstrous smiles. "I'm so sorry, but you do understand that you must be punished."

He really seemed to be sorry. It was horrible.

He came toward her, and she tried to lean away from him. But there was no escape. He caressed her hair. His touch made her skin crawl.

"I thought about having you, but you understand why I can't, not with his semen inside you." He let go of a long sigh. "Such a shame. I would have liked to have you."

He leaned down and gave her a kiss on the cheek. And then he viciously knocked over the chair so that she ended up on her side, bound, gagged, and just like a frigging turtle on her back.

"Hey y'all," Ross said, "I know it's the wee hours of the morning and y'all are tired, but would you mind if we make a quick stop at Dash's place to pick up Sparky?"

The LCFD pumper was approaching the long gravel drive that led to Painted Corner Stables where Sparky was vacationing. Since the honeymoon was off, Ross kind of wanted to get his buddy back. It had been really lonely last night without him. Until Sabina had shown up wearing that incredible dress.

His whole body flushed hot. If he were certain she was still waiting for him at the Smith house, he'd probably bypass the dog. But Sabina was a careful woman. She probably would have gone home.

He'd call her after the sun was up.

"Sure," Dash said. "To be honest, I'll bet ol' Sparky will be happy to see you. He wasn't all that thrilled when you left him. Walter said he had to put him out in the dog run."

"Really?" Guilt percolated through Ross. "I'm sorry. He's not all that well trained."

"Don't sweat it, man," Bubba said. "You've been busy these last days."

"Bubba! Shut up." This from Matt.

"Okay, guys, let me make something clear. I'm fine. Really. You don't have to walk on eggshells around me. That would drive me crazy."

It was getting on to four in the morning when they arrived at Painted Corner Stables. Dash told everyone to wait and slipped from the truck and headed into the barn.

Four or five minutes passed, and he didn't return. And then a light came on in the cottage beside the barn where Walter Taylor, Dash's horse trainer, lived.

"I have a bad feeling about this," Bubba said.

Bubba had a strong grasp of the obvious. A moment later Dash came back shaking his head. The dog wasn't with him.

"Where's Sparky?" All the emotion Ross should have felt yesterday when Lucy failed to show kind of descended on him all at once. His first, totally crazy thought was that Lucy had taken the dog. But then he remembered that Betsy was the one who had chosen to strike at him in that way. Lucy wouldn't have taken Sparky.

"He's gone," Dash said. "Walter said he'd never seen anything like it. About midnight the dog just went kind of nuts or something. Walter figures it was a raccoon or a possum or something. Anyway he started barking and carrying on. Walter went out to the dog run out back to see what was up. He told me that he'd never seen a dog that size jump the way Sparky did. He cleared a fence that no dog should have been able to."

"He jumped the dog fence?" Matt, who knew dogs, was really impressed.

"He didn't hurt himself, did he?" Ross asked.

"I don't think so, because Walter said he took off like a bat out of hell. He ran right across the pasture that way." Dash pointed toward town.

"I'm sure he was just chasing a coon. I'll go looking for him on horseback just as soon as it's light." Dash's hand came down on Ross's shoulder. "Looks like that dog wants to hunt, boy. Maybe we should organize us a coon hunt one of these days."

"Don't worry, we'll find him," Matt said quietly. Matt, of all the guys, understood. In a few short weeks, Sparky had become Ross's buddy. He couldn't bear to lose another dog.

And besides, in the last hour or two, he'd been entertaining a wonderful fantasy about him and Sabina and Sparky together.

So he didn't want to lose Sparky now. Sabina loved Sparky. And Ross loved both of them. He wanted them to be in his life. He wanted to live in the Smith house and have Momma come sit on the porch and drink sweet tea. One day, he wanted to have a little girl with long, curly black hair and blue eyes.

Yeah. Sparky was part of the plan. And that was kind of amazing because, until right this moment, Ross didn't even realize that he had a plan.

The dog running away was a bad omen or something. Or maybe it was a metaphor for Ross and his fear of commitment. But either way, Sparky needed to settle down, and so did Ross. And somehow that didn't seem nearly as frightening as it had a few days ago.

Layton had taken the light with him. Sabina was in the dark now. And she might have only minutes to live. All her plans for vacationing in Europe were done. All her dreams of finding love and a home with Ross and Sparky were finished. The house she'd dreamed of bringing back to life was about to be erased from the face of the earth.

And all she could do was pray for forgiveness?

Damn it, she might have been cruel to Layton when she was fourteen. But what fourteen-year-old girl hasn't been cruel to someone? This wasn't her fault. Lucy's scars were not her fault. If she wanted forgiveness, she had better start forgiving herself because everyone else, probably even God Himself, had already forgiven her for the stuff she'd done as a stupid teenager.

And after she forgave herself, she needed to fight for her life.

Had she ever fought for her life?

The answer was pretty clear. Not until last night, when she'd come here intent on getting what she wanted.

And now Layton wanted to take it all away from her as a punishment?

Damn.

She rocked the chair from side to side. It was amazing how desperation could make a person's body do impossible things. She managed to roll the chair over and get onto her knees. The position wrenched her back and put pressure across her chest where the duct tape bound her. But that pressure meant she was still alive and breathing.

She started hopping across the rough plywood subfloor in the direction of the back door, praying that it was still missing its knob. The action bruised her knees and sent pain up her spine. Splinters embedded themselves in the delicate fabric of her dress and then, when the dress shredded, they found her skin. Her progress was excruciatingly slow.

The tape across her mouth and nose combined with the pressure on her chest was taking its toll. It was hard to catch her breath, and she started seeing stars and swirls in her vision, even though the room was dark.

The dark was kind of scary, but it beat the idea of flames. She started to wonder if the fire would start with a big bang or if it would creep toward her.

No. No. No. She wouldn't think about that. The back door was maybe six feet away. She could get there.

Just then Layton returned, bearing his blue LED lantern. "Oh, no, sweetheart, we can't have this. I thought you might try something. That's why I fooled you into thinking I'd gone. I'm not stupid enough to give you a way out." He let go of a creepy sigh. "You've always underestimated me, you know that, don't you?"

He righted the chair, taking the pressure off her chest and knees. Then he dragged it all the way into a small closet that had once been a butler's pantry. The closet door hadn't been removed, even if the walls had been taken back to the studs, which were set a little more than a foot and a half apart. There was no way Sabina could maneuver the chair through those spaces while hopping on her knees.

If Layton shut the closet door, the lack of solid walls would be irrelevant. She wouldn't be able to get out. With her hands bound behind her back and virtually no room to turn the chair, she would be trapped. Another wave of panic washed through her. She was utterly helpless, and her only avenue of escape was being slowly closed.

Just then, as if in answer to her deepest prayers, someone came up the back porch steps and barreled through the unlocked back door with such force that the door slammed against the wall with a sharp crack.

Ross. He'd come for her. Relief flared inside her chest. She was going to be okay.

And just as quickly her hope faded.

The dog came into the kitchen and gave a tentative bark. She could just see his white spots in the dim light, through the open wall studs.

"Goddamn it," Layton swore and turned on the dog.

Bad move.

Sparky's hackles rose, and he gave a growl that made the hairs on Sabina's neck rise. She'd seen Sparky react that way before. The dog had never liked Layton. She didn't stop to wonder why; she merely accepted this gift.

Sabina had only a moment's grace before Layton came back and shut the closet door. She dug in her heels and pitched the chair forward again. She was back on her knees, gasping, but Layton was busy in the kitchen with the dog. She prayed that he didn't have a weapon. It would break her heart if Layton hurt Sparky.

But she couldn't worry about that yet. She needed to get free. She inched her way forward on her knees, the rough floorboards scraping her flesh anew. The lantern was sitting on the floor in front of her. Darkness would help her. Darkness would help Sparky.

She hopped on her knees toward the lantern and

knocked it over. It fell with the push-button power switch faceup. Luck or providence was with her. Sabina managed to lean her knee into the switch.

Praise God. The light went out.

Behind her in the kitchen the dog's growls had reached a level that verged on vicious. Sparky had let his wolf out, big time, and she was glad of it. She continued to inch her way toward the parlor and the foyer beyond. Blast these Victorian homes, why did their public spaces have to be so large?

She was beginning to despair of ever reaching freedom when a huge crash sounded in the kitchen. It was followed by a spine-tingling scream loud enough to wake the dead.

Or better yet, the neighbors. Although she wasn't above asking the help of Evelyn Smith's ghost if that particular dead person was still around and willing to help.

And then Layton started screaming curses at the dog while simultaneously wailing about his leg. The dog had obviously subdued the man. And now that Sparky had the bad guy where he wanted him, he went into alarm mode.

If Layton's screams didn't wake the neighbors, the dog's barking surely would.

Dash was just about to swing the LCFD's pumper around to back it into the firehouse when the radio crackled to life and everyone's pagers went off.

"Possible injury at Three Seventy-Two Baruch Street. LCPD is on its way. The Allenberg Volunteer Ambulance Service has been called, but you guys are closer."

Ross's body went ice cold. "That's the Smith house," he said.

Dash responded. "On our way, ETA in about a minute and a half." He floored the accelerator, and the pumper took off.

They arrived at the scene before the police. Inside the house a dog was raising the alarm. And someone was screaming. It wasn't Sabina.

"I think we found Sparky," Matt said as he and Ross jumped from the truck.

"Take care, y'all. Walter said something got into that dog," Dash said as they headed toward the front.

"Hey, wait," Bubba called from behind, pointing down the street. "That's a 7 Series BMW. A white one. There's only one person I know in this town who drives a car like that. Layton Webster. What's he doing here this time of morning?"

Adrenaline hit Ross's system. He turned and rushed the front steps, taking out his flashlight as he ran. "Sabina," he hollered at the top of his lungs. "God help me. Sabina! Are you in there?"

He got no answer as he came through the front door like a crazy man. It wasn't locked. None of the doors were locked. The place was a fricking construction site, not a place where a woman should have been sleeping.

He forgot his training. He just rushed right into a dangerous situation without sizing up the incident. Without going through a checklist. Without being in control.

It was the kind of foolish thing that could end in disaster.

But it didn't matter.

If Layton Webster's car was down the street then Sabina was in danger. And just like that, Ross knew in his gut that Layton Webster had set that fire out at Nelson's farm. He'd done it to get Ross out of the way.

His flashlight split the darkness. Sparky came bounding out of the kitchen. He came halfway across the room when he stopped barking and started whining.

Ross trained his flashlight on the dog.

Oh God. Oh God. Oh God.

Sabina. On her knees. Her dress torn. Her hair falling forward. And the duct tape...

Suddenly Dash was right behind him, taking charge as if he were the chief. "Stop. Ross. Don't be stupid," he said. Then Dash stepped carefully toward the dog, "Good dog," he said, as if he wasn't quite sure.

But Sparky made no threats. Instead he turned and wuffed and headed back into the kitchen where someone, presumably Layton Webster, was screaming.

The dog was the hero of the moment. Clearly Sparky had held the fort until the cavalry could arrive.

Dash followed the dog. Ross rushed toward Sabina, fumbling as he searched through the borrowed suit for a utility knife. He found it in the wrong pocket. He righted the chair, not really able to see her face in the gloom. He was angry enough to want to kill that bastard in the other room.

He didn't want her to see how crazy he'd become. He didn't want to look at what that bastard had done to her.

He started at her ankles and worked his way up, slicing through the tape while people moved in and out of the house behind him. Someone set up a light so he wasn't working in the dark anymore. When he finally reached the tape on her mouth he looked into her eyes.

They were filmed with tears. But they looked surprisingly strong. Like she'd come through this okay. She'd been trying to get away. There were splinters from the rough subfloor in the shimmery fabric of her dress and embedded in her flesh. He needed his med kit.

But he didn't have it.

He yanked the tape from her mouth. He knew it hurt her, so he tried to make it quick.

She sobbed.

And then she was in his arms. And he crushed her to him.

"Oh my God, Ross, I thought Layton had hurt you. And then I knew he hadn't, and I thought I'd never see you again. I thought I'd never have the chance to tell you that I've fallen head over heels in love with you." She sniffled against the front of his big, cumbersome old turnout suit.

Holy crap, Sabina Grey, the best-looking girl in his high-school class, the queen of the prom, loved him. It was amazing. It was incredible.

He nudged her back and looked her square in the eye. "I love you right back." The words were so easy this time. Like he'd been waiting his whole life to say those words to this particular woman.

Sparky took that moment to join the group hug. He came over to where they were still kneeling on the floor, leaned his head into their shoulders, and let go of a long, tired, doggy sigh.

Sabina released her death grip on Ross so she could give Sparky's ears a little caress, gigantic tears still running down her cheeks. "Someone needs to give you a medal, Sparky," she said in a shaky voice. "You saved my life."

"He saved my life too," Ross whispered.

And then Ross was done talking for a while. He drew Sabina up into his arms and kissed her with all of his heart and soul. Yesterday he'd been left at the altar, but today he was luckiest man in the world.

EPILOGUE

The little room off the narthex of the First Methodist Church contained a full-length mirror so brides could make final adjustments to their dresses and veils.

Sabina stood before the looking glass, transformed by the vintage dress and veil. It was almost astonishing how well the silk of Evelyn Smith's gown had weathered its long storage in that steamer trunk. And the dry cleaner had done wonders in restoring it. The veil was gorgeous, and the Juliet cap allowed Sabina to wear her hair down. Ruby and Jane Rhodes had done a terrific job of making her look radiant.

Unfortunately the old suit of morning clothes that she and Ross had discovered that day hadn't fared as well. Moths had gotten to the wool. Which was just as well, since the suit was too small for Ross, and besides, who wanted to remember the guy who left Miz Smith at the altar anyway?

Lucy came up behind her. She wore her hair down, just like Sabina, and they did look almost like twins. You could see how an old lady with poor eyesight could make a mistake. Today Lucy looked drop-dead gorgeous in a pale blue dress with lace sleeves and neck. Ruby had done her hair this time. And there weren't going to be any last-minute changes of heart.

Lucy had a big, fat diamond ring on her left hand. Her wedding was scheduled for next June. In the meantime, she'd followed Zach to Kansas City, where he'd been transferred. She was working in a home furnishings store at the moment, and searching for jobs as a designer and stager.

Momma sighed. "Y'all look so beautiful, I think I might start crying right now." And she did have tears in her eyes. But this time they looked happy. Momma wasn't all that wild about Lucy living with Zach in Missouri, but, on the other hand, it was time for Lucy to grow a pair of wings.

And time for Sabina to finally start living her life.

Tomorrow Ross and Sabina were going to Spain on their honeymoon. And then they'd come back to their almost renovated house, which might actually be finished in time for Christmas. And Ross would, once again, resume his paid job with the LCFD. The election two weeks ago had changed a lot of things.

Daddy came into the room. "All right, y'all, this it's for real." Momma left with him, and Lucy and Sabina were alone.

Lucy gave Sabina a big hug. "If you say you're sorry about anything today I'm going to pop you in the mouth. You hear me?"

Sabina nodded.

"Now come here and let me fix your veil." Lucy rearranged it so that it covered her face. "I'm glad Ross ended up with you. You're perfect together. And I can see you're happy. And believe me, I am completely in love with Zach." She grinned. "I'm telling you, girl, you should see the way he handles a gun."

They giggled. Daddy returned. Ella Miles started up the wedding march.

And Sabina headed down the aisle to the two loves of her life: Ross, wearing his rented gray cutaway suit, and Sparky, sporting a cute bow tie on his collar and a little pillow strapped to his back, where the rings had been attached.

There was no way she and Ross were leaving Sparky out of the fun. He was the hero of this particular love story.

High roller Mike Taggart has
always been willing to take a gamble—
except when it comes to love.
But sexy Charlene Polk is out to
prove that she'd be the best stroke
of luck he's ever had...

**Please see the next page for
an excerpt from**

Last Chance Family.

CHAPTER 1

The kid should have been named Stormy, not Rainbow.

She didn't wear pink or have girlie cartoon characters on her shirt. She didn't have cute pigtails or a precious smile. No. Rainbow wore faded Goodwill clothing that didn't fit her. Her hair stuck out in all directions in a big, nappy mess that thwarted all efforts to brush it. The five-year-old sat in the rented Hyundai's backseat with silent tears running down her cheeks. She had an equally bedraggled tiger-striped cat clutched in her arms. The cat was also weeping but only out of its left eye. Occasionally it would sneeze.

Mike Taggart, Rainbow's reluctant uncle, figured the kid had plenty of reasons for crying. Ten days ago her mother had been killed in another case of senseless gun violence on the streets of Chicago. A few hours ago, Rainbow had lost her grubby stuffed elephant, probably in the men's room at the Atlanta-Hartsfield Airport, where they'd made a pit stop before boarding their connecting flight to Columbia, South Carolina. And then the final blow fell at the baggage claim, when the cat arrived sneezing.

Mike swallowed down the acid churning in his stomach. He should have done more to rescue Angie, his half sister, from the life she'd been living. But Angie hadn't wanted to be rescued. And her five-year-old daughter had paid the price.

He needed to make amends for his failure. Which explained why he'd brought his niece here to the middle of nowhere, determined to find her the kind of family that he'd always dreamed of as a little boy. Reverend Timothy Lake, Mike's half brother and Rainbow's other uncle, was exactly the kind of upstanding citizen Mike wanted for Rainbow's new father.

The cat sneezed again, and the kid clutched it to her chest in a death grip that the animal tolerated with amazing patience. Clearly the cat played favorites, because it had pretty much shredded Mike's right hand when he'd battled it into the cat carrier in Chicago this morning. But it seemed to love the kid, and vice versa.

He didn't understand cats. Or little girls.

"Don't worry," he found himself saying. "We're going to find a vet right now."

This announcement did nothing to stop the silent flow of Rainbow's tears.

It would have been so much better if the kid had wailed or made even the smallest of sounds. But no. Rainbow had been silent from the moment she'd witnessed her mother's murder ten days ago.

He hoped he hadn't promised something he couldn't deliver. They had to have vets out here in the boonies of South Carolina, didn't they? They needed them to look after the cows. Not that Mike had seen a lot of cows during his drive south to Allenberg County. But he'd sure seen a lot of fields planted in various crops. There had to be cows someplace around here.

He touched the screen of his smartphone and keyed in a search for veterinarians. Lady Luck smiled on him. He had a bar and a half of service and managed to activate his GPS and set a course for Creature Comforts Animal Hospital, only ten miles away, just south of the little town of Last Chance.

It didn't take him more than two minutes to motor through the town, which was still swagged out in yards of red-white-and-blue bunting from yesterday's Memorial Day celebration. They probably had a parade or something down Main Street, which, in Mike's estimation, made Last Chance perfect in every way.

The vet's, a building of tan-colored cinder blocks with a green roof, stood about half a mile past the retail district. It could have been a medical building in any small town or suburban location, except for the collection of animal statues in its front yard.

A life-sized cement German shepherd, collie, and boxer guarded the front door. Half a dozen cats in a variety of colors frolicked on either side of the walkway. A squirrel and a raccoon peeked out from the bushes planted along the front of the building, and a collection of plastic birds hung on strings tied to the eaves. The tacky menagerie didn't inspire confidence.

Mike helped the little girl out of her booster seat, enduring the cat's hisses and dodging its claws. The cat refused to go back into its carrier, which was a moot point because Rainbow refused to let the animal go. She carried the cat right below its front shoulders, with the bulk of its body dangling over her little arms. Why the cat tolerated this was one of life's greatest mysteries.

In any case, Rainbow had control of the cat, which was more than Mike could say about himself. They made their way to the air-conditioned waiting room, where his luck ran out.

A fifty-something woman with obviously dyed red hair sat at the reception area guarding the inner sanctum like a bulldog. "We're about ready to close. Y'all will have to make an appointment for tomorrow. We don't have late hours on Tuesdays," she said in a drawl so thick Mike could practically slice it.

"This is an emergency. We just got into town. The cat is wheezing."

The woman arched her eyebrows and gave the cat a quick look. The cat fixed the woman with its strange, green-amber eyes and sneezed. "Hmm, upper respiratory infection," she said. "You know, if you didn't let your cat outside he wouldn't get sick."

Mike put on his poker face and gave the infuriating woman a smile. "We'll try to do better in the future, but for now, the cat is sick."

"It's a kind of herpes virus that causes this, you know. Once your cat gets it he'll have it for life."

Great. Rainbow's cat had herpes. It figured. It had lived in one of the poorest and meanest neighborhoods in Chicago. Mike remained calm and continued to give the receptionist the blank, emotionless stare that he used in poker games. "I'm happy to pay for emergency services. Are you the vet?"

The cat sneezed again, and the woman peered over

the side of the reception desk at Rainbow, who seemed to know exactly what was required of her. She stood there looking pitiful with tears running down her cheeks.

"Oh, you poor thing," the woman said. "I'll just buzz Dr. Polk and see if she can see y'all. She's got a meeting she needs to get to, but I know she'll make time. In the meantime, fill in this paperwork." The receptionist handed Mike a clipboard with a patient form.

It didn't take Mike more than a few seconds to realize that he couldn't fill in most of the blanks on the form. He only knew the animal's name because the cat had a collar with a name tag and rabies vaccination date. On the opposite side of the name tag was a phone number that didn't belong to anyone. He had no idea about Tigger's age or whether the cat had been fixed. And since Rainbow refused to talk, Mike was in the dark.

He couldn't even fill out an address because he didn't know where the cat would ultimately end up. The cat should have been sent to the animal shelter. But Rainbow had pitched a fit, and Rachel Sanger, her caseworker in the Chicago Department of Social Services, was a cat lover. Ms. Sanger had broken all the rules and found a way for Rainbow to take the cat with her to the foster home where she'd stayed for a week before they were able to locate Mike.

And really, now that she'd lost her stuffed elephant, the cat represented an important link to Rainbow's former life. Not that living in the slums with Angie had been all that idyllic.

Hopefully, Timmy could take both the kid and her cat. The management of the hotel where Mike hung his hat didn't allow cats. And besides, a man who made his living as a professional poker player and part-time day trader didn't need a cat.

Or, for that matter, an unhappy little girl named Rainbow.

Cindy, the receptionist, had said something about a sick cat. But when Dr. Charlene Polk walked into examination room two, all she found was a tall, redheaded, blue-eyed man with a square jaw, cleft chin, and oh-so-carefully groomed stubble.

He looked like a fashion plate standing there with his Ralph Lauren polo shirt open at the neck and his hands jammed into his AX jean pockets. He didn't look like your typical cat owner.

But then the missing animal spoke, giving forth an anxious *meeeooowwww*.

Charlene blinked and turned to find a little girl standing at the opposite side of the room. She bore no resemblance to the man with her. The child was maybe five and had brown skin and dark, frizzy hair. Unlike the logo-wrapped guy, the child wore a grubby-looking blue T-shirt and a pair of jeans with holes in both knees. The only clue to the child's gender was her long, delicate hands.

Her mixed-race looks grabbed Charlene right where she lived. This could have been Derrick's child. Except that she was about ten years too young.

Tears trickled down the girl's cheeks. She hugged her tiger-striped cat as if the animal were a toy. People who carried their cats into the office were one of Charlene's pet peeves. A cat should always be transported in a carrier. But in this case, Charlene decided to forgo her usual lecture.

She squatted down to be on the same level. "What's the matter?"

The child said nothing. But the cat let out another slightly squeaky meow.

"She doesn't talk," the man said.

Charlene looked up. "Oh, I don't know. By the shape of her face and pointy ears, I think she has a bit of Siamese in her, or maybe Abyssinian. They are notoriously talkative."

"No." The man shook his head, his blue eyes looking oddly animated in his otherwise expressionless face. "I mean Rainbow. She doesn't talk."

"Rainbow? That's a nice name for a cat."

"No." The man gestured toward the little girl. "Tigger is the cat's name. Rainbow is Tigger's owner. And Rainbow doesn't speak. I mean, she hasn't spoken for about ten days."

Charlene's disquiet grew. Something wasn't right. "Ten days?"

"Yeah, ten days. Since her mother died."

"Oh." Just a four-word sentence but it sure packed a wallop. The little girl had lost her mother. Charlene's heart turned in her chest. Rainbow's tears seemed endless. They left long tracks across her brown skin.

Charlene held her hands out toward the girl. "May I take Tigger?" she asked.

The girl sniffled once and then reluctantly allowed Charlene to take the cat, who promptly sneezed. Charlene stood, put the animal on the examination table, and turned her attention back to the man. "I'm Charlene Polk, the assistant vet here. And you are?"

"Mike Taggart. We just arrived in town. I'm Timothy Lake's brother. Do you know him?"

She didn't see a resemblance, except that both men were tall. Pastor Tim had blond hair and a classically handsome face. This guy looked way more rugged, like he spent a lot of time out in the sun surfing or mountain climbing. "I'm acquainted with Pastor Tim," Charlene said. "But I don't know him well. I'm not a Methodist."

Mr. Taggart's face remained utterly impassive. The lack of emotion creeped Charlene out.

She began a routine examination of the cat while Mr. Taggart folded his arms and observed in an intense and unsettling manner. Rainbow watched, too. She stood on tiptoes, looking up at Charlene out of a pair of amber-green eyes that were almost the same shade as Tigger's.

"Uh, Mr. Taggart, Tigger is not a male cat," Charlene said as she checked the paperwork where the cat's sex was marked as male. Besides the cat's name and incorrect sex, the patient information sheet was entirely blank. What was going on here?

"Uh, its name is Tigger. Who names a girl cat Tigger?" he asked.

Who indeed? "Has Tigger been eating?"

"The cat was eating just fine before we put it on the airplane. *She* wasn't sneezing until we picked her up at the baggage claim," Mr. Taggart said.

"The cat was transported recently?" Charlene asked.

"Yeah, today, from Chicago to Columbia by way of Atlanta. We were transported the same way."

The poor cat. She'd obviously been stressed. Her placid demeanor might also be a warning of more serious conditions.

"How old is Tigger?"

The child remained silent. The man let go of a long breath. "I have no idea. Up until a few days ago, I wasn't even acquainted with the cat."

Charlene gave him a stare. He stared back, giving nothing away. Alarms went off. Maybe she should stall this guy and give Sheriff Rhodes a call. Things were not adding up. The man seemed not to care very much about the cat or the child.

Their gazes remained locked for a long moment before he eventually looked away. "Look," he said stabbing his hand through his fiery hair. "I know what you're thinking, but here's the situation. Rainbow's mother died about ten days ago. I'm her uncle, and Timmy is my half brother. I am not parent material. But Timmy's a minister. So I'm here to leave Rainbow with her uncle. The cat got sick along the way, so you can call this an emergency fly-by-night visit. If you can fix it up, that would be great. But don't ask me any questions about it. I don't know anything, except that it has sharp claws." He ran his finger along a nasty scratch on the back of his hand.

"You should put some antiseptic ointment on that," she said.

"I will when I get to a stopping place. The animal didn't want to go into the cat carrier this morning." Mr. Taggart had the temerity to glare at the cat. The cat glared right back at him, obviously unimpressed and unperturbed.

Wow. The gossip mill in Last Chance would be running overtime once the members of the Methodist Altar Guild got wind of this. Those busybodies had been trying to find a wife for their minister since he arrived last winter. Even Charlene's aunt Millie, who wasn't a Methodist, had broadly suggested that a single woman of any faith would be crazy not to set her cap for the young, handsome pastor. If Pastor Tim agreed to adopt a child, the Altar Guild would have to go into hyperdrive or something.

"Does Reverend Lake know you're coming?" she asked.

"No."

"No?"

"No. I doubt that he remembers me at all. The last time I saw him I was five and he was three. But he turned out okay. And that's why we're here."

Charlene shifted her gaze to the child. Rainbow stood with slumped shoulders, her body language tragic. In that moment, she looked like the personification of every unwanted child who had ever lived.

Mike Taggart was a jerk. He seemed to have no idea how his words hurt Rainbow. And even worse, he didn't seem to care.

Familiar guilt tugged at her. She wanted to fold the little girl up in her arms and tell her that everything would work out fine. But she couldn't do that because Charlene knew that things might not work out for Rainbow.

Charlene quickly finished the exam and handed Tigger back to Rainbow. "She's going to be fine. I'm going to give your uncle Mike some medicine for her."

The child took the cat, hugging the animal as if she were a stuffed toy. Tigger allowed this indignity as if the cat knew how much Rainbow needed her.

"Now I need you and Tigger to go sit quietly in the room outside. There are some yummy oatmeal cookies out there and a few cat treats. I'll be right here with Uncle Mike. I need to tell him what he needs to do for Tigger."

She ushered Rainbow into the outer office and handed her one of the cookies the receptionist baked for staff and pet owners. She also gave Rainbow a treat for Tigger. When they were settled, Charlene returned to the examination room and shut the door behind her.

"Tigger's lungs are clear, so this is not an upper respiratory infection. It's probably a herpes virus outbreak brought on by stress. My guess is that the sneezing is probably a reaction to the lack of humidity in the airplane. The cat may be dehydrated, so make sure she has plenty of water. If the sneezing continues, you'll need to bring her back for a follow-up.

"In the meantime you'll need to put some drops in Tigger's eyes twice a day, and I've got some antiviral meds for her to take by mouth. The meds are disguised as cat treats so you probably won't get scratched trying to dose her."

She paused for a moment, wondering if she should go on. Every instinct told her that she should. But who was she to give parenting advice? She didn't know the first thing about kids.

Still, she couldn't let her concerns go unvoiced. She already had enough guilt to haul around. So she squared her shoulders and looked him right in the eye. "I'm equally concerned about Rainbow, who is probably one of the sources of the cat's stress. Have you any idea how frightening it is for a child to hear that you're planning to drop her off with someone she doesn't know and who doesn't even know that you're coming?"

That got a reaction. The mask he'd been wearing slipped, and anger flared in his eyes. "Look, lady, I came in here for vet services. I know precisely how sad Rainbow feels. And I'll bet you a thousand dollars that you have no clue. I'm sure you had a nice, middle-class upbringing and never once worried about whether you'd go hungry. I'm sure you didn't have a parent with a drug problem. I'm sure you got your clothes new, instead of from the Salvation Army. But Rainbow and I have both known that kind of thing. And I'm here precisely because I want her to have a better life. So butt out, okay? Just give us what we need for the damn cat and we'll be out of here."